COLI

CROSS

GAME THEORY

A KATERINA CARTER FRAUD THRILLER

GAME THEORY
A Katerina Carter Fraud Thriller

Colleen Tompkins writing as Colleen Cross
Copyright © 2012 by Colleen Cross, Colleen Tompkins

ISBN: 978-0-9878835-2-0   Paperback
ISBN: 978-0-9878835-1-3   Ebook

Published by Slice Publishing
Cover art: Streetlight Graphics
Author Photo: Trevor Hallam
For information contact Colleen Cross: http://ColleenCross.com

EPIGRAPH

Laws are spider webs through which the big flies pass and the little ones get caught.
Honoré de Balzac (1799-1850)

PRAISE FOR GAME THEORY

"If you like a good conspiracy theory, you'll LOVE Colleen Cross' financial thriller, *Game Theory*. Financial fraud investigator, Kat Carter, is confronted with the very real possibility of world order conspiracy in this smart and compelling read that relates hauntingly to the current global economic and political climates. Was the economic crisis created? Is the news we are fed designed to mold our opinions and actions? Are we all just pawns in someone else's game? You'll begin to wonder after reading *Game Theory*. Thought provoking and wonderfully entertaining!"

—Karen Cantwell, author of the Barbara Marr mysteries

"Another gripping page-turner from Colleen Cross. Suspense-charged to provide one plot twist after another, this credible tale of global fraud and currency domination draws you in and never lets go. An intelligent and exciting read!"

—Sandra Nikolai, author of False Impressions

ALSO BY COLLEEN CROSS

Exit Strategy

Find out more at http:///www.colleencross.com

CHAPTER 1

H E DIDN'T LOOK LIKE A man about to die. They never did. Part of the thrill was deciding their fates. It just required a bit of planning.

"Back up. Just a little." She focused him in her sights. He was easily twice her age, but surprisingly fit for sixty. He had matched her step for step as they skied and then snow-shoed up the steep Summit Trail. Wanted her in bed, just like every other man. She had decided long ago to use that to her advantage.

He stepped back, moving closer to the cornice slab of snow that jutted out unsupported from the cliff. She'd been careful to take the eastern approach so he wouldn't notice the dangerous overhang. Her pulse quickened as she anticipated what was to come. Whiskey jacks flew past on reconnaissance, the small gray birds circling as they swooped in to scavenge muffin crumbs from the man's outstretched hand.

It was a Wednesday morning and the backcountry was deserted. Another man on snowshoes had passed them in the opposite direction more than an hour ago. They were alone.

"Smile." She zoomed in, clicked the shutter, and felt a rush of exhilaration. Hers would be the last face he would see, the last voice he would hear.

He grinned as he shifted his weight and unzipped his Gore-tex jacket. The sun shone through the low clouds, creating strange shadows across the snow.

A split second later his face contorted, confidence replaced with unmasked fear. His mouth dropped open as his eyes hollowed with terror. It was her favorite part: the hunter now the prey, and her victim knowing she had something to do with it.

Realization froze on his face as the ground beneath broke into pieces, unable to support his weight. The snow overhang snapped off the cliff, sending him hurtling down to the valley two hundred meters below.

His screams echoed down the canyon. Then silence, except for the whiskey jacks circling back for seconds.

She smiled. Almost too easy. She tossed the camera over the edge. No bullets, no mess. No trace, unless someone came looking before the next snowfall, forecasted to start in a few hours. Even if they found him before the spring melt, it would look like an accident, a tourist unfamiliar with backcountry snow conditions. She scattered the rest of the muffin to the birds. They pecked at each other, fighting for what was left of the crumbs.

Just like she once did. Not anymore. She would get her fair share, even if she had to kill for it.

CHAPTER 2

KATERINA CARTER SHIFTED IN THE hard plastic chair and tucked her hands under her thighs. Her fingers were crossed on both hands, knuckles crushed into the unforgiving seat. It defied logic, but she did it anyway. What did she have to lose?

Uncle Harry hunched forward beside her, elbows on knees, poised for Dr. McAdam's next question. His first mini mental health exam had been six months ago, right after the accident. The early-stage Alzheimer's diagnosis meant the loss of his driver's license and the independence that went along with it. He'd been depressed ever since, his memory dramatically worsening.

The tiny examination room barely held the three of them. Since the diagnosis, the doctor had insisted a family member accompany him. That was Kat given Aunt Elsie's heart attack and sudden passing a year ago.

"What city are we in, Harry?" Dr. McAdam rolled back on his stool as he waited for an answer.

"Vancouver." Her uncle pulled a hanky from his pocket and

wiped his brow. A thin sheen of sweat covered his forehead.

"Good. What is your home address?"

"Easy—418 Maple." Harry beamed.

"All right. What year is it?"

"It's 1989."

"Hmmm. What month?"

"June."

"What day of the week?"

"Saturday."

December 5, 2012, a Wednesday. The Weather Channel finally got it right today. Wet snow, chance of freezing rain tonight.

Kat checked her watch. Most of the afternoon gone with a full day's work waiting for her at the office. Like most days lately—plans derailed, whole days and weeks evaporated in an instant. Keeping Harry safe, fed, and calm was practically a full-time job.

"You better get yourself a calendar, doc. Now will you help me get my license back?"

"Let's deal with this first, Harry." Dr. McAdam pointed to a drawing. "What do you see in this picture?"

Harry cast a furtive glance at Kat. "A watch."

"And this?" Dr. McAdam smiled at him.

"A pen. See? Easy-peasy."

"Now some arithmetic. Starting at one hundred, count down by taking seven off each time."

Harry wrung his hands together. "How is this getting my license back?"

"Just bear with me, Harry." Dr. McAdam shifted his gaze to Kat.

"Uncle Harry, just relax. Take your time." Kat's mother had failed a similar test twenty years ago when she was first diagnosed with Alzheimer's. The mood and memory changes were unmistakable, even to a fourteen-year-old.

Kat's father had accompanied her mother to the appointment. Shortly thereafter, he had walked out on both

4

of them for good. That's when she had moved in with the Dentons. Alzheimer's was a cruel death sentence.

At least Harry got twenty more years of sanity than his sister. Early-onset Alzheimer's like her mom's supposedly ran in families. Did she inherit the gene? She'd rather not know.

"One hundred."

Silence.

"Ninety-three." Harry's brows creased.

Kat squeezed her fingers together as her stomach growled. Kat's lunch plans had been foiled by a two-hour delay to convince Harry to leave the house. Harry had all his meals with her and Jace now, partly because he always forgot to eat on his own.

"Twenty-three."

She pulled one hand free and glanced sideways at Harry. She wasn't that hungry after all. Matter of fact, she felt a bit sick to her stomach. Harry had complained of stomach cramps for the last few days too. Must be that flu going around.

Harry counted down to three and turned his gaze to the door. He hummed under his breath.

"Harry?"

"Doc? Are we done now?"

"Not quite." Dr. McAdam sighed and handed him a pencil with a clipboard. "I want you to draw a clock face. Then draw the clock hands pointing to ten before two."

Easy enough. Harry didn't read or do his morning crossword anymore, but he still knew what time it was. He always chided Kat for being late.

Harry tapped the pencil against his lip and stared at the blank page on the clipboard. Slowly he lowered his arm and started to draw.

A shaky, oblong circle, but it *was* a circle.

Kat exhaled.

Harry dropped the pencil on the clipboard and brought his hand to his face. He brushed his index finger back and forth against his lip. Finally he picked the pencil up again and pressed the lead to paper. One line. Then a second one.

Upside down, marking *6:35*.

"Now can I get my license back?"

"Harry—you remember your car accident?" Dr. McAdam removed a pen from his pocket. "You can't have your license back unless you retake and pass the driver's exam."

Harry had crashed his prized 1970s Lincoln through the front window of Carlucci's Pasta House after mistaking the gas pedal for the brake. Luckily the accident happened just after the lunch crowd had dispersed. No one was hurt, but the damage was done.

His life had spiraled downward since then. He had missed numerous appointments, accused his neighbor of stealing, and most recently, set his kitchen on fire after forgetting to turn the stove off. Luckily Kat had arrived in time to smother it, limiting the damage to a blackened wall. She shuddered to think of what might have happened.

Harry thrust the clipboard back into the doctor's hands. "One accident in almost sixty years! You pulled my license for that? Not fair. I've got the reflexes of a thirty-year-old." Harry motioned to Kat. "Tell him, Kat."

Kat pretended to search her purse for her cell phone.

"Kat?"

"Less to worry about, Uncle Harry. I can drive you to your appointments."

"I don't want you driving me places. I'm perfectly capable of driving myself."

"No, you're not. You get lost and—" The words tumbled out of her mouth before she could stop them. "I just think it would be easier on you, that's all."

"So you two are in this together? Maybe I'm retired, but I'm not dead. Or stupid." He flushed and turned to Dr. McAdam. "Let me retake the road test."

Dr. McAdam pursed his lips. "I'm not sure that's a good idea."

"You're not safe out there, Uncle Harry. What if it

happens again?"

"It won't. If you won't help me, fine. Hillary will."

Kat opened her mouth, then caught herself before answering.

Dr. McAdam frowned. "Hillary?"

"Harry's daughter." She shuddered just thinking about Hillary. Her cousin had vanished ten years ago, shortly after reneging on a six-figure loan from Harry and Elsie. They had refused to advance her any more money. Not that they could have, since it had wiped out their savings and taken them years to recover. Harry sure talked about her a lot lately. Alzheimer's stripped away recent memories and regenerated ancient ones, like river rocks eroded underwater.

Dr. McAdam stood and brushed his palms on his white lab coat. "Your troubles are much bigger than driving, Harry. I suggest you get your affairs in order, and soon. Alzheimer's can progress very quickly."

"Alzheimer's? That's ridiculous. I don't have Alzheimer's." Harry jumped from the chair and brushed past Dr. McAdam. He turned at the doorway. "Go to hell. Both of you!"

He threw open the door and slammed it behind him.

The Harry she knew never would have done that. Kat blinked back tears as she stood. She grabbed the chair back, overcome by dizziness as black dots darkened her vision.

Dr. McAdam held up his hand, oblivious to her condition. "Wait—he'll cool off in the waiting room. We should chat anyways. What else have you noticed?"

Kat's vision cleared and the shakiness passed. "He has delusions. Talks about Aunt Elsie like she's still alive. He thinks squatters have moved into his house and are trying to kill him."

"Typical." Dr. McAdam scribbled something on his prescription pad and handed it to Kat. "Have him try these. They could help with the hallucinations and might slow down the progression of the disease. You also need to start exploring caregiving options now, because the disease requires a great deal of expertise and attention. The better places have waiting lists, which you'll need to get on. Call my office tomorrow and we'll arrange for Harry to see another doctor."

"A specialist?"

He stood in the doorway and stared at his shoes. "I won't be able to keep seeing Harry. With his Alzheimer's and all..."

"You're dropping him as a patient? Right when he needs you the most?" Kat swallowed the hard lump in her throat.

"It's complicated. He'll be better off with a geriatrician anyways."

"But he's been your patient for close to forty years. How is seeing a doctor he doesn't know better for him?"

"It's not going to matter much. But I'll recommend someone—just call the office tomorrow." He checked his watch. "I am running a bit behind right now, so if you'll just excuse me..."

"But—"

"Good luck." Dr McAdam pulled the door shut behind him.

After forty years, that was some goodbye.

CHAPTER 3

T HE AFTERNOON'S WET SNOW HAD turned to freezing rain with nightfall. It stung Kat's exposed face and hands and soaked through her leather soles. She punched in Jace's cell number but got his voicemail for the umpteenth time. Where was he?

She hung up without leaving another message. She had been purposely vague in her original message, asking only for him to meet her in front of the medical building.

Harry had been alone in the waiting room for less than five minutes. Now he was gone, and it was completely her fault.

"Kat."

She jumped at the voice, barely audible above the driving rain.

Jace waved from a half-block away as he hurried towards her. Even in his bulky ski jacket he was tall and athletic looking. "Sorry—I was out on a call. I got here as soon as I could."

He held her close and kissed her. "Out-of-bounds skier. Broken leg—he's lucky we found him before the snowstorm hit. Never would have lasted the night." As a search and rescue volunteer up in the North Shore Mountains, Jace often had callouts for lost skiers and hikers.

That same weather system in the city meant endless torrential rain. Vancouver rain smothered you in stealth mode, in a chokehold lasting weeks and months. Slow but relentless, west coast weather beat you into submission before you even knew it. It was why there were more suicides here.

The rain roiled diagonally in sheets as the wind circled through the tunnel carved from the downtown high rises. Kat couldn't remember—had Uncle Harry worn his raincoat or his lightweight, non-waterproof windbreaker?

He pulled back to look at her. "What's up? Where's Harry?"

She avoided his gaze. "Gone."

"Gone? What do you mean, gone?"

She broke from his embrace and pointed to the concrete high rise behind her that housed the medical office. "We were at his doctor's. He disappeared from the waiting room."

Jace didn't know about Harry's Alzheimer's diagnosis six months ago. They had only rekindled their romance a few months before that, and she was waiting for the right time to tell him. Only there never seemed to be a right time, and it'd been too easy to hide the depth of Harry's problem—older people are just expected to grow fuzzy.

"Is he still sick? The flu should have passed by now—"

She changed the subject. "He's been gone four hours. I don't know where he could possibly be." Kat explained how she had repeatedly combed the building and the surrounding streets. She had searched everywhere. But no Harry.

Four hours later she had nothing to show for her exhaustive grid search. She was completely soaked, exhausted, and at a loss on what to do next.

She tensed as her stomach cramped. She must have caught Harry's flu.

"Why didn't you mention Harry in your message? I might've got here sooner. Four hours is a long time. He could be anywhere by now."

Kat pushed him away. "You think you can do better?"

Jace's lips pressed into a frown. "No—I'm just saying two heads are better than one. Just involve me, before things get out of control."

She stepped back and crossed her arms. "Things aren't out of control. I can handle it." The more she kept Jace out of it, the better. Men left when things got uncomfortable. Like her dad did after her mom's Alzheimer's diagnosis.

"No, you are absolutely not handling it. You're a wreck." He touched her cheek. "Why won't you let me help you?"

Jace already did Harry's home repairs, grocery shopping, and much more. Would their relationship survive, or would the burden of his care strain it beyond repair?

She shrugged, not knowing what to say. Jace was right. She had just never expected Harry to be out of her sight. Especially since his doctor's appointment was the sole reason for the trip. Now he was gone, a mistake she couldn't undo.

He softened his voice. "Did you tell the doctor how he's been forgetting things?"

Kat nodded. Jace simply thought Harry was forgetful.

The endless crisis management of the last few months wore on her and she was exhausted from lack of sleep. Caring for Harry and running her full-time fraud investigation practice was impossible. She worried she would make critical errors in her work. She couldn't afford to lose clients, or her reputation. More importantly, she couldn't lose Harry.

Kat tucked a lock of hair behind her ear as she struggled to hear Jace over the wind. It whistled through the high-rise towers, the gusts increasing with each passing hour. She grew increasingly worried about Harry. Was he safe?

Kat studied Jace. His inner calm pulled her in and embraced her like an aura. His steady gaze rested on hers as if no one else existed. It was what she loved most about him. Only now his face was tinged with worry, despite his efforts not to show it.

Dr. McAdam wanted Harry in long-term care. Kat bristled at the thought. Harry had cared for her; now she needed to do the same for him. She wanted to hang onto him as long as she could. Kat dropped her gaze from Jace's clear blue eyes and followed the water rivulets coursing down the front of his waterproof jacket.

"I didn't want to bother you. Besides, you were working on your story deadline." She had to raise her voice to be heard above the wind.

"Bother me? I'm not important enough in your life to be included?"

"I didn't mean it that way, Jace. It's just that I—I just didn't know what to do."

"You still should have called me." Jace pulled her closer. Even through his jacket, she felt the strength of his embrace. Her fingertips traced the curve of his bicep as his strong arms encircled her.

One more thing and she would break apart and shatter into little pieces. Pieces too small to be made whole again. She broke from Jace's embrace. "I will. But we can't waste any more time. "

Where would she go if dementia clouded her mind? Home. But Uncle Harry wouldn't remember the way, and it was too far to walk from downtown Vancouver. Not that it would stop him. He wasn't very logical.

"Don't get mad at me." Jace stepped back and turned away. "I'm only trying to help."

Now she felt even worse.

The streetlights cast a cold yellow light on Jace as he faced her, arms crossed.

Gore-tex and Timberlands, ready for anything, always under control. She felt a twinge of resentment, though she was grateful. No one else dropped everything when she needed help.

"Sorry," she said. "I'm beat. The Barron hearing's tomorrow and I'm not ready." Zachary Barron's future net worth rested entirely on her.

Forensic accountants like Kat specialized in fraud detection and uncovering hidden assets. Or, in high-net-worth divorce cases like his, providing valuations and expert testimony. A nasty divorce battle, a hedge fund tycoon with a short fuse, impossible expectations, and millions at stake meant no room for error.

"You'll be fine."

"I don't know—I've still got hours of work to do." If things went wrong, Zachary Barron could ruin her reputation with a phone call. If, on the other hand, he won—the publicity would be priceless.

"It'll work out."

It always did for Jace. Her mind slipped back to the doctor's office. What if Harry was hurt somewhere, or worse? She would tell Jace about the Alzheimer's—once Harry was safe and sound. She winced as another cramp gripped her stomach.

"Kat?"

"Huh?"

"I said, yes—let's go to the house. But we should call the police first. They'll be much more effective than the two of us on foot. I know you don't want to ..."

Harry had been calling the police at least twice a week lately for imagined break-ins and thefts. Not all cops were sympathetic when called out for what inevitably turned out to be an old man's delusions, a false alarm. Harry wanted to keep living in his home, and as long as Kat kept an eye on him, she figured he'd be safe. Until now. Things were getting much worse, faster than she ever imagined.

"No—it's okay. Call them."

Jace punched in the numbers on his cell phone as they strode to the underground parking garage.

Kat checked her watch again as they headed down the ramp. The hearing was in less than eleven hours.

As they rounded the corner onto the first level of the

parking garage, the glare of the bright fluorescent lights played shadows on the gray concrete walls.

Then she saw him. In the far corner, a figure curled up in a fetal position. He faced them, his back nested against the corner where the two walls met. His upper body was partially covered by a piece of cardboard. She couldn't be sure, but he seemed to be wearing a gray windbreaker.

"Uncle Harry?" She broke into a run.

The man sat up and pulled back the cardboard. He grinned. It was Harry.

Kat reached him and held out a hand to help him up.

"Can we go home now?" Harry said without missing a beat.

CHAPTER 4

THE JUDGE YAWNED AS KAT finished her testimony. Bad sign. Financial analysis was often the difference between financial windfall and complete financial ruin in high-profile divorces. As a forensic accountant, she knew it was always a numbers game. High stakes were decided by the stroke of the judge's pen. In this case, a bored judge.

No matter how often Kat provided expert testimony, she always got nervous. And felt personally responsible if things went sideways for her client. Zachary Barron's case was no different. She cursed herself for her lack of preparation. She was off her game. If she lost such a high-profile case, she'd ruin her reputation and maybe even her business. It was the last thing she could afford. She needed cash more than ever for Harry's care, and she couldn't blow it over a lack of sleep.

Zachary Barron's eyes bored into hers. Why was her client staring at her like that? Had she missed something? Said something wrong? No. She had to stop second-guessing herself.

Finally Zachary glanced away.

She exhaled. *Relax.*

In court just ten minutes and things were already out of control.

"Looks like you forgot a few zeros on your calculator, Ms. Carter."

Kat half-expected Connor Whitehall to wink like she'd just performed a parlor trick—a gray-haired lawyer chastising a much younger expert witness. His aging television-anchor looks, expensive suits, and thirty-something years on her created a powerful impression. An impression he used to discredit her.

"I haven't missed a thing." Kat tried not to sound defensive. She clenched her hands together as she sat inside the witness box. The courtroom was empty, save for the warring Barron spouses and their lawyers. Victoria and Zachary Barron sat on opposite sides of the courtroom, studiously avoiding eye contact.

Whitehall shook his head. He shifted his gaze to the judge and sauntered towards him. The judge's head jerked up from whatever he was reading as the sound of Whitehall's footsteps filled the silent courtroom.

Kat thought she saw a look pass between them. The judge probably figured she was stupid too. Maybe that's why he wasn't listening.

What if she had made a mistake? With less than three hours sleep and no time for a dry run this morning, she was hardly on top of her game. She'd brought Uncle Harry with her to the courthouse again, having run out of options. Leaving him home alone was too risky. He was convinced squatters in his house were trying to kill him. This time she'd parked him at the coffee shop in the lobby and bribed the waitress to watch him. She felt guilty about it, but she'd exhausted all other alternatives.

She hadn't missed anything, she reassured herself. Whitehall was just using old lawyer tricks to make her crack. She was the only forensic accountant in the courtroom, and the only qualified fraud expert. Still, tracing a tycoon's assets was never straightforward.

"You've missed hundreds of millions of dollars!" Whitehall spun around as the corners of his mouth turned up into a mischievous grin. "Yet you call yourself a forensic accountant?"

Whitehall paused before strolling back to where Kat sat in the witness box. He leaned in close, exhaling coffee breath into her personal space. Kat held her breath. Why did she feel like the one on trial?

"Objection!" Zachary Barron's lawyer sprang into action. Finally. Kat felt like she'd been left to the wolves, or worse, a predatory lawyer.

"Sustained." The judge's voice was devoid of emotion as he checked his watch. Counting the minutes till lunchtime.

Divorces brought out the worst in people, more than criminal fraud, white-collar crime, or anything else. But these little wars were the bread and butter of her forensic accounting practice, providing steady cash flow.

For once she was on the side of the client with money. He would pay her bill on time, in full. In her weeks of groundwork, she'd identified all the assets, verified the valuations, appraisals, and legal titles, and even turned up a few surprises. She just had to follow through and it would be over in twenty minutes.

Kat glanced over at her client. Zachary Barron sat head down as he thumb-tapped yet another message on his BlackBerry. He was in his mid-thirties, just like her, but with more money than she'd ever see in a lifetime. He could potentially lose most of it in the next ten minutes if Whitehall got his way. So much was at stake, yet he treated the hearing like a distraction. She, on the other hand, was breaking into a sweat, and it wasn't even her money.

"Ms. Carter?" Whitehall asked.

"Are you asking a question?"

"Yes, I'm asking you a question. I'm disputing the valuation you have assigned to the matrimonial assets."

17

"That doesn't sound like a question." Kat returned Whitehall's stare with her best look of puzzlement and consternation. *Cheeky maybe, but two could play at this game.*

"Ms. Carter! This isn't *Jeopardy*. You valued the matrimonial assets at thirty million. Why have you excluded the family business?" He tapped his pen against her exhibit, a little harder than necessary to make his point.

Good. She'd finally got Whitehall riled up.

Even Zachary glanced from the file he was reading and smiled. One thing she was sure of—if she had millions at stake, she sure as hell wouldn't be catching up on office paperwork.

Victoria Barron, Zachary's ex-wife, ex-part-time financial manager, and walking billboard for plastic surgery, sat at the opposing table, crossing and uncrossing her legs. Her expression remained impassive, except for a slight ever-present smile. Kat concluded it was a remnant of too much plastic surgery.

"May I?" Kat asked.

She rose from her seat and strode over to the easel holding her exhibit of the Barrons' assets. Kat focused her laser pointer on the Zachary's side of the financial organization chart.

On Edgewater Investments.

It was complicated. Operating companies, holding companies, and offshore trusts. Zachary had been careful to keep very little in his own name. She spent the next ten minutes explaining the complex web of agreements and relationships amongst the entities.

Whitehall raised his eyebrows, then walked away and slumped into the chair beside Victoria Barron. He crossed his arms and gave Kat a look of contempt.

She smiled back at him. "Shall I go on?"

He glared at her.

Victoria Barron, Zachary's soon to be ex-trophy wife, was gunning for not only half the matrimonial assets, but also half of Zachary's business. A hundred million rode on Kat's interpretation of what was or wasn't included in matrimonial assets. But Zachary had a pre-nup.

"Edgewater Investments is Mr. Barron's business. It is certainly not community property, so I have excluded it from the matrimonial assets to be divided." She traced the pointer above the Edgewater box, to two other boxes, both holding companies. One was owned by Zachary Barron, the other by his father, Nathan Barron.

"Not true. My client is entitled to half of that."

"If that's the case, we should apply the same logic to Mrs. Barron's business."

"That's hypothetical," he snorted. "She has no business."

Actually, she was in the business of getting married. And marriage number three was about to end. "Are you sure about that?" Kat asked.

"Of course I'm sure!" Whitehall jumped up from his seat and marched towards her. "And I'm the one asking the questions, not you."

"You really should talk to your client. According to my records, she has sizable investments, as well as a healthy income. Didn't she tell you any of this?"

Whitehall stepped back, obviously surprised. He flashed an angry glare at Victoria Barron. Her eyes widened and her mouth opened into a perfectly round Botox *O*.

Kat flipped to a second chart and rolled through the details of Victoria Barron's winning wine and real estate investments, endorsement deals from her plastic surgery reality show, and recent fragrance deal with a cosmetics company. She had hidden it well, with profits funneled to offshore companies in the Caymans. But a spreadsheet was a deadly weapon in the hands of a good forensic accountant.

"Those aren't investments," Whitehall scoffed. "It's personal property."

Kat glanced over at Victoria. Her perfectly sculpted shoulders slumped and her eyes closed momentarily. "A few bottles of wine, maybe. But she made a two-hundred-thousand-dollar profit last year on her wine investments alone. And her real estate portfolio is eight figures. That's some hobby." Her analysis had dispelled the dependent housewife myth—now it was up to the judge to decide.

"It hardly compares to a hundred million." Whitehall's tone was flat and defeated.

"What else isn't she telling us?" Kat turned to smile at the judge, but his head was down, reading the newspaper Kat had noticed earlier. He had hidden it under a file folder on the side of his desk.

Whitehall flushed as he strode back to his seat without saying anything. Flying by the seat of his pants, probably assuming he'd never be questioned. Unprepared. She had him and he knew it.

"That's just one of the dozens of sales she's had over the last year. Or didn't she tell you?"

His face reddened to a deep crimson. Even from twenty feet, Kat saw his knuckles whiten as he dug them into the weathered oak table.

Silence.

"Why don't you ask her yourself?" Kat pointed with her pen. "As you can see here, she actually owes Mr. Barron, instead of the other way around."

No answer.

Zachary fidgeted.

Kat felt her face flush. Had she pushed things too far?

"Not a chance, Ms. Carter. Your numbers are bogus."

Kat took a deep breath and flipped to her final chart. She was about to explain why Whitehall was wrong when the courtroom doors swung open with a bang. She looked up, startled.

"Kat!"

Uncle Harry stood in the doorway and waved his keys.

"You've got to help me! I've lost the Lincoln."

Uncle Harry—again forgetting the accident.

Kat motioned for Harry to sit down. Judges were unpredictable. This was exactly the sort of thing that could turn the tide against her client.

Uncle Harry threw his hands up in the air in an exaggerated flourish, but then slumped down in a seat in the second row. She hoped he could stay quiet for the next few minutes.

"Friend of yours?" Whitehall raised his eyebrows.

Kat ignored him.

Harry's voice rose again, an unfortunate result of the room's acoustics.

"Damn towing companies! Why can't they leave a note or a phone number or something?"

The judge motioned to the bailiff standing at the back of the room.

"Your Honor, I'm sorry. Give me a minute, please." If she hadn't already blown it, she surely had now. She strode towards Harry as fast as possible without breaking into a run.

"Where, Uncle Harry? On the curb?" Kat whispered as she patted his arm. "Ten more minutes. Then we'll search for your car." The Lincoln was safely parked in Harry's garage. She'd disconnected the garage door opener as an added precaution since he'd refused to part with his car keys.

"They could at least call me." He pouted and crossed his arms.

Whitehall turned to face the judge. "Your honor, do we really need to listen to more?"

"No counsel, I don't think we do."

Whitehall gloated.

Kat returned to the witness box. She glanced at Victoria Barron, who was smiling into a handheld mirror, checking her makeup.

Victoria's smile faded when the judge spoke.

"Judgment for three million in matrimonial assets to be divided equally. Case dismissed."

Zachary Barron snapped his file shut and straightened, suddenly at full attention. Like someone had flipped a switch.

Kat should have felt good, but divorce cases always got her down. How could two people fall in love, then hate each other within three years? Money brought out the worst in people. They would die for it, lie for it, and even kill for it. She'd seen it countless times in her line of work.

That's why she'd never get married. Not even to Jace, despite his proposal. They'd had heated discussions about it, even broke up over it two years ago. They'd been testing the waters as a couple again for the last year, and she wasn't screwing that up by getting married.

She shoved her papers into her briefcase and made a beeline for Harry.

"Let's go outside." She linked arms with her uncle and steered him out to the lobby. It was the second time today Harry had thought he'd lost his Lincoln. "Uncle Harry—maybe it's time you—"

Harry held his arm up in protest.

"Will you stop it, Kat? It's my God-given right to drive. I drive better than all those other yahoos on the road. They're the ones creating problems."

"Driving's a privilege and a convenience. But when we get older, sometimes it's better to be—"

"Don't use that 'we' tone with me, young lady! I might be old, but I will not be patronized!"

Harry's rising voice echoed in the cavernous marble foyer. Groups of lawyers, plaintiffs, and others turned and stared, most giving her suspicious glares.

"Don't be upset, Uncle Harry. I'm just worried about you."

"I know." His voice cracked. "But it's frustrating. What's happening to me, Kat?"

Harry rubbed a hand over his bald head.

"It's okay, Uncle Harry." Kat touched his arm. "You've just been busy. We all forget sometimes."

Aunt Elsie's unexpected heart attack right after the Liberty Diamond Mines case had hit Harry hard. Dr. McAdam figured the stress accelerated the decline in his mental health. Now Kat was his only family to speak of. What might be next on the dementia journey scared her too.

"It's easier to take the bus. No car or parking tickets to worry about." Kat squeezed his hand. "I can drive you wherever you need to go."

"After you drove your car into the Fraser River last year?" Harry pulled his hand away. "No thanks."

His long-term memory was still remarkably intact.

"Kat—wait."

Kat spun around. Zachary Barron emerged from the crowd and marched towards her. People parted on either side, opening a path for him like he was royalty. A clean-cut man in an Ermenegildo Zegna suit whispered success and power. Kat's arm-in-arm journey with Harry a minute earlier had been more like a jousting match, as she elbow-bashed and zigzagged through the crowd.

Zachary couldn't possibly be mad about the settlement. Or could he? Save a client a hundred million and they'd still find something to complain about. He hadn't even seen her bill yet.

"Kat? We need to talk."

"Sure. You do realize you got a very good result. It's hard to—"

"It's not about the divorce." He glanced around to see who was within earshot, then leaned closer. "You handle fraud, right?"

"Yes, of course." Corporate fraud and divorce were both big areas of her forensic accounting practice. But Harry was agitated; she had to calm him down and distract him from his Lincoln.

Harry. Kat spun around, but he had vanished. The lunchtime crowd had swallowed up Harry's path. Her eyes searched the crowd, a life-sized *Where's Waldo?* puzzle. Nothing. A wave of panic washed over her. How could she find a short, balding octogenarian in the sea of people?

Out of the corner of her eye, she saw him. A flash of gray hair, a beige raincoat. Harry—or at least someone who resembled Harry—disappeared around a corner.

"Zachary—can I call you later this afternoon? Something's just come up."

She pressed speed dial on her cell, trying to call Uncle Harry and corral him back. Even if he had his phone, he probably wouldn't answer, but it was worth a try.

"It's urgent," Zachary said. "I'll come by your office this afternoon. Two o'clock."

It was more of a command than a question. Kat glanced up from her cell phone to protest, but Zachary Barron was gone.

CHAPTER 5

KAT AND HARRY PICKED AT the remains of the Chinese takeout she'd ordered after finding Harry on the courtroom steps two hours before. The food seemed to settle her stomach and it felt good to finally be back at Carter & Associates after this morning's courtroom drama. Her office's hundred-year-old brick walls wouldn't withstand a strong earthquake, but today they felt like a fortress. The sketchy neighborhood and rustic furnishings felt comfortable, especially with her uncle finally safe and sound.

"She's back, Kat. It's like she never left." Harry's eyes shone as he spoke.

Hillary's return was one of Harry's delusions Kat could do without.

She shuddered as she remembered her first week living with the Dentons. She had arrived home from school to find Hillary by the fireplace, grinning. She stood in front of the roaring fire, Kat's photographs in her hand while she beckoned Kat over with the other. Then she dropped them into the flames, one by one. The pictures of her mother gone forever. All she had left were memories, and those faded further with each passing year.

"Really?" Kat played along. Despite her feelings, reminding Harry it wasn't true only caused mental anguish. No one wanted to know they were losing their mind.

"Yup. Great, isn't it?"

Kat reached for a second egg roll. "When did she come back?"

"A while ago. She's moving back home. I wish Elsie was here to see her. She would be so proud."

Harry manned the front desk while Kat sat cross-legged on the couch, feeling more relaxed after a quick run. She'd moved a treadmill into the spare office so she could still fit in a workout despite keeping an eye on her uncle.

"Proud?" Proud his daughter had the nerve to show her face after what she did?

"She's got a new job."

"Doing what?" Hillary had never worked a day in her life. Unless you counted cheating and manipulating people out of money a career. She'd convinced Harry and Elsie to lend her all their retirement savings, promising to pay it back. They never heard from her again. Some things were better forgotten.

"Can't remember. But it's something really important."

"I'm sure it is," Kat said. If it wasn't, Hillary would be quick to embellish, or more likely, fabricate the whole thing.

"And she's looking forward to catching up with you."

Kat felt a stab of fear. Nothing about Hillary came without a cost. But that was silly—Hillary now existed only in Harry's imagination.

"Business lunch?"

Kat snapped to attention at the man's voice. She wasn't expecting anyone for another hour.

Zachary Barron stood in the doorway, staring at her. She was suddenly conscious of how she appeared: stringy auburn hair, dried sweat on her face from the run. If he got any closer, he'd smell her damp, stinky running clothes. She chewed her mouthful of Chow Mein as fast as she could, and then Harry rescued her.

Harry swung around the reception desk, surprisingly fast for an eighty-year-old.

"I don't think we've met. I'm Harry Denton, Kat's associate."

Harry held out his hand. Zachary shook it and had the good grace not to mention their meeting earlier in the day.

The nameplate on the office door read Carter & Associates, but in reality Kat had been associate-less since opening the office two years ago. Nevertheless, Uncle Harry had always drummed up excuses to come by, so Kat had made it official.

At least his presence at the office allowed her to keep an eye on him, important since he had lost interest in just about everything and everyone else. His buddies at the curling rink swept the ice without him now, and weeds were all that grew in his once well-tended garden.

As their time together increased, she became acutely aware of his declining mental state. No matter what, she enjoyed having him at the office and figured the people contact was good for him.

"Mmmm, sorry." Kat swallowed a mouthful of noodles. She stood up and wiped her hand on her shorts. "I don't usually—"

"No need to explain. I'll make this quick."

Quick riches, quick marriages, quick divorces. Was there any other way with Zachary Barron?

"Didn't you say two o'clock?"

"I don't really do appointments. Can we talk or not?" Zachary asked.

CHAPTER 6

ZACHARY BARRON SAT ON THE edge of the leather armchair opposite Kat's desk, his designer suit and tie at odds with her office's shabby chic décor. He seemed oblivious to the furnishings and the million-dollar view outside.

Kat's office windows framed a view of the Vancouver harbor, spectacular even in the rain. The docks were deserted, though. The giant cruise ships that sailed the Alaska Inside Passage run were gone for the season. The only waterfront activities today were a dozen plump seagulls scavenging for food.

Zachary leaned forward, his elbows on Kat's desk. "I want you to investigate my partner."

"Your partner? But isn't he your—"

Zachary's mouth hardened into a frown. "Nathan Barron. Yes, he's my father. That doesn't make him any less capable of fraud."

"He founded Edgewater." Kat knew about the father and son's tangled web of inter-related companies from Zachary's divorce proceedings.

"Twenty years ago. But the company he started is nothing like Edgewater today. Back then it was just small trades, mostly table scraps his university buddies threw his way. And business was drying up."

"What changed?"

"Ten years ago I joined the company. I built Edgewater into what it is today."

Modest he was not. "How so?"

Zachary leaned back and straightened his tie. "My proprietary trading model turned Edgewater into the second-biggest hedge fund worldwide. The financial results point to our success, but where's the money? I had trouble settling a trade last week. The bank said we didn't have enough money. How can that be?"

"Maybe it was a timing issue?"

"No way. For a multi-billion-dollar hedge fund, our business is very simple. We buy and sell currency using my proprietary model. Trades settle a few days later, and the brokerage fees are paid as part of the trade settlement. Besides office rent, salaries, and expenses, there's nothing else to spend the money on." Zachary handed Kat the most recent Edgewater annual report.

"Nathan's always handled the back-office stuff, and I've done the trading. I never paid attention to the administrative side until last week when the bank said we were short. Where's all the money going?"

Kat knew the preliminary year-end results: they had been part of the Barron divorce proceedings. She flipped the report open to the income statement page. Her mouth dropped open. She hadn't seen the final, audited results until now. "Edgewater made two billion dollars after tax? Much higher than I thought."

Had Zachary timed the annual report's release to favor his divorce proceedings? Whether he did or not, it had certainly worked out that way.

"That's my point. Where did the money go? Two billion in earnings, yet only a few million in the bank. Edgewater's fully extended on our line of credit. Why is there so little cash when most of our trades are hundreds of millions of dollars?"

"That doesn't necessarily mean fraud, Zachary. It could be mismanagement." Kat was suddenly aware of Uncle Harry hovering just outside her office. He paced back and forth, his forehead creased in a frown.

"That's supposed to make me feel better?"

"No, but we need to consider all the possibilities. At any rate, I'll check it out. When do you need this?" Kat hoped to stretch the deadline. She glanced out to the hallway. She needed a diversion for Harry pronto.

"Yesterday. Without access to cash, Edgewater can't operate for more than a few days."

"You've talked to Nathan about this?" Kat knew things were tense between father and son from Zachary's divorce proceedings. Her valuation of Edgewater Investments assumed an equal partnership. However, Nathan disagreed and was even contemplating legal proceedings against his son.

"No. I want you to poke around first before I talk to him. I need all the facts."

"I can do that. What about investment losses? That could also wipe out your cash balances." Kat craned her neck towards the hall just as Harry disappeared again.

"Impossible. We've had a great year. At least three home runs, and double-digit returns. We should be tripping over cash. Instead, we're practically broke. I'm not involved in daily operations—Nathan does that—but at the trading level, I know exactly what I've bet on, and the percentage return."

"What about redemptions? A few big investors cashing out could decrease your cash on hand." Uncle Harry was back outside, clutching his checkbook. She should have known. He'd been trying to balance it for weeks, but had refused any help.

Zachary scowled. "No, exactly the opposite is happening.

Investors are scrambling to get into our fund. Matter of fact, new investments outnumber the redemptions by more than two to one. The Evergreen fund has stellar returns—all due to my trading model. Our investment return is way better than our competition's."

Uncle Harry peered anxiously around the doorframe.

"Uncle Harry? Everything okay?"

"Uh, yeah." Harry checked his watch and then disappeared down the hall again.

Kat turned back to Zachary. "I'll need access to your office and all of Edgewater's financial records, payroll—anything else involving payments or receipts. And access to the accounting system." She checked her watch. It was just after three. "I can start tonight."

"Great. I'll be at the office till about ten. Nathan's away again, so come by as soon as you can." Zachary rose. "I should go."

"Before you leave—why are you so sure there's a fraud? Nathan founded Edgewater. Why would he steal from it?"

"Why else would the money vanish? Nathan is a thief." Zachary spat the words out.

Apparently not on good terms. How did father and son manage to work together every day? A recent grudge, or a long-standing one?

"Any proof of your suspicions?" Kat leaned back in her chair, studying Zachary. Forensic accountants were a little like financial shrinks. Her psychoanalysis was based on open-ended questions. When people talked freely, they always revealed more.

"No, but you'll find it. I'm sure of that."

"If there really is a fraud, why all of a sudden now? Why not five or ten years ago?"

"The more successful I am, the more resentful he gets. It can't be the money itself. He's got all he needs. You can't even spend the kind of money we're bringing in."

Harry was back again. Only this time he didn't wait in the

hall. "Kat—sorry to interrupt. You gotta help me. We need to get to the bank before it closes. I need a loan."

"Uncle Harry, give me a minute." Kat felt bad asking Harry to wait, but a paying client was sitting right in front of her. She turned back to Zachary. "If Nathan is stealing, maybe it's his way of evening the score with you. Like you said, billionaires like Nathan don't need more money."

"You'd think he'd be grateful. The funds grew astronomically when I joined Edgewater. My proprietary trading model picks winners, and our performance is better than anyone else's. He gets to bask in the glory without any effort."

"What's so special about your model? Why couldn't he do it without you?"

"Currency speculation is part technical analysis and part gut feel. My model crunches the numbers—GDP, government debt, interest rates, and other economic data. Then it uses game theory to evaluate every possibility."

"Game theory?" Kat remembered the mathematical model from school. Players either competed or cooperated to maximize their own individual payoffs.

"In the simplest terms, it means everybody's out for their own personal gain, even at the expense of others."

"I know what it means, Zachary." Kat fought to control her annoyance. "My question was about how it factors into your model."

"You don't need to understand the details." Zachary dismissed her with a wave of his hand. "My model determines the likelihood of any event happening or not, based on how rewarding it is to the players involved. Then I make my bet and corner the market. My bet alone will move the currency, because our fund is so big. But the real payoff is when traders follow, thinking it's a sure thing. It becomes a self-fulfilling prophecy, making Edgewater even bigger profits. The other traders still score, as long as they get out before I sell my position. Then fortunes reverse."

"You're manipulating the currency."

"Absolutely not. I'm just taking a position. A huge one, perhaps. But I'm no Pied Piper; other speculators don't have to blindly follow me. Just because they do doesn't mean I'm manipulating them."

"But most of those followers will lose. Like a hot potato, the big players or insiders reap profits at the expense of those who buy when they're ready to sell. Whoever's late to the game suffers. Is that fair?" Zachary and his father were each billionaires in their own right. They had more money than ninety-nine percent of the world's population. What more did they need?

"There are no victims here. They know my motives are to make a profit."

"Thus weakening the currency further."

"It's a free world, Kat. Free choice, free will."

"And then the government intervenes?"

"In theory. They buy up their currency to prop it up. But they can't really control it—the currency markets do. The markets trade about four trillion dollars per day—run mainly by speculators like me. Government reserves are less than a tenth of that."

"Huge," Kat agreed. "So you place a bet, say, that the U.S. dollar will drop. What happens next?"

"All currency trades in currency pairs. Say I bet against the U.S. dollar. I'll sell it at the same time I'm buying another currency—or betting it will go up. Let's say that's the Euro. The U.S. dollar will drop because I've sold more than other people are buying. The Euro will rise against the U.S. dollar simply because I've just bought a huge position in it."

"Supply and demand," Kat said. "An exclusive game only a few can play."

"Anyone can play."

"Only with enough money. You need a huge amount to move the market. Smaller players can only be followers."

"Technically, yes. But people who follow me can potentially make a lot of money."

"If they get the timing right."

"Of course. Timing is everything. Or they can just invest in Edgewater's hedge fund instead."

"Isn't the minimum investment five hundred grand? That's too rich for most investors."

"Maybe." Zachary stood. "I can't worry about other people. I focus on what I do best—making money."

"You sure you don't want to talk with Nathan first? Maybe there's a logical explanation."

"No point—he's never around. He's off on one of his sailing trips, or maybe big game hunting in Africa. He doesn't tell me where or when he goes."

Zachary probably liked it that way. He ran the business without much interference from his father. Most fraud was kept quiet. No one wanted to take responsibility for theft on their watch, and unless it significantly impacted their business and the profits of their shareholders, management usually forced the perpetrator to quietly resign. Retribution was rare: usually the money was already spent.

Kat scribbled a few notes on her legal pad. "What if your suspicions are confirmed and I do find fraud? What happens next?"

"I'll destroy him."

CHAPTER 7

KAT AND HARRY WAITED IN the tiny windowless office while the bank manager retrieved Harry's bank records. An inbox stacked six inches high with files and paper-clipped documents sat on the left side of the worn wooden desk. Beside it a brass nameplate read *Anita Boehmer*. Several diplomas and a child's drawing hung on the only wall. Three glass partitions with half-open venetian blinds enclosed the rest of the room.

No wonder Harry was so distressed. According to his bank statement, he was flat out broke. Kat pointed to a transaction halfway down the page. "It says here that you already have a loan."

"It does? Let me see that." Harry traced his finger beside Kat's. "Ten thousand dollars? That's got to be a mistake."

Kat thought so too. Uncle Harry was frugal to the point of madness. He shopped at thrift stores, re-used Saran Wrap, and had worn the same pair of re-soled shoes for as long as Kat could remember.

She scanned the rest of the statement. A number of

checks for amounts in the thousands were listed as well. She flipped through the stack of cancelled checks. They were all made out to cash. Her pulse quickened. This was completely unlike Harry.

Anita Boehmer returned with a couple of manila folders. She dropped them on her desk and smiled at Harry. She sat down in her high-backed chair behind the desk. "I see what the problem is."

"So do I." Harry crossed his arms. "Your records are wrong. I didn't take out any loan."

"I'm afraid you did, Mr. Denton. I remember, because I approved it. Last month. You said you needed money for renovations. Don't you remember?"

"That's impossible," Kat said. Harry never financed anything. And he certainly didn't renovate.

"Here's the loan agreement." The bank manager pulled it out of the file and turned it upside down so Kat could read it. Sure enough, it had Harry's signature at the bottom, signed a month ago. Harry really had taken out a loan. But why? Where was all his money going?

Kat studied the document. It *was* his signature, though his big loopy *y* was shakier now. "That is your signature, Uncle Harry. I guess you forgot."

Harry uncrossed his arms and leaned forward to study the document. "No, I did not." His voice rose as his face reddened.

She patted the top of his hand. It felt brittle and trembled under her touch. "Look at the signature."

"Let me see." Harry jerked the paper away from Kat. "It does look like my writing. But it can't be. It must be forged."

Kat sighed. Harry was being paranoid again about someone stealing from him, another Alzheimer's delusion. But his signature was right there on the form, in blue ink. The real question was why he needed the money. And who drove him to the bank. She turned to Anita. "This is completely out of character for Harry. Didn't you think to ask him why he's taking out a loan for the first time in his life?"

"Katerina, I am very sorry, but we can't interrogate everyone who asks for money. We take them at face value unless there's a glaring error."

She was right of course. Harry's dementia wasn't obvious. Until you talked to him for about two minutes. Surely the loan application had taken longer than that. Didn't Anita notice how often Harry repeated himself? It was too late to do anything about that now.

Kat refocused on the bank statement. She pointed to the next line on the statement. The same ten thousand dollars transferred out the next day. "Anita, where did this money go?"

"Transferred out to another bank. All we have is the bank and the account number. I'm afraid you'll have to contact them. Sorry."

Kat circled the transaction with her pen. If she could identify the recipient, she would be one step closer to finding out what was going on.

CHAPTER 8

KAT FOLLOWED HARRY UP THE creaking steps to her front door. Kat and Jace had purchased the old Victorian at a tax sale last year. The stairs were just one of many repairs listed on their never-ending to-do list.

While their renovations weren't on hold, the *for sale* sign was. Kat and Jace originally planned to fix and flip it for a quick profit, but they had grown attached to the Victorian house. It was one of the oldest houses in their Queen's Park neighborhood, conveniently located just two blocks from Harry's.

"Jace? We're home." She paused to inhale the restorative aromas of basil, oregano, and tomato.

"In here. Hope you're hungry."

Kat followed Jace's voice into the kitchen. He stood at the stove, stirring the source of the wonderful smell. Kat's gaze drifted from his muscled arms to his form-fitting black t-shirt. Even in an apron he looked hot.

He winked at her. "Spaghetti?"

"Love some." She kissed him, wishing she could stay. "You seem happy."

"I am. My real estate fraud story is running on the front page. Tomorrow's paper."

"Hmmm, wonderful. Does that give you rock star status at the *Sentinel*?" Jace had uncovered a real estate fraud involving dozens of high-end properties on Vancouver's affluent west side. The ruse used inflated appraisals to flip properties.

"Not quite. But I'm in McCleary's good books again. He thinks I can get a series out of it." Jace's hard-nosed editor was notoriously difficult to please.

"Good news." Kat glanced over at Harry. He sat at the kitchen table, head slumped forward onto his chest as he snored.

She lowered her voice and told Jace about the bank loan and the never-ending search for the Lincoln. But not about his Alzheimer's. Not yet. Saying it out loud made it all too real. "Harry's problems are much worse than I thought."

"Can't the bank find out where the money went?"

"No, and I don't know what to do. It's obvious Harry can't manage on his own anymore. First the fire, and now this." She felt a catch in her throat and turned away, hoping Jace hadn't noticed. Living alone was becoming a serious safety issue.

He dropped the spoon on the counter and circled his arms around her waist. "He could move in here. We've got lots of room."

"I—I don't know, Jace. It will be a big change for you." Kat pulled away from his embrace. Jace didn't know what he was offering, what he was getting himself into. Overnight he would be plunged into Harry's paranoid world. A world that worsened with every passing day of dementia. It might be too much for Jace.

"It's no big deal. We're at Harry's place all the time anyways." Jace tapped the spoon against the rim of the saucepan. "It might even be easier on both of us."

Kat tiptoed over to the kitchen table to avoid waking Uncle Harry. She detoured around the section of the floor that creaked, but it was no use. Harry jerked awake just as she pulled out her chair. "Sleepy?"

"Now, why would I be sleepy? It's barely lunchtime." Harry rose from his seat and shuffled towards the bathroom. "I'm going to freshen up."

It was actually after six, but Kat didn't bother to correct him. "I know. I'm already hungry." Harry had already forgotten his day at court and Kat's office.

Jace carried over two heaping plates of spaghetti and set them on the table.

"I can't stay long, Jace. I'm starting on the Edgewater case tonight."

"Now you're working nights? Zachary Barron doesn't waste any time, does he?"

"Guess not." Kat picked up her fork and twirled some pasta around it. The portion on her plate could feed a small army. "Anyways, it will be good to get a head start and see what this case is all about. Especially while Nathan Barron's out of town." She filled him in on the Barrons—Zachary's suspicions and Edgewater Investments.

Harry emerged from the bathroom. "You're telling Jace about my bank loan? Geez, the bank's robbing me blind. Would you believe ten thousand dollars, Jace? Criminals!"

Kat raised her eyebrows at Jace, surprised Harry still remembered. "We were just at the bank. They said Harry took out a loan last month."

"Really?" Jace glanced at Kat. "What are you buying, Harry? Real estate?"

"I didn't buy anything. Those crooks forged my signature! You know what? I can't wait—I'm calling the police." Harry grabbed the kitchen phone. "What's the number, Jace?"

"Uh, Harry, why don't we eat first?" Jace returned to the stove and spooned out another plate of spaghetti. He sat down at the table, opposite Kat and Harry. "We'll call the police after dinner."

"Mmmm, this is good, Jace." Kat hadn't realized how hungry she was. Harry would forget all about calling the police in a few minutes. But that didn't solve the problem of who orchestrated the loan. Harry couldn't visit the bank on his own since he had to be driven. He rarely left the house at all anymore. He never went anywhere alone, except maybe the supermarket or coffee shop. Had he met someone at either of those places?

"I busted a fraud ring, Harry. It's tomorrow's top story." Jace grinned. "They bought houses and faked real estate appraisals to inflate the property values. They took out huge loans against the houses, then took off with the money."

Kat made a slicing motion across her neck. Loan was a four-letter word.

Jace's smile vanished and he mouthed *sorry*. But then he continued nonetheless. "They let the banks foreclose on them. I traced at least two dozen high-end houses on the West Side and exposed them. Until my story, they weren't even on the cops' radar."

"Humph," Harry said as he twirled pasta around his fork. "You know, I feel a bit sick right now. I think I've had enough."

"Eat, Uncle Harry." Kat studied her uncle. No wonder he felt sick—he hardly ate anything. His face was drawn and pale; that recent flu was really taking a toll. He needed all the calories he could get.

"All right."

They ate the rest of the meal in silence. Despite her profession, Kat often felt money was the root of all evil, or most of it, anyways. This was one of those moments.

"I'm just happy to have my story finished." Jace set down his fork and checked his watch. "Now I can relax. Hey, the hockey game's on. Want to watch the game, Harry?"

"And watch a bunch of carefree millionaires chase a puck? No thanks."

CHAPTER 9

KAT FOLLOWED ZACHARY THROUGH THE heavy wood doors that guarded Nathan's office. She had timed her visit for after-hours so it wouldn't raise suspicions among Edgewater's employees.

A massive, richly carved mahogany desk dominated the center of the room. To the left, built-in bookcases overflowed with leather-bound volumes and more recent hardcovers. In the right-hand corner, a dark brown leather sofa and chair faced a table with an alabaster chess set. The wall above was lined with pictures encased in heavy wood frames. The windows were framed with partially closed, heavy damask drapes.

Despite being twenty floors up, Kat felt transported to the study of a nineteenth-century country estate. The air carried the faint scent of cigars. Even with Zachary's presence, she felt uneasy, like she'd trespassed into a hunter's lair. A hunter who might return at any moment.

Kat's shoes sank into the thick Berber carpet as she wandered over to study the pictures. Nathan Barron was in every one of them. Various locations, poses, and locales, but they all involved Nathan posing with something he had just shot or speared. Mostly bears, lions, other cats. A predator among predators.

Kat moved down the wall to the last picture, which judging by the frame, was the most recent. A stocky sixty-year-old man stood beside a hippo. Shirtless, wearing just khakis and a rifle slung over his shoulder. With a grin that said *top of the food chain*. It sent chills through Kat.

"Last year. Selous Reserve. Tanzania. It's considered poaching to kill a hippo, but he doesn't care."

Kat jumped at Zachary's voice, then recovered. "I've got to ask the obvious. Why would a billionaire steal from his own company? He doesn't have to do this."

"Simple. Nathan's a cheap bastard. Edgewater is fifty percent mine. If he pays through Edgewater, he gets a fifty percent discount."

"And risk going to jail?" Kat didn't buy it. Something more than money was driving the fraud. "Why? He's already got more money than he can spend in a lifetime."

Kat sat down in Nathan Barron's chair, trying to get a feel for a man she hadn't met yet. The desk surface was bare, save for an empty inbox and a telephone. It contrasted with Zachary's office, where disorganized stacks of paper and three computer screens competed for attention.

Kat opened the side desk drawer. She pulled a thick sheath of papers out of a manila file. She studied the top sheet, a spreadsheet. A series of numbers were added and subtracted in each of about a dozen columns.

She flipped through the pages underneath. They were all in the same format, only the headings and numbers were different. "What's this?"

"I don't know," Zachary said. "Yesterday was the first time I'd been in here. He always keeps his office locked."

"You don't have a master key?" Odd that Zachary, as co-owner, wouldn't have keys to every office. She turned her attention back to the first spreadsheet. Heading each column was a set of initials and numbers. It was a code of some sort. If so, it must be cryptic for a reason. What did Nathan Barron have to hide?

Zachary shook his head. "Nathan had a special lock made for his office door. I brought a locksmith in yesterday to make me a key."

Kat set the spreadsheet aside. She had arrived at Edgewater almost two hours ago. Before searching Nathan's office, she had reviewed all checks issued from Edgewater Investments itself and from its hedge fund, Evergreen. It had been strange to look at them, as many carried Victoria's signature—she'd only left the company's accounting department upon formal separation from Zachary. Aside from the usual payments for expenses like rent, office supplies, and payroll, Kat noted some very large invoices and cancelled checks for investment research. She pulled the file with the documents from her briefcase and handed it to Zachary. "What do you know about these?"

Zachary sat down at his father's desk and opened the file. He sifted through the first few pages. "Research Analytics? Never heard of them."

"Shouldn't you know about them?"

Zachary looked up from the invoices, clearly puzzled. "Why would I?"

"They're Edgewater's biggest expense," Kat explained. "They provide research analysis on currency, your area of expertise. Shouldn't the name be familiar to you?"

"You're right. But it isn't." Zachary unlocked Nathan's bottom drawer and tabbed through the files.

"May I?" Kat exchanged places with Zachary and powered up Nathan's computer. She attached a portable hard drive to the computer and mouse-clicked to start copying Nathan's files. While she waited for the data to copy over, she pulled the files one by one from his desk, searching for more clues. Other than his files and office supplies, the desk drawers contained a few credit cards and some loose change. She wasn't too hopeful—Nathan hardly spent any time at the office. That likely meant he had very little on his computer.

After Nathan's files had successfully copied onto her portable hard drive, she clicked a few of them open one by one. Nothing significant jumped out, just a few marketing letters about Edgewater's fund performance.

Zachary stood behind her chair as she closed the last file. "Nothing?"

"Nothing. But there's one more place I'd like to check." She opened Nathan's email and accessed his contact list. Hundreds of contacts came up, in stark contrast to the paucity of computer files. She scrolled down the list, noting billionaire philanthropists, royalty, and heads of state. Nathan moved in a rarefied circle.

Near the bottom of the list something caught her eye. A group listing under *W* for something called the *World Institute*.

"Zachary, what's the World Institute?"

He leaned closer and squinted at the screen. "World what?"

She clicked open the entry to reveal a list of names within it. "This World Institute group listing—ever heard of it?"

"Not sure...I think it's some sort of global think tank Nathan belongs to."

"What exactly do they do?" She scanned the list. Current and former heads of state. The head of the International Monetary Fund—along with members of at least two royal families.

"Something to do with currency theory, I think. Nathan mentioned it once or twice, back when we actually spoke to each other."

"Currency theory—wouldn't that interest you?" Why didn't Zachary know more about something clearly related to his field of expertise?

"Not really. I trade currency—I don't theorize about it. Theory is for academics." He rested his hand on the back of her chair as he scanned the list of names.

Kat scribbled a note to herself to find out more. She disconnected her hard drive and placed it in her briefcase. She'd sift through the remaining records byte by byte back at her office.

"Look at this." Zachary bent over and plucked a paper out of Nathan's waste paper basket. "He's not even hiding it."

Kat studied the paper.

"What's wrong with a flight to London?" It was a travel itinerary. A flight and six nights at a luxury hotel.

"For starters, he's supposed to be meeting with our New York bankers, London's got nothing to do with our business. Of course, he doesn't care about that."

"The lines between personal and business travel sometimes blur. That's common in family business."

"Family business?" Zachary spat out the words like poison. "We're family in name only."

"The flight was yesterday. Any idea what's going on in London?"

CHAPTER 10

KAT'S BREATHING QUICKENED AS SHE climbed the hill, unable to concentrate on anything more than her slow jog up the ten percent grade. Uncle Harry's house was halfway up, close but still an impossible thirty meters away.

Her legs burned, unaccustomed to running up the long incline. Already Friday and it was her first run this week. With Harry's increased needs and her growing workload, it was difficult to get a decent run in, or to find any time for herself. This might be her longest run for a while, so she wanted to make it hurt, to make it count.

The steep grade gave the illusion of a road to nowhere, rising almost vertically until it touched the horizon, ending abruptly. At least that was the view from the bottom. When she was growing up, after her dad left and she went to live with Harry and Elsie, she'd wanted to just keep on going. Up to the top of the hill, where she would pretend there was nothing above the asphalt but sky. There she'd drop off the face of the earth—away from her past, present, and most especially, away from Hillary.

She'd started out early to fit in a two-hour run before Harry woke. The steady downpour had trickled to a shower. Not that it mattered anymore. Her clothes were soaked, and her running shoes squished from landing in too many puddles.

Kat finally crested the hill and slowed to a walk at the top. Harry's Cape Cod house came into view a half-block away. It was a far cry from the immaculate condition Harry had always kept it in. Moss had overtaken the lawn, and paint peeled from the window frames.

After the car accident, she'd taken to checking in on Harry every morning, getting him breakfast and bringing him to the office, or to her house on weekends. She knocked on the door and waited a few minutes. No answer. The television was blaring. Judge Judy was berating someone about a convertible that didn't belong to them.

She bent down and flipped up the letter slot, her legs already stiffening.

"Uncle Harry? It's me, Kat."

Footsteps shuffled behind the door. Metal clicked as Harry unlocked a half-dozen bolts.

"Nice to see you!" Harry smiled at her.

As if they hadn't seen each other in ages. As if she didn't do this check-in every morning.

"What brings you here?" Harry wore a short-sleeved Hawaiian shirt and wool pants cinched with a belt. He'd lost so much weight since Elsie died last year.

"Just checking in. Feeling better than yesterday?"

"Why? What happened yesterday?"

"You were feeling sick." Kat dropped her gaze to Harry's forearm, purple with bruises. "Did you fall?"

"Now why would you ask that?" Harry closed the door and frowned.

"Your arm." She held it and pointed to the bruises.

Harry stared at his arm in wonder. "Yup, I guess I did. But I guess everything's fine now."

Harry motioned Kat inside. "It's about time you came by, Kat. I haven't seen you in weeks!"

She followed Harry inside the hall, where a wall of heat assaulted her. A stack of mail sat on the side table. She picked up the envelopes and sifted through them, looking for bills or anything else that needed prompt attention. Two Visa bills, a MasterCard bill, a phone bill, and his latest bank statement.

She opened the first Visa statement and almost gasped when she saw the balance.

Twenty-two thousand dollars and change. The other two credit card statements had similar transactions. All together they totaled thirty grand. That amounted to a lot of pension checks.

Her heart thumped in her chest as she pocketed the statements. She walked into the bathroom, closing the door behind her so she could examine them without arousing Harry's suspicion.

Six thousand at Tiffany's. What on earth could Harry possibly buy at Tiffany's? Another four thousand at various designer clothing stores. Troubling, since Harry only shopped at thrift stores. Interest and a balance carried forward made up the rest of the amount owing. Was it a mistake? Probably not, in light of the suspicious loan. And now she discovered three different credit card balances.

She opened the latest bank statement and checked the ending balance. Harry's overdraft was much higher than she remembered seeing in Anita Boehmer's office. But, then, the statement Harry had brought to the bank had been a month old.

She held her breath and flipped to the last page. A mortgage, taken out almost three weeks ago, was listed along with the home reno loan. Anita Boehmer never mentioned it. What the hell was going on?

Kat sighed. The loan, checks made out to cash, and now credit card bills and a mortgage. In just a few months, Harry's finances had completely spiraled out of control.

She emerged from the bathroom and checked the thermostat. Eighty-four degrees. She turned it down to seventy-two and trudged into the kitchen.

The small television on the counter blared out the morning news. "...Fredrick Svensson plunged to his death in a snowshoeing accident." The CBC reporter lifted a hand to brush stray hairs from her face as the wind whipped across.

"The accident in the mountains is thought to have occurred two days ago, when Svensson was last seen in the back country. Search and rescue located his body early this morning but will delay the recovery operation at least to tomorrow, due to the approaching storm front."

The sky behind the reporter was dark, with low clouds obscuring the peaks of the snow-covered mountains behind her. Several men laden with backpacks and skis on their backs stood off to the right of the camera.

Kat turned the volume down and joined Harry sat at the kitchen table. Stacks of books were piled on the table, barely leaving space for his orange juice glass.

"Did you eat, Uncle Harry?"

He sipped his juice. "Oh, a long time ago."

The heat inside the house was oppressive. As usual, all the windows were closed tight. Kat unlatched the window in the breakfast nook and pushed it open.

"What did you have?" She stuck her head out and inhaled the cool air.

"Can't remember. Don't open that window—the burglars will get in."

"It's stuffy in here. How can you breathe?" Something smelled rotten. She opened each cupboard one by one. A half-eaten hamburger inside the third door had sprouted gray fur. She picked it up with a paper towel and gingerly carried it to the trashcan.

"Want some orange juice, Kat?" Harry picked up his glass from the table and motioned to Kat.

"Sure." Kat grabbed a glass from the cupboard and walked

over to the table. She located the orange juice carafe behind a stack of newspapers and poured herself a glass. She froze as she noticed his bare ring finger. "Where's your ring, Uncle Harry?" He hadn't removed his wedding ring since Elsie died, or in the forty years of marriage before that.

"Oh." Harry raised his hand to his mouth. The corners up his mouth turned up into a bashful grin. "I think it dropped down the drain."

"Really? Which sink?" If it was still in the trap, Jace might be able to fish it out. She'd ask him to have a look tonight.

"Uh, the kitchen sink. No, it was the bathroom."

Kat gulped her juice. Usually it refreshed her after a run, but this batch tasted a bit off. Harry had probably kept it out of the fridge too long. She pushed aside a pile of books and set her empty glass down on the table. "Coming to the office today?"

"Sure."

"Great. We can carpool. We'll stop at my place for breakfast. I've got to pick up a few things." Jace would watch Harry while she showered and changed for work. It was part of their routine to ensure Harry was eating. Food might help calm her stomach too. She winced as another cramp gripped her stomach.

Kat's thoughts slipped to Harry's Visa bill. It was unexplainable, just like the mortgage, renovation loan, and thousands of dollars in checks made out to cash in his checkbook. Everything was spiraling out of control, and she felt powerless to stop it.

CHAPTER 11

K AT YAWNED, DROWSY AFTER HER nap. This morning's examination of Edgewater's financial records had turned up nothing. Between keeping tabs on Harry and trying to make sense of Edgewater, she felt both physically and mentally exhausted.

She glanced at Harry. He sat at the reception desk, head bent over as he scribbled in that damn checkbook of his. It had completely consumed him. She'd better distract him or it might kill him too.

The noonday sun streamed in through the tall windows, illuminating dust specks as they drifted to the floor. She still puzzled over Research Analytics. Edgewater had paid the company fifty million this year, and two hundred and twenty million last year. Yet Zachary knew nothing about it. Whatever business service Research Analytics provided, it was obviously lucrative.

She dialed the phone number listed on the Research Analytics invoice and gazed out the window while she waited for an answer. The storm clouds had finally dispersed outside, exposing the North Shore Mountains in all their snow-dusted splendor.

Kat counted six rings and was about to hang up when a woman answered, sounding breathless. A slight accent? Kat couldn't quite place it.

"Yes, I'd like some information on your investment research."

Long pause, just breathing on the other end.

"I can drop by this aft—"

Click.

Kat redialed. This time her call went unanswered, fuelling her suspicions. Legitimate businesses didn't ignore customers or hang up on them.

She flipped through the Research Analytics invoices a second time. Many of the invoice numbers were in sequential order. A fraud red flag. Most real businesses had more than one customer. Especially businesses with hundreds of millions in annual sales.

Either Research Associates had no other customers, or the other customers they had were very infrequent. Kat bet it was the former.

The Research Analytics invoices showed an address on East Broadway, just a few minutes' drive from her office. She'd pay them a visit later this morning. She searched online to see what else she could find on the company. Nothing, not even a website.

"Trouble?"

Kat had been so engrossed in her thoughts that she hadn't even heard Jace come in. He stood behind Harry, bent over.

"It's right here." Jace pointed at Harry's checkbook. "You forgot to carry the one."

Harry muttered something under his breath. Kat shot Jace a warning look. Harry got worked up whenever anyone tried to help.

Kat's thoughts returned to Nathan's computer data. Trolling through the data all morning had uncovered nothing of substance in his remaining computer files. Except for his impressive contact list, a who's who of global movers and shakers. The World Institute entry in particular intrigued her. Aside from wealth and power, what did all its members have in common?

She glanced at Harry as he shielded his checkbook with his right arm. Jace stood behind Harry, looking over his shoulder. Only now Harry was more animated.

Kat waited for Harry's inevitable eruption. Dr. McAdam was at least right about one thing: it was better to agree, even if you didn't.

"Stop it, Jace," Harry growled. "You make me want to pull my hair out."

Not a good time to remind Harry he'd been bald for decades.

"Fine." Jace pretended to pout. "I'm just trying to help."

"Give it a rest, Uncle Harry," Kat said. "Let me help you."

"Damn bank! The loan was bad enough. All these other charges are mistakes, too. It says I have an overdraft, but that can't be right. Why can't they make their statements less complicated? It's like reading Greek!"

Harry threw his pen down and got up from his chair. "Leave me alone, both of you!"

"Uncle Harry—I can sort it out in an hour. Hand it over." Kat rose from the couch and walked to the desk. She glanced down at his desk drawer. It was pulled all the way open, doing double duty as a do-not-cross line. The drawer was filled with tangled elastic bands and bundles of clipped papers. And of course, a metal strongbox, his version of a safety deposit box.

"No." He crossed his arms and glared at her. "I want to do it myself. It keeps me sharp."

"But you've been working on it for weeks. I review bank statements all the time. Just let me get your checkbook up to date. I'll add up all the bank's mistakes so you can call them."

"I've almost got it. Just a couple more hours..."

"I need you to work on something else," Kat said. "It's time sensitive."

"When you put it that way, I guess we should each

concentrate on our area of expertise." He drew out the last syllable in a long *teeease* as he gathered up his papers.

"Great. I need you to put these invoices in date order." Kat handed him the Research Analytics file, knowing Harry liked feeling indispensable a lot more than he liked math.

"Okay, boss." His scowl vanished. "You need anything else, just holler."

Kat held out her hand. "Better give me those."

Harry reluctantly handed over his checkbook and bank statements. "Promise you won't undo my work so far? I need to keep track of where I left off."

Kat smiled at him, but secretly worried about what other financial surprises his checkbook might hold. "Promise."

She stole a glance at Jace, but he avoided eye contact. Instead he plodded over to the reception area couch, his broad shoulders slumped in defeat. He sat down and loosened his tie. Something was wrong. The nicely pressed suit he had left the house in this morning was now wrinkled and creased. His hundred-amp smile was absent, too.

"Is this your disheveled journalist look? If it is, you're pulling it off perfectly."

No answer.

"Jace, I really need to talk to you." She motioned him to follow her. Jace's steps fell in behind hers as they headed for her office.

"An assignment for me too?"

"It's Harry." She lowered her voice. "Harry's got some big financial problems—even bigger than I found out about yesterday. He's got high credit card balances. He's practically bankrupt. Look at this." She handed him a copy of Harry's bank statements, showing the massive mortgage for the full value of Harry's house. "He's mortgaged to the hilt and has nothing in the bank. Every time I turn around there's a new loan or credit card charge. Yet he's with us night and day. Where is he finding the time to do these things?"

Jace shrugged. "Maybe online?"

Kat shook her head."He's close to losing his house."

"Like I said before—Harry can move in with us. He can sell the house."

Jace wouldn't feel the same way once he realized what was in store. "He refuses. Says I'm betraying him. He doesn't understand anymore, and he has no recollection of taking out a mortgage. Meanwhile his finances have spiraled out of control. What do I do, Jace?"

"I don't know." Jace collapsed into the chair opposite her and let out a sigh.

Something *was* wrong. Jace always had an answer for everything. And he looked miserable. She felt sad just looking at him. "What's wrong with you? You look like someone died."

Kat cleared a spot on the desk and deposited Harry's paperwork. It could wait a few more minutes.

Jace bent forward, elbows on his knees. He held his forehead in his hands, still silent.

"Jace? What's wrong?"

"*The Sentinel* just sacked me."

"No! Why you?"

Jace leaned back and brushed his fingers through his hair. "I think I know why. That real estate story? It must be connected to someone important."

"Who?" She felt selfish for putting her problems ahead of his.

"That's what I can't figure out. They not only pulled my front page story—they told me my services are no longer required."

"That's crazy. Your editor loved that story." Jace had investigated the company for over a month. Kat had helped with the analysis that ultimately exposed the crooked real estate appraisals.

"I don't think it was his decision. Someone higher up must have killed it. No one's telling me anything. They escorted me from the building, Kat. After ten years. Too contentious, I guess."

"Isn't that what news stories are supposed to do? Stir the

pot, invite discussion? Expose wrongdoings?"

"Apparently not at the *Sentinel*. But why tell me to go with it if they planned to kill the story in the end?" He dropped the paper on her desk. "See this? They'd rather have advertorials about real estate developments than even a whiff of controversy." The full-page spread showed a twenty-something couple draped on a couch with a set table and gourmet kitchen in the background.

"They can't even tell me the truth about it. They said they were replacing the reporters with syndication. But I was the only one turfed."

The Sentinel's reporting staff had already been downsized when a global media group bought it last year.

"They can't fire you. You're not an employee, you freelance." Kat jumped up from her chair and came around the desk. She leaned over and kissed the top of Jace's head. She hated to see him so dejected. Journalism was his life.

"Semantics. It's the same end result—no more income. And as a freelancer, I get no severance. The newspaper's been my only income for more than a decade. What am I going to do, Kat? They're the only game left in town."

It was true. Nobody read newspapers anymore. Everything was online, dumbed down to monosyllabic words, and free.

Kat sat on the edge of Jace's chair and gave him a hug.

"There's lots of online magazines." Kat tried to sound upbeat, though she didn't believe it herself. "You could do something there."

"Doubt it. Everything's syndicated now, and they pay pennies a word. It's not enough to live on. I need to pay the bills."

"You'll find something. You're a good journalist." Jace had won industry awards three years running.

"I'm not so sure. With all the mergers, everything's owned by fewer and fewer people these days. No one's hiring."

"I can cover our expenses, Jace. I just got a nice retainer from my new case. You'll get work soon—I'm sure of it."

He shook his head. "I should have picked a different career. Who'd have thought journalists would go the way of blacksmiths and typewriter repair people? Obsolete."

"You're not obsolete. People still need to hear the objective truth."

"It gets worse." Jace flipped the paper open to the financial section. "Read this."

Kat scanned the headline. *Bargains Abound in Local Real Estate.* "It's the polar opposite of your story about appraisal fraud and an overheated market." She shook her head. "It doesn't matter, Jace. It's their loss."

"Of course it matters. They fired me because of some sort of cover-up. I want to know what it is."

"It's better for your peace of mind to drop it." Jace never knew when to quit. He was as tenacious as a dog with a bone. Sometimes that was good, like when dealing with contractors on their never-ending house renovations. But facing off against powerful people rarely worked out in the end.

"That's exactly what they want me to do. There's obviously more to the story than what I've uncovered. I'm going to find out what that is. They can't muzzle me. The truth is always worth fighting for."

"Sometimes, but it's always at a cost, Jace." Kat wanted to believe. But ruthless people gained at any cost, and often at the expense of idealists like Jace. They thought nothing of stepping on the bodies, hearts, and minds of others to get ahead. Confront them and they'd bury you, in a hole sometimes too deep to dig out of.

Like Uncle Harry and his money. Or those smaller investors who followed Zachary's currency gambles. Jace would be better to cut his losses and move on instead of making it worse. You had to pick your battles. The black-and-white ones. The ones too precious to lose.

CHAPTER 12

KAT MARCHED INTO THE BANK, ready for combat. She ignored the tellers' stares and made a beeline for Anita Boehmer's office. Jace was right. Some things were worth fighting for. And since Harry couldn't do that himself, she would. How could the bank put their own self-interest ahead of blatant financial abuse? Was making a buck really that important to them? It was criminal. She inhaled, focused her thoughts, and willed herself to keep calm. Do Battle With Banks hadn't been on her to-do list today.

Jace had taken Harry grocery shopping, which gave Kat a chance to work on Harry's checkbook. She wanted to have it reconciled for him when he returned. His finances were much worse than she realized.

After a closer look at his statements for the last six months, she noticed something more. Both mortgage payments had been reversed due to insufficient funds. Harry had always been a saver, yet suddenly he was stretched to his overdraft limit.

Kat stared down a startled Anita Boehmer in the bank manager's office. "Why didn't you mention Harry's mortgage when we were here yesterday?"

"We were talking about his renovation loan. There was no particular reason to mention the mortgage." Anita rose and stood by her desk.

"No particular reason?" Kat dropped Harry's bank statement on the bank manager's desk. "We came in here to discuss an unusual transaction. What would be a good reason to mention other suspicious transactions in an eighty-year-old pensioner's account?"

Anita sighed and sat down. She motioned for Kat to do the same. "Like I told you yesterday, he seemed perfectly normal when he took out the loan. As for the mortgage, that would have been done by the loans officer." Anita's held her arms up, palms facing Kat. "I don't see what's so susp—"

"He's eighty years old, Anita! Living on a fixed income, with money in the bank. Suddenly all his money's gone, and he's in debt. Would you let your elderly parents mortgage their house?"

"I can't tell him not to do it—it's none of my business."

"He's got Alzheimer's. If you don't help him, who will?"

Anita just stared blankly, like she heard it all the time.

"Silence is just as bad. But I suppose you earned a few more points towards your monthly quota." Kat really had no idea whether bank employees got incentives or not.

Anita's face reddened. "I *am* sorry his finances are in such a state. Really I am. It's simply not our business to manage people's money."

"No? When does it become your business? After you've sold them every bank product under the sun?" Kat pointed at Harry's bank statement. "After you ruin them?"

"I'm sorry, but I don't see how the bank is responsible for any of this."

"Anita—you helped him fill out the loan application." Kat pointed to the form. "This isn't my uncle's writing."

"I do remember him having trouble filling it out." Anita bit her lip.

"Exactly my point. He can't remember things from one hour to the next. He can't balance his checkbook and can't do the paperwork. Yet you're comfortable giving him a loan?" Harry's checkbook had been riddled with errors. His calculations indicated a balance thousands of dollars higher than his bank statement.

"I couldn't refuse him. He qualified, and the numbers work. But that's not my writing on the loan application. Someone else helped him."

"Who?" She'd give them a talking to.

"No one from the bank. He took the form home."

"That just doesn't make sense." Kat said it more to herself than Anita. Even if Harry remembered to complete the application, he would have forgotten to return it. Aside from the fact that he no longer drove and with her almost twenty-four-seven. "Who was with him?"

"Nobody. He came by himself. Both times." Anita handed Harry's statement back to Kat. "I know this must be hard for you, but the bank hasn't done anything wrong."

Kat stood. "Maybe not legally. But morally, I wouldn't give a senior with dementia a mortgage and a loan to make a buck. If you and the bank don't have a conscience, who does?"

Anita just stared at her, speechless.

"Who watches out for vulnerable people like Harry?" She needed to not only get Harry out of this financial disaster but also to find out who got him into it in the first place.

Five minutes later Kat sat in her Subaru in the bank parking lot, furious. Like most people, Anita put her own needs first—her quota ahead of a vulnerable person's welfare. Technically Anita was right; she was just doing her job. Legally, she couldn't exercise moral judgment over her customers. But that was part of the problem. Laws and rules never applied until someone got burned. People like Harry, the most vulnerable in society, got used and abused repeatedly before anyone made the laws in the first place.

Her keys dangled from the ignition as she tried to pull herself together. While she didn't agree with the bank, she probably shouldn't have launched into a tirade with Anita. Better to focus on who did this and get the money back. But with Harry's faulty memory and no clues, where to start?

As a forensic accountant, Kat always considered the fraud triangle of motive, rationalization, and opportunity. It almost always pointed to the fraudster. Except in Harry's case there was no opportunity. Harry was with her or Jace constantly, except when he went home to sleep. She was pretty sure he hadn't seen anyone in his social circle for months, since most of them had called her to express concern about his absence and his forgetfulness.

At least in her Edgewater case, she had a likely suspect. But one thought tugged at her since reviewing the audited statements this morning. Even if Zachary hadn't noticed the missing money, how had it escaped the auditors' scrutiny? With so much money unaccounted for, the annual audit should have raised alarm bells. Auditors didn't sign off on company financial statements without verifying account balances. Either they hadn't checked the bank balance, or they purposely allowed the deception.

She grabbed the Edgewater annual report from the passenger seat and flipped it open. The auditor's report was signed Beecham & Company. Strange that a company the size of Edgewater would be audited by a small local firm instead of one of the big international accounting firms.

She checked the address. Just a few blocks from the bank. She decided to pay Beecham a visit. She put the Subaru in gear and pulled out of the parking lot.

Minutes later she had an answer, just not the one she expected. She pulled up to the curb of 422 Cedar Street and got out. Instead of a glass and metal high rise, she faced a vacant lot, locked behind a chain-link fence.

CHAPTER 13

I<small>N LATE AFTERNOON,</small> K<small>AT EXITED</small> the elevator and entered Edgewater's plush, quiet offices. The receptionist buzzed Zachary and motioned Kat to an overstuffed chair in the waiting area. Zachary wasn't expecting her, but the revelation on the auditors demanded immediate attention.

If Beecham didn't exist, then Edgewater's financial statements hadn't been independently audited. Purposeful deception meant only one thing: bogus financial results. Someone was hiding something. She grabbed her cell phone and punched in Jace's number. She left a message, asking him to do a background check on Beecham.

Ten minutes later, Zachary greeted her at reception and ushered her into his spacious office. He pushed a stack of papers to the side of his desk and motioned to sit down. Kat filled him in on Beecham's fictitious address and her suspicions.

"That's impossible. The regulators require us to have audited statements. Not to mention our clients. They wouldn't invest in unaudited funds." Zachary shook his head.

"Did you ever meet with the auditors? Check them out?"

"Never had to. Like I said, Nathan handled the back-office side."

"But you said your trading model was complicated. The auditors would need to understand it in order to audit Edgewater. Who explained it to them? Nathan?"

Realization dawned. Suddenly Zachary focused laser-like on Kat.

"Nathan never came back to me about it. And he's used Beecham for years, even before I came onboard." He slumped forward and rested his forehead in his hands. "This can't be happening."

"Well, it is. Unless Beecham operates from a vacant lot."

"Maybe they moved?" Zachary wiped a thin sheen of sweat from his forehead.

Kat raised her eyebrows. "Beecham probably doesn't even exist. I've got someone checking on that right now."

"But the auditor's signature is on the statements. You're telling me that was faked?"

"Anyone can cut and paste a signature. Edgewater's year-end was a few months ago. Weren't there any auditors in the office?" Auditors normally worked in their clients' offices for part of the year-end audit. For a company of Edgewater's size, the fieldwork would last at least a few weeks.

"Not that I remember. We don't get many visitors, not even auditors. Back-office stuff isn't exactly my strong suit, but still—how could this happen right under my eyes?" He pounded his fist against the desk as he stood. "How could I be so stupid?"

"It might seem obvious in hindsight. But until you ran short on cash, you had no reason to question anything." Just like Uncle Harry and his loans.

Even Zachary looked small as he paced back and forth against the backdrop of the large windows. "I've got to stop this thing. What's next?" His shoulders hunched forward in defeat.

"Think of why the financial statements were faked. I'll reconstruct the results from your financial system to see what the real numbers are."

"The real numbers?" He stopped abruptly and stared.

"If the financial statements are faked, you can be sure the actual numbers are different. I'm guessing not in a good way. I need complete access to your books and records. We'll work at night while your staff is gone." As if she had other staff to help. Reconstructing the financials could be hugely time-consuming. Maybe Jace could pitch in.

Zachary's forehead creased. "Holy crap. No wonder Edgewater has no money. I'll call my lawyer, get a court order. Freeze the bank accounts and the funds."

"Zachary, that would be my first reaction too, but—"

"Don't tell me to wait and see. I've got to shut him down." Zachary headed for his office door, cell phone in hand.

"Okay, call your lawyer. But he'll want proof too. Something Nathan can't explain away. Especially if you want any charges to stick."

"That could take days. In the meantime, Edgewater gets plundered?" Zachary turned abruptly and faced Kat. "Can't afford it. We'll go with whatever you dig up by Monday."

"Monday?" Friday was almost over. Considering Zachary's entire future rested on her investigation, a few days was ridiculous. "I need a week or two minimum just to reconstruct the financials. Edgewater is a multi-billion dollar company."

"Monday." Zachary exited into the hall before she had a chance to answer.

CHAPTER 14

KAT SPENT THE EVENING HOURS in Nathan's office extracting data from Edgewater's client records system, the first step in validating the company's revenue. Edgewater earned its fees as a percentage of their clients' investment performance. If their clients' investments grew, so did Edgewater's revenues. But if they lost money, or even broke even, the hedge fund earned nothing.

That was the problem. According to her calculations, Edgewater's fees amounted to a fraction of what was actually reported on the financial statements. Barring an undiscovered source of income, the company's revenues were overstated by billions. Did she miss something? Unlikely after her exhaustive analysis. Something fishy was going on. She needed to talk with Zachary before progressing further.

There was also the problem of Beecham's vacant lot address. On a hunch, Kat typed in Beecham's 422 Cedar Street address into Snoopy, her proprietary audit analytics software. She pressed enter and waited while the software scanned all of Edgewater's accounts payable data. She was surprised to see the results contained not one, but two vendors with the same address. The second name sounded familiar, but she couldn't quite place why.

"Zachary?"

No answer. She'd head down the hall to his office in a minute. But first she'd do some more digging. Finding two Edgewater vendors at a nonexistent address was a fraud red flag.

She stared at the screen for a moment, wondering where she had heard the name *Svensson* before. Then it came to her: Fredrick Svensson was the man who had died in the snowshoeing accident. She was certain that was the name she'd heard on Harry's radio this morning.

She typed *Svensson* into a search engine and pressed enter. Sure enough, at the top of the results page were half-dozen stories on Wednesday's snowshoeing accident. She clicked on the first one. A sixtyish gray-haired man with a neatly trimmed beard and John Lennon glasses gazed out from the photograph. The caption underneath read *Nobel–Nominated Economist Dies in Snowshoe Tragedy.*

Why would Edgewater pay a Nobel economist? She pulled up Svensson's vendor record in Edgewater's accounting system and clicked on the transaction details. A series of invoices had been paid in the last two years, all for similar amounts of eight or nine thousand dollars. She clicked on one and read the description: consulting fees. Consulting for what? What did Svensson and Beecham have in common?

More importantly, what did Svensson and Edgewater have in common? Kat scrolled through the rest of the stories. Aside from his love of the outdoors, Fredrick Svensson had very particular views on currency.

She clicked on another article, dated last year.

One World Currency—Does It Make Economic Sense?

Fredrick Svensson, the Nobel–nominated economist and pioneer on currency reform, spoke today at the Davos

Economic Summit. His work on currency reform is well known and controversial, arguing that numerous currencies create inefficiencies and barriers to world trade and overall economic well-being. Svensson says these barriers result in higher transaction costs and put developing countries at a disadvantage. He spoke about the need for one world currency as a step towards global prosperity.

Kat skimmed the rest of the article. Edgewater and Svensson had currency as a common denominator. Edgewater traded currencies, and Svensson was the pre-eminent global expert. But their currency views differed dramatically. Svensson's theories, if adopted, would directly impact Edgewater. Edgewater exploited currency exchange rates, the very thing Svensson recommended eliminating. So why would Edgewater pay Svensson consulting fees?

Kat pressed the print button and grabbed the article from the printer. She paused for a moment at Nathan's massive marble chess set, then headed out to the hall. Zachary might be able to make sense of it. He had retreated to his office a few hours ago.

She noticed for the first time that the walls were lined with dark wood frames, each one containing an antiquated bank note or bond of some sort. She scanned the names— Mississippi, the South Sea Company, and others. Worthless, except as collector's items. How ironic that Edgewater's walls were lined with financial instruments of earlier financial scams. Had Nathan or Zachary had chosen them? The hall was eerily quiet. No voices, no typing, just the sound of her shoes sinking into the thick carpet.

"Zachary?"

No answer. She called out again, louder this time. She had assumed Zachary was somewhere else in the office since she hadn't heard anyone come or go. Kat turned the corner into Zachary's office. He wasn't there. She'd assumed wrong.

She pulled out her cell phone and punched in Zachary's number. She jumped as she heard the ring nearby. Zachary's cell phone sat on the desk, but his coat was gone.

Kat swore under her breath. Why hadn't Zachary told her he was leaving? Was he returning, or had he expected her to work here all night? She didn't even have a key to lock up. She left a message for him to call as soon as possible, knowing it probably wouldn't do much good.

She returned to Nathan's office and shut down her laptop. She gathered up Edgewater's financial statements, account listings, client statements. While she hadn't even begun to reconcile fully the client totals to the financials, there was one total in particular that troubled her.

The Edgewater bank account now held a balance of less than a hundred thousand dollars. For a billionaire who invested heavily in his own company, that amount was unthinkable. Not only that, but it differed from the amount on Zachary's net worth statement for the divorce. If the balance was accurate, his net worth was much less than he had believed since it was wrapped up completely in Edgewater. That meant Victoria Barron's divorce settlement had been based on money that didn't actually exist.

Could Zachary really be so oblivious to the value of his own holdings? How would he react when he found out the truth?

She stuffed the documents into her briefcase and grabbed her coat. Although Zachary's deadline loomed, she was past the point of concentration. Aside from her stomach ache, she felt a fever coming on. She needed sleep before this flu got the better of her. And to check in on Harry and Jace.

She paused at the door, then turned back into Nathan's office. She re-opened her briefcase and studied today's ending bank balance. According to her rough calculations, Edgewater's cash would run out on Tuesday—mere days from now, and one day after Zachary's deadline.

Zachary's sense of urgency was real. Monday might even be too late, if she had under-estimated Edgewater's cash burn and Nathan Barron's greediness.

A key clicked in the front door lock.

Now was as good as time as any to tell him. Kat dropped her coat and briefcase on Nathan's couch and started for the door.

But it wasn't Zachary. A woman's laugh broke the silence.

Kat froze. Her heart pounded as she scanned the office for a place to hide. Then she realized: she knew that voice. It was Victoria. But why was she here now? After such an ugly courtroom battle, why hadn't Zachary changed the locks?

The front door slammed shut. Kat spun around and searched for cover. The only door led straight out into the reception and Victoria. Behind the sofa? No. Victoria might come in the office. If she sat down, it would be on the sofa or the desk.

Victoria's stilettos clicked across the reception's marble floor, then grew silent as she reached the Berber carpet in the hallway. Kat stifled a sneeze as strong perfume wafted towards her. She dove behind the heavy damask curtains. They were in the current fashion, long enough so they draped in a puddle on the floor, and luckily covered her feet.

Victoria whispered something—Kat assumed into her cell phone. She was in Nathan's office now, too close for comfort.

Kat glanced down in horror. Light seeped in under the curtain by her feet, and she realized the toe of her shoe was outside the carpet. She slowly slid her foot in, hoping the movement didn't attract attention.

Who was with Victoria? She hadn't heard any other footsteps. A drawer opened and papers rustled.

Kat flattened herself against the wall, wishing she hadn't eaten such a big lunch. Did she bulge through the curtains? She couldn't tell.

"Okay, got it. Call you later."

Kat barely made out the whispered words. Victoria must be talking on her cell phone. *Got What?*

She breathed a sigh of relief as Victoria's heels echoed off the foyer's marble floor. She had a lot of nerve to come here, as she hadn't worked at Edgewater since the separation.

Didn't she care if she ran into Zachary? Or did she somehow know he wasn't here?

The outer office door slammed. Kat held her breath as the key clicked in the tumbler.

She listened for the elevator bell, then waited a full five minutes before emerging from behind the curtains. Victoria's heavy perfume lingered, tickling her nose. She sneezed.

As Kat searched for a tissue, she spotted her coat and briefcase sitting on the couch. Had Victoria seen them? She jumped as her cell phone rang. She checked her call display as she shut the ringer off. It was Jace. She didn't dare call him back from here. Victoria might return, and Kat would be home in twenty minutes anyways.

CHAPTER 15

KAT'S EYES TWITCHED FROM FATIGUE. It was almost three a.m. She longed for some shuteye, but couldn't rest until she tallied up the damage for Zachary. Edgewater appeared to be the victim of a massive fraud, bigger than anything she had ever seen.

Since arriving home from Edgewater several hours ago, she continued to analyze the individual client accounts against the statement copies she had found in Nathan's office. It was a painstaking, eye-straining process. She had checked over a hundred and fifty accounts so far but had yet to come up with a single account where the paper statement matched the computer records. The paper copies boasted double-digit returns, yet most accounts in the computer had balances close to zero, with investment losses instead of gains.

The investment returns of the paper accounts were also remarkably consistent. Too consistent, as a matter of fact. Every account she checked earned exactly a twelve percent return, regardless of the timing of the client's investment. Such consistency was statistically impossible given that the fund itself fluctuated. It invested in different currencies with constantly changing gains and losses.

The wind gusted outside, and she longed for the warmth of her bed.

"Still at it?" Jace stood in the doorway of the upstairs study, holding two cups of steaming coffee.

"Come see this, Jace." She waved him over to her computer screen. "The client accounts only total about one hundred and fifty million dollars. Not the billions showing on Edgewater's financial statements. I've crossed referenced them with the account statements I found. It doesn't look good." She had found files of paper statements in a locked filing cabinet at Edgewater. None reconciled to the balances in the computer system.

Jace handed her a coffee and pulled up a chair. "A hundred and fifty mil out of three billion? You mean 2.8 billion missing? How can it be so different?"

"It appears that Nathan's been operating a giant Ponzi scheme. He takes investors' money and transfers it out as soon as it comes in. These must be copies of the fake statements. It's how he keeps track. See this?" Kat pointed to the computer screen where she had reconstructed investment returns for a sample group of twenty Edgewater investors. "All these investors earned exactly twelve percent per year for the last three years."

"That's impressive. I make less than two percent at the bank. Maybe I should move my money?"

"It's fake, Jace. All made up. Each of these clients invested at different times. Some have been in the fund the whole time, and others just invested in the last year. Yet they made exactly the same return on investment."

"Coincidence, maybe?"

"No. I've compared dozens of clients and their investments in the fund. The fund supposedly invests in all types of currency speculation, yet I can't reconstruct the transactions in each of their accounts, or any of the other trades in

Edgewater's hedge fund. I've traced all the trade settlements from the bank statements *and* reconstructed the gain or loss in each currency that Edgewater trades in. Know what I get?"

"What?"

"A loss, Jace. There is no twelve percent return. Zachary thinks his currency model works, but it doesn't. There are no trades. Nathan simply doesn't execute them. He's not investing the money, and Zachary's oblivious to that fact because he never reviews the accounts."

"You mean it's all faked? Don't other people work here? How could that go unnoticed?"

"Nathan is very hands-on, which is surprising with his frequent trips and absences. An executive doing administrative work is another fraud red flag. The work is much too junior for a billionaire founder." Someone had to be helping too. The extent of the manual account manipulation was too much work for just one person.

"Zachary really has no clue about this?"

"He says he doesn't. As hard as it is to believe, I think he's telling the truth," Kat said.

"But how could Nathan get so much money without Zachary or anyone noticing?"

"I don't know. This fraud has been operating for at least ten years. Look at this." Kat held up a statement. It had the Edgewater name and logo on it, but it was in a different format than the computer-generated statements. The client name was glued to the statement.

Jace took the statement and rubbed his finger over the logo. "Sloppy. This cut and paste job wouldn't fool anyone."

"He doesn't use this version—he scans and emails an electronic copy, so no one knows it's been doctored. He tallies everything on a spreadsheet and just adds a percentage increase to each account every quarter. Everyone's happy." The cryptic spreadsheets Kat had found in Nathan's office finally made sense. It was his manual accounting system of sorts.

"How does he ensure the real statements don't go out?"

"Someone else must be in on it. When the system prints the real statements, they are destroyed. The doctored statements are mailed to clients instead."

Jace whistled. "All this money goes where?"

"A good chunk of it has gone to a company called Research Analytics. I'll pay them a visit tomorrow." Kat pointed to the pile of Research Analytics invoices. "Fifty million was transferred so far this year, and two hundred and twenty million last year. I'm still searching for the rest."

"What if a client wanted to cash in their investment? Wouldn't that expose the fraud?"

"Only if Nathan doesn't give them their money. As long as more new money comes in, he can pay redeeming investors without the fund going broke. He just moves the money from one investor account to another to cover it." Kat caught a movement out of the corner of her eye. She turned around to see Harry in the hallway, dressed in shorts and a golf shirt. "Going somewhere, Uncle Harry?"

"Just out for a stroll."

"It's the middle of the night. And it's raining." Harry had decided to stay over after watching the game with Jace. Had Harry been on these nighttime excursions before?

"It is? Maybe I'll just stay in, then."

Kat and Jace exchanged glances. What if she hadn't been awake? Harry would have gone out in the sub-zero weather without a coat. "Okay, Uncle Harry. See you in the morning."

Harry shuffled back down the hall. The doctor was right: Harry wasn't safe on his own. But moving him to a care home was out of the question. She'd figure something out tomorrow. She turned back to Jace.

"Would you redeem your investment if you were earning twelve percent a year for five years running?"

Jace shook his head. "No way. I can't get that kind of return at the bank—or anywhere else."

"That's exactly what Edgewater's clients think too. Year

in and year out, they've earned fantastic returns. No one redeems their investment unless they're in dire straits. You'd be crazy to pass up that income. Nathan's banking on very few redemptions. Investors always cash in less profitable investments first."

"So Nathan just needs enough money to cover off the few accounts that did redeem."

Kat nodded. "Yes, and that hasn't been a problem. Investors are practically banging down the door to invest in the hedge fund. The fund has an air of exclusivity about it. Nathan doesn't let just anyone invest, so people consider themselves lucky to invest in the first place. If they redeem their investment, they might not be allowed back in. And you have to be rich to invest in a high-risk hedge fund with a minimum five hundred thousand investment."

"It sounds like there's no risk at all. The investors get a hefty return, year over year. The markets haven't been anything like that. It's too good to be true."

"It is—as long as Edgewater keeps earning those stellar returns. Zachary thinks it's due to his secret trading model."

"Sounds like you doubt him."

Kat sipped her coffee. "I think *he* believes his model works. Trouble is, it's never been proven, since Nathan isn't processing the trades. And Zachary never checks. I guess he assumes twelve percent overall sounds about right. Zachary's suspicions are bang on, though. Nathan is clearly defrauding Edgewater. The fake client statements and Beecham & Company prove that. I just don't get how Zachary could be so disconnected. There's more." She filled him in on Edgewater's unlikely association with Fredrick Svensson.

"The Nobel economist guy? Maybe there's a good reason to pay him. Even with different views, he might have some good currency predictions."

"It's too weird, Jace. Svensson's push is for a common currency—like the Euro—only on a global scale. Edgewater exploits and profits from the very discrepancies Svensson seeks to eliminate with his model. It makes no sense."

"Maybe Zachary has some ideas. Since he's so smart." Jace smirked.

"I doubt it, Jace. Zachary insists that all trades are based on his proprietary trading model. He says they don't use any outside research. There is one more thing I can't figure out."

"What's that?" Jace asked.

"How is Nathan pulling this off? Zachary says he enters his trades into the system himself. But when I checked, those trades aren't being pulled into the accounting system. It's like it's not connected to anything."

Jace never got a chance to answer.

They both froze as a loud crash followed by shattering glass came from downstairs.

Kat dropped her pen. Heavy footsteps thudded on the front stairs. She jumped up and peered out the study window. A dark figure ran down the walkway to a black sedan idling at the curb. She couldn't tell whether it was a man or woman as they slammed the passenger door. The car's tires squealed as it tore away from the curb.

She ran to the hallway with Jace close behind. They both slammed to a stop on the upstairs landing when they smelled the gasoline.

CHAPTER 16

KAT AND JACE STOOD ON the landing, transfixed by the scene below. The remnants of a homemade Molotov cocktail smoldered on the center of the hallway rug. Gasoline fumes fused with smoke, and glass from the side window covered the wood floor.

Suddenly the bottle exploded.

Fire shot out in all directions. Within seconds their view of the front door was obliterated by the rising smoke. Flames licked the stairway banister.

Gasoline burned Kat's nostrils. She jumped as a second explosion followed, ballooning into a fireball.

"Oh my god. Uncle Harry—get out here! Hurry!" Kat spun around, about to head to the guest bedroom.

But Harry was already in the hall. "What's happening?" Harry rubbed his eyes. His eyes widened when he saw the flames. "Holy crap!"

Kat ran into the office to call the fire department. But the cordless phone wasn't in its cradle. She cursed and ran back into the hall, wondering where it could be.

"I'll try and smother it." Jace raced down the stairs, pulling off his sweatshirt.

"Jace! Be careful." Kat watched from the top of the stairs. In less than a minute, the flames had grown to several feet across. It was too late to do anything. Soon it would block the stairwell, and their escape.

She turned. "Harry—let's go!" She waved and descended the stairs with Harry right behind her.

"Let me give you a hand, Jace." Harry pulled his golf shirt over his head and headed towards Jace.

"No!" Kat grabbed her uncle's arm and pulled him back. She turned him towards the kitchen and away from the fire. "Keep going, Harry, out the back door. Jace, you too. Just leave it."

The fire now engulfed the entire front hall, too big to be smothered. It was out of control.

Suddenly Kat remembered the papers upstairs. Nathan's spreadsheets and the customer statements. She had the original copies.

If she ran upstairs now she could get them in time. No—that was stupid. "Jace, leave it!"

Her face flushed from the heat.

"I can put it out." Jace winced as he pulled his scorched sweatshirt up from the rug. He inched over and dropped it on the fire. He stomped on it with his boots, trying to extinguish the flames.

Kat stopped at the kitchen door. Jace's actions might have worked a minute ago, before the flames doubled in size. Now it had little effect, other than being dangerous.

"It's too much, Jace. Let's go."

Jace jumped back and shielded his face just as a third explosion increased the flames. Flames now blocked the staircase they had just descended. Jace turned and fell in behind Kat, waving her on.

Kat veered into the kitchen, only to find Harry motionless by the stove, wringing his hands. He seemed lost. "We're going out the back stairs, Harry. Just follow me to the kitchen door." Kat grabbed the cordless phone off the kitchen counter as she exited, trying to stay calm. She opened the kitchen door and filled her lungs with the cool, clean air. She punched in 9–1–1 and descended the stairs, pulling Harry behind her. When she glanced back, her heart stopped.

Where the hell was Jace? He should have been right behind her and Harry. Only he wasn't.

"Wait here. Talk to them." She pushed the phone into Harry's hands and ran back.

"What do you mean, wait here?" Harry held up his hand. "Don't go in there, Kat."

She turned back. "I have to find Jace." The downpour drowned Harry's pleas, or maybe she blocked them out.

"No!" Harry screamed louder and wrung his hands together. "Wait for the fire department."

But Kat was already up the stairs. She crossed the threshold only to be met with thick smoke. She gagged and ducked, hoping to find fresher air lower down. Why hadn't Jace followed her outside? He had been right behind her. It was obvious the fire was too big to be extinguished—what was he thinking? She crawled along the kitchen floor, low against the thick smoke.

Harry was right—going back had been a mistake. But a few seconds could make all the difference before the fire department arrived. Her Edgewater papers were one thing, but she couldn't leave Jace. She coughed as the smoke invaded her lungs. It stung her eyes and she blinked away tears.

She crawled through the kitchen into the hallway, unable to see more than a foot in front of her. While the flames had died down, the thick smoke permeated every inch of the corridor, making it impossible to see.

She inched closer to where she had last seen Jace, her breath heavy with exhaustion. She couldn't get enough air.

Then she heard the fire engine's sirens coming down the block as she gasped for breath. The truck screeched to a stop outside. Doors slammed and men's voices drifted up through the broken window. She still felt hope until the fire truck's flashing lights penetrated the darkness. The hall was empty. Jace was gone.

CHAPTER 17

KAT SHIVERED AND PULLED THE wool blanket tight around her shoulders. She sat on her front steps, listening to the water drip down the eaves troughs. The rain had abated, and the fire was out. She coughed in spasms, a result of the smoke inhalation. Harry sat beside her and nodded his head while the fire chief chastised her for going into the house. One by one, neighbors returned to their houses and extinguished their lights, relieved the fire hadn't spread.

Jace trudged across the lawn, past a pair of firefighters busily packing up their equipment. His right hand and arm were bandaged and wrapped in white gauze. He had smashed the living room window and jumped through it into the front yard. Kat rose and descended the stairs to meet him.

She hugged him, grateful he had escaped the fire. "Don't ever do that again, Jace. I thought you died in there."

He pulled back to study her. His eyes narrowed. "You shouldn't have gone back in. I can take care of myself."

Kat disagreed but didn't say anything. She was just

relieved he wasn't more seriously injured. She locked her arm in his un-bandaged one. Together they climbed the stairs to the front door. She stood just outside and peered into the front hall.

"Why would someone do this?" Kat studied the smoldering remains of the Molotov cocktail. It appeared homemade, a blackened rag still sticking out of the broken wine bottle's neck.

Jace didn't answer. He squatted down and studied the damaged floor.

A burnt black circle was all that remained of the antique British India rug. It had been as old as the house. The stairway banister and hallway wainscoting were blackened and charred, and the floorboards Jace had so painstakingly restored now sat under puddles of water. The firefighters had quickly extinguished the blaze, but the damage was done.

"I don't know." Jace stood and turned to her. "Maybe it's a case of mistaken identity. They hit the wrong house."

"Most of our neighbors are over seventy, Jace. I can't imagine them as targets for anything." The pensioners in their Queens Park neighborhood did mocktails, not Molotov cocktails.

"Someone's got it in for you guys." Harry came up behind them. He peered inside at the mess. "Maybe I shouldn't stay."

"What's this?" Jace poked at a metal canister with the toe of his boot. It lay partially hidden under the hallway armoire, unnoticed by the arson investigators. He bent down and picked it up. He unscrewed the lid and pulled out a scrap of paper.

"What is it?" Kat asked. "Maybe you should leave it there."

Jace ignored her. His face darkened as he read it, then shoved the paper in his pocket.

"Let me see that." Kat held out her hand.

Jace shook his head. "It's nothing."

"What do you mean, nothing?" The metal canister must have been inside the Molotov cocktail. "I live here too. I want to know what it says."

Jace shrugged and pulled the paper from his pocket. He handed it to her.

Kat read the typewritten note. *Stop the story.* "So it is about your article. But didn't the *Sentinel* pull it?"

"They did."

"Is there another story I don't know about?" Kat shivered as she handed the note back. She pulled the blanket tighter around her shoulders.

"No, that's the only one I was working on. But it didn't go to press. No one even knows about it."

"No one except people at the *Sentinel*. The same people who fired you."

"You think someone at the newspaper firebombed us? That's crazy, Kat."

"Maybe it's not the *Sentinel*. Somebody could have leaked your story. To the people you're accusing, maybe?"

"Why would they do that?" Jace glanced at the paper before stuffing it in his pocket.

"Who knows? Maybe the same reason your story got pulled. That still means the *Sentinel* is connected to your story somehow. They must figure you're going to publish the article anyway."

"You know, that's actually not a bad idea. *The Sentinel*'s not the only game in town."

"It's not worth it, Jace."

"Why not? I'll sell the story to someone else. There's obviously more to it, and they're not going to muzzle me. Maybe I should dig a bit deeper and see where it goes."

"And be targeted again?" Kat wished she'd never mentioned it. Jace was like a bloodhound on a scent. He'd never stop until he found out who was behind the firebombing.

"Whoever it is has to be stopped, Kat. Especially violent attacks like this. If I don't stop them, what's next? Will everything controversial be stifled? This is how oppression starts."

Kat sighed. She wanted to know who was behind the

attack too, and she wanted justice. But sometimes it was better to let sleeping dogs lie. It was something she'd learned growing up in the Denton household.

She certainly didn't feel like arguing after everything that had happened. She changed the subject. "Did you find out anything about Edgewater's auditors last night while I was at their offices?"

"Matter of fact, I did," Jace said. "Beecham & Company is a registered company, even if it does operate out of a vacant lot."

At least that was progress. Fire or no fire, she still had a job to do.

"So it does actually exist."

"Beecham exists alright, but in name only. It's owned by a holding company. Which in turn is owned by Nathan Barron."

Kat's worst fears were confirmed. "That explains why the auditors didn't pick up on the fraud. There are no auditors. It's all a sham."

Of course Nathan Barron couldn't risk a legitimate auditor uncovering his fraud. But with billions at stake, why hadn't he covered his tracks better? An address at a vacant lot and a disconnected phone number was just plain sloppy.

"Don't millionaire investors check these sorts of things out more than the average person?" Jace asked.

"You would think so, but with twelve percent returns year in and year out, maybe not. Zachary tells me investors are practically tripping over each other to invest in the fund. And another thing—someone else in Edgewater's records has the same address as Beecham."

"Really? Who?"

"Fredrick Svensson. I need you to help me find out what they're paying him for." That, and how on earth Zachary could trade with no money. Something didn't pass the smell test.

CHAPTER 18

KAT AND JACE SAT IN Kat's downtown office, exhausted from last night's fire. Aside from the broken window, the fire had undone hundreds of hours of painstaking restoration to the carved banister and wainscoting. Luckily there was no structural damage, but it was just too hard to look at right now. By the time they finished cleaning up and boarding the window it was early Saturday morning. They'd come to the office to escape the smoky air still lingering downstairs.

"Tell me I'm not crazy, Jace." Kat pointed to Edgewater's trade confirmations for the last two months. "Edgewater's broke, and there aren't any trades to begin with. How could Zachary not know that?" Kat grimaced as she sipped her coffee. It was ice cold.

"You're really sure he's not in on it? Of course he'd be crazy to hire you if he was." Jace winced as he propped up his injured right arm on his knee.

"Exactly. But why didn't he notice that his trades weren't going through? Edgewater Investments seems to be nothing at all like how he's described it. It's about to implode."

"Could the trade confirmations be faked too?" Jace asked.

"Yes, but doesn't Zachary talk to other people? Other traders? His broker?" Despite the fire, last night's work had paid off. With proof the money was diverted, Kat figured she could meet Zachary's deadline. If she could follow the money through to its ultimate destination, Zachary would have an airtight case against his father. But this latest question had her stumped. "Doesn't he execute the trades on a computer trading platform? It's an elaborate ruse if that's all faked too. I'll have to watch him do it."

"You said Edgewater paid Research Analytics about two hundred and twenty million last year?" Jace scratched his chin.

"That's right."

"That's almost exactly Research Analytics' total revenues for the year. I downloaded their annual report," Jace said. "It was surprisingly easy to get."

"That means Edgewater might be their only customer." Kat thought back to Beecham's vacant lot address and the hang-up phone call. Research Analytics was probably a front too. But a front for what? What was Nathan hiding, and why did he need all that money?

Kat rose from her desk and grabbed a thick file from atop her filing cabinet. "These are copies of all the bank deposits over the last year. Almost all of the deposits are clients investing their money. No trading that I can see."

"Further proof no trading is going on."

Kat nodded. She perched on the arm of Jace's overstuffed armchair. "Unless there's a bank account I don't know about." She opened the file. "The deposits are immediately transferred out again, almost as soon as they come in. All to the same account number at the Bank of Cayman."

"I bet that's Research Analytics' account." Jace looked up at her. "Want me to confirm?"

"Sure. I also want to review the inter-relationships." Kat

rose and dropped the file on her desk. She walked over to the whiteboard. "It helps to see who's related to whom."

She pointed at the diagram sketched out on the board. A box labeled *Edgewater* sat at the top. The two boxes below were marked *Research Analytics* and *Svensson* respectively. Lines marked *payments* connected them to Edgewater. A line marked *reporting* ran to the right, connecting *Edgewater* to a box identified as *Beecham*.

"What's all this for?" Jace stood and held his arm as he followed her to the whiteboard.

"To get an idea of the cash and information flows. What do they all have in common?" Kat traced her forefinger along the top of the diagram.

Jace raised his eyebrows but didn't say anything.

"We know how much Edgewater paid to Research Analytics. And how much money in total they have from their annual report." Kat tapped the document on her desk. Together with the Cayman Islands Registrar of Companies and online searches, the diagram represented all the information she could glean on the company.

She pointed to the *Research Analytics* box. "Almost all the money Research Analytics receives—about two hundred and twenty million annually—goes to one non-profit organization. The World Institute. Nathan's a member." Lucky for her, the World Institute had a website. A website that proudly listed its donors and members.

She drew a circle below the diagram and wrote *WI* inside it. She drew arrows downwards from *Research Analytics*. "Research Analytics is simply a conduit from Edgewater to The World Institute."

"That's a fortune. If it all goes to one place, why wouldn't the donors just pay the World Institute directly?"

"You mean like Edgewater?" Kat tapped the board.

Jace nodded.

"Good question. It's non-profit, so there's no tax advantage to funneling it through the Caymans or any other tax haven."

"Research Analytics is just a front." Jace held his arm as he returned to his chair. "Edgewater's money ends up in WI without anyone tracing it back there."

"Exactly. I'm betting some donors have something to hide. Maybe they want to remain anonymous."

"They're obviously covering their tracks for a reason." Jace shifted in his chair and winced. He rubbed his injured arm.

"It's that sore? You should see a doctor, Jace."

Jace waved her off with his left hand. "It's fine for now."

"Suit yourself." Kat sat back down at her desk and typed *World Institute* into the search engine and pressed enter. The search results came back with a dozen entries aside from WI's official website. She clicked on the first one. "Apparently they also hold an annual conference."

"I thought it was a secret organization."

"It is. No one knows what they discuss inside the conference, or even where it's held. Just that they hold one every year." For such a clandestine organization, she was surprised at how easy it was to find information online. Perhaps to inspire additional investors.

"Who are the members? Investment types?"

"No—that's what's interesting. It's anyone and everyone. Business tycoons, philanthropists, royalty, future presidents, and even well-connected talk show hosts. People with money."

"Future presidents? How can they predict the next head of state before it happens?"

"They don't have to foresee the future," Kat said. "They decide it. At least that's what some people say." She scrolled to the financial statement page. "See this? Total inflows last year were four hundred million. That meant Edgewater's two hundred and twenty million via Research Analytics is more than half of all their cash inflows."

"Wow. Very influential. Who's kicking in the rest?" Jace leaned forward.

Kat frowned. Like a dog with a bone, he smelled a story. Still, Jace was the best at sniffing out secrets.

"I don't know. Can you check further to see who else is affiliated with them?" Kat's quick investigation had found all sorts of conspiracy theories related to the World Institute. While the WI referred to itself as a *think tank* in the annual report, others were less complimentary. At best it was considered a secret society of global elites, the rich and powerful determining policy and law to suit their needs. At worst it was described as a global shadow government undermining national sovereignty by backing politicians friendly to big business.

But she'd let Jace form his own opinions. No one was better at uncovering dirt. She just had to ensure he wasn't sidetracked once he saw the story potential.

"I'll get right on it." Jace leaned back in the leather armchair and stretched his long legs out in front of him. He pulled a laptop out of his briefcase and powered it up.

Kat glanced at her inbox, where Harry's bank statement caught her eye. It sat atop his checkbook and other statements. Another task she needed to tackle quickly. Whoever was behind his financial mess needed to be stopped, but she was quickly running out of time on Zachary's deadline. She'd work Edgewater for another hour and then concentrate on Harry's stuff. She needed to get his affairs straightened out tonight once and for all. She picked up the pile to deposit in her briefcase when one line jumped out at her. It was a monthly transfer to the same account as the recent loan.

Jace shifted in his chair. He was silent, other than the odd tap on his keyboard.

She turned back to Harry's bank statement. Sure enough, regular monthly transfers had occurred for at least six months, as far back as Harry's checkbook records went. But as far as she knew, he didn't have another account at the same bank. She scribbled a note to ask Anita Boehmer.

Thirty minutes later, Jace beckoned Kat over. "Kat, this is fascinating. I can't believe I've never heard about the World Institute. Says they're trying to start a new world order."

Kat scanned the article. The caption under the author's photograph read *Roger Landers, author of Currency Conspiracy and the New World Order.*

"We can uncover what's behind the World Institute later," Kat said. "Since we don't have much time, let's focus on how Edgewater's payments end up there."

"The membership list is impressive," Jace said. "I traced all the attendees since first meetings in 1954. That year, one hundred of the world's elite met with the sole purpose of establishing one world government. In every year since then, about a hundred or so very powerful people have met to advance their cause."

"That's a conspiracy theory if I ever heard one." Kat realized her mistake too late. Jace was off on a tangent already.

"There are a lot of interesting facts to back it up. For instance, the last three American presidents, the British prime minister, and the Canadian prime minister have all attended. Right before they were elected."

"They were voted in by the people, Jace. Democratically." How could she get him back on track?

"True," Jace said. "Except who decided which people would be running in the first place?"

"You think those nominations were fixed?"

"Heavily influenced at the very least. Ninety-three percent of all the World Institute political attendees ended up in office a year or two later. That's more than a coincidence. But how and why are they connected to the WI? I'd never even heard of the organization until now."

"What does this have to do with the money?"

"Background, Kat—background. I'm guessing the only reason we haven't heard of the WI before is because they don't want us to. Of course a few journalists *are* writing a lot of the stuff I'm reading, but they've been dismissed as crackpots."

"Except you don't think they're crackpots." Kat sighed.

"There must be an element of truth to it. From what I can see, the WI is all very hush-hush. The meetings are closed to media. At least the regular media. A few high-profile journalists have been invited, but with the understanding that they are bound by secrecy. Break the silence and they won't be invited back—or write a book like Landers and you'll be completely shoved out. None of the more accommodating journalists have ever leaked anything. Not in over fifty years. Any journalist worth his salt would write a story on this."

"Yet no mainstream journalists have." Kat turned more fully to him. "Pray, why is that?"

"They've been silenced." Jace raised his brows. "Paid off—or something worse."

"Or, maybe there's nothing to write about."

"Maybe—maybe not. Don't kid yourself, Kat. This is a big story. There's a reason we haven't heard of it until now. These are some of the richest, most powerful people in the world. They control banks, governments, and even countries. Their objective is to consolidate power even more. The European Union? That was the first step. They've got plans for an Asian union and a North American one next."

Jace pointed to the World Institute Annual Report on Kat's computer screen. "Their mandate is one world currency. Edgewater is one of the biggest global currency traders."

"That doesn't make sense to me," Kat said. "Fewer currencies ruin Edgewater's business. They would have nothing to trade."

She turned back to her computer screen. "At any rate, we don't necessarily need to know Nathan's reasons for diverting the money. Just proof he embezzled the money."

"Don't you want to know the motive behind the crime?"

"Sure, it's interesting, but we don't have time, Jace. I need to wrap this up by Zachary's Monday deadline."

It was as if Jace hadn't heard a word. "Perfect example—the European Union. What happened after that? The Euro.

One currency."

"So what?"

"That's just the start, Kat. What if the credit crisis happened on purpose?"

"You mean, like someone planned it?"

"Exactly. What if currency was worthless? What would you do?"

"I'd keep my money in a stronger currency. Or, if that wasn't enough, in something like gold or diamonds. So would everybody else. But why would anyone orchestrate a currency devaluation? It hurts everybody."

"Not everybody—only the people who don't see it coming."

"Sounds just like every other conspiracy theory I've heard of," Kat said. "And it has nothing to do with Edgewater and Zachary's assignment."

"That's where you're wrong, Kat. Regardless of Zachary's low opinion of his father, Nathan Barron is a well-respected currency expert. What if the goal were to switch to one world currency? How would you get people—or governments—to do that?"

"You'd have to make it worthless," Kat said. "Then everyone wants out of the weak currency. They'd exchange it for a safer, more stable currency."

"Exactly. Devalue the dollar, the pound, the yen. Everyone panics, and *voilà*, you offer one global currency to get them out of the mess they're in. On your terms, of course."

"Where do you get this stuff, Jace? You're completely off the wall."

"I don't think so. Look at these lists." Jace handed Kat a printout of the attendees for each conference. Every year was like a Billboard Top 100. Except it wasn't the year's hit songs. It was the year's heavy hitters—the richest, most powerful, most influential people in the world, for every year going back to 1954.

"The queen of The Netherlands? She's a philanthropist. The World Institute is a think tank. Nothing strange about that." Kat skimmed the list. Heavy hitters all right, but nothing that indicated sinister motives.

"She controls one of the biggest oil companies in the world," Jace said. "It's more than an interest in humanity. It's a concentration of power."

"Even if you're right, how exactly does this relate back to Nathan Barron and Edgewater?" Kat felt herself being pulled in.

"There's money to be made, Kat. If you happen to know a currency is about to fall, you can profit from that knowledge."

"Meaning speculate on it? As in Edgewater's trades?"

"Exactly," Jace said. "That's why we have to expand the scope to include the World Institute. We know Research Analytics plays a major role in Nathan's fraud. At the very least, we should investigate Research Analytics' relationship with the World Institute."

"No, Jace. We only need to provide background on the World Institute and show the money going there. Anything beyond that is out of scope."

"Why? Aside from the fact the money Nathan's contributing isn't actually his, there must be a reason he contributes secretly in the first place. Wouldn't Zachary want to know that Nathan's funded an organization that undermines their business?"

Kat sighed. "Fine, as long as Zachary agrees." She was already certain Zachary would be onside with anything that exposed Nathan's wrongdoings. "Just keep it focused."

"We need to go to that conference."

"Jace, no." Kat held up her arms to protest. "I don't mind helping you with a story, but we're getting sidetracked. We don't need to go to the conference."

"But I think it's in a few days. At least it appears that way, given the information you found in Barron's email and calendar. It's held somewhere different every year, usually in a resort just outside of a large city. Last year it was at a Swiss resort, the year before, just outside of New York."

Kat tapped her forehead in realization. "Nathan's trip to Geneva this time last year." She remembered it from his calendar.

"Exactly. The meeting takes place at the same time every year. I'll bet if you go back a year before that you'll find a New York trip too."

"My fees don't include international travel, Jace. If you want to go on your own dime, fine. Where is it being held this year?"

"I'm not sure. The secrecy extends to not even telling attendees until the last minute. Don't want a bunch of journalists snooping around." Jace smiled. "But those are the best places—obviously they've got something to hide."

CHAPTER 19

KAT STILL COULDN'T GET JACE off the subject an hour later.

It was already noon, and Kat wasn't any further ahead. She stared at the diagram on her office whiteboard, trying to make sense of the money flows and how they connected to Edgewater.

Jace, however, had become an expert in World Institute affairs.

"Where exactly is Nathan Barron?" Jace asked. "That might give us a clue where to search next."

"I don't know. His calendar showed the flight to London yesterday. But Zachary checked with his secretary and confirmed he wasn't on it. He is out of town, though."

"Where is he?"

"Don't know. His secretary didn't know either. At least that's what she told Zachary. And Zachary hasn't seen him in almost a week."

"Do you think he made a run for it?"

"Doubt it." Kat remembered the trophies in Nathan's

office. His ego was too big to leave them behind. "He's been doing this for more than a decade. I'm sure he has no idea we're investigating him. It's just business as usual as far as he's concerned."

"Suppose that's true, and also assume he's a member of the World Institute. He must be, since he's diverting all this money to them. That means he'll be attending the conference."

"Maybe that's what was taking place in London," Kat said.

"When was the ticket booked?"

Kat pulled out a copy of Nathan's flight ticket. "It was issued six months ago. Why does that matter?"

"Can't be for the World Institute. They arrange everything at the last minute—a month or two before the actual conference. To keep the location secret. But it's always held this time of year. I think he's not going to London because he has something more important. The World Institute annual conference."

"Assuming he is, how do we find out where?" Kat asked.

"There's another way to view this. Hand me the conference list." Jace grabbed a handful of pushpins. "If I'm searching for someone in the back country, I start with his last known whereabouts. That gives me a pattern to define our search area. Then it's a process of elimination."

"This isn't a search and rescue mission."

"No, but the same principles apply."

⁓⁓⁓

An hour later they stood in Kat's spare office downtown, staring at the wall in front of her treadmill. It was the only space available to pin up the map Jace had bought from the dollar store.

Pushpins marked the location of all fifty-something conferences to date. They were concentrated in Europe, but there were plenty on the east coast of the U.S. and Canada. Blue pins marked conferences that had taken place in the last ten years, yellow for the decade before, and so on.

The map resembled a budget version of something you'd find in the war room at the Pentagon.

"Interesting concept," Kat said. "But how will this help us find the location?"

"I'm guessing it's like the Olympics. You don't choose the same continent or country over and over again. To be fair to everyone."

"That rules out Europe."

"North America seems a bit sparse," Jace said.

True. There were only seven pins, all in eastern North America.

"They're always held at exclusive resorts under heavy security—armed guards, soldiers, secret service, police," Jace added.

"Makes sense. Somewhere they can secure the perimeter."

"And clear the surrounding areas of residents and visitors."

"Really?" Kat arched her eyebrows in surprise. "They go to that extent?"

They stood in silence and studied the map. While the places and players had changed through the years, those controlling the strings behind the scenes hadn't. Changes in government, civil wars, and even democracy hadn't altered the real power structure. The play was the same, just a different cast of actors on stage. Some things never really changed at all.

CHAPTER 20

KAT STARED AT JACE'S MAP. Its clusters and webs reminded her of neural pathways and the dementia overtaking Harry's brain. Plaques and tangles breaking through his last lines of defense, smothering synapses and trapping memories. Battle lines were redrawn daily as dementia encroached further into his mind and body.

Harry slammed a file cabinet in the outer office and muttered something unintelligible.

Kat jumped.

"What's wrong with you?" Jace asked. "Didn't you hear me?"

Kat met his eyes and couldn't answer. Her lower lip trembled.

"Why are you staring at me like that?"

Kat burst into tears. "Harry's got Alzheimer's."

Jace didn't hesitate. He pulled her close, holding her against his chest as the tears flowed down her cheeks. "So, now the diagnosis is official."

"You don't seem surprised."

Jace pulled back to meet Kat's eyes. He stroked her cheek. "C'mon, Kat. We both know what's been happening to him. His delusions and accidents. It's more than just forgetfulness. But why didn't you talk to me?" He pulled her towards him. "You knew before—at the doctor's office?"

"Yes." She didn't mention the first appointment. Her tears soaked his shirt as she burrowed her face into his chest.

"But you kept it from me? Why?"

How could she tell him why? Tell him she was afraid he would leave her? He would be insulted at the suggestion. But her father left. Maybe Jace would too.

"I was waiting for the right time."

"The right time was the minute you knew, Kat. You didn't want to tell me—you know how that makes *me* feel?" Jace turned away, a hurt expression in his eyes.

"I didn't know what to say." He was right of course, but she was scared.

Jace pulled her close and kissed her. "Kat, I love you. I have a right to know. You just can't leave me out of things like this."

"I know, but talking about it—it just scares me. It makes it too real. I can't deal with it right now." Kat willed herself to stop crying. Crying never solved anything.

"Your mom had Alzheimer's."

She nodded as tears streamed down her face.

There—he'd said for her, out loud. She was just fourteen when her mom died and she'd moved in with the Dentons. Uncle Harry and Aunt Elsie. And Hillary.

"Does Harry know?"

"I'm not sure. He seemed to understand, but now he's forgotten all about it."

"Everything will be fine, Kat. We'll deal with it." Jace stroked her cheek and wiped away a tear.

"I don't want Harry to end up like her, Jace."

She still held out hope that the diagnosis was a mistake.

But in her heart she knew otherwise.

"I'll help with Harry. Don't worry about anything."

They were interrupted by a crash coming from the reception.

"Uncle Harry?"

Kat ran down the hall, with Jace close behind her.

Harry lay on the floor. His upturned chair was beside him, wheels still spinning. He held his shoulder and winced in pain.

"I'm okay. Just lost my balance."

"Never stand on a chair with wheels, Uncle Harry."

"I had to help her. The file was on the top shelf." Kat's office previously housed a dental practice, with floor to ceiling filing. She didn't use the top rows, but hadn't got around to renovating yet.

"Help who? Nobody's here but you."

"Hillary," Harry explained. "She needed a file for her school project. It's due tomorrow."

"Right," Kat said. "I don't see her. Where is she now?"

"She had to go. Or she'd be late for school."

Kat fought the urge to cry. Jace had no idea what he was in for, and she couldn't expect him to help for long. It was too much to ask of anyone.

CHAPTER 21

K AT FINALLY FOUND TIME TO drive over to check out Research Analytics. She pulled up to the curb and put the Lincoln in park. The only space big enough to park Harry's boat-like Lincoln was a block away. That was okay, since parking down the street allowed her to observe Research Analytics without drawing attention.

Harry insisted they take his car, which of course meant she had to drive. Despite losing his driver's license, he'd repaired the Lincoln after the accident and refused to sell it. He sat beside her in the passenger seat, rolling his thumbs. He fidgeted constantly now, although seemingly unaware of it.

"Watch the whitewalls, Kat. You're going to scrape them." Harry sucked in his breath. "Why do you always park so close to the curb?"

Kat turned to Harry. "I'm six inches away. Open the door and see for yourself." She always parked further away to avoid this endless debate, but Harry's perception of space and proximity to things seemed off now.

Harry averted his eyes and rolled his thumbs faster. "Why are you arguing with me, Kat?"

"No, you're right, Uncle Harry. I am too close." Kat suddenly realized why he was agitated—the door handle. Dementia's mental erosion was uneven. Harry remembered lyrics from the hit songs of his youth, yet forgot how to work a door handle. Even in a car he had owned for thirty-plus years. "I'll try to be more careful next time."

Kat jumped out of the car and ran around to the passenger side to open the door. She studied the street front while she waited for him to exit. This part of the city was a jumble of storefronts and three-story apartment buildings, built mostly in the forties to the seventies. Except for the faded paint and disrepair, it remained almost unchanged from its heyday. Even the people here oozed tiredness. She shut the car door. "Ready?"

Harry nodded and they plodded up the street. It was his old neighborhood, just three blocks from the house he grew up in.

"Where are we, Kat?" Harry glanced around in wonder. "I've never been here before. It's sure busy around here."

"I know." Kat didn't correct him. It would only upset him, and they were already at their destination. Research Analytics' corporate headquarters appeared to be a stucco apartment building with a vacancy sign out front. She walked up to the front door and inspected the suite listing. None of the names were even remotely similar to Research Analytics. The closest thing to suite fourteen hundred was number twelve, listed as belonging to A. Knopf.

Just as she had suspected, Research Analytics was a complete fabrication. The phone number hadn't checked out either—it turned out to be a disconnected number. Fictitious vendors were a common method of insider embezzlement. Kat pulled out her cell phone and snapped a picture of the building as evidence for her report.

An hour later, Kat sat across from Zachary in the Edgewater Investments' boardroom. Despite it being a Saturday, half the offices were occupied by people talking on the phone or typing on their computers. Snippets of hallway conversations drifted in through the open boardroom door as people sauntered by with their morning coffees.

She pulled a thick stack of documents from her briefcase and set it on the table.

"What have you got? Enough to nail him, I hope." Zachary appeared almost happy. An odd reaction since discovering his partner—and father—was stealing from him.

Kat's investigation had brought more questions than answers. One thing was certain: Edgewater and the Barron family would never be the same again.

She drew in her breath. Zachary wasn't going to like what she had to say. "I'm working on it. Here's what we've got so far." Kat recounted how the money had moved from Edgewater to Research Analytics.

"The investment research company you told me about? How much money are we talking about?" Zachary stared at her.

"Fifty million so far this year. Two hundred and twenty million last year." She help up her hands and shrugged. "Before that—I'm still working on the number."

He shot up out of his chair. "That's impossible. I know something's going on—but a quarter of a billion? That can't be right."

"Remember you said there was no money in the bank?"

"But that much? It's impossible."

"I'm afraid it is possible, Zachary."

His smug expression morphed into panic. "How can we get it back?"

"I'm trying to figure that out right now. What I know so

far is that Research Analytics is a sham. The address on the invoice is a seedy run-down apartment building on the eastside." She spun her cell phone around to show him the photograph of the derelict building.

Zachary scoffed. "I knew it. Nathan's a thief. I want to press charges, run him out of Edgewater."

"Nathan didn't act alone, Zachary."

He stiffened and his eyes narrowed. "What do you mean?"

"He had help. Someone had to issue the checks to Research Analytics. He doesn't have the security access to do that."

"Well, who does?"

There was no avoiding it. "Victoria did. Edgewater's auditors are suspect, too." Kat explained the sequential invoice numbers and Beecham, including its connection to Nathan. Victoria was the only other person at Edgewater with access to the checks.

"They don't exist? Nathan set up a fictitious auditing firm?" He didn't seem all that surprised. Zachary's lack of emotion troubled her. Didn't he understand the implications? Or maybe he did, but was in denial.

"It's very serious, Zachary. Everything about Edgewater is suspect. The financials, the investment performance—everything." There was no way to sugarcoat it. "Edgewater's broke, and so are you."

"What do you mean, broke?"

Kat pulled the bank statement out of her briefcase and slid it across the boardroom table.

Zachary snatched the paper and was silent for a moment as he read her analysis. "I'll kill the bastard." He pounded his fist on the table.

Kat jumped, even though she had expected his reaction. "The hard part will be getting the money back. Do you have anything in reserve? Any lines of credit?"

Zachary shook his head. "Isn't there any money left?"

Kat shook her head.

"You're telling me I'm ruined?" Zachary jumped up from

the table and paced in front of it.

Zachary was even more broke than Harry. He just didn't know it yet.

CHAPTER 22

KAT AND JACE SAT IN her office and stared at the twenty-seven names on her whiteboard. Many of the World Institute conference attendees were also on Nathan's contact list. To the right of the names were columns, one per year for each of last five conferences. Saturday afternoon was slipping away, and they were inching ever closer to Zachary's Monday deadline.

Outside, seagulls squawked as they circled the overcast sky, searching for scraps on the harbor docks below. A large gull swooped down on smaller bird on the wharf, stealing his catch.

They had decided to focus their efforts on Research Analytics. But that just meant following the money to its ultimate destination, the World Institute. Every step brought more questions, and Zachary demanded answers for all of them.

"Who *are* these people?" Kat asked herself as much as Jace. She stood and walked over to the white board.

The World Institute conference attendance list hadn't

been difficult to get. Conspiracy theorists had documented the comings and goings of the attendees for years, following a few key players to hone in on the location. That was about all they found out. Since nonmembers weren't allowed in, they couldn't report on the meeting agendas. The security detail for a World Institute conference rivaled a G8 summit, replete with police SWAT teams, air and ground surveillance, and the personal security details of each of the attendees.

"Most are rich," Jace said. "Almost all of them are famous. All are important public figures. Aside from being World Institute invitees, all these names have something to do with money."

"That's true." Kat studied the list. "Treasury secretaries, central bank heads, bank CEOs, and hedge fund principals. They either develop policy, regulate it, or are impacted by the rules."

"Agreed," said Jace. "And they're all global experts in monetary policy. But why all the secrecy? Why meet as a supra-national group, outside of government?"

"Governments are obstacles to them. They involve voters, laws, and discussions. Democracy and consensus. Powerful people like Nathan Barron and the rest of the World Institute want things done their way, on their terms. As a bloc, their multi-national corporations are also bigger than most governments." Sometimes it was better not to know how the world really worked.

Jace didn't say anything.

"That sounds kind of paranoid, doesn't it?" Kat asked.

"It does, but there's a ring of truth to it. More and more, big multi-nationals set the rules. They use paid lobbyists to influence lawmakers, and eliminating trade barriers equals higher profits. Foreign currency transactions are simply another hurdle that costs them time and money."

It was the only connection they'd made in the last hour, and it was troubling. Kat still couldn't understand why Nathan would be part of it. Fewer currencies meant fewer opportunities to arbitrage the differences, and that's where Edgewater Investments profits were made.

"What kind of a conference organizes itself at the last minute?" Kat asked.

"A secret one. One that wants to achieve its aims without outside interference."

"Right." Kat tapped the white board with a dry erase marker. "Let's review each name and see what else they have in common."

"Jason Blackstone," she said, "U.S. Federal Reserve Chair."

Jace read from his laptop. "He's been at the conference for the last three years."

Kat placed three X's beside Blackstone's name.

"Jean-Claude Bruneau."

"Attended for the first time last year. He heads the International Monetary Fund."

"Since when?" Kat asked.

"Six months ago. Before joining the IMF he served as France's finance minister." Jace emptied a packet of sugar into his coffee and stirred it with the end of his pencil.

Kat shot him a disapproving glance. "You're going to get lead poisoning. Can't you just grab a spoon?"

"No time." He smiled sweetly at her.

"Whatever. The timing sure is interesting. Bruneau was invited just prior to his appointment as IMF chief. Just like the current U.S. president and Canadian prime minister were."

"Invited before they became heads of state," Jace recapped.

"That's right. And finance ministers like Bruneau don't usually attend."

"Unless the World Institute had bigger plans for them."

"It's starting to seem that way. The World Institute decides who gets on the slate. Your choice is made even before you vote." Kat went on:

"Gordon Pinslett."

Jace choked on his coffee. "Who?"

"Gordon Pinslett. He's a media tycoon—Global Financial."

"I know who he is, Kat. He owns the *Sentinel*."

"Really? You never mentioned him before."

"He's never set foot in our humble office. Technically, he owns the conglomerate that owns the *Sentinel*."

"Oh. What's he doing at the World Institute?"

"I don't know, but I intend to find out." Jace scratched his bandaged arm. "Maybe he's the reason the editor killed my story. Criticizing the rich hits too close to home, I guess. But if stories like mine aren't told, we never know the truth. What kind of world is that?" He didn't wait for her answer. "A censored one."

Kat shrugged and smiled, hoping to drag him out of his dark mood. "None of that matters now, since you don't work there anymore."

"It matters to me, Kat. People like Pinslett can't just buy up all the media and stifle us. Stories like mine have to get out."

Kat sighed. "Okay, but for now, let's focus on the story at hand. Why Nathan is diverting money to Research Analytics and The World Institute." Discussing democracy with Jace could last for hours. If she wanted to meet Zachary's deadline she needed to steer him in the right direction. Seeing Pinslett's name had got Jace all riled up again. "You're better off, Jace. You said yourself things have been going downhill at the *Sentinel* for a while. This is a chance for a new start."

Jace shrugged. "I suppose. But I still need to earn a living."

"I've got it covered." That was debatable. They had won their run-down heritage house with their bid at the city tax sale last year. Won was the wrong word. The old Victorian was a bottomless money pit, consuming endless time and money with repairs and remodeling. The city's strict heritage rules meant expensive and drawn-out renovations. It was a constant challenge to stay onside with the zoning bylaws.

"Let's get back to the list."

They reviewed the remaining names as the sky outside darkened. It started to rain.

"Svensson," Jace said. "Invited for the last three years. His

Nobel nomination was the basis for most of the one-world-currency theories out there."

Kat wrote Edgewater *payment* and *snowshoe accident* beside his name.

"The guy who died in the mountains, right?"

Kat nodded.

Jace tapped on the keyboard. "He fell through a cornice." Cornices formed under heavy snow conditions, causing snowpack to extend a few feet past the edge of a cliff. It was only obvious from underneath that there was no ground supporting it. Above it appeared to be snow-covered earth. It was a common cause of falls in the backcountry.

"I remember hearing about the accident, just not the details," Kat said.

"The details weren't on the news. Kurt told me. He was part of the recovery operation." Jace's friend, Kurt, was also a search and rescue volunteer. Kurt worked on the Sunshine Coast, while Jace's territory was the North Shore.

Jace typed something on his keyboard. "Hold on a sec— says here the coroner now suspects suicide."

"Suicide? When he's up for a Nobel?" Kat asked. "Winning a Nobel would be the pinnacle of anyone's career. It's only two weeks away. Definitely worth waiting for, even with depression."

"Depression does strange things to people. They also found narcotics in Svensson's system. Too much to have hiked there. He must have taken it after reaching the spot where he fell. The story goes on to say he had money troubles."

"Lots of people have financial difficulties, Jace. The Nobel prize money would fix that."

"This article says he left a note. They just found it in his hotel room." Jace tapped his computer screen.

"I'd like to see that suicide note," Kat said. "He's in a foreign country in the middle of winter, and he hikes for hours just to jump off a cliff? That's a lot of effort for someone who wants to end it all."

"True," he said.

Kat stared out the window. An old man in a yellow slicker scattered bread crumbs along the wharf. A few dozen pigeons swarmed around his feet, pecking at the crumbs.

"Wait a sec—it's not just your average suicide note. Says here that he apologized."

"Apologized? For what?"

Jace tapped away at his keyboard. "Svensson changed his mind. He decided one world currency was wrong after all."

"But that was the whole basis of his Nobel nomination."

Jace held up his hand as he read from his screen. "An excerpt from his note was printed in the *Herald* today."

Kat rushed to Jace's side to read over his shoulder:

A single global or supra-national currency undermines the sovereign rule of nations. Money is a fundamental tool in monetary policy. Governments need it to adjust interest rates, debt, and money supply to manage their economies.

The Herald was the other daily paper in town, the *Sentinel*'s competition.

"I have to agree with him," Kat said. "Take away the tools and suddenly you lose control over your economy and, to some extent, your destiny."

"Of course his new theory is completely at odds with the World Institute. One global currency is the World Institute's *raison d'être*."

"I wonder what changed Svensson's mind?" Kat stared out the window. Two of the larger pigeons had attacked a smaller bird. It flew up to a post, watching helplessly as the two bigger birds devoured its share.

"I don't know, but I intend to find out. There's a story here—I can feel it." Jace punched some keys on his laptop. "Another thing—Svensson's now out of the running for the Nobel. Apparently you can't win if you're dead."

"Doesn't winning a Nobel include money?"

"Ten million crown. One and a half million dollars."

"That's a hefty sum," Kat said. "Some people would kill

for it."

"You think he was murdered?"

"Possibly. I don't know. At any rate, we have to find this year's conference location and get the proof of Nathan's involvement. Svensson's been to the last three conferences, so he's probably still invited to this conference, even if he did change his mind. I think I know where it is."

"Where?"

"Right here," she said. "See these dots on your map? It's due for a west coast venue. It also explains why Svensson was here. See if you can find out if any of the others are here. Check all the high-end hotels. They might arrive the day before and stay in a downtown hotel. Then check all the local conference centers. Places outside of the city, where the perimeter can be secured. Preferably ones with limited access. We don't have much time if they're already here."

"Got it."

That was the easy part. The hard part was getting in.

CHAPTER 23

KAT'S HUNCH WAS CONFIRMED TEN minutes later.

"The Tides Resort at Hideaway Bay," Jace said. "Close, yet hard to reach."

"On the Sunshine Coast? I can't imagine these VIPs coming in on the ferry."

The Sunshine Coast was ten miles north of Vancouver, yet it was accessible only by boat. Getting there involved two short drives with a forty-minute ferry sandwiched in between.

Locals relied on government ferries to stay connected to the rest of the province—still, British Columbia ferries were for the proletariat, not global elites accustomed to five-star service. Kat couldn't imagine them lining up behind SUV's and minivans in two-hour ferry line-ups, sipping coffee from commuter cups while trying to keep warm.

"They don't have to take the ferry," Jace said. "They can fly from the Vancouver Airport in a matter of minutes on a small charter plane or helicopter. The Tides Resort has a landing strip."

"We'll need to confirm it somehow."

"Done. I already called the hotel because Monsieur Bruneau forgot his medication." Jace grinned. "I arranged to have it couriered immediately."

"You're so devious." Kat circled her arms around his waist and hugged him.

Jace bent his head to kiss her. "When do we leave? Bruneau checks in tomorrow."

∽๛๛๛๛∾

Two hours later Kat, Jace and Harry sat on a worn bench seat in the Sunshine Coast ferry's forward cabin. The ship's interior hadn't changed since it first set sail in the sixties, aside from the scarring of the powder blue naugahyde from generations of passengers and not nearly enough upkeep. The cabin windows were fogged, a result of damp clothing meeting the warmth inside.

"That's him." Kat dropped her newspaper and pointed across the aisle to the opposite side of the ship. A tall, thin man balanced a coffee cup with one hand while he fished a notebook out of a knapsack.

Jace leaned closer as the recorded safety message crackled over the ferry's ancient, distorted speakers. "Who?"

"Roger Landers." Kat locked her eyes on Landers. He wore jeans, and his unzipped ski jacket revealed a fleece pullover underneath. "We're definitely in the right place."

Kat was surprised Jace hadn't noticed him first. Landers had tracked down the last dozen or so World Institute conferences and tried to get into every single one There could be only one reason for his presence on the ferry.

The journalist glanced up and met Kat's gaze. He jumped from his seat and winced as he spilled coffee on his hand. He dropped the cup and brushed his hand against his jacket. Then he turned and strode back towards mid-ship, headed for the parking deck stairs.

"I've got to meet him." Kat rose and followed.

115

Jace frowned and shook his head, clearly embarrassed. She ignored him.

Harry spun around in his seat. "Where are you going, Kat?" Kat didn't answer.

Landers glanced back at her. He reached the stairs and broke into a run, taking the steps two at a time.

"Wait!" Kat shouted. "I just want to talk to you."

Landers' pace quickened as he disappeared around the corner. Kat bounded down the stairs, reaching the door to the parking garage as it closed halfway. She pushed it open and gazed out at the sea of vehicles. Landers was gone.

Somewhere down the long lines of cars and trucks, a dog barked, its cries echoing under the low ceilings of the car deck. Aside from the dog it was eerily quiet, a stark contrast from the mayhem thirty minutes ago when they boarded at Horseshoe Bay. She had to catch Landers before the boat docked in twenty minutes if she wanted to talk to him. Maybe they could combine forces.

She jumped as footsteps sounded somewhere in front of her. Landers's silhouette was outlined under a beam of harsh white fluorescent twenty feet ahead. He spotted her and ducked behind a Ford F-150 truck. She weaved in and out of the vehicles, tracking her eyes on where she last saw him.

"Mr. Landers? Please don't run. We can help each other." Silence.

Kat ran to the truck but Landers was already gone. She craned her ears for footsteps but heard only a dripping pipe beside her. What reason did he have to run from her? He didn't even know her. More importantly, where did he go?

Kat jumped as something crashed at the front of the boat. It sounded like it came from the section where they parked the bicycles, but of course there weren't any at this time of year.

Then she saw Landers. His back faced her, silhouetted against an ocean backdrop. The front of the car park level was completely open, except for a barrier of double ropes that were removed when the vehicles disembarked. He turned and met her gaze for a split second. Then he jumped.

CHAPTER 24

THE FERRY DETOUR MEANT ANGRY passengers and a schedule to make up. The ferry captain's onboard announcement practically accused Kat of staging a hoax. The police seemed skeptical too, finding no evidence of a man overboard.

Kat couldn't wait to disembark to escape the angry glares of delayed passengers. She drove the Subaru off the ferry ramp and followed the vehicle traffic out of the ferry terminal and up the steep hill that led to the highway. It was the same route they often travelled to Kurt Ritter's cabin. Like Jace, Kurt was also a search and rescue volunteer.

"Why would Landers jump?" The brush opened up to a panoramic vista of Howe Sound beyond the edge of the highway, but Kat barely noticed. She still couldn't figure out how Roger Landers had disappeared into thin air right before her eyes.

"Running scared," Jace said. "I'd be scared too, if you ran after me like that."

Kat rolled her eyes. "I just wanted to talk to him. I don't

understand why he took off, or jumped for that matter."

"He obviously thought you were someone else," Jace said.

"He'd rather drown than be caught?" Landers wouldn't last five minutes in the frigid ocean waters. "What on earth is he running from?"

Several nearby passengers had practically attacked her when she pulled the emergency alarm. Apparently their schedules were more important than a maritime accident. But the fact remained: Landers had gone over the edge. She knew what she saw, even if she was the only witness. Weren't you supposed to help a man overboard?

"We don't know he's gone for sure. Only that he's disappeared."

"Jace, he just vanished. There's nowhere for him to swim to. No land, no boats." Landers was gone without a trace, despite the captain's efforts in turning the ferry around and the coast guard's almost immediate arrival.

Kat stole glimpses at the water as the Subaru hugged the curves along the coastal highway. Whatever secrets the waters held would remain that way, at least for now. She steered off the highway onto an unpaved, hilly logging road. An hour later, the ruts and rocks finally gave way to smooth pavement, and the property came into view.

The Tides Resort was built into the hillside like a bunker. Large stone boulders anchored huge, old-growth cedar beams that rose three stories, framing a stunning view through its center. Kat saw a large lobby through the large glass panes, and beyond that, the ocean. The great room was dominated by a massive stone fireplace, the hearth giving off an orange glow. Several people sat around it, sipping drinks.

On the left was a second building that Kat took to be the conference center. Beyond its glass and steel façade was ocean and nothing else. Tall Douglas firs flanked the two buildings like sentinels. A garden and walkway sat between them, beyond which the cliff dropped off into the ocean far below. Even on a wintry day, it took her breath away.

"You remember the plan, Jace?"

"I'm the technician setting up the audio visual equipment. A last-minute replacement."

Kat had uncovered both the company and employee name with a phone call to the hotel to verify the technician's onsite accommodations.

Then she called the video company and canceled the gig. They were now free to take the company's place. It was the perfect cover. They got a room, and no one had ever seen the company's employees. As long as the A/V stuff was basic, they would be fine.

Jace, however, was uneasy. "I'm not so sure about this, Kat."

"I thought you were an investigative reporter." She pulled the Subaru into the long circular driveway and pulled to a stop.

"Why me?" Jace's face darkened as the valet approached the car. "This is never going to work. I don't even know what the guy looks like. How can I disguise myself like him?"

"You don't have to. The resort staff have never met him either. Besides, you're a guy. I could hardly pass for what's-his-name. And Harry's too old."

That got Harry's attention from the back seat.

"Too old for what?"

"Never mind." Kat handed the keys to the valet and opened her door.

"Oh. We're staying here?" Harry's eyes widened. "Wow."

"Grab your stuff, Harry." Jace opened the passenger door. "Let's go."

"Remember," she whispered to Jace as they went inside. "You're tired and want to check in as quickly as possible. Act irritable so they won't want to talk to you."

Kat steered Harry to a pair of low leather couches. Her eyes followed Jace as he headed to the check-in desk. She'd insisted he wear a suit. Even if he was only the A/V technician, it was important to blend in. She figured global power-broker types probably slept in their suits.

She was glad she had insisted. Jace was dressed just like the two other men at the lobby bar—except Jace was decidedly fitter and hotter-looking. She couldn't help but admire the way the well-cut jacket defined his broad shoulders and slim waist. Most definitely not a nerdy A/V technician.

She studied the two men sitting at the bar. They were engrossed in conversation, angled towards each other, making it hard to get a good look at them. Likely two of the hundred or so guests. One of them waved his arms emphatically, almost spilling the drinks on the bar. Kat pulled out her cell phone and held it up.

"Isn't this beautiful?" she said loudly to Harry in what she hoped would pass for some sort of European accent. She snapped a picture, making sure the two men appeared in the frame. It might come in handy later on.

Ten minutes later Kat, Jace, and Harry admired the ocean view from the balcony of their third-floor suite. They sat bundled in their winter jackets, their backs to the gas patio heater that Jace had turned on full blast.

"Are you sure about this, Kat? They didn't even ask for my credit card. Someone's bound to find out."

"Not if we keep a low profile. The people who made the arrangements probably aren't even here. Even if they are, with so many other details and people to keep track of, room assignments are the last thing on their minds. Besides, they rented the whole resort, so it's not going to matter. No one will notice."

"I'm not so sure. What if we get caught?" Jace peered over the balcony railing.

"We won't. We'll get proof Nathan's here, maybe even the level of his involvement. We can be out of here tomorrow, with enough time to wrap up the Edgewater case." Suddenly she was hungry. She rose from her chair and went inside to investigate the mini-bar fridge. She chose a package of toasted almonds, three Coffee Crisp chocolate bars, and a bottle of Merlot.

She carried the wine and three glasses outside, along with the snacks.

"Let's order room service so no one wonders why we're not dining with the other guests."

"I guess that's me again?" Jace unwrapped a Coffee Crisp.

"You're the boss." Kat tossed the room service menu across the table. She poured the wine into glasses.

"None for me." Harry stood. "I'm bushed. I need a nap."

Kat rose and showed Harry to his room. The suite had two adjoining rooms, each with a fireplace.

"Remember, don't go anywhere without us."

"I won't. Good night, Kat."

Kat shut the door and returned to the main suite. Was it right for her to bring her uncle here? Probably not, but she certainly couldn't leave Harry alone for days at a time, especially not after his kitchen fire.

Jace came inside from the balcony as she checked her watch. It was six o'clock and she switched on the television, hoping for an update on Roger Landers and his disappearance from the ferry. The news anchor cycled through the local news with no mention of the missing journalist. World news dominated the broadcast. Greece and Portugal had failed to meet International Monetary Fund loan terms they had agreed as part of their earlier bailouts.

"Isn't the IMF head here at the conference?" Jace placed the telephone receiver back in its cradle. He'd ordered steaks for the two of them and a Monte Cristo sandwich for Harry in case he woke up.

"Jean-Claude Bruneau?" Kat didn't like the expression on Jace's face. "Don't even think of following him, talking to him, or confronting him, Jace."

"I'll be discreet. It's the opportunity of a lifetime."

"No way. Not until I get the goods on Nathan. Promise?"

Jace pouted. "Alright. I guess."

"Wonder how he feels about bailing out these countries."

The fate of so many in the hands of a few. It reminded Kat of feudal lords in medieval times, where the elite lived in castles, and the serfs lived outside the walls. A lucky few got to live inside the castle walls, leaving the rest unprotected and vulnerable.

"Bruneau? He doesn't care one way or the other. It's the IMF's mandate. He doesn't have to care to do it."

"True, but you've got to wonder if the global financial system actually caused the failures in the first place. A few countries set the rules for everyone else to follow. Rules that favor themselves." Kat turned her attention back to the television. The weather forecast was for mixed rain and snow tomorrow. Still no mention of Landers and his ferry disappearance.

"Loan defaults don't exactly bolster their case," she said. "Unless, of course, they wanted them to fail." The Research Analytics payments proved money was being diverted for something other than legitimate research fees. Assuming Research Analytics was a front, what was the World Institute using the money for? Was it really a conspiracy to destroy the world's currencies?

Kat grabbed the remote just as she heard a man's voice outside their room. Her pulse quickened. It was too soon for room service. She muted the volume and realized it wasn't coming from the hallway. It was just Uncle Harry talking in his sleep in the adjoining room.

CHAPTER 25

KAT AWOKE TO A KNOCK on the door. Jace must have ordered breakfast room service. Her mouth watered as she envisioned eggs Benedict and waffles. She rolled over and reached across the bed.

She rested her arm on Jace's stomach and traced her fingers over his taut abs. If Jace was still in bed, then he hadn't called room service. Her disappointment turned to apprehension. Had they been discovered already?

"Jace," she whispered. "Someone's at the door."

"Hmmm." He rolled over and stroked her shoulder with his hand. Her skin tingled as his hand moved down her arm. The knocks came louder. She snapped back to attention.

"Jace, answer it."

"Okay. Don't go anywhere." Jace rose and threw on a shirt and pants. He walked to the door and peered through the peephole. He turned and padded back to the bed and sat down, shaking his head.

"You're never going to believe this." He buttoned his shirt.

"Believe what?" Kat bounded out of bed and threw on sweats and a t-shirt.

The pounding grew even louder, like someone was throwing their weight into it.

"It's your cousin Hillary." Hillary, Kat, and Jace had all been in the same grade at school. Jace had taken an immediate dislike to her, despite Hillary's best efforts to send him swooning.

Kat's pulse quickened as she flashed back to her last confrontation with Hillary. Aunt Elsie's diamond rings had been stolen. Hillary insisted there had been a break-in, but Kat suspected otherwise. Soon after the robbery, Hillary sported a new Rolex, no doubt bartered for the missing rings. She was nothing but trouble. "Impossible. She's been gone for ten years. Besides, how would she even know we're here?"

"I know, but I'm positive it's her. Maybe Harry hasn't been imagining things. Come here and see for yourself."

Kat tiptoed up to the peephole and held her breath as she peered through the viewfinder.

The years had added wrinkles, a sagging chin, and a ton of makeup. Hillary's eyes hid behind Chanel sunglasses with an oversized logo. Worn like a label to advertise her status and impeccable taste, despite the fact she was indoors in the dead of winter.

Kat opened the door and her cousin steamrolled past her, practically knocking her over. She wore a low-cut sleeveless dress, even though it was sub-zero outside. White salt stains formed circular patterns on her brown stiletto boots. An exaggerated D&G zipper tag hung off each boot. It was Hillary all right.

"Where the hell is Dad?" Hillary headed straight for the patio sliders, pushing her giant sunglasses up onto her teased and hair-sprayed hair. "What have you done with him? You kidnapped him!"

"Hillary?" Kat asked. "What are you doing here? Why would you think—?"

Jace's mouth dropped as Hillary stormed past him onto the deck. A gust of cold air rushed in.

Finding no one on the balcony, Hillary marched back inside, leaving the sliding door open to the cold. She headed to the closet, practically ripping the door off its tracks.

"Tell me where he is. Now!"

Jace walked over to the patio door and closed it. He arched his eyebrows at Kat but said nothing.

"He's in the next room. What's going on?" Kat asked, still in shock.

Hillary yanked on the knob, and when it didn't open, pounded on the adjoining door.

"Dad! Open the door."

"Take it easy," Kat said. "You'll break it."

Hillary just glared at her. Then the door opened from the other side.

Harry emerged, looking sleepy.

"Hillary!" He smiled. "What a nice surprise."

Kat stole a glance at Jace. He threw daggers at Hillary, who didn't seem to notice.

"How did you know we were here?" When they were teenagers, Kat sometimes thought Hillary stalked her.

"Wouldn't you like to know?" Hillary glared at Kat from across the room.

Kat studied Hillary. Heavy brown eye shadow framed her eyes. They resembled a pair of burnt-out sockets.

"I'm calling the police and having you charged." Hillary grabbed Harry by the arm. "You'll never work another day in your life once I'm through with you."

"Charged with what?" What the hell was she doing here?

"Forcing him here against his will."

"Uncle Harry, did I force you to come here?"

Hillary cupped her hand over Harry's mouth just as he started to speak. She turned to Kat. "Don't talk to him. You've done enough."

"Hillary, I had to bring him with me." She glanced at

Harry, wondering how to explain to Hillary without hurting Harry's feelings. "The dementia—it's getting worse."

Harry glanced down at the carpet, crestfallen.

"I'm sorry, Uncle Harry."

"It's okay. Kat's right. I know I'm not as sharp as I used to be."

"He's not safe on his own, Hillary. If you'd been around the last few years, maybe you'd know that."

Hillary didn't know about Harry leaving the stove on and almost burning down the house. Or driving his Lincoln through the front window of Carlucci's Pasta House. Or did she? Harry had been talking about her for months, and more frequently of late. Then there was the Tiffany's charge on his credit card. But even Hillary wouldn't stoop that low—would she?

At any rate, Kat had to focus on Harry. Unplugging the stove and disabling the garage door opener and the car battery were only temporary fixes. Harry needed full-time care, and Kat had run out of options. Hillary surely wouldn't help. Suddenly it dawned on her—Hillary's reappearance must be for a reason. Harry's dementia was obvious—was Hillary here to take advantage of the situation? Why else had she returned after a decade?

"You kidnapped Dad against his will. How can you live with yourself? You're a criminal."

"How can you live with yourself, Hillary? You're the criminal—you stole his and Aunt Elsie's life savings."

"It was a gift."

Kat rolled her eyes. "Whatever."

Harry stared at the floor, saying nothing.

"You don't understand, Hillary. Harry forgets to eat. He's here because I take care of him. I wouldn't leave him alone for a few days."

"Oh, I understand, alright. You kidnapped him to take advantage of him. I'm putting an end to that right now."

Harry must have been talking on the phone with Hillary

last night. She must have called his cell phone. Harry wouldn't remember the name of the resort, but he could still read. Hillary only had to ask him to find something with the Tides Resort name on it.

"Kidnapped? Are you serious?" Kat glanced at Harry. He had zoned out, oblivious to the argument. "He wanted to come along."

"We're finally all together again." Harry smiled. "Let's go for breakfast and celebrate."

Kat was just about to explain why they couldn't when Hillary jumped in.

"No, Dad. We're leaving. Get your things." Hillary pushed Harry back into the other room and slammed the door.

Kat glanced at Jace, stunned. A wave of helplessness swept over her as she thought of Hillary taking Harry. Would Harry even survive the ride home before Hillary, with her short fuse, tired of him and dumped him on someone else? That is, if she was really taking him home.

"Let her go." Jace embraced her. "He'll be all right. We'll be home tomorrow."

"But she doesn't know how bad he is." Hillary was too self-centered to deal with his medications, delusions, and confusion.

"I don't believe that for a minute," Jace said. "She knows exactly what's going on."

"Then why is she saying those things?"

"To get to you. And to divert anything negative from her onto you. To hide what's really been happening."

Kat pulled away. "I know she's selfish and I know she stole from him. But she can't possibly think I'm harming him," Kat said. "She doesn't really mean it."

"C'mon, Kat, it's all about her and getting what she wants. You of all people should recognize fraud when you see it. Those mysterious bank withdrawals, the Tiffany's charges? Explain that."

"I thought about the Tiffany's charges too. But isn't that

... too obvious?"

"A series of mistakes about Harry's finances when she re-appears after ten years? Too much of a coincidence for me. Call her on it—I'm sure she'll insist they were all gifts."

"You think she's back because I cancelled those credit cards? Her supply was cut off?" Kat sat down on the bed. "She wouldn't go to that extreme—it's fraud and it's elder abuse."

"Open your eyes, Kat. Harry doesn't shop at Tiffany's. Why do you think she's back?"

Jace was right. "But to steal from her own father?"

"Most people wouldn't," Jace agreed. "But Hillary's not most people. She'll do whatever she can get away with."

"Jace, even if it's true, there's nothing left. I've cancelled the credit cards, and all his money went to pay the bills. There's nothing left to steal."

CHAPTER 26

KAT AND JACE HUDDLED IN their warm parkas on the balcony and sipped their morning coffees. The sun had risen just over the horizon, and a burnt-orange glow peeked through the tall evergreens. Eerie light reflected off the fresh dusting of snow and contrasted with long shadows from the trees.

Kat swallowed her last bite of French toast. Overnight her flu symptoms had passed, and she was surprised at how hungry she was. "Do you think Harry's okay? Hillary's got such a short fuse. His dementia's going to frustrate her."

"She won't stick around long once she finds the money's gone. All Hillary cares about is Hillary." Jace stood and peered over the railing. He motioned Kat to lean forward.

Two security guards had just emerged from the hotel's kitchen door below them. They talked in voices too low for Kat to make out the conversation.

Kat first noticed the two beefy thirty-somethings outside the building this morning. They stood below on the frozen ground, securing the entrance. Every few minutes they talked into their sleeves, apparently in radio contact.

Security had materialized gradually at Hideaway Bay as the conference attendees arrived. Even in suits, the security men seemed more like army commandos. A stark contrast to the aging, overweight conference attendees they guarded.

"There must be a dozen guys on this side of the hotel alone," Jace whispered. "I'm going for a walk—a VIP must be arriving."

Kat held up her hand, not wanting to risk being overheard by the men below. But Jace was already inside, changing into his suit. Kat jumped up and followed him, sliding the patio door closed.

"Do I really need to wear this suit the whole time I'm here?" Jace sat on the bed as he slipped his shoes on.

"You can't go out there, Jace." Kat dropped her parka on the bed.

"Why not? If I truly am the technical support, shouldn't I be out there? The hotel staff must wonder why we haven't left the room." Jace came up and circled his arms around her waist. He pulled the curtains closed.

Kat cupped her hands over his. "Can't we just relax and enjoy the place? Once the conference starts, the security detail will relax a bit. Give them a few hours to settle in." She felt anything but relaxed. Now that they were in, she didn't want to do anything that would risk discovery.

"You said yourself they're not checking out anyone already inside."

Security had seemed strangely absent until now. After all, Hillary had managed to get in. Kat realized they were lucky to have arrived one day before the conference started. Otherwise, they might not have even made it up the driveway into the resort.

"I'm more worried about you. That you might confront Pinslett or something. I need to close this case and meet Zachary's deadline. Ideally before Edgewater runs out of money tomorrow or Tuesday. We can't risk tipping off Nathan

Barron. Don't jeopardize my case, Jace."

Jace shook his head. "C'mon, Kat, give me some credit. Of course I won't—but I also can't pass up an opportunity of a lifetime. No journalist has ever been inside a World Institute conference before."

"Except Pinslett."

"He's not a journalist. He just owns a stable of journalists. I want to expose him, make him pay." He punched his fist into his hand.

"Okay, you're really not going out there. You're too worked up. You'll arouse suspicion and get us kicked out of here."

"You're holding me prisoner? What if I miss something?"

"Jace, you know what I mean. First things first. Let's get proof of Nathan's involvement. Once we have that, you can have a field day with Pinslett and the rest of them. I'll even help you. The problem is, I can't go into the conference. Almost all the delegates are men."

"And they'll soon know I'm an imposter."

"Maybe—maybe not. At any rate, we need a way to get the proof that Nathan's here and his involvement. Otherwise, short of videotaping, it's still only our word against theirs." She needed something more ironclad.

"So what do we do?" he asked.

Kat quickly dressed and stepped into a pair of running shoes.

"I've got an idea." She pushed her long hair under a baseball cap. "Give me fifteen minutes."

She opened the door to the hall and peered outside.

Clear.

She turned to the right, the direction she figured she was least likely to run into other guests. After following the corridor to its end, she doubled back to another hallway and peeked around the corner. A housekeeping cart was parked halfway between where she stood and the stairs.

She strode towards the cart, head down in case she ran into anyone. She scanned the cart, momentarily tempted to pick up extra conditioner.

All the hotel room doors were shut, which meant the housekeeper probably wasn't in any of them. She turned the corner and saw the door marked *Housekeeping*. The door was slightly ajar, and she pushed it open. If she were discovered, she'd pretend to search for extra pillows.

No one was inside. It didn't take long to find what she was searching for. A housekeeper's uniform hung on a hook behind the door. She grabbed it and quickly changed, stuffing her sweats and t-shirt into a laundry bag. She pulled the too-tight shirt sharply down to try and cover her stomach—no matter, she wouldn't be in the hallway long.

The hallway was still empty. She emerged and strolled towards the cart. She grabbed two bottles of conditioner just as something hard scraped against her hip. As she pulled it out of the pocket she couldn't believe her luck. Not only did she have a housekeeper's uniform, she now had a master key card to all the rooms in the resort.

She turned and sped away, anxious to make it down the corridor without seeing anyone. She reached the elevator bank that divided the two building wings just as the elevator dinged. Then she heard a voice. A voice she'd know anywhere.

CHAPTER 27

KAT SLAMMED TO A STOP, almost running into the wall. She fought the urge to turn around and head back the way she came. It was too late. She'd been spotted.

Victoria Barron stood by the elevators and tapped her Gucci sandaled foot impatiently as she checked her watch. Her size 2 frame was enveloped in a thick cotton robe just like the ones in Kat's room. Somehow it looked more glamorous on Victoria.

"Don't you dare walk away from me," Victoria barked.

Kat froze. She glanced down at her scuffed running shoes and wondered what was next. Why was Victoria here? The World Institute had booked the entire hotel, and Victoria wasn't exactly delegate material.

"Do not ignore me! I'm not going away, and I can get you fired in a heartbeat."

Kat slowly lifted her gaze to meet Victoria's. Was it possible that Victoria didn't recognize her in her housekeeper's uniform?

"You people never do more than the bare minimum."

Victoria pointed a manicured nail at Kat. The shade matched her lipstick exactly. "There's too much dust in my room and not enough shampoo. Do you realize how lucky you are to work here? You'd never get a job like this in your own country, wherever that is. I'll bet you're not even legal."

Kat hadn't even opened her mouth and Victoria already had her pegged as lazy, illegal, and incompetent.

"Yes, ma'am," Kat said in what she hoped would pass as the same Eastern European accent she'd used earlier. "I get you more shampoo. Your room number is?"

"Room 216. I'm going to the spa." The elevator doors opened and Victoria got in. "I expect shampoo in my room when I get back. Anything less is unacceptable."

"Yes, ma'am." The elevator doors closed. It was a relief to not be recognized, but also demeaning. After all, she had faced Victoria in court—even been her undoing. She fingered the master key card in her pocket. With Victoria gone, she might as well search her room. Maybe discover why she was here in the first place.

Kat stood outside room 216 and knocked. No answer. She slid the key card into the reader. A flashing green light and a click greeted her. She opened the door and let it click shut behind her.

The room was similar in layout to hers, but reversed. The curtains were drawn and two suitcases were stacked by the window. Even in the dim light, she saw clothes strewn everywhere: on the floor, on the unmade bed, and folded over the armoire doors and ironing board. How could Victoria have found dust? There were no bare surfaces for any to settle on.

She walked over to the desk, almost tripping over a pile of high heels in the middle of the floor. Papers were strewn haphazardly across the surface of the desk. She switched on the lamp and quickly leafed through them. She couldn't believe her luck. Below the hotel check-in information was an agenda for the World Institute meeting. She shoved it down the front of her uniform.

Then she noticed the rest of the documents, a thick pile held together with a bulldog clip. She flipped through the pages. On top was last year's meeting minutes, followed by some financial statements and other papers.

Was Victoria really a delegate? Hard to believe, but why else was she here? And why did she have a World Institute agenda? Kat pulled out the agenda and scanned it. No mention of Victoria as an attendee. She glanced at her watch. According to the agenda, the meeting started not tomorrow, but in thirty minutes. Victoria certainly wouldn't be attending in her robe.

Kat shoved the clipped papers into the folded towels under her arm.

She jumped as the bathroom door clicked open. Men's cologne and humid shower air wafted towards her. She quickly shoved the agenda down her top. Then she sneezed.

"What the hell are you doing in my room?" Nathan Barron emerged from the bathroom. He was naked, except for a towel cinched around his waist. He was much smaller in real life than in his predator portraits. Of course, in the pictures, his trophies were dead mammals, not live people, so it was hard to get a sense of scale.

Kat broke into a sweat. Nathan stood between her and the door, blocking her exit. Her throat tightened and her heart pounded in her chest as she scrambled to come up with an excuse for being in the room. Then she remembered: she had only met Nathan in pictures. He hadn't been at Edgewater when she visited. He had never laid eyes on her and wouldn't know who she was. And in her maid's uniform, she had a perfectly plausible reason to be here.

"I—I'm sorry, sir. I thought the room was empty. I was just checking the towels."

"Leave them on the bed." He crossed his arms and stared her down.

She couldn't. Tucked into the towels were the papers she had just pinched off the desk. She tried to keep her voice calm. "These are dirty. Let me get you some fresh ones."

"Fine." Nathan scowled as he turned. He stormed back into the bathroom and slammed the door behind him.

Kat let out a sigh and realized she had been holding her breath. She wiped a thin sheen of sweat from her forehead and opened the door to the hallway. These surprise encounters were stressing her out.

Nathan and Victoria had to be lovers. Why else would they share a room? Did Zachary know his ex-wife was having an affair with his father?

It wasn't exactly within the scope of her investigation. Still, didn't he deserve to know? On the other hand, if she told him, he would know she had trespassed in their hotel room. Maybe there was good reason for Zachary's hostile feelings towards his father. What kind of man got involved with his son's ex-wife?

Kat let herself out. The door clicked shut behind her as she stepped into the corridor. Her mouth dropped open as she almost collided into a slight, blonde woman in a housekeeping uniform.

"Who are you?" she asked in heavily accented English.

Russian, Kat guessed. The woman appeared to be about five-six, maybe a hundred and ten pounds. Her ill-fitting uniform hung from her shoulders. It was meant for someone much bigger.

"I'm new." Kat held out her hand, willing it not to shake. "Name's Marcie. Today's my first day."

The woman studied her without saying anything.

Kat pulled her hand back and wiped her palm on the front of her ill-fitting uniform. It was meant for someone six inches shorter, and she didn't need a mirror to guess how ridiculous she looked. She tugged the blouse down to cover her midriff and extended her hand again.

The housekeeper glanced at Kat's waistband and clasped her hand lightly. "Angelika. You here for conference? Dorothy didn't mention you." Angelika's English was peppered with missed pronouns and omitted plurals. She glanced nervously down the corridor and tucked a stray blonde hair behind her ear.

"Yes, the conference." Kat couldn't help but notice how beautiful she was. High cheekbones and translucent ivory skin.

Angelika stole another glance down the hall.

"Looking for someone?"

Angelika shook her head. "No, just checking rooms. Which one to do next."

"They only called me this morning." How many housekeepers worked a shift? Five? Two dozen? One of them could be searching for her uniform right about now. "With the conference and all."

Angelika still looked puzzled.

"I'm not on this floor," Kat added quickly. "Just came down for some extra shampoo." Hopefully Angelika wouldn't ask what floor she was working on.

"Of course. There's box of shampoo in storage room." Angelika smiled and pointed down the hall in the direction Kat had just come from. "Help yourself. You taking Annie's place?"

"Yeah, Annie. Couldn't remember her name. What's this conference all about?"

"Dorothy didn't tell you? Maybe not, if you just fill in today. It's top, top secret. We can't talk to anyone about it. You sign non-disclosure agreement?" Angelika leaned on her cart, knocking a box of tissue off the cart and onto the carpet.

Kat bent to pick it up. "Not yet. I'll sign it on my break."

She handed the tissue to Angelika without taking her eyes off the housekeeper's shoes. Her designer pumps sported a two-inch kitten heels—totally impractical for cleaning hotel rooms.

"I'll be glad for Friday," Angelika sighed. "The security guards everywhere, and guests—so demanding."

"Friday?"

"When conference ends. Things go back to normal."

Friday was also the due date for Harry's next mortgage payment. If he couldn't make it, the bank would foreclose. How could she deal with his loans and Zachary's case at the same time?

She dreaded Friday and hoped for it all at the same time.

Kat's thoughts drifted back to Uncle Harry as she headed for the storage room. Once Hillary found out Harry was flat broke, what would she do? Her return after all these years must mean she was desperate. How far would she go to get more of Harry's money?

Kat swiped her card key in the door to the storage room. She opened the door and froze as she came face to face with Roger Landers.

CHAPTER 28

KAT JUMPED BACKWARDS AS THE door slammed behind her. The towels fell from her hand and unfolded as they fell to the ground. The bulldog clip must have broken somewhere between Nathan's room and here. It clattered in pieces to the floor as the papers scattered. She kicked the papers with her foot and pushed them under the towels.

"Shut up and don't move." Roger Landers brandished the broom handle high above his head, ready to strike.

Kat remained still while her mind raced, trying to figure out what to do next. Her hand gripped the knob of the door. Landers was close enough to strike but not near enough to grab her. If she acted quickly, she might be able to open the door and escape down the hall. Landers probably wouldn't chase her, especially if he was in hiding. But that meant leaving the papers behind.

How did Landers get in? Given that he was *persona non grata* from earlier conferences, he'd never make it past security without being recognized. Not to mention the fact he was presumed drowned, his lifeless body floating somewhere in Howe Sound.

Maybe he had been invited to the conference after all. Even if he hadn't, security had seemed pretty lax before the burly suits arrived. After all, she, Jace, Harry, and Hillary had managed to enter the resort without any problems. Jace only had to give the name of the A/V company.

"I thought you were dead," Kat said.

"You wish." Landers was still trying to impale her. But at least he had relaxed his grip on the broomstick handle.

"I've got no opinion one way or the other. I was just trying to talk to you," Kat said. "Why jump ship? You don't even know me."

"I know who you represent."

"I don't represent anyone. I'm here for the same reason you are—to find out more about the World Institute." Kat bent down over the towels and gathered them up, hoping Landers hadn't spotted the loose papers.

Had the towels been intact when she entered the storage room? What if the clip had broken earlier? Scattered papers in the hall outside would be a dead giveaway.

"Oh really?"

"I'm investigating one of the members." Kat held Landers' gaze for a few seconds before he shifted his focus to the door behind her, a worried expression on his face. The room was like a closet.

"You're lying. These guys don't get investigated. They're above the law."

"No one's above the law." Not even the rich and powerful— or self-entitled daughters. People kowtowed too much to the first group, and gave the second free rein. The double standards really pissed her off. "Especially not this guy."

"Prove it."

"I don't have to prove anything. Besides, it's confidential." However, she didn't want him to expose her, either. She exhaled and shrugged her shoulders. Better to have Landers as an ally, not an enemy. "It's one of the World Institute members. I'm not saying who."

Landers shoulders dropped. She took his relaxed stance as a sign that he believed her. He probably worried that she was competing with him on a story. Still, he didn't lower the broom, which remained motionless above her head. "Give me one good reason to trust you. How do I know you won't tell them I'm here?"

Kat sighed. "I'm trying to work with you. But if you don't want to, fine. I'm leaving."

She turned to the door, but the broom handle came down in front of her, barring her exit.

"Wait. I'm listening. Who are you, and why are you here?"

"Kat Carter. I'm a fraud investigator." She slowly held out her hand. Landers didn't take it, but at least he lowered the broom handle.

Kat described how the trail of Edgewater payments to Research Analytics had led her to the World Institute.

"Research Analytics? Never heard of them."

"You must know the name. Didn't you write a book on the World Institute? Surely you checked their finances? If you did, you'd know that Research Analytics is one of the World Institute's biggest donors. It's all in their annual report." Kat had been surprised at the World Institute's financial transparency, given they hid everything else. If their hidden agenda was really true.

"The World Institute doesn't publish an annual report."

"Sure they do. You can find it online. Don't you have a copy?" Kat patted her chest. Nathan's documents were safely tucked under her uniform. She couldn't wait to read them.

"Is that what you've got there?" Landers arched his brows. "Show me."

"I don't have it on me. But what I do have is even better."

She tugged on the papers so just the top corners were visible. Her uniform was so tight that she risked a popped button with any movement. She flushed. A sheen of sweat coated her skin and held the World Institute agenda in place. A hidden agenda, she thought as she smiled.

"What's with the grin?"

"Inside information. Are you in or not?" Kat hadn't had more than a glance at the agenda, but could guess what was likely attached. Multi-million dollar organizations had financial statements, most likely attached to said agenda. The statements would be discussed at the annual meeting, so delegates would get a copy. She was anxious to return to the room to check her bounty for every mention of Nathan Barron and Edgewater.

"Why should I cooperate with you? You'll only draw attention to me. Chasing me on the ferry, and now here." Landers rested the broom handle against the wall. "For an investigator, you're rather flamboyant."

Kat laughed. "It's all about you, isn't it? You're holed up in a supply room and you think I'm stalking you? You're nuts." She threw her hands up in the air. The arm of the too-small uniform ripped and she swore under her breath.

Kat had hoped to work with Landers. His knowledge gleaned from ten years of following the World Institute could have saved her some time, but he obviously didn't want to cooperate.

Landers gave her a once-over. "No crazier than you in that skimpy maid's outfit. Are you cleaning rooms here too?"

"Sort of." *More like cleaning out rooms.* The stolen papers under her uniform stuck to her skin as she turned to the door. To hell with Landers. She didn't need his help. She pulled her key card from her pocket and dangled it in front of him. "This is a master key. I can go anywhere, get almost anything. Are you with me or against me?"

"You've got a point," Landers conceded. He leaned the broom against the wall. "Two heads are better than one."

"You've finally come to your senses. Now, how did you get ashore before dying of hypothermia? I saw you jump off the ferry. You wouldn't last more than a few minutes in that frigid water."

"Ah. But you didn't witness me land—only disappear." A faint smirk crossed his face. It was just as quickly replaced with the same dour expression.

"If you didn't jump, where did you go?"

"I slipped through a rope hole at the stern. There's a handhold and a ledge on the other side. You just assumed the obvious—that I went in the water. You never considered anything else. I simply hung on for a few minutes until the ferry docked, and got off before the cars and foot passengers. Ahead of traffic. At the front of the line-up. Saved a lot of time, actually."

"Smart." Kat still couldn't figure out why he ran in the first place. She picked up her towels, carefully tucking the papers inside so Roger Landers wouldn't notice them.

"I thought so too."

They made plans to meet back in the storage room in thirty minutes. Kat decided not to tell him she was staying in the hotel. He hadn't earned her trust just yet.

CHAPTER 29

JACE JUMPED UP IN BED and pulled the covers up to his neck. His eyes widened with panic.

"Relax. It's just me." Kat sat down on the bed beside him and glanced at the nightstand clock's LED display. So much had happened today, yet the clock read only eight-thirty in the morning. "You went back to bed?"

"What else can I do? You've trapped me in this hotel room. Hey, why are you dressed like that?" He relaxed his hold on the covers to reach for her.

"Long story." Kat kicked off her shoes and dropped the towels on the foot of the bed. Then she squeezed in beside Jace on the bed. "While you've been lounging, I've been gathering intelligence."

"Hmmm, this is nice. Tell me all about it." Jace pulled her towards him. Then he stopped. "Wait a minute—why are you rustling like paper?"

Kat squeezed her chest together with her hands on either side. It was the only way she could remove the thick wad of documents without popping the buttons on her too-tight blouse. She carefully extracted the documents. "See what I got?"

Jace stared at her chest.

Kat exhaled, finally able to breathe again. The towels dropped to the floor as she shifted her weight on the bed. She held up the papers to show Jace. She'd pick up the towels and the rest of the papers in a minute.

"Let me see that." Jace took them with his outstretched hand and skimmed the top page. "Gordon Pinslett's on the agenda! He's got a lot to answer for. Like why he's a delegate, instead of covering this farce of an institution. I'm going to talk to him."

"No, Jace." Any hint of romance in the air had been replaced by blind ambition. "Facing off against Pinslett jeopardizes my case. Besides, his company sacked you."

Kat turned onto her side to face Jace. "It's just a bad idea on so many levels." Just as she had feared: Jace smelled a story and would do anything to get it.

Jace's face darkened. "It's a perfect example of the media in bed with business."

Kat traced her fingers down his arm. "You mean like us?"

A hint of a smile played on Jace's lips. "You know what I mean. Pinslett and his cronies are taking over everything. They already influence government, make laws, and control trade. Freedom of the press? It doesn't work when the press are in bed with the politicians."

Kat laid her head across Jace's chest. "I'm not letting you leave this room."

"Okay. But I'm writing that story the minute we leave."

"Don't worry—there'll be lots to write about. You'll never believe who I ran into." Kat recounted her run-in with Victoria, then her run-in with Roger Landers.

As she described Landers paranoid behavior, someone knocked on the door. They both froze.

"Get the door, Jace." Kat dove under the covers. "Hurry."

"I'm not dressed. Whoever it is will go away."

The door clicked open. "Housekeeping."

Jace bolted upright into a sitting position. "Hello?"

Angelika the housekeeper entered the room. "Oh—I'm sorry, sir."

Kat flattened her body against the mattress, wishing she hadn't eaten such a big breakfast. Would Angelika notice her outline under the covers? She sucked in her stomach and held her breath.

What was worse—a housekeeper in bed with a guest, or a guest impersonating a housekeeper? No matter what, her cover would be blown in more ways than one.

Kat lifted the cover just enough for a line of sight. Angelika stood by the television screen at the foot of the bed.

"Oh, sir." Angelika's hand went to her mouth. "So sorry. I thought you already left for conference."

"I'm feeling a bit sick. I'm going to stay here and rest a bit." Jace coughed. "Don't worry about cleaning the room today."

"You sure? I come back this afternoon?" The housekeeper appeared doubtful as she scanned the room. Clothes hung off the chairs and were heaped on top of the suitcases.

Kat spotted the two coffee cups on the table. Would Angelika notice? She shifted slightly under the covers to get a better view as the housekeeper backed towards the doorway.

Angelika stopped as she caught the movement. She stared at the bed, seemingly puzzled by the extra mounds under the covers. Or maybe it was all just Kat's imagination.

"No need, but thank you," Jace said.

"Okay, sir." Angelika bent to pick up the fallen towels.

The towels with Kat's papers tucked inside. Papers she'd barely looked at yet.

Kat kicked Jace under the covers.

"Ouch! Uh, leave the towels, please."

Angelika looked puzzled. "I have fresh ones outside in cart. I bring back in one minute."

Kat kicked Jace again.

"No! I mean, I want those ones. Just leave them."

"Okay, sir." Angelika smiled. She dropped the towels on the foot of the bed and backed towards the door. "Hope you feel better soon."

After asking about soap and shampoo supplies for the umpteenth time, Angelika finally left. Kat checked the clock. Her meeting with Landers was in less than five minutes.

CHAPTER 30

"THAT WAS CLOSE. NOW, WHERE were we?" Jace lifted the covers and kissed the top of Kat's head. "Before you started kicking me, I mean."

"You were about to get dressed." She'd love to play hide and seek all morning in the luxurious linens, but there simply wasn't enough time.

"That's not how I remember it." Jace stroked her stomach and burrowed his lips into the crook of her neck.

"I've got to go." Kat pushed herself up and rolled over to kiss Jace. She glanced at the nightstand clock radio. "Landers is waiting."

She jumped out of bed and retrieved the rest of the papers from the towels. She carried them back and placed them underneath the agenda and other papers Jace had placed on the bedside table.

"Fine." Jace sighed and sat up. He pulled his legs over the side of the bed and clicked on the television remote. "You're totally obsessed with this guy."

"We'll have more time later." She kissed him on the cheek and grabbed her running shoes. She sat on the bed to tie them. "Promise."

"I'll be waiting." Jace stood and grabbed his clothes from the bureau. He froze in front of the television.

Kat followed his gaze. Roger Landers stood in front of the Hideaway Bay RCMP station. The camera panned to show a police constable beside him, squinting in the sunlight.

"When did you determine Svensson was murdered?" Landers held his mike in front of the police officer. He wore jeans and a Gore-Tex jacket, unzipped.

Kat's mouth dropped open as she met Jace's eyes. "Impossible. How can Landers be on TV? I just talked to him half an hour ago, holed up in the housekeeping room. We're at least five miles from town."

"Maybe it was taped earlier," Jace said. "He'd never be able to sneak in and out of the resort right now. Not with all the security around."

Jace spun around and grabbed a pen and paper off the desk. He started scribbling.

Kat studied the screen.

The police officer turned to Landers. "We suspected murder early on in the investigation, just didn't have enough evidence. We now have several promising leads and hope to lay charges very soon." Officer Kravitz squinted into the camera as the sunlight glinted off his nametag. He puffed out his chest and adjusted his belt.

Kat turned to Jace. "First suicide, and now a murder? I wonder if they actually have a suspect?"

Jace ignored her, mesmerized by the television.

"I'll bet nothing this big has ever happened in Hideaway Bay," Kat said. "First a world conference, and now all this international intrigue with the murder." She still couldn't believe the World Institute had chosen the sleepy hamlet for the conference. But maybe that was the attraction. It was close to an international airport, yet remote and difficult to reach, except by private plane. Under the radar.

"The motive?" Landers was asking Kravitz.

"We think it was a robbery. Hideaway Bay is a very safe place and I want to assure everyone that—"

Jace switched off the television. "I need to meet this Landers guy. Let's go."

Angelika's unexpected visit unsettled Kat. Since when did housekeepers clean rooms at eight-thirty in the morning? The news on Svensson added a new twist, too. Was it related to his monetary policy theories or something else?

As Kat stood, she noticed several cards on the carpet, jutting out from under the bed. She bent down to pick them up—a room key card and a MasterCard. They must have slipped from her pocket when she laced up her shoes.

Jace saw them at the same time and motioned Kat to hand it over. She gave him the room key. He stretched the elastic cord attached to it between his fingers. "This isn't our room key. It's a different color. Where did you get this?"

"It was in the pocket when I put on the uniform. It's a master key." Kat held out her hand and motioned with her fingers. "Can I have it back?"

"How do you know it's a master key?" Jace handed the key card to her and walked over to the bureau. "Wait a minute—are you breaking into rooms?"

"Using a key isn't breaking in." She flashed what she hoped was her most charming smile. "How else do you think I got all this World Institute material?"

"It's not okay for me to snoop around, but you can pilfer from people's rooms? Not fair."

"Remember why we're here in the first place, Jace. Edgewater. I need to solve the case. Without you stirring things up."

"You talk about *me* doing questionable things..." Jace stood by the door, arms crossed.

"Don't act innocent with me. You do stuff like this all the time to get stories."

Kat hadn't noticed the second card in her pocket. She studied the MasterCard. It had no customer name on it. Tiny writing above the MasterCard hologram read *debit*. It wasn't a credit card at all, but a prepaid credit card instead. Prepaid cards were often used by people without credit ratings or bank accounts. She wondered if any cash remained on it. If so, the owner might look for her uniform.

"You're wrong, Kat. I've never stolen a uniform or master keys. You're investigating one crime and committing another one to do it."

"I got the goods on Nathan, didn't I?"

"How exactly did you get it? You're a little short on details. Even I wouldn't sneak into someone's room for a story."

"It's not like I planned to. It just sort of—happened." After all, Victoria had insisted she replenish the shampoo. Which she had forgotten to do, she realized. At least it gave her an excuse to return, if necessary.

"Stuff like that doesn't just happen."

Kat tapped her watch. "I'll explain later. We're late."

Ten minutes later, Kat and Jace returned to the room with Roger Landers. Landers sat in the desk chair, his long legs stretched out in front of him. Jace and Kat sat on the edge of the bed. The storage room had proven too cramped, and meeting there just heightened the risk of discovery.

"Tell us what you know about Svensson's murder," Kat said.

Landers didn't answer. Instead he tilted his head back and drained his second cup of coffee in less than five minutes.

Kat opened the mini-bar fridge and grabbed a can of Pringles. She tossed it to him.

Landers caught the can with one hand and tore off the foil top. He wolfed down the chips like a starving animal. "Not much to tell. The police say the motive was robbery, which is ridiculous. A two- or three-hour hike from the middle of nowhere? Criminals usually like easier targets."

"When did you talk to the police?" Kat was certain the interview had been taped earlier, but when? The weather yesterday had been cloudy, and the sun at daybreak had quickly turned to cloud.

"A while ago."

"Can you be more specific? Is this where your conspiracy theory sets in?"

"It's not a theory, Katerina. It's fact." Landers placed the almost empty Pringles can back on the table. "Svensson's theories are the keystone of the World Institute's mandate. The basis for his Nobel nomination. Until he backtracked, that is. Guess they didn't like their star economist switching sides."

"You think the World Institute is involved in Svensson's murder?" Jace asked.

Why had she introduced Jace to a conspiracy theorist like Landers? Terrible mistake. Now both journalists smelled a story and would stop at nothing to get it.

"How else can you explain it?"

"There are lots of possibilities," Kat said. "The police called it a robbery. Why aren't they exploring your theory?" They were rapidly veering off track. The idea of quickly getting the goods on Nathan Barron was evaporating along with Kat's patience.

Landers scoffed. "In this hick town? The police haven't a clue where to start for a murder investigation. Hideaway Bay's biggest crimes are stolen canoes or cabin break-ins. It's the perfect place for the World Institute to get away with murder."

"What's the motive?" Jace asked.

"To silence a dissenting voice," Landers said. "Svensson was a World Institute member, yet he spoke out against their platform. Not only does he have cachet as a Nobel–nominated economist—he's also the world's leading expert in currency reform. He left them no choice."

"No choice?" Kat was surprised at Landers somehow rationalizing Svensson's murder.

"Not if they want to achieve their mandate." Landers pulled his sweater off over his head, revealing a blue plaid shirt. "It's stifling in here."

Kat walked over to the thermostat and notched it down. "Other World Institute members are also influential. All they had to do was discredit him. The World Institute has enough money and power to counteract his claims. They didn't need to murder him."

Kat's remarks fell on deaf ears. Landers and Jace stared at the television, transfixed by a story on CNN. Jace always had the news on; she barely noticed it anymore. She sighed and glanced at the television.

A wealthy movie star cradled an Ethiopian baby in her arms. She couldn't remember the star's name, just her annual adoption forays to orphanages in African countries. Kat wondered: did the parents really want to give that infant up, or did they have to? What would it be like to deny your child a life of untold riches? Some choices really weren't choices at all.

She glanced at Landers, wondering how he had become so obsessed with the World Institute. Despite covering the WI for ten years, his work had been largely discredited. She had discovered many unfavorable reviews and comments on his book when researching background on the Institute.

Then she noticed Landers's shirt. It was light blue; the same shirt he had worn on the ferry. Not the red shirt he had been wearing on television. So the interview had been taped after all. That, along with the difference in the weather, was significant. The clouds here contrasted with the sunny weather during Landers's interview with the RCMP officer. Hideaway Bay was only a few miles away, certainly not enough to account for the difference in the weather.

Given the interview must have happened earlier, when exactly did Svensson's death change from a suicide into a murder investigation? And why hadn't Landers mentioned it earlier? Despite her best efforts, she was getting sidetracked too.

CHAPTER 31

"**L**OOK AT THIS." JACE UNCLIPPED the documents and spread them out on the small table in their suite. He pointed to the first item on the agenda. "One global currency."

Kat shot him a sideways glance. They hadn't discussed how much to show Landers, and she resented him showing the meeting documents without asking her. Five hours had passed since Landers arrived in their room, yet he still hadn't shared any information of his own. All take and no give.

"Where did you get these?" Landers bent over to study the documents. "They can't be real."

"Of course they're real." Jace pulled the paper back like he'd been stung. "Straight from a World Institute delegate."

"Which one?" Landers looked up. "I've never been able to get my hands on any of their meeting materials before."

"That's confidential." Kat snatched the papers away just as Landers reached for them. It had been a mistake to invite Landers to their room. Now he knew their whereabouts, but had offered up nothing in return. She certainly wasn't going to incriminate herself by revealing the papers she'd stolen from Nathan and Victoria's room. She tried to catch Jace's eye, but his head was down, engrossed with the agenda.

"Even if it's legit, it's hardly news." Landers tipped another handful of chips out of the Pringles canister. "One world currency has been on the World Institute's hit list for years."

"Maybe as a theory, but now they're ready to implement," Jace said.

"You don't know that." Landers brushed potato chip crumbs off his palms. "All the agenda shows are topics for discussion."

"We've got proof." Jace pointed to one of the piles spread out on the table. The documents from Nathan's room promised a treasure trove of information—if Kat could get some privacy to properly go through them. She'd barely gotten a glance as of yet. Jace, meanwhile, was just flipping through them—with Landers looking intently on. "They've got a pretty impressive media campaign here. They're planning a financial meltdown. First, a debt crisis, which will devalue all major currencies. Initially Europe, then North America. Once those are underway, Asia and the rest of the world will follow."

"Let me see that." Landers held out his hand.

Jace looked at Kat.

She tilted her head. *Not now.*

Jace flipped through the documents. "Once currencies lose their value, a common global currency will be much more palatable. At the brink of disaster, The World Institute swoops in and saves everyone. No one will guess they orchestrated the whole thing themselves, or even question them. It's a new wild west. Everyone who stakes a claim gets a piece."

Landers turned to Kat. "This is exactly what I've been predicting. Now do you understand the murder motive?"

Kat shook her head, exasperated. She wasn't a naïve sixth-grader. "That's for the police to decide. I'm here to solve a fraud."

"It's all related. You think this hick town police force even has the World Institute on its radar?" Landers didn't wait for her answer. "They don't have the sophistication or the manpower. We have to guide them. By exposing the WI's mandate."

"We?" Kat said.

"He's right, Kat." Jace pointed at the papers. "Pinslett and his cronies are part of a creeping media takeover. His conglomerate already owns sixty percent of the major newspapers in North America and Europe. He's got television and radio stations, too. Between him and a couple of other guys, they control most of the significant global media. They only report what they want to."

"Only what they want us to hear. Money and information are two keys to power," Landers added. "With it they can control politicians, governments, and society."

Kat felt bullied. She had lost Jace to a conspiracy theory nutcase.

"First they engineered the European Union, then made a case for the Euro," Landers said. "Their next step is to create the same thing in other world regions—North America, Asia, and South America."

"What about Africa?" Jace asked.

"No need to do anything. At least that's the World Institute's view." Landers grabbed another handful of Pringles. His eyes darted to the paper piles on the coffee table. "It's already controlled or exploited—depending on your politics—by the rest of the world. There's no stable, dominant currency to dismantle. Trade is mostly in greenbacks or Euros, and China's got most of the natural resources locked up."

Everything Landers said was confirmed by last year's meeting minutes. But why was it up to them to save the world? Maybe cutting off Landers's food supply would make him go away. Judging by where the conversation was headed, it was probably too late.

"Svensson's argument last year was for a common global

currency," Jace said. "That's why he was nominated for the Nobel. Then, just before he died, he changed his mind. A powerful murder motive. What I don't get is—why all the secrecy? The Euro works. Why not put it to a vote?"

Kat started to speak but realized an answer only fueled the discussion for another few hours. Instead she headed back to the fridge and opened it. She rummaged through mini-bar snacks. In the end she grabbed everything and dumped it on the table in a pile.

Landers grabbed a Mars Bar and smiled at her. The CNN news anchor had switched to a story on household debt and instant gratification.

"Not everyone's in favor, Jace," Landers said. "Most governments aren't, since one global currency takes away their power. Only the dominant countries want it, because it removes trade barriers and lowers transaction and foreign exchange costs. They call the shots, so rules always end up in their favor. You're practically forced into a common currency if you want those trade barriers to come down. But prices can increase dramatically when you switch. Suddenly you're paying wages in a stronger currency. That drives up inflation."

"Which makes your domestic goods more expensive and less affordable." Jace padded over to the window. The clouds outside had thickened, and the dark sky threatened to burst at any moment. "A good argument, but the pain's just temporary. Instead of leveling the playing field, it makes it more unequal in the long run."

"That's why Svensson changed his mind," Landers said. "It's too bad about the accident—I mean, murder. His was the only moderating voice."

"What proof do the police have that it's murder?" Jace scribbled on his notepad.

"Toxicology report. Coroner said he couldn't have possibly made it there with the amount of drugs in his system."

"Maybe he took the drugs after he got there," Jace said.

"No. Another hiker saw him on the Summit trail at two p.m." Landers unwrapped the last chocolate bar and bit into it. "He wasn't impaired. The coroner's report says he ingested the drugs around three p.m. Based on when the hiker passed him, he was still a few hours' hike away from where he died. He couldn't possibly make it there after taking the drugs. They were too powerful."

"Nobody else saw him?" Kat had hiked the trail many times with Jace en route to Kurt's cabin. There was heavy snowpack this time of year, and they often walked for hours without passing another soul.

"No, although someone remembered seeing him with a woman earlier in the day," Landers said. "Another snowshoeing hiker passed them. No one reported him missing until the next day. That's when searchers retraced his steps and found him. A three-hundred-meter fall."

"I know that trail," Jace said. "What about the woman? Who is she?"

"Nobody knows. They never found her. There weren't any cars in the parking lot, so she must have been okay," Landers said.

"No missing person report?" Kat knew the only way to get to the trailhead was by car. It was far too impractical for anyone to be dropped off. "Don't you need a backcountry pass?"

"You do," Jace said. "But they don't ask your name. There's also no system to check who comes out. I know some of the search and rescue guys. I'll find out what they know about it." Kurt headed up the Hideaway Bay area search and rescue and would likely know the details.

"Why would she leave without reporting anything?" Kat was suspicious. "Unless she was involved in the murder."

Landers pulled a pen and notebook from his back pocket. He rose and grabbed a pen from the desk when he couldn't get his started. "Svensson's change of mind didn't go over well. His expert opinion was the basis for their entire argument on currency reform. A Nobel nominee in economics is a heavy hitter."

"A dissenting one is even bigger," Jace said. "Instead of an asset, he became a roadblock. Now there's no debates and no dissenters. Easy."

CHAPTER 32

AFTER LANDERS ATE HIS WAY through their mini-bar like a rescued hostage, they'd ordered room service. He promptly devoured a ten-ounce steak dinner and two desserts in minutes.

One detail still bothered Kat. Landers had arrived at Hideaway Bay on the same ferry they had. Assuming he had taped the interview in advance, when had he done it? The weather in the interview had been sunny. It hadn't been sunny the whole time they had been here.

Then there was the discovery of Svensson's body. It was only recovered yesterday, and the autopsy completed today. Landers arrived on the same ferry they did, before the autopsy results were announced. If the interview was taped ahead of time, when did Landers and the police get the autopsy results?

Kat was tired of playing host to an opportunist like Landers. After eating their food and absorbing all their information, he'd offered nothing tangible in return. It was already eleven p.m. She'd been holed up in the room all day and couldn't work on the case with Landers present.

Kat turned to the television. The late news was on. Even with the volume muted, she saw that Paris was in a state of siege. The camera panned to the Latin Quarter where an angry mob had set several cars on fire, including a police cruiser.

"France is the next one to fall." Landers followed Kat's gaze. "It's following in the footsteps of Greece and Portugal. People won't accept the austerity measures they're proposing. Especially not the French."

Jace turned up the volume. The television footage moved to the Champs Élysées where several men disguised with bandanas kicked in store windows. A crowd had formed behind them, cheering them on.

"Why are they so mad?" Jace asked. "It's their fault for overextending themselves on credit. Now they've got to pay for it."

"Sort of," Kat said. "The government and the banks share some of the blame with their monetary policy. The government, for keeping interest rates so low. The banks, because they lent to everyone, regardless of creditworthiness. When people defaulted, everything unwound. It's not just the people who over-extended, but the country itself." Kat understood why Svensson changed his mind. A common currency made theoretical sense, until you factored in the self-serving behavior of fewer and fewer people who controlled it. Concentration of power lent itself to corruption.

"Why didn't the banks just stop lending when things got ugly?" Jace asked.

"They were making too much money." Kat said. "The banks offloaded their risk by packaging the good and bad loans together to make a new investment product. As long as most of the loans packaged together have a high credit rating, they can apply the high rating to the group. In reality, the loans have been re-packaged so many times that no one remembers who or what the loans are for."

"Or who isn't making payments," Landers said. "The

banks made money on the way up by loaning to anyone with an address outside of a cemetery. Yet they expect government bailouts when people default. Giving a seasonal berry picker a mortgage on a million-dollar home with zero down is a disaster waiting to happen. When it implodes, the bankers want to make money on the way down too."

"What exactly *are* you working on, Roger?" Kat asked him point-blank so he couldn't avoid the question. If she was feeding this marooned castaway, she wanted something in return. How could she trust him when all he did was take, take, take?

"You hadn't heard of me before? My work is quite well known."

Kat feigned ignorance. "Not until I researched the World Institute and discovered you're a World Institute groupie."

Jace frowned at Kat.

At least she finally had his attention. He was practically fawning over Landers, convinced they could do a story together. Kat was certain Landers would never share credit with anyone. He was a user, a taker. Why couldn't Jace see it?

Landers puffed out his chest. "I'm a journalist, not a groupie, Katerina. If you had read my book, you would understand how serious this all is."

Kat ignored the snub. "Isn't your World Institute theory just a bit overblown? You have to admit, making up all this stuff boosts sales of your book. You've probably got enough filler for a sequel." Landers' book sales had languished, and a bit of controversy wouldn't hurt his book sales. Bruising his ego might make him show his true colors.

Landers's face reddened and he crossed his arms. "I don't need your opinion."

"Let's call it a night." Kat turned and headed into the bathroom. Maybe Landers would leave if he were ignored.

She started to close the bathroom door, but Jace followed and slipped inside. "Kat, why are you acting like this? It's the opportunity of a lifetime. Landers has researched the World

Institute for ten years. Together with what we've already got, we can expose this thing. It's a huge story about greed and corruption."

Kat pushed past him to the partially open bathroom door. "You left Landers out there with all the documents? Jace, how could you?"

Jace blocked her and held his forearms up, palms facing outwards.

"Landers won't do anything," he whispered. "I'll make sure of it."

"Of course he will. He's an opportunist." Kat turned on the tap to muffle their conversation. "See where this is headed? He's just using you until he gets what he wants. Then he'll dump you and take all the credit."

"Why are you always so negative?" Jace stood beside her at the bathroom sink, looking at her in the mirror.

"I'm just being realistic." Kat squeezed toothpaste onto her toothbrush, furious. Her head pounded, and she was upset that their conversation had deteriorated into an argument. All because of Landers. Why had she talked to him in the first place? There were better ways of getting information, and now that she had dragged Jace into it, things would only escalate. "I have to wrap this case up before I meet with Zachary at noon tomorrow. I can't afford any complications or delays." Zachary had already left her several messages, and she needed concrete proof before revealing the World Institute connection. It sounded too unbelievable otherwise.

"Can't you give me credit for anything, Kat? We're staying here tonight anyways—what's wrong with taking advantage of an opportunity? I'm going next door." Jace turned and slammed the bathroom door behind him.

Couldn't Jace see Landers for what he really was? Kat clenched her teeth and stared at her reflection in the mirror. She disliked the person she had become.

While she didn't begrudge Jace an opportunity for a story, she couldn't let it be at the expense of her own investigation.

Kat turned off the bathroom tap and pressed her ear to the door. She strained to hear the snippets of conversation.

"Let's go to the adjoining suite." Jace said to Landers. "Kat's tired, and we can continue our discussion there."

"Sure."

"You can sleep there too. The room's empty, and it's better than the storage closet."

Kat's mouth dropped open. How could Jace offer the room to Landers? Even if he was trustworthy, which Kat doubted, one more person just increased their odds of discovery.

She rinsed her mouth and opened the door, ready to voice her objections. But Jace and Landers were already gone. The World Institute papers were gone from the table too.

Kat pressed her ear to the adjoining suite door and listened. She heard their voices in the next room, animated as they carried on their discussion. She considered knocking but decided against it.

Let Jace have his story. She had to trust him with the papers. Although she didn't agree with full disclosure to Landers, she also knew Jace would never part with them. As long as it didn't interfere with her investigation, it was good to see his enthusiasm return after being sacked from the *Sentinel*. She shuffled over to the bed and collapsed. He'd get what he needed tonight, and tomorrow they could wrap up and go.

CHAPTER 33

KAT AWOKE WITH A START, bathed in sweat. Her heart pounded as she kicked her legs free of the covers. Then she saw the flash of the hotel room's smoke detector above the bed. Her panic subsided as she realized where she was.

It was just a bad dream. Hillary had bulldozed Harry's house and left him at a homeless shelter. Even Hillary wouldn't go to that extent, she thought as she rubbed her eyes.

She turned to the bedside clock. Three a.m., and the bed beside her was empty. Then she remembered: Jace had gone next door with Roger Landers. Their World Institute discussion and their ensuing argument flooded back to her. Jace's new alliance with Landers was unsettling, but she shouldn't have been so upset with him. He had every right to pursue what could be a breakout story, yet she had put up roadblocks. Didn't she trust him enough to use his discretion? Of course she did. She felt ashamed of her selfishness.

After pulling on a t-shirt and jeans, she slipped on her running shoes, just in case. She padded over to the adjoining suite door and listened. No voices. Were they asleep? No—Jace would have returned to the room, regardless of their argument.

She knocked softly on the door and waited.

A few seconds later she heard soft voices. "Jace?"

She tried the door handle, but it was locked. She tapped lightly a second time. The door opened a crack. The back of her neck tingled when she realized the room was dark. It was too dark to tell if the shadowy figure was Jace or Landers.

"Jace? Is that you?" The door opened wider. Suddenly a hand grabbed her and pulled her into the adjoining suite.

"Hey—?" Strong arms gripped her shoulders and pushed her further into the room. She stumbled forward and almost tripped as her rubber soles stuck to the carpet. Jace wouldn't do this. "Roger?"

"Shut up." He struck her across the face. "Someone will hear you."

Kat regained her balance and turned to face him. Her instincts had been right. Landers was no friend. "You're hurting me! What are you doing—?" Kat never got the chance to finish her sentence.

Landers slammed the door behind her. The lights flashed on and Kat stared straight into the eyes of evil.

Nathan Barron was fully clothed this time, in a black tuxedo under a trench coat. He also wore latex gloves.

Kat's heart pounded when she saw his hands. Gloves meant only one thing: no fingerprints and no evidence. Her legs buckled under her and she stumbled back a half step before recovering.

"You came all this way just to check up on Victoria?" Nathan Barron grabbed her as Roger Landers released his grip. He stood by the nightstand, blocking Kat's view of a third person who sat on the bed. "How touching."

"What do you want from me?" Was is possible Nathan didn't know about her fraud investigation? Kat surveyed the room.

Jace wasn't in the room. She didn't see the documents she had lifted from Nathan's room either.

Landers remained behind her, blocking the adjoining suite door. Nathan moved slightly to the right, revealing the person behind him.

Victoria sat on the edge of the bed and smirked at Kat. At least as much of a smirk as her Botox allowed. "It took me awhile, but I recognized you. You know something? You are one lousy maid."

"This doesn't have to be unpleasant, Ms. Carter," Nathan said. "You leave now, quit the investigation, and we'll both put this behind us." Nathan's lips turned up at the corners, but his cold eyes pierced hers. "If you fully cooperate."

Kat returned his glare.

Calm down.

She inhaled and exhaled twice, blowing the air out slowly and willing her pounding heart to slow. She would not succumb to his scare tactics. She could think her way out of this.

Did Nathan really think she was here as part of Zachary and Victoria's divorce? No. The judgment had already been made, so it had to be a bluff. Landers would have told him about her investigation.

"Cooperate how?" At least she hadn't told Landers which World Institute member she was investigating. Jace wouldn't betray her confidence, but Landers might have found other clues from the documents themselves while they were unattended on the table in Kat and Jace's room.

"Roger told me everything." Nathan loosened his grip but still didn't release her. "You won't get away with this."

Nathan Barron was a businessman, not an enforcer. Kat was certain he wouldn't dirty his hands with messy details. But one look at his gloved hands and she doubted her conclusion. Did he butcher his kills in the wild, or did someone else do his dirty work? She felt like trapped prey.

"Get away with what?" So he knew about her investigation.

169

So what? He couldn't intimidate her. She scanned the room again for clues of Jace's whereabouts and spotted her laptop with the screensaver engaged.

She cursed under her breath. How much had Jace shared with Landers? The presence of her laptop here also meant Nathan, Victoria, and Landers had potentially accessed her Edgewater files stored on the computer.

"Your investigation, or whatever you call this idiotic field trip of yours. You're wasting your time and ours. But I like you. I'll help you out of this mess you've created for yourself."

"How?" Kat kept her voice even. Had Nathan Barron asked the same of Jace? Of Svensson?

Nathan released his hold on Kat, and she shook out her arms.

"Cease and desist. Whatever Zachary's paying you, I'll double it. Leave now, and quit the case. Then you'll work for me."

Switch sides for double her fees? Zachary's fees were already generous. Double equaled a year's worth of billings. Of course it was almost laughable now that she knew he wasn't good for the money. No wonder Nathan and the World Institute operated with impunity. And got away with murder.

"What exactly did you have in mind?" Svensson's death was somehow connected. And it was a murder. She doubted he would sell out. But Landers would.

"Investigate Zachary for fraud. He's been operating a Ponzi scheme, and I've got the evidence to prove it."

"You'd frame your own son for your crimes?"

Nathan's eyes narrowed. "He's guilty, and I've got proof. Zachary's careless and aggressive trades have almost ruined Edgewater. We'd be bankrupt if I hadn't restricted his access to cash."

"You mean the hundreds of millions of dollars you embezzled and diverted to Research Analytics and the World Institute?" No point in keeping secrets. It was obvious Nathan knew he was the subject of her investigation. Kat turned to

Landers. "Where's Jace?"

Landers leaned against the door. He remained silent, his eyes focused on the floor.

Kat lunged at Landers, but Nathan grabbed her arms and pulled her back.

"Your friend Jace had a bit of an accident." Nathan tightened his grip. "Is that what you want?"

"You won't get away with this. The police know what you're doing."

"The police?" Nathan laughed. "I haven't done anything illegal."

"I disagree." Kat tried not to show any emotion. She refused to give him the satisfaction.

Victoria smiled at her. Only the Botox turned her mouth into more of a crooked smirk.

"You think I'm the criminal?" Nathan shoved her down on the bed. "Edgewater's my company, and I'll spend my money as I please."

"It's the investors' money, not yours. But you don't care, do you? You're not only screwing the general public, but you're paying for it with other people's money."

"That's ridiculous!"

Kat sat up. "Is it? One global currency, controlled by an institution beyond government? It's simply too dangerous to allow to happen. It's the downfall of democracy. Svensson thought so, and you silenced him so you could carry out your plan."

The words stung as she spoke them. That's what Jace was trying to tell her, but she'd been more interested in her investigation.

"Whatever—it doesn't even matter anymore. The wheels are in motion and there's nothing you can do to stop it."

She faced Nathan as panic rose in her gut. "Let me go."

Nathan tightened his grip and squeezed her wrists together. He pushed her back down with ease. "You want the same treatment? Keep this up and you'll get it."

Nathan had practically admitted his involvement in Svensson's death. He held her wrists tightly as he fished for something in his pocket. Rope. The nylon strands burned her skin as he coiled it around her wrists and cinched it taut. He knotted and tightened it until she screamed in protest. Kat's chest constricted as she felt the room close in on her.

"Got the needle?" Nathan waved his hand at Victoria as he sat on Kat's legs, holding her down.

Victoria stood. "I do, honey," she said in a sickly sweet voice. She fished through her oversized designer bag and produced a syringe.

Kat tried to kick free, but it was no use. Her thoughts raced through all the things Roger Landers had said last night. Was it an act from the start, or had he capitulated to a shark, circling in an ever-smaller tank?

"How much did he give you, Roger? What's your price?" She squirmed on the bed to face Landers. No one appeared to be holding him against his will.

Silence.

"Shut up, bitch." Victoria tapped the syringe with a manicured nail. "Time for your medicine."

Kat winced as the needle pricked her skin. Then icy hotness pumped into her bicep and coursed through her veins. It burned into her chest, then flowed upwards to her neck and head. Everything hot, hot, hot, then the voices faded. No sound, no color, and nothing mattered anymore.

CHAPTER 34

KAT CRIED OUT AS SOMETHING sharp poked her ribcage. She rolled sideways so her back faced the assailant.

"Get up," the man said in heavily accented English.

Kat pulled her elbows up in front of her face in self-defense. Then she realized: her wrists were no longer bound together. Nathan and Victoria were gone. No Roger Landers either. Instead she faced a turbaned Securicor guard in bright yellow Gore-tex. He stood over her, looking uneasy.

Kat squinted into the beam of light from the security guard's Maglite.

"I said move along, miss. Now."

Kat's mouth dropped open as she scanned her surroundings. Voices echoed as people scurried across the tiled floor to their destinations. She lay on a well-worn oak bench, one of several that bordered the open area. Carved moldings arched above Canadiana landscape paintings of mountains and forests. It took a moment before she realized she was at the Waterfront Train Station in downtown Vancouver. Judging by the hordes of commuters, it was rush hour, maybe seven-thirty or eight in the morning. Monday morning. Only a few hours until Zachary's noon deadline.

"Sorry, sir. I'm going." Kat stood and inhaled the aroma of fresh coffee and muffins that wafted over from the Starbucks across the great hall. She reached into her pants pocket, searching for change to buy a coffee. Nothing. She glanced down at her clothes. Same sweats and t-shirt she had worn last night. Thank goodness she had put on shoes before going to the adjoining hotel room.

She reached into her other pocket for her cell phone but came up empty. Of course it was still at the Tides Resort, along with her purse, money, laptop, and World Institute documents. Had Nathan, Victoria, or even Landers found her Edgewater report? She shivered at the thought.

Would they have caught her if she hadn't gone into the adjoining suite last night? Probably. Landers knew where she was and was obviously cooperating with Nathan and Victoria. Then there was Jace. Gone, perhaps suffering a fate worse than hers.

Jace would never leave without her, despite their argument. The only people that knew his whereabouts were the ones in the room last night—Nathan and Victoria Barron and Roger Landers. Had they had dumped Jace somewhere too? Her mood lifted as she realized it meant she would be able to find him. The only question was where.

Kurt's cabin was a distinct possibility, as it was within hiking distance of Hideaway Bay. Unlikely, since the sub-zero alpine temperatures required winter clothing and he hadn't taken his jacket. Had they dumped him at the train station too? Then he might have made his way home. And called her, but of course her phone was still at the resort. Finding Jace at home was a long shot but not impossible.

Her spirits lifted when she realized how close she was to home. She just needed bus or cab fare to get there. She might be able to scrounge up some change at her office eight blocks away.

Kat exited the train station, only to be met with a blast of cold air as she pushed the heavy door open. The rain pelted sideways, driven by the wind. Sleet stung her face as her hair whipped across it. Commuters trudged by, faces turned into their coats for protection. She shivered as the frigid air penetrated her thin t-shirt.

A panhandler accosted a couple as they strolled by. The man held out a baseball cap, hoping for loose change. The couple quickened their pace and waved him off. Kat strode through the parking lot towards the street where the vagrant stood. His cup reminded her that she needed at least a couple of bucks for bus fare home. Forget about a cab.

The panhandler caught her stare and pulled his cup protectively closer, as though she might to grab it. "My corner. Git your own." He scowled, revealing missing front teeth.

"Huh?" It suddenly dawned on her that he thought she was a panhandler too. Competition. Did she really look that bad? Only eight a.m., but for the second time today she felt utterly worthless.

Kat walked along Water Street to her Gastown office building, arms crossed against the cold. The cobblestone sidewalk was slick beneath her sneakers as the snow turned to slush. It seeped into her shoes, reminding her of her warm boots still at Hideaway Bay, abandoned with the rest of her belongings.

Despite the above-zero temperature, the bite of the wind and rain chilled her to the bone. Her teeth chattered and she shivered as she made her way along the deserted street. Most of the homeless people had gone inside, seeking shelter from the damp cold. She passed the Café Marseilles as a group of vagrants stood against the building, hands wrapped around paper coffee cups.

By the time she reached her building, she was completely frozen. Her hands were so numb she couldn't feel her knuckles knocking on the glass doors. The building was usually locked in the mornings, particularly in the wintertime when homeless people searched for shelter from the cold.

After what seemed like forever, the building super finally came out of the side door to investigate the noise. He glanced over quickly and waved her away.

"Marcus, it's me—let me in." Kat waved at him frantically, but he retreated back through the doorway. Carter & Associates had been a tenant at Hudson House for almost three years. How could he not recognize her? She pounded again on the door, as loud as she could. "Marcus!"

Several passers-by in raincoats and umbrellas scowled at Kat and scurried by. She avoided their eyes, ashamed of her appearance. She didn't need a mirror to know that her torn clothes, stringy hair, and lack of makeup made her look like a homeless person. Is this what it felt like to have people hate you all day?

Marcus finally reappeared. He stormed towards the door and swung it open.

"Get going or I'll call the—"

"Marcus, don't you recognize me? Kat? From upstairs?"

Recognition dawned on his face and he stopped in his tracks. His mouth dropped open. "What the hell happened to you?" He held open the door and motioned her in.

"Can't talk right now." Kat brushed past him and shuffled to the elevator as the feeling slowly returned to her legs. She pressed the up button and waited, turning her back to Marcus. She wasn't in the mood for explanations right now, and he didn't deserve one anyway.

He trailed after her. "Kat—I'm sorry. I had no idea it was you."

She ignored him and stepped into the elevator. This was a side of Marcus she hadn't seen before, and she wasn't sure she liked it. She pressed the button for the fourth floor.

Nathan and Victoria weren't getting away with this.

What had they done with Jace, and why had he disappeared

but not Landers? She doubted Nathan would take Landers at his word if he simply said the documents were not his. Nathan would want to get rid of them both, as they had both seen the World Institute plans. Unless Landers was already in on the conspiracy, whatever it was. Obviously Landers had cooperated with them. Looking out for himself, as usual.

Nathan Barron had said Jace had met some sort of "accident." That sounded more ominous than what had happened to her. She was relatively unscathed except for a few bruises and a headache from whatever they had injected her with. Could Jace have suffered a fate similar to Svensson? Despite different occupations, both had spoken out against the World Institute and the power elite. Was it reason enough to die? Kat shuddered at the possibility.

Svensson met his demise shortly after he reversed his position and disagreed from the World Institute dogma. Jace's disappearance could be related to his exposé on the mortgage fraud. After all, they had been fire-bombed because of it. But Jace's disappearance had happened at Hideaway Bay. Did that mean the suppression of his real estate story was connected to the World Institute? If so, how? Or maybe the goal was something simpler—like silence of dissent against any of its members. With voices silenced, the WI could carry on with impunity. That was how things worked in the corridors of power. Eliminate the roadblocks. Greed did ugly things to people.

Maybe it wasn't the World Institute documents they were after. While they were damaging enough, it wasn't just Jace's story they wanted to suppress. It was more powerful than that. It was his opinion, his voice. He was a respected journalist people listened to, just as they did Svensson. Their voices could not be discounted or denied. But they could be eliminated.

Although she hadn't looked at the rough draft he'd been working on at the resort, she knew his World Institute exposé meant to implicate all the World Institute members, although giving star attention to Nathan and Gordon Pinslett in particular—Nathan for diverting investor funds from Edgewater to fund WI's mandate, and Gordon Pinslett for suppressing coverage unfavorable to WI. It was one thing to try to push through a politically unpalatable theory. It was quite another to profit exorbitantly from it with currency manipulation and insider dealings. Then there was the media censorship and fraud that went along with it.

One thing was clear. Those with the courage to speak were silenced. Jace had been fired, and had his story killed by the *Sentinel*, which happened to be owned by Gordon Pinslett. Had Jace been silenced in more ways than one? She shuddered at the thought.

Jace was right. It was fine to say nothing until it happened to you. But then no one would defend you either. With silence came the risk of losing your freedom, economic well-being, and right to free speech. If she didn't take a stand, who would?

Some things were worth fighting for at any cost.

CHAPTER 35

HILLARY STOOD IN THE KITCHEN doorway and
watched her dad unload the dirty dishes from
the dishwasher. One by one they went in the
cupboard: dirty plates, coffee cups, and glasses.
Loading and unloading, the same unwashed dishes. Like
pressing the rewind button over and over again. Boy, was he
losing it. Is this what his life had become?

"You need to move, Dad." She checked her watch. It was
already after one and all they'd done all morning was drink
soapy-tasting coffee. She had better things to do on a Monday.
"Into one of those care homes."

"Care home? Over my dead body." Harry dropped dirty
knives into the cutlery drawer. "I don't need a care home. I'm
just fine here."

"Look at you—you're a crazy old man! Can't even figure
out a dishwasher. Look at this mess!" Hillary waved her arm
at the cluttered kitchen counter. "It's too much for you."

"No, it's not. It's my mess and I like it." He wiped his
forehead with his sleeve. "I'll keep my house the way I want it."

Not if she had any say. So pathetic—was he really going to cry? Hillary swiped her arm across the stacks of books on the kitchen table, knocking them off and sending them cascading to the floor. She sat down, annoyed. Can't pay his bills or even clean the house. Since when did that become her problem? "I can't even find a spot at the table. How can you eat in this pigsty?"

"Aw, Hillary, why'd you do that? I said to leave them." Harry closed the dishwasher door and shuffled over to the table, a dishtowel draped over his shoulder. His gaze dropped to his books splayed open on the linoleum. Wounded soldiers, all creased pages and banged up spines.

"Because you're nuts, Dad. You're living in a pile of junk." Hillary rolled her eyes. Why was he creating all this trouble for her? She certainly wasn't going to cook and clean for him.

"It's not junk, Hillary. Some of these books are collector's items. Put them back," Harry said. "We'll eat in the living room."

"No way am I eating here. This is disgusting." Hillary slammed her coffee mug on the table. "How can you live like this?"

"Easy. I like my things just the way they are. You're not living under this roof, so don't tell me what to do."

"What if I was living here? Then would I get a say in how things go?"

His face lit up.

Just the effect she had intended. "Maybe I'll move back home."

"Really? That would be wonderful. It's been real lonely around here since your mom died."

"I'd consider it. But we'll need some ground rules." Hillary rose from the table and headed to the fridge. She could stand maybe another week of this, tops. Just long enough to wrap things up and get her overdue Porsche payments caught up again.

"We can work something out," he said.

"Good." Hillary pulled a pitcher of orange juice from the

fridge and poured a glass. She dumped in a tablespoon of the powder, stirring until it dissolved. She pocketed the vial before turning back to face Harry.

"Here. Drink this." She handed the glass to her father. Not that she really had to sneak around. She could have shot a freaking cannon through the kitchen and he wouldn't have noticed. Stupid.

"Thanks." He sipped the juice and smiled.

Hillary sighed. Five more minutes and he'd pass out in his ugly plaid chair. Then she could start tossing some of his crap. She sure as hell wasn't waiting till he died to do it. The clutter was smothering her.

He cared more about this junk-filled hovel than her, even though she'd put her life on hold to come back to this shithole, to this crappy little neighborhood. For what? Nothing had changed in ten years. Except the neighbors were older and crankier, and Kat's tentacles dug in even deeper. Kat pretended she cared about Dad, but Hillary knew better. As if. He was nothing but a demented old man.

Kat had another thing coming if she thought sucking up to Harry was going to give her a cut. That's why the checks had stopped; Kat was keeping all that money herself. She was sure of it. Why else would she hang around here at thirty-four years old? Wasn't it enough that her parents had adopted Kat after her father abandoned her? Who adopted fourteen-year-olds? Next thing Kat would be contesting the will.

She'd put a stop to that.

CHAPTER 36

HILLARY SHIFTED HER WEIGHT FROM her right foot to her left. She didn't dare take off her shoes in this dump. Her four-inch Manolo Blahnik's were killing her, but she couldn't possibly remove them. Who knew what vermin were crawling around this dive?

"Eat it, Dad," she said, depositing another glass of orange juice beside his plate.

"I did. Can't eat any more. I'm full." Harry sat at the kitchen table, fork in hand and napkin tucked into his shirt collar.

"You have to. Finish it." Hillary felt her face flush. He needed the same dose every day. It was cumulative, and missing a day meant starting over again. She sure as hell wasn't investing any more time or money than she already had.

"I did, Hillary. I'm not hungry anymore. You want the rest?" Harry pointed at the hash browns with his fork.

"I already ate." Hillary imagined her life a few weeks from now. Sell this dump and she'd be flush in cash again. Maybe skiing in Switzerland, like the royals did. She might even meet a prince.

"When? I didn't see you."

"Of course you did. You forgot. You've got Alzheimer's, old man." Hillary drew circles around her ear with her forefinger. "You're nuts, remember? Or did you forget that too?"

Harry shook his head and he put his fork down.

She grabbed it and shoveled a forkful from Harry's plate. She held the fork an inch away from his mouth. "Open up. Eat the rest."

Harry held up his hand to protest.

"I said—eat!" Hillary shoved the potatoes in her father's mouth as he opened it to object.

"Stop it!" Harry deflected her hand with his forearm. He spit out the potatoes, scattering hash browns all over the table and floor.

"Look at what you've done!" Hillary screamed as she slammed the fork down on the table. "Who's going to clean up this mess? You don't deserve to have anyone taking care of you."

Her father lowered his arm and shrank into his chair. This was a total waste of time. The house was disgusting, with clutter, dirt, and dust almost as bad as the houses on that *Hoarders* TV show. Except Dad's worn out Sears furniture was still visible amongst the outdated seventies décor. It sickened her just to stand in it.

Each day in the Denton dump was one more stolen from her new life, the life she deserved and had waited far too long for. After months of hiding from the neighbors and Kat, her plan had worked perfectly. A new life awaited. It was just within her reach, now that she'd met the man she was going to share it with.

She just needed Harry out of the way first. And to keep him away from that prying bitch, Kat. There was no time to waste.

CHAPTER 37

HILLARY STOOD IN THE DOORWAY of the living room and studied her father. His snores reverberated throughout the house, competing with CNN on the television. He slouched in his La-Z-Boy, head drooped to his chest. It bobbed up and down with each snore.

The reporter droned on about the Paris riots, interviewing a tearful shop owner in the Latin Quarter while masked thugs kicked in windows behind her. It was nighttime and raining. A police car's siren wailed, the siren lights leaving streaks of color as the car raced by in the background.

Hillary jumped at the sound. She tiptoed into the room and grabbed the remote from the arm of the La-Z-Boy. She turned down the volume, worried it would wake up Harry. She relaxed when she remembered the dose. Enough to knock out an elephant.

She had at least a couple of hours. Where to look first? The safe? She decided on the bedroom first. That way she'd be finished by the time Harry woke up. She could convince him to go upstairs for a nap while she searched the rest of the house.

She changed into sneakers one foot at a time, careful not to let her feet touch the dirty floor. Then she took the stairs two at a time to her father's bedroom, anxious to get started.

She searched the drawers of his bureau first, then his closet. Her efforts yielded nothing but old clothes, shoes, and a box of photographs. She dumped the box contents onto the bed and sifted through them. Baby pictures of her, then pictures of the whole family, later on with Kat. She snapped open a plastic garbage bag and tossed the photographs in. Harry wouldn't need those where he was going. Soon he wouldn't recognize the people in them anyways.

It didn't take long to realize that what she was searching for wasn't here. She padded out to the hallway, reassured by the sounds of her father's snores drifting up the staircase. She opened the hallway linen closet and felt along the wall until she found the safe. She pulled on the door. It was unlocked. She opened it and pocketed the papers and five hundred dollars in crisp new fifties. It would be hers sooner or later anyways.

She needed to keep Kat away for a few days while she worked her plan. She hauled the black plastic garbage bags down the stairs in pairs and carried them out to the back lane. Sixteen bags, all just from one room. The old man wouldn't even notice the missing junk. She returned to the kitchen, wiping sweat from her forehead.

The kitchen calendar was still on June. She flipped it over to December and ripped off the notes in Kat's handwriting. Kat's phone number, Jace's phone number, a grocery list, and reminders of meals in the fridge. That ingratiating bitch had her claws dug in everywhere, and she was sick of it. She ripped the notes off and crumpled them into a ball.

Then she took a deep breath and reminded herself: this time was going to be different. She needed to keep her cool and work her plan. Get rid of the old man, and she would be on her way to her new life.

She glanced back at the calendar. December featured an amateurish watercolor of poinsettias that looked like it had been painted by a two-year-old. Piece of garbage. As she tore it from the wall, she saw what she'd been hunting for. Behind the calendar was the key. The one that would unlock her future.

CHAPTER 38

KAT RUBBED HER HANDS TOGETHER as she exited
the elevator onto the fourth floor. She shuffled
towards her office, grateful to be out of the cold.
She stopped when she saw her office door. It was
partially ajar, and it was obvious from the damaged doorjamb
that it had been forced open. Someone had been here.

She debated calling Marcus before entering. But that
would only invite more questions and delays. She didn't
have time for that right now. First she needed to change,
pull her Edgewater report from the remote data storage, and
change passwords to minimize Nathan and Victoria's access
to her files.

She pushed the door open slowly and listened. Hearing
no one, she entered and searched around, starting with
the reception area and then the kitchen and two offices.
She relaxed a bit when she realized whoever had been here
was gone.

The office looked exactly as it had before, except Harry
and Jace were conspicuously absent. The thought of Harry

gave her a twinge. At least he was with Hillary.

Kat punched in Jace's cell phone number. Her anxiety grew when she realized there were no messages from him on her office phone. There were, however, half a dozen messages from Zachary. Angry messages, asking why the hell she hadn't called.

She knew she should call Zachary. Calls to her cell phone would have gone unanswered too, and given his tenuous financial straits, he had every right to an update. But he'd have to wait until their meeting a few hours from now. Right now she had more urgent things to worry about. Like finding Jace.

Jace would leave a voicemail here and at home, after being unable to reach her on her cell phone. She was sure of that. Dread enveloped her.

She hung up after a dozen rings and glanced at the message pad beside the phone. Furious indecipherable scribbles ran off the page. The few words she could make out were misspelled and repeated. Harry had always been a stickler for penmanship, but the tangles of dementia had overcome him in just a few short months. It broke her heart to watch him deteriorate.

That was when she noticed a square-shaped bare spot on the desk. Harry's desktop computer was gone. Kat swore under her breath. Without her laptop or Harry's computer, she couldn't retrieve her Edgewater report or the supporting documents from the remote server. She had to go home.

Kat called home, only to hear a recording of Jace's voice. Tears welled up as she listened. What if she never saw him again? Wherever he was, he'd be counting on her to find him.

She looked up the number for the Hideaway Bay RCMP and waited uneasily. After six rings, her call went to voicemail. She slumped in Harry's chair. What kind of cop shop didn't answer the phone? She left a message and then slammed the handset down, fuming. Jace was missing, and she was completely at a loss on what to do next.

Harry's house and cell numbers went unanswered too. She realized she didn't even have Hillary's phone number. Harry no longer remembered phone numbers, so it was unlikely he'd call the office, even though her office and home numbers were programmed into his phone. He'd had difficulty using his new phone, a replacement for the one he had lost a few months ago. Maybe Hillary would call. At some point her patience would wear thin, and she would want to dump him off so she could concentrate on her social life.

She had second thoughts about Zachary and called him to postpone the meeting. She was relieved when she got his voicemail instead. For a guy conjoined to his BlackBerry, Zachary was surprisingly impossible to reach. She decided against leaving a message. She had just enough time to get home and back. Besides, she needed to talk to Zachary in person about Nathan and Victoria and last night's events. She also needed time to figure out her approach. What if Nathan's accusations about Zachary were true?

How else could Zachary trade fictitious amounts and not know it? How could he be unaware of such a huge Ponzi scheme? You'd have to be an idiot not to know the trades weren't being executed.

She checked her watch and realized she needed to get moving if she was to be back in time. But first she did a quick walk-through of the office. Nothing else appeared to be missing.

She paused at the bathroom mirror. Her tangled hair framed a grubby face covered in scratches from her struggle with Victoria. Where the dirt on her face came from she had no idea. No wonder Marcus had backed away.

She rifled through the wicker basket she kept her running clothes in and managed to find a tracksuit, socks, and an old jacket. Enough to get her home without freezing to death again.

She still needed bus or cab fare. After coming up empty in her office, she padded down the hall to Harry's desk. She rifled through his desk drawer, hoping for enough loose change for bus fare.

Harry's top drawer was a mess. Elastics and paperclips tangled together in clumps. She pulled out everything one by one and deposited it on the desk. Two staplers, tape with grit stuck to it, three pairs of reading glasses, and a bottle of expired ibuprofen. She opened the bottle and popped two of the pills, hoping to dull her aching head.

Kat picked up a small metal Sucrets© box and shook it. It was rusted from age, but the clinking sound was promising. A masking tape labeled *change* was affixed to the top. She opened it and found loose change and two twenty-dollar bills. She counted it, pocketed the money, and dropped an IOU into the box.

Then she noticed the two keys. The first was a spare office key. The other appeared identical to Harry's house key—same as the one on her keychain. It suddenly occurred to her that her own house key was in her purse, which was still up at the resort. She grabbed Harry's key. At least it allowed her to retrieve her own spare key at Harry's house if he wasn't home.

She closed the drawer and opened the second one. It was almost empty, a sharp contrast from Harry's usual clutter. As a matter of fact, it was spartan. Completely different from his other drawers. Odd. She remembered that Harry kept something there for safekeeping but couldn't recall exactly what it was. It had to be something important, though, since Harry never left empty spaces. Just as he filled up a room with his presence, so did his stuff. She had never been more conscious of that emptiness than she was right now.

CHAPTER 39

TWENTY MINUTES LATER KAT PAID the cab driver and trudged up Uncle Harry's steps. She knocked on his front door and waited.

No answer.

She tried again and peered through the side window. No signs of movement. She descended the stairs and headed for the back yard. Harry might be in the garage, puttering around with the Lincoln. Or maybe in the garden, even if it was December. The stranglehold of dementia meant nothing surprised her anymore.

She opened the garage door and froze. The Lincoln was gone. Had Harry figured out how to unjam the door? Unlikely in his current mental state. Someone must have done it for him. Her heart skipped a beat as she thought of Harry out driving in the snow. A disaster waiting to happen no matter how she looked at it.

Hillary's Porsche wasn't out front either. Harry could still be with her. But Hillary wouldn't be caught dead in a late-seventies Lincoln, whether driver or passenger. Kat pressed her thumb on the opener and the door swung open. Just as she feared: someone had reconnected it.

She exited through the open garage door into the lane, hoping to somehow find it. Instead, she discovered dozens of plastic garbage bags stacked against the back fence. Dread burned in Kat's stomach as she walked over for a closer inspection. Threadbare brown plaid peeked out from one corner. She hoisted a bag up and tossed it aside. Harry's La-Z-Boy recliner was rain-soaked and closer to ruin. Why was his favorite chair out here, discarded like garbage?

Kat's chest tightened. Her uncle would never part with his recliner. The chair and his other furnishings fit him and the house like a well-worn shoe. Hillary must be behind this, and the Lincoln's disappearance. Hillary always overstepped boundaries, and Kat was certain Harry had no idea his prized possessions were out in the trash. He would be heartbroken.

The garbage truck rumbled down the lane one block over and it dawned on her that today was garbage day. She checked her watch. First things first. She had to save Harry's things from the dump.

She grabbed bag after bag from the laneway and heaved them into the empty garage. She stopped counting at four dozen trash bags. Barely a dent in the pile, just enough of an opening to slide Harry's recliner through. There had to be hundreds of bags.

At least she'd arrived in time to save his belongings, but now what? She'd worry about that later. She slid the recliner back, scraping the legs along the uneven asphalt as she dragged it inch by inch out of the rain into the garage.

She tossed the last bag into Harry's garage just as the garbage truck turned into the lane. She stopped and wiped the sweat off her forehead with the back of her hand. The rain had turned her hair into a frizzy mess, but she didn't care. At least she'd managed to do something right today.

The garbage guy waved at her. She raised her arm in a slow motion wave that felt more like surrender. Not even nine a.m. and she was already weary from battle. Jace was still missing, along with the World Institute documents, her laptop, and the Edgewater case files. Her client was mad at her, even though it really should be the other way around. She had assumed that at least Harry was still with Hillary, but now she was beginning to wonder. Whatever the case, she had to get home.

She trudged back into the garage and tapped the garage door opener to close the door behind her. It creaked shut as she ran her hand along the shelf above Harry's workbench, searching for her spare house key. She breathed a sigh of relief when her hand touched the metal. Two keys. Her spare house key and another of Harry's spares. At least Hillary hadn't got her hands on that.

She pocketed her key and exited the garage, then bounded up the back stairs to Harry's kitchen door. She knocked and waited a minute, just in case he was sleeping. Highly likely, with all his worldly possessions dumped in the lane. She had a bad feeling about it all.

Long enough. What if Harry was inside, hurt, or worse? She slid the key in the lock and opened the kitchen door.

Empty.

Gone were Aunt Elsie's cookbooks in the shelves beside the fridge. The figurines above the kitchen sink had also disappeared, as had the calendar Harry planned his life by.

Even the kitchen table was missing, though she hadn't seen it in the pile of furniture out in the lane. Had scavengers already sifted through Harry's belongings? What the hell was going on?

She already knew the answer. A lifetime's worth of simple possessions meant nothing to Hillary. Especially those of a frugal old man who had scrimped and saved to give her the best of everything.

Hillary's designer labels and expensive cars were regularly tossed too, replaced with the latest status symbols at any cost. Everything and everyone was disposable after it had served a purpose. Her entire existence revolved around re-inventing her image, positioning herself as an available female of a certain socio-economic class. Except she needed others to finance her brand.

Harry's favorite chair and mementos were simply junk to her, a reminder of where she came from. So she discarded them, despite knowing perfectly well how he treasured them. Kat felt a slow burn in her gut. Hillary didn't have the right to decide what stayed and went in Harry's house. Even if it was cluttered, it was *his* clutter, and he had a right to live how he chose.

But Hillary's self-centered nature was only part of the problem. Kat's bigger concern was the underlying reason for her actions. How did tossing Harry's stuff fit into Hillary's bigger game plan?

Was Harry aware of what she had done? Either way it spelled disaster. Familiarity was very important to a person with dementia. Just a small disruption to Uncle Harry's routine might put him over the edge. Assuming he was actually around when she had tossed his stuff. Kat shuddered at the alternative.

Her thoughts returned to the Lincoln. She ran to the living room and looked out to the street. Maybe she'd missed Hillary's Porsche. She hadn't. The only vehicle outside was a neighbor's F–150 truck.

The living room had been stripped bare too. Not only was the La-Z-Boy missing, but so was everything else. The house had been completely cleaned out, stripped down to the oak floors and bare walls. An empty pail and mop sat by the fireplace.

Her mind raced. If it really was Hillary's doing, where was Harry? It would be terrible for him to see his empty house, but even worse if she had left him alone somewhere. Her cousin's sudden reappearance after ten years was a shock. Hillary had always felt this town, and the Denton family, was beneath her. Now she was back like a curse.

"Hello?" Her voice echoed through the empty house.

She went upstairs. What if Hillary had disappeared again and taken Harry with her? She dismissed the thought. He would cramp her lifestyle.

Kat realized all this had been her own doing. By cancelling Harry's credit cards, she had brought Hillary back to the feed trough. Once she got some money, she would disappear again and leave Harry heartbroken. Which would be soon, since Harry's money had all but run out.

Hillary was capable of loving no one but herself. On some level Harry knew that, yet he still gave her money. His way of keeping the truth at bay, a form of denial.

Kat jumped as she heard a click in the lock. They were back. She breathed a sigh of relief and ran downstairs.

But it wasn't Harry or Hillary standing in the hallway. A stranger faced her instead.

CHAPTER 40

T HE MAN WAS THIRTY-SOMETHING AND clean-shaven. His suit jacket strained at the buttonholes to contain a body packing too many business lunches. He slipped his cell phone back into his suit pocket and stared back at Kat.

"Who the heck are you? How'd you manage to get in here?" He smiled at her, but cold eyes betrayed him. A couple in their early thirties came up behind him, the woman obviously pregnant.

Just because she looked like a vagrant didn't give him the right to talk to her that way.

"I should ask you the same. I'm Katerina Carter, Harry Denton's niece." Harry couldn't have done this. He hadn't been out of her sight until he left Hideaway Bay only yesterday morning with Hillary.

Hillary.

What was Hillary up to?

Why was she explaining herself to strangers?

"Denton? Oh, right. Aren't you supposed to be someplace

else? Because I'm showing the house." His pupils dilated like bloated dollar signs.

"You're a real estate agent?" Kat crossed her arms and blocked the hallway. "Harry's house isn't for sale."

"It is for sale, and Hillary told me it was vacant. Now, if you'll excuse us..."

The woman sniffed and hugged the wall as she waddled past Kat.

"Hillary doesn't own this house." Kat didn't move. "Harry Denton does. Unless you have permission from him, I suggest you leave. We'll straighten this out later."

"Katerina?" The real estate agent didn't wait for Kat's confirmation. "Hillary—the owner—listed the house, and these nice folks—" he gestured to the couple, who were already discussing how to gut the kitchen, "—want to look at it." He pulled out his cell phone again. "Uninterrupted. I don't want any problems, so if you'll just leave quietly..."

Every ounce of energy she had left evaporated. She started to protest, but had nothing left inside. So Hillary had her hands on Harry's house now too? That might explain Harry's possessions in the lane. One thing was clear; the real estate agent wasn't about to divulge the details. She was too afraid to hear them anyway.

In the end she did leave. Even if it was Harry's house, this was not the time or place to fight. She would confront Hillary, but right now she had more pressing things on her plate. Like finding Jace and getting the truth from Zachary.

CHAPTER 41

KAT TURNED THE CORNER ONTO her street and
breathed a sigh of relief when her house came into
view. The old Victorian was sandwiched between
a forties bungalow and a turn of the century
Craftsman house. Even from half a block away it was obvious
Jace wasn't home. His truck still sat in the same spot it had
been in when they left for Hideaway Bay. A thin slab of half-
melted snow slid partway down the windshield. The absence
of tire tracks in the driveway meant the Subaru hadn't been
here either. No one had come or gone since their departure.

She trudged up her front steps as the weight of her
troubles burned in her stomach. Harry's house, Jace gone,
and the increasingly sinister tone of the Edgewater case was
wearing on her.

Jace was right about the World Institute. Why had she
dismissed it as a half-baked conspiracy theory? Retaining
those WI documents to help prove Nathan's fraud might have
led down a different road, but the end result was the same.

More than anything, she regretted ever going to Hideaway

Bay. Landers obviously played a role too. If only she hadn't been so anxious to talk to him.

Kat turned the key in the lock and pushed the door open. She braced herself for another break-in. Instead the front door lodged against a pile of mail and flyers and it was obvious no one had been here. She bent to pick up the mail off the fir floor and stopped, suddenly aware of the tick-tock of the kitchen clock. She had never noticed the quiet before.

The silence just reminded her of Jace. He could be hurt, or worse. What if she never saw him again? The thought washed over her like rain.

Every inch of the house had so much of Jace in it. Especially the carved woodwork and wainscoting he had spent hours restoring, now bearing the scars of fire damage. A few strands of the ruined rug were all that remained, scattered across the floorboards now warped from water damage.

Kat swallowed the lump in her throat. Arguing with Jace about his World Institute exposé seemed so pointless now.

She dropped the mail on the on the bird's eye maple side table and headed down the hall for the kitchen. Worrying wouldn't help. She needed to *do* something. But what? Reporting Jace missing hadn't spurred the RCMP into action, and she couldn't afford to wait.

The kitchen was also undisturbed. No one had been here, including Jace. The same dishes sat in the sink, and the newspaper still opened to where Jace had left it. *The Sentinel*. Now the newspaper stirred feelings of anger rather than indifference.

Her sense of urgency returned when she remembered her missing laptop. If Nathan and Victoria hadn't dissected its contents yet, they would soon. She'd better change her passwords and retrieve her data from her remote data storage before Nathan or Victoria figured that out. No doubt they'd destroy all her files.

Kat bounded upstairs to the study and powered on the desktop computer. While she waited, she called Marcus, the building super, and left a message about her broken office door.

Finally the computer booted up and she logged in. She breathed a sigh of relief and quickly changed her password. She clicked on her Edgewater file, noting the last access date was early yesterday evening, before she went to bed. Her files were untouched and safe, at least for now. She selected all of her laptop files and copied them onto the desktop computer, as well as to her portable hard drive.

As she waited for the files to copy, she realized she needed a computer at the office, since both hers and Harry's were gone. She grabbed Jace's laptop from the desk along with the portable hard drive and shoved both in her bag. Now she could finish and pull off the Edgewater report for Zachary. She checked her watch. Exactly forty minutes until her meeting with Zachary.

Thirty minutes later Kat was back at her office. The door was still broken, so she jotted a note for Marcus, hoping he'd just go ahead and fix it. She really didn't feel like speaking to him in person right now. She returned Harry's key to his desk drawer.

In a flash she realized what else was missing. Harry had kept a key behind his kitchen calendar. It was the key to the metal strongbox in Harry's second drawer. Both the key and the box were gone. Harry was too thrifty to pay the bank fees for a safety deposit box, preferring to keep important documents in the metal strong box. The box contained his passport, will, and legal documents. It also contained his house deed.

Harry's second drawer had been open when they reviewed his checkbook. She was certain the box had been inside.

Kat's stomach dropped at the realization.

Harry could only retrieve the box if someone brought him

to the office. That meant Hillary had been here with him.

Then there were the realtor's comments—that the house belonged to Hillary, not Harry. A growing sense of dread enveloped her. She'd better talk to a lawyer. Harry needed protection.

Kat booted up Jace's laptop and called Harry's cell phone while she waited. It went straight to voicemail. Either powered off or a dead battery. Kat's sense of unease grew. It had been close to twenty-four hours since Harry and Hillary had left the resort. Too long. Hillary would tire of Harry within hours. Where were they?

Kat copied her Edgewater files from the portable hard drive onto the laptop. That's when she saw it. Buried in her Edgewater investigation files was a document that wasn't hers.

Her heart skipped a beat as she studied the file. The file was updated last night, after midnight. That was after she went to bed, after Jace went next door. She held her breath and clicked it open.

It was Jace's real estate story, the one that was pulled from the *Sentinel* just before press time:

Global Financial Implicated in Real Estate Fraud

Global Financial, a holding company, used fraudulent real estate appraisals that overstated the value of dozens of downtown Vancouver commercial properties. The holding company purchased properties, which were then flipped several times to numerous straw buyers at ever-increasing prices. As the buyers were all related, these prices were artificially inflated.

Once the property values had been substantially inflated, the accused obtained large mortgages against the properties and then subsequently defaulted on the mortgage payments. The extent of the fraud is still being determined, but is estimated at more than four hundred million dollars. No one at Global Financial could be reached for comment. The company's address of record is 422 Cedar Street, but a complex web of holding companies makes it difficult to trace the ultimate ownership.

Kat almost fell off her chair. 422 Cedar Street was the address of the vacant lot she had visited earlier. The same address Nathan Barron used for Edgewater's auditors, and where Fredrick Svensson's payments were sent. That connected Jace's real estate fraud to Edgewater and Research Analytics, which was directly connected to the World Institute. No wonder Jace's story was crushed.

Had Jace made the connection too? Unlike her, he hadn't visited the vacant lot. She doubted he would have paid attention to the address, knowing she had already checked it out.

She shivered. World Institute membership wasn't the only thing Gordon Pinslett and Nathan had in common.

It might explain why Jace was specifically targeted. There was just one problem. The only people who knew Jace was at the resort were Roger Landers, Hillary, and Harry. Hillary was too self-absorbed to worry about, and Harry wasn't an issue.

That left Roger Landers. In just two days, Jace had emerged as new competition on the story Landers had been writing about for years. At least that's how it probably appeared in Landers's eyes.

Knowing Jace, he likely asked Landers, a fellow journalist, for feedback on his mortgage-fraud story once he uncovered the Beecham connection. Had Landers betrayed Jace? Why hadn't Jace come to her?

Kat shivered and drew a sweater around her shoulders. It sounded farfetched, but was it?

Then there was the issue of Fredrick Svensson, formerly a World Institute member, also tied to the same address. Someone had silenced Svensson. Would Jace be silenced too?

CHAPTER 42

"WHERE THE HELL HAVE YOU been?" Zachary paced back and forth in Kat's office, his face flushed with anger. "I've been trying to reach you for two days. First you tell me I'm financially ruined, then you don't return my calls. Do you have any idea what I've been going through?"

Zachary faced billion-dollar losses, but Kat faced a hell of her own. Not knowing where Jace was, or how to even find him. It was all her fault. None of this would have happened if she hadn't asked for Jace's help.

"I'm sorry, Zachary. I would have called you, but I couldn't." Kat told him everything, starting with Research Analytics and ending with Nathan and Victoria.

"You couldn't pick up a phone?"

"I tried but—" Didn't he care that his father and ex-wife were having an affair?

"I have no idea where you are with your investigation, what's going on at Edgewater—whether there's enough money to last another day or another hour. You've left me paralyzed."

"Well, I could have been killed, Zachary. And Jace is still missing. Fire me if you want—I don't care anymore." Kat broke into a sweat. Why had she expected him to understand in the first place? Edgewater and the World Institute was way more than she bargained for. As a matter of fact, she should be mad at Zachary. If he weren't so oblivious to his environment, none of this would have happened in the first place.

"Fine. Tell me what to do and I'll do it. But don't keep me out of the loop."

Hadn't he listened to anything she had just said? How on earth was she supposed to call him when she was drugged and dumped on a bench without money or a phone to call on?

"The short answer is—you're broke, Zachary. You've got to halt all payments and redemptions, and freeze the bank accounts if you can."

"How much time have I got?"

"None. You need to stop things immediately." Kat outlined Nathan's faked results, starting with the doctored client statements and their overstated investment returns, then the siphoning of funds to Research Analytics and its ties to the shadowy World Institute.

"How can Nathan get away with this?" Zachary leaned forward and pounded the desk. "Why didn't the auditors notice?"

"I mentioned this the last time we talked—those auditors actually don't exist. Beecham is a company Nathan made up, and Research Analytics appears to be a front for the World Institute. Nathan's been taking money out of client accounts and funneling it through Research Analytics. He hides the client transfers by doctoring their investment statements. Don't you ever read any of the administrative stuff? You should."

Zachary sighed. "I know. But I can't be everywhere. Besides, the deal was that I concentrated on the trading while Nathan managed the back office. At least I was making stellar returns with my proprietary trading model."

Kat sucked in her breath. "About that trading model of yours—it doesn't quite work the way you think." Now he'd really want to fire her.

"What are you talking about?"

"I recreated all your trades for the last two years. It's not the twelve percent average return you advertise for your hedge fund. It's much lower—a loss, actually."

"That's ridiculous. I don't believe you."

Kat passed her analysis to Zachary. "Over the last two years, you've actually lost five percent. But there's more. None of your trades were processed." She paused, waiting for Zachary's reaction. "Not one. Nathan didn't put them through."

Zachary rose, angry. "That's insane. I'd have to be an idiot not to notice that. How could all this be going on under my nose?"

The fund performance seemed to bother Zachary the most, even more than hearing he was broke or that Nathan and Victoria were romantically involved. Kat couldn't believe Zachary was so unaware of his father's deceit, but his surprise appeared genuine.

She handed Zachary a thick file of bank statements. "See for yourself. The only transactions you'll find are investments into and out of the funds by clients. Nothing else. No records of buying or selling dollars, yen, pounds, or any other currency."

Zachary opened the file and flipped through it. His shoulders slumped and he didn't say anything. He looked defeated. "This can't be happening."

"It's a Ponzi scheme, Zachary. There's no trading. As a matter of fact, there's not much of anything going on, except Nathan siphoning off all the money. No wonder everything ran smoothly when he was away on his frequent trips. It's because no real trades were taking place."

Zachary Barron's face reddened. "A Ponzi scheme? That's impossible."

"I'm afraid it's true." What seemed impossible was

Zachary's unawareness of the massive fraud operating under his eyes. "Nathan has been withdrawing money from client accounts and paying it to Research Analytics. In fact, he's been doing it for years."

She watched Zachary for a reaction. "As long as there are lots of new investors, the scheme works. Nathan simply pays the redeeming investors with new investor money. The scheme works fine if more money comes in than goes out. And it did work until the recession hit. Suddenly investors lost their jobs, had to cover loans or losses in other investments. They needed cash and were forced to redeem even their best-performing investments. Like Edgewater's hedge fund."

"How could this happen to me?" Zachary stood in front of the window, his back to Kat.

"You had no reason to question anything. No one does when things are going well. Nathan's doctored statements gave clients a twelve percent return, so no one ever redeemed their investments. Why would they? The returns were better than anywhere else. That is, until the financial crisis. Then a lot of your investors faced a cash crunch of their own. That caused them to redeem even their high-performing investments. Like Edgewater. That's when the bank balance dropped."

"It can't all be faked. Surely you've missed something—a bank account, some accounting records. Prove it to me."

Kat pulled out the cut-and-pasted client statements. "Here are the client statements. Nathan's been operating this fraud for at least ten years—probably since before you joined the firm. As long as new investor money was greater than the amounts redeemed, everything worked." Kat swallowed. She was telling the world's number one hedge fund manager that everything about his success was a lie.

"I don't get it. What about all my currency trades? I'm entering them myself—right on the trading terminals."

"It's all a sham, Zachary. An expensive, elaborate fraud. Those terminals? They're not connected to an exchange. It's a sophisticated software program running on Edgewater's local-area network. Money's no object when you're covering up a billion-dollar fraud."

Kat had found the software on the trading terminals after a search of Edgewater's computers. Her suspicions were further confirmed when she found no vendor for the custom-developed software program.

"You're telling me it's all a shell game?" Zachary slammed the report down on Kat's desk and strode to the doorway. He turned to face Kat. "I just don't know what to believe. Either you're completely incompetent, or I'm the biggest idiot in the world."

"I'm sorry, Zachary. I've checked and double-checked. I wish I was wrong." Kat winced as she handed Zachary the Research Analytics file. "The money goes to Research Analytics first. Then it's almost immediately transferred to the World Institute."

"You're telling me that Edgewater is part of a global conspiracy?" Zachary pursed his lips together like he was going to explode. But he didn't.

"It appears that way. I also think anyone could fall for this. Stellar returns mean happy investors. Happy investors don't ask questions or redeem their investments. As long as new money keeps coming in, Nathan perpetuates his fraud."

Zachary dropped back into the chair opposite Kat. He said nothing, just stared vacantly ahead. Beads of sweat formed on his forehead.

"There is a silver lining," Kat said. "Your divorce settlement was based on fraudulent representation. We might be able to get it overturned."

Zachary pulled a handkerchief from his pocket and wiped his brow. "We'll worry about that later. Where's Edgewater's money right now?"

"The money's in the Caymans, at least if it's still in the World Institute coffers. Whether it's recoverable is another story. The bank secrecy laws in the Caymans make it difficult to trace."

"Why would the World Institute even want Nathan as a member?" Zachary rose and walked to the window. "It doesn't make sense."

"Look at the money he brings in," Kat said. "He gets to rub shoulders with the world's most powerful people."

Zachary scoffed. "Nathan's not in their league. He's only rich because of me. Where's the proof of all this?"

Zachary still didn't get it. Kat grabbed a stack of papers off the printer and handed it to Zachary. It contained a summary of her findings, but unfortunately not the documents retrieved from Nathan's hotel room. "There was more, but it's still at Hideaway Bay." She described what she had read in the World Institute agenda and last year's meeting minutes. "Jace is missing too," she reminded him.

Zachary said nothing as he flipped page after page of the report. His surprise seemed genuine. Ten minutes later, he finally spoke.

"You actually followed Nathan?" Zachary's eyes widened.

"Not quite. I just followed the money—literally. It led me to him and the World Institute. Since the conference was nearby, it was only natural that I should attend."

"Only natural." Zachary raised his eyebrows. "You sure don't mess around. What happens now?"

"We need Nathan's documents—the World Institute agenda, minutes, and annual report. It's the audit trail we need to prove Nathan's fraud. Not only that—we need to prove you weren't involved. Without those documents, people will assume you were part of it." Kat didn't tell Zachary how she got the documents. Sneaking around Nathan's hotel room wasn't exactly something she was proud of.

"I don't even know where to start." He rested his elbows on her desk and rested his head in his hands.

"Don't worry about that part—I'll figure it out." Maybe Jace had somehow escaped with the documents? She felt bad for Zachary. His whole world and sense of worth was crushed. She saw the defeat in his eyes. "But there is something you can help me with. Jace is missing, and I think Nathan is somehow involved." She hesitated. Could she trust Zachary? She had no other choice. "I also suspect Nathan might be tied to Fredrick Svensson's murder."

Zachary nodded. "If what you say is true, he would silence anyone about to expose him."

Nathan's world was so ruthless that mere differences of opinion could lead to murder. Svensson's death seemed to lend credence to that theory.

Kat mouse-clicked on a podcast and turned the laptop screen around so it faced Zachary. In the clip, Svensson discussed currency reform. He was speaking at a European economic summit, just days before he left Sweden for Canada. It was his last public speech, ten days before meeting his demise at Hideaway Bay.

Zachary waved the screen away. "I'm familiar with Svensson. Did you see the story in the *Herald?* His note said he backtracked on his one world currency theory. Finally came to his senses."

Kat shrugged. "Odd, since it was his life's work." She turned the screen back towards her. She froze when she spotted the petite figure standing behind Svensson. Kat had noticed the group of people standing around him during the half-dozen times she had viewed the clip, but hadn't given them more than a passing glance. But the woman seemed familiar. Kat zoomed in until the woman and Svensson filled the screen.

Kat froze the frame. Svensson seemed uncertain and turned to the woman for reassurance. She nodded back at him. It was an expression so intimate Kat knew at once they were lovers. Unmistakably so—as was the woman's identity. Without the video, Kat would never have connected them in a million years.

CHAPTER 43

KAT NEVER EXPECTED TO FACE Connor Whitehall again so soon. Yet here she was in his office Monday afternoon, as soon as she could race over after Zachary left. At least Connor Whitehall and she weren't facing off in a courtroom again.

She was out of options and out of time. Aside from being the only lawyer willing to see her without an appointment, Connor Whitehall specialized in elder law. Kat sat across from him, studying her surroundings as she waited for him to finish his call. His office walls were a relaxing pale green, lined with framed landscape photographs. Several photography books sat on the corner of his desk. She had never even considered that her court adversary might have outside interests, let alone an artistic bent.

"Sorry about that." Connor replaced the telephone receiver and smiled at her. "I remember your uncle from court. He's a bit, uh—forgetful?"

Kat nodded. The lawyer was completely different than he had been in court. In a good way. She leaned over and extracted Harry's financial records from her briefcase. "His dementia has worsened in the last few months. I've been helping him more lately—balancing his checkbook, making sure he eats, that sort of thing. That's when I realized he wasn't paying his bills. Not only is he almost bankrupt, but he's about to lose his house."

Kat recounted her run-in with the real estate agent at Harry's house, his bank loan, and the unusual credit card charges. And her suspicions about Hillary.

"You can prove Hillary's receiving the money?" Connor peered over his glasses at her, raising his eyebrows.

"Yes." Kat was well aware of Hillary's parasitic tendencies but hadn't suspected outright fraud until it hit her between the eyes thanks to Jace. She handed Connor photocopies of Harry's bank statements highlighting the numerous transfers, all to what appeared to be Hillary's account.

"I called the bank the money was transferred into, pretending to be her. That all but confirmed it since they agreed to look into the missing transfer. Harry's bank had rejected the transfer due to insufficient funds in Harry's account. Hillary also reappeared about a week ago, the same time as the failed transfer."

Whitehall's brows furrowed as he scanned Harry's bank statements. "Harry can do what he likes with his money. Including giving it away, even if it seems self-destructive to you or me. Are these transfers still happening?"

"They would be—except there's no money left in his account." She explained about Harry's overdraft and large loan. "Unless the bank decides to lend him even more." She shuddered at the thought. They'd probably do it in a heartbeat and repeat it until they squeezed every last drop of equity from his house.

"Nothing illegal about that."

"I've got to stop the carnage, Connor." Kat explained Harry's maxed-out credit cards, all issued within the last six months. She described that and the thousands of dollars of clothes, entertainment, and luxury trips he had been paying for. She shuddered to think of the charges Hillary was probably racking up right now, unchecked. "Can't the courts help him? Can't you do anything?"

"That's up to Harry. Unless he says he didn't authorize it, we have to assume he did."

"But he's not in his right mind. If he were, he would never allow this to happen. As a matter of fact, money is what made Hillary leave in the first place. When he cut her off. He would never go into debt, or mortgage his house." Kat threw up her arms. "Fifty years of savings, completely erased in months. He desperately needs help."

"Poor judgment alone isn't enough to take over someone's affairs. It's a serious step, Kat. There are different degrees of Alzheimer's. He's assumed competent unless proven otherwise. "

"It's more than that. He can't remember things from one minute to the next, and he's not even safe anymore." She described his recent kitchen fire, delusions, and complete lack of awareness of his surroundings. "Someone has to step in and help him. He can't manage the simplest things anymore. And he never set up a power of attorney, either."

"It's not that easy. There's no legal recourse unless Harry's proven incapable of managing his affairs. It does sound like he might be near that point. Have you talked to him about his situation?"

"I've tried, but it's difficult. At first he's in denial, but when I show him the statements, he realizes what she's done. It upsets him, but dementia complicates things. He forgets our conversation within minutes, and then it's back to square one. Meanwhile, he's losing everything. His bank account has been drained and even his line of credit is maxed out."

"The bank should freeze his account."

"I asked them to, but they won't listen to me. They said it has to come from Harry, but he doesn't understand what's happening. It's a vicious circle."

Just thinking of all the debt piling up under Harry's name sent shudders through Kat. "How can his own daughter steal from him?"

Connor sighed. "It happens in the best of families. I see it all the time."

Kat pointed to Harry's Visa statement. "All his life he's scrimped and saved. For what? So everything he's worked for can be squandered on jewelry from Tiffany's, trips to Las Vegas, and car repairs at the Porsche dealership? Harry doesn't own a Porsche. But Hillary does. Now he's about to lose his house." She checked her watch. "If he hasn't already. It's financial abuse."

"Quite possible. Sad how common it is." Whitehall peered over his glasses at her. "You should talk to him about his mental state before we take any legal steps."

"And tell him what? That he might be declared incompetent? It will kill him." Kat rose and gazed out the floor to ceiling window. It framed a spectacular view of the Lions Gate Bridge with the snow-capped North Shore Mountains in the background.

"He deserves to know as much as possible. Besides, you're helping him."

"But Harry's so proud of his independence. He'll be humiliated."

"Maybe. But the alternative is far worse."

Kat knew Whitehall was right. But Harry's first reaction to the doctor's most recent confirmation of his Alzheimer's diagnosis had been to flee from his doctor's office, get lost, and almost freeze to death in an underground parking lot. She couldn't risk that again.

"He needs to be evaluated by medical doctors familiar with geriatric patients. They'll interview him and run a series of tests. If they don't think he is competent, he can be declared as not responsible for his actions. That will protect him going forward. The bank can't loan him more money, and Hillary can't take it from him. Of course, that means he can no longer make any financial decisions for himself either."

Kat rubbed her forehead. She already had a splitting headache. "How soon can we get this done? I think there's an offer on his house." Kat had found Whitehall's calm demeanor soothing a moment ago, but now his lack of urgency grated on her nerves. "What can we do? Can't we call the police?"

"It's not that simple."

"It seems simple to me. Hillary's taking advantage of him."

"We're dealing with a person's mental state, Kat. The law says that Harry has the right to manage his own affairs as long as he's mentally competent. Taking away that right is a very serious step."

"It's obvious he's not competent. A rational person would never do this."

"Maybe, but a legal assessment of Harry's mental competency rests on the medical opinions of two doctors. His family doctor can be one."

"His family doctor just dumped him as a patient. Where will I find two doctors willing to examine him on short notice? I don't even know where to start."

"I know of some." Whitehall patted her hand. "I'll make some calls."

Kat felt physically ill. "What about the damage so far? Won't Hillary be prosecuted? Doesn't she have to return the money?"

"Probably not since there's no proof of his mental incompetency at the time of the transactions."

"So she gets away with it, just like that?" Kat scoffed. "It's easier than robbing a bank."

Whitehall sighed. "The law may not seem fair, but Harry's competency has to be objective and verifiable. There's no turning back to fix past injustices. I'm afraid financial abuse is very common in families."

"I thought laws were supposed to protect vulnerable people like Harry."

"If the medical assessments do show he is mentally

incompetent, we'll apply to the courts to have him declared legally incompetent. It will protect him going forward. We can't do anything about the past. It could be in place in as little as three weeks."

"Three weeks? By then he'll have nothing left."

Whitehall studied her sympathetically. "I'll work as fast as I can. Now, when is Harry available?"

"That's the problem. I don't know where he is."

CHAPTER 44

OUTSIDE THE RAIN CHANGED TO hail. It clattered against the kitchen window, rising in crescendo as Kat stirred the boiling pasta. The steady tapping on the window grew louder, finally exploding in a cacophony of noise, drowning out everything except her thoughts. She was grateful to have made it home before the storm started.

Low clouds loomed in the late afternoon sky. Kat shivered, wondering if Jace was outside alone somewhere. He would never leave without contacting her. And why hadn't the police called yet? The knot in her stomach grew larger. Was he hurt? Or worse, had he met a fate similar to Svensson? She didn't dare think about it, yet she could think of nothing else.

Kat jumped as a loud bang broke into her thoughts. Probably branches from the strong winds outside. She turned the stove burner down and dumped the pasta in the colander to drain in the sink.

The banging started again. This time she realized it was the front door. Her heart skipped a beat as she spun and ran to the door. It might be Jace, or more likely, Hillary. Ready to offload Harry. But it wasn't either of them.

Connor Whitehall stood at the threshold, water droplets beading on his London Fog raincoat. His hair was wet, though the front porch was just steps from the curb where his Volvo was parked.

Kat invited him in and hung up his coat in the hallway armoire that had fortunately escaped the fire. She motioned him to follow her into the kitchen. "I was just making dinner. Can you stay?"

Connor eyed the charred wainscoting and stairway banister.

"Afraid not. But there's something I thought you should know as soon as possible." Connor stared down at his shoes. "I did a title search on Harry's house."

"And?" Kat felt the blood drain from her face. It was already heavily mortgaged, and it was all Harry had left. "It's sold? Hillary sold it?"

"Not exactly. Hillary's on the deed. Harry transferred the title to her." He studied Kat. "In essence, it is already sold. To Hillary. Harry's no longer the owner."

"That's impossible! He would never do that." She hadn't expected such blatant fraud, even from Hillary. On the other hand, it explained a lot. Hillary's recent appearances at Kat's office, Harry's missing lockbox with Harry's house deed and other papers, and the missing key from behind Harry's calendar. Hillary was manipulative all right, but Kat never dreamed she would go this far.

Connor dropped his briefcase on the kitchen table and extracted an envelope. He pulled out a sheaf of papers and handed them to her. "Have a look."

Kat studied Harry's signature, with its big loopy *y* and the slash across the *t*. It was his writing, all right. And it was dated two days ago.

It really was too late.

"He's not in his right mind. He wouldn't understand what he was signing. This can't be legal."

"Oh, I'm afraid it is. Without proof of his incompetence or any sort of coercion, it's perfectly legal."

"Wait a minute." Kat held the signature up to the light. While it was Harry's autograph, it was more in line with how he signed his name a year or two ago. The handwriting matched his documents and identification, but it didn't resemble his shaky penmanship of late. She'd been barely able to decipher his handwriting at work for months. Same with the spidery scrawls in his checkbook, which had been almost illegible for the better part of a year. Even his renovation loan sported the same shaky scrawl. "This is too perfect. It has to be a forgery."

"Forged? How can you be so sure?"

"Harry's hand shakes when he writes. This signature is smooth and fluid, like he wrote a couple of years ago." Hillary had stooped to a new low.

"You're sure Harry wouldn't sign this? Sometimes parents do add their children to the house to avoid probate fees and such. Did he ever mention doing that?"

"No, and he would never do that." Especially not with Hillary. Despite his love for his daughter, even Harry knew of self-centered Hillary's dark side.

"Well, I'm truly sorry to be the bearer of such bad news." Connor Whitehall checked his watch. "I'd best be going."

Kat followed him out to the hall and handed him his coat. "You've got to stop her."

"First you've got to track Harry down, Kat. I can't help until we get him assessed." He turned and descended the front steps to his car.

It was dark now. The Volvo pulled away from the curb, brake lights reflecting in streaks on the wet asphalt. The gusting wind swayed the bare tree branches back and forth in front of the streetlight. It changed the light into intermittent flashes, like a Morse code signal. Kat shivered and closed the front door. It was already too late to save Harry financially. The only good thing about dementia was oblivion. You never had to know how big of a mess you were in. Eventually, you wouldn't care either.

CHAPTER 45

KAT ARRIVED AT THE OFFICE just before six a.m. Tuesday morning, the building dark and eerily quiet. She climbed the stairs to her office and fumbled to unlock the door in the dim light. Marcus had repaired the door, although it took several tries with the key to turn the tumbler.

She wasn't an early riser, but after a fitful sleep and waking up alone for a second morning, she couldn't bear to stay in the house any longer. It just reminded her of Jace.

She was also haunted by Svensson's podcast from the Swedish conference. The woman with him bore a striking resemblance to Angelika, the Hideaway Bay housekeeper. As a matter of fact, she was positive it was her. But why was she in Sweden? Was she somehow connected to Svensson's death?

Kat closed the door behind her and leaned against it. Across the room the floor-to-ceiling windows framed the silhouette of the North Shore Mountains. A few lights twinkled across the water as the sun rose over the horizon and the harbor slowly came to life. She had a meeting with Zachary for the second day in a row. This time it was to determine a strategy to disclose the fraud to investors and the bank. As soon as she finished her early morning meeting with Zachary, she would head to Hideaway Bay.

Her numerous calls to the RCMP there remained unanswered and she couldn't understand why. What kind of a police station screened calls with voicemail? Jace was missing and she deserved an answer, even if only to state there were no developments. It was simply unacceptable. If the police couldn't take this seriously, she'd hold them accountable. And start a search for Jace herself.

But before she left, she needed to better define her search area.

Kat studied the map pinned to the wall. What was she missing? The map of Hideaway Bay was simple. The only land access was a single road. It originated at the ferry, cut through town, and then continued on to the turnoff for the Tides Resort. Water or air access were possibilities, but less likely. She'd heard a helicopter land during their stay. Certainly a second helicopter landing would have awakened her. That meant Jace must have left on foot or by boat. The high bank waterfront meant no dock or moorage, especially not at night. A number of trails connected to the resort, including the Summit Trail, where Svensson had fallen to his death. Not an easy hike in winter but possible with the right gear, including a headlamp at night. Had Jace met a similar fate to Svensson's?

There was one other scenario, one she thought the police were unlikely to check. Jace might have gone to Kurt's cabin nearby. Kat doubted Jace wouldn't leave without proper equipment for a winter-night hike. He wouldn't leave the resort without telling her either. Unless he had no choice.

She couldn't rule it out without visiting Kurt's cabin herself, since it was out of cell phone range and had no telephone connection.

Had Landers's enthusiasm been a ruse? Had he intended

all along to entrap and expose Kat and Jace?

Kat stabbed pins into the map for every trail that branched off from the resort road. She'd drive back up and check the most likely ones later today. Her heart sank as she pushed in the last pin. Was Jace even alive?

Daylight gradually suffused the office. Outside it reflected off the white frost that clung to everything but the harbor waters. Traffic noise, machinery, and voices drifted upwards as the city awoke. Kat shivered. The heat was finally pumping into her office, but it couldn't compensate for the draft that seeped through the ancient single-paned windows.

A crane in the harbor below lifted a Maersk container from a Chinese freighter and lowered it onto the shipyard dock. The containers were stacked three high, filled with electronics, furniture, and who knew what else. Port traffic never seemed to slow, fueled by cheap imports and insatiable consumer demand.

Kat jumped as the outer office door scraped open.

"Zachary—in here."

But it wasn't Zachary. It was Hillary. Her stilettos clicked as she appeared in Kat's office doorway. As much as Kat didn't want to see Hillary, her reappearance at least meant Harry could be found. Now she could start the wheels in motion to curb Hillary's financial abuse.

"Hey, cuz." Hillary pointed to the map and laughed. "Are you in kindergarten? Is this really what you do all day?"

"Hillary, what are you doing here? Where's Harry?" Kat stood and headed Hillary off at the map. She stood in front of it, holding her arm up to block Hillary from plucking a tack off the map.

"Can't I drop by for a visit without your stupid questions?" Hillary lifted her right foot and then the left, dusting the soles of her Gucci pumps with the palm of her hand. She grimaced as she wiped one palm against the other. "Don't you ever clean in here?"

"The janitor cleans every night." She had to get rid of

Hillary before Zachary arrived. The thought of Hillary crossing paths with any of her clients gave her the creeps. She was too manipulative and unpredictable.

"Where's your dad, Hillary?" She wouldn't mention Harry's house just yet. She couldn't risk Hillary running off without disclosing Harry's whereabouts.

Hillary ignored her. "This office is filthy. And your furniture looks like thrift-store rejects. All this clutter." She picked up the half-dozen magazines on the side table and tossed them into the trashcan. "No wonder no one takes you seriously."

"My office is fine. Where's Harry?" Hillary had arrived less than a minute ago, and Kat's stomach was already in a tight knot. She reminded herself that only one of them commanded six-figure retainers, and it certainly wasn't Hillary. At least she earned her own keep. "I called him and he wasn't home. He's not answering his cell phone either."

She had a million other questions, like where the hell Hillary had been for the last ten years. But now wasn't the time.

"How would I know where Dad is? I'm not his keeper. He probably went shopping or something."

"Hillary, you know as well as I do he's not shopping or at home. You were with him." Was Hillary really that irresponsible, or was there something more at play? Anytime Kat gave Hillary the benefit of the doubt, it backfired. At any rate, she was certain Hillary's reappearance wasn't out of concern for Harry.

"What makes you think he's not home?" Hillary frowned and her face darkened.

Kat motioned to the leather armchair. Confronting Hillary was futile, so she changed her tone. "Have a seat. You must be tired."

"You expect me to sit on that flea-infested crap?" Hillary smoothed her hair with a manicured hand. "I don't think so."

"It's perfectly fine. But if you want to stand, suit yourself."

Hillary inspected Kat, taking in her clothing, hair and

makeup. "You really should think about a makeover." She grimaced. "Head to toe. Your wardrobe went out of style five years ago. How could you leave the house in that get-up? You seriously need an upgrade."

Kat said nothing and turned to the board. Hillary couldn't stand to be ignored.

"What are you doing with those thumbtacks?"

"Just experimenting." Kat glanced out the window. In mere minutes the sun had vanished, replaced by low clouds. Snowflakes swirled past the window and she could barely make out the North Shore across the water. Where the hell was Zachary?

"Some experiment." Hillary pulled hand sanitizer out of her purse and squirted a dollop onto her hand. She rubbed her palms together and stared at the map. "Hey, that's the place you were hiding my dad."

"Hillary, cut it out. I wasn't hiding him and you know it."

"Sure you were. Isn't it near the place that Nobel economist guy disappeared?"

"Fredrick Svensson?" Kat was shocked that Hillary had even heard of him.

"Yeah, that guy. Pretty hot for an old guy."

Hillary's hot scale was measured by net worth, not looks. "Whatever. He's dead now." Svensson had to be in his seventies.

"Dead right. Never even knew what hit him." Hillary laughed at her own joke.

Enough. Kat was ready to explode. "Where is he?"

"The Nobel guy? How the hell would I know?"

"Harry, for crying out loud!" Kat massaged her temples, feeling the start of a headache coming on.

Across the inlet, a second storm front was gathering in the direction of Hideaway Bay. Kat shivered despite her heavy wool sweater and tights. She had to leave soon or risk road closures. Jace's truck sat parked outside, packed with warm clothes, outdoor gear, and whatever she thought she could possibly need.

"Don't get snarky, Kat." Hillary pulled a nail file from her purse and began filing her nails. She pointed the nail file at Kat and narrowed her eyes. "Or have a breakdown. How should I know where he is?"

"The last time I saw him he was with you. If Harry's not with you, then where is he?"

Hillary's eyebrows arched and the corners of her mouth turned up in a smirk. "Calm down. What do you care? He's my dad, not yours."

The words always stung, no matter how many times Hillary uttered them. The Dentons had legally adopted Kat when her mother died and her father left. Once Hillary realized the arrangement was permanent, she did everything she could to make Kat feel unwelcome.

"Kat—it's none of your business what Dad and I do." Hillary pursed her lips. "Get over it."

"Oh, it's very much my business." Kat crossed her arms. "He's not at home. He's not with you and he's not here with me. Wherever he is, he's confused and lost. I've got a right to know."

"You don't have a right to anything. Go find your own family to look after." Hillary raised her hand to her mouth. "Oops, I forgot. You don't have one."

"Hillary, Harry is my family too. I'm the one who's been taking care of him while you've been away. You've been out of his life for years."

"That's about to change." Hillary scowled at Kat.

The outer office door opened, and a few seconds later Zachary strode down the hall and into Kat's office, talking into his cell phone. A light dusting of snow still coated the shoulders of his wool coat.

Hillary's jaw dropped and a smile slowly transformed her face.

"Hello." Hillary turned towards him and smiled, sucking in her cheeks. She scanned Zachary from head to toe, noting his tailored clothing, leather-soled shoes, and unencumbered ring finger.

Kat watched dollar signs dance across Hillary's field of vision.

Zachary didn't seem to hear Hillary. He stood transfixed in front of Kat's television. New York protesters had blockaded Grand Central Station, demanding government intervention and lower food prices. The screen faded to a commercial and Zachary glanced over, noticing Hillary for the first time. He ended his call. "Sorry to interrupt. I didn't see you there."

"No need to apologize." Hillary stepped forward and held out her hand, palm down, as if she expected a prince to kiss it. "I just dropped by to see if I could take my cousin out for breakfast."

As if, Kat thought. Hillary's act was reserved for men with benefits, whether cut-rate auto repairs or potential husband income streams. Men saw through it eventually—but only after Hillary had taken them for a ride.

"Of course, if you two already have plans, I'll come back another time." Zachary smiled at Hillary, who now sat in the leather armchair. Apparently she had overcome her previous thrift-store objections.

"No." Kat waved her hand. She had to talk to Zachary pronto. "Hillary was just leaving."

Hillary crossed one leg over the other, allowing her skirt to ride up and show off some leg. She didn't appear to be going anywhere.

"Why don't we all go for breakfast," Zachary said. "We can discuss the case and eat at the same time."

Kat stood. This was quickly turning into a nightmare. She needed an hour with Zachary before leaving for Hideaway Bay, and the worsening snow lessened her chances of getting there every minute. Any more delays and she wouldn't make it at all. "Hillary—can I call you later instead?"

"Nonsense. She can join us." Zachary motioned towards the hallway with his thumb.

Kat had to get rid of Hillary. She couldn't discuss the case or Jace's fate in front of Hillary. She wasn't sure exactly how, but Hillary was sure to use Jace's disappearance against her. Why would Zachary even consider discussing his personal financial situation in front of Hillary, a stranger?

She stopped in the doorway and faced Hillary. "I thought you were going to pick up your dad. Where is Harry, anyway?"

"The old guy with the Lincoln?" Zachary asked. "He's a bit confused, isn't he? He shouldn't be alone."

Hillary's eyes narrowed.

"I was just telling Kat that. Kat, where is he?" Hillary twirled her hair around her finger and raised her eyebrows at Kat, an expression of mock concern on her face.

Kat pursed her lips and unclenched her fist. How could anyone not see right through her? "I thought you were picking him up. Where did you say you left him?"

Hillary glared at Kat. "At the seniors' center. I was just headed over there."

"That's what I thought." At least Hillary was forced to behave in front of Zachary.

"I'll be back right after lunch." Hillary smiled at Zachary.

Just enough time for Kat to brief Zachary and get on the road to Hideaway Bay.

CHAPTER 46

KAT GLANCED OUT HER OFFICE window, impatient and frustrated at her lack of progress. Snow blanketed the city once again, and still Zachary wouldn't budge.

"Let's hold off reporting anything, Kat. I know I can make back most of the money back."

Zachary remained convinced his trading model was infallible. "What are you going to trade with, Zachary? There's no money."

"I've got connections—people that will lend me funds. Enough to make some trades and recover some of the losses." Zachary dropped her report on top of the stack of folders on her desk. As he did, the pile slid, sending several of them to the floor.

Zachary bent to pick them up.

Kat waved him away. "I'll get it later." She stood. "What about the investors, Zachary? It's their money. Don't they deserve to know about the fraud?"

He stood. "Sure they do—but I'll recover their losses before they even know about it. It's in their best interests, even if they don't realize it yet. I'll get the money back and they'll never even know there was a problem. Just a few good trades and things will be back to normal."

Whatever normal was. Amazing what people will do on a sinking ship. "No, Zachary. You have to shut it down."

"Kat, you said yourself we're missing some of the proof. If we alert Nathan without proof, won't it jeopardize the case? He could make a run for it before the authorities have enough evidence to arrest him."

Zachary was right. Waiting also meant she might be able to recover Nathan's missing World Institute agenda and her backup documents. If she found Jace and he happened to still have them. It was unlikely at best. And—it just felt wrong to not immediately disclose the wrongdoing.

On the other hand, it was still an active investigation, and if Nathan and whoever else were prosecuted, she'd better have her ducks in a row. Right now that wasn't the case. And closing in now could somehow worsen Jace's situation, whatever that was. It also gave her more time to search for Jace. If she could find him.

She sighed and bent to pick up the files. Why did Zachary have to push the limits? She supposed it was why he was so rich. And relentless.

Her hand felt something rigid in the gutter of one of the Edgewater folders. She opened the folder to find a bundle of credit cards, held together with an elastic band. In her haste she hadn't noticed them before. She undid the elastic that bundled them and examined the top card. No name. She shuffled through the rest. They were exactly the same— prepaid credit cards. Just like the one she had found in the housekeeper's uniform at Hideaway Bay. Was there a connection?

⌒⌒⌒⌒

Two hours later Kat was finally on the road. She drove north towards Hideaway Bay, thankful for the truck's four-wheel drive. Deep ruts had formed in the snowpack on the highway, and the snow fell heavier now, reducing visibility to a few feet in front of her.

Traffic then slowed to a crawl en route to the ferry, and she missed the sailing. She was lucky to get on the next one. Once across, she followed the crowd exiting the ferry until the turnoff for Hideaway Bay.

Here the traffic was nonexistent. Despite the unplowed roads and low visibility, she felt much safer driving with no other cars on the road. She relaxed her hands on the steering wheel and bit into an apple. She glanced at the rearview mirror and spotted a snowplow round the corner a few hundred feet back. It was the only other vehicle she had seen since the turnoff.

Her biggest worry was the limited time until nightfall. Daylight disappeared around four p.m. this time of year. That gave her only a few hours to search for Jace on the trails. He might have hurt himself and fallen off the trail. She shivered. If he had, chances of survival in the frigid temperatures would be slim to none after a couple of hours.

Kat's thoughts drifted back to Svensson and his speech in Stockholm. The snowplow was about fifty feet back now, growing larger in the rearview mirror.

Svensson had changed his views from one global currency to the status quo of many sovereign currencies. Why would Nathan Barron find issue with that? Exploiting differences between the various currencies was how Nathan Barron, and Edgewater, made money. The World Institute's goal of one global currency actually killed his business rather than helped it. Which begged the question: why Nathan would even join an organization that thwarted his financial ambitions?

She was certain both Svensson's murder and Jace's disappearance were connected to the World Institute and Nathan Barron.

Was the woman standing with Svensson really Angelika, the housekeeper? A more logical explanation was that the woman was a look-alike. After all, she had been standing behind Svensson and slightly in the shadows. Of all the billions of people on the planet, there were likely a few doppelgangers. Or was it too coincidental?

Kat glanced at the rearview mirror. The snowplow was right on her bumper, the driver probably anxious to finish work and get home. Kat gripped the steering wheel, not wanting to go any faster but feeling the pressure. There was nowhere to pull over. A sheer rock face to her right and, across the oncoming lane, a steep drop-off to the water below. Couldn't he just pass her? There was no traffic coming the other way.

Suddenly the snowplow tapped her bumper.

She lurched forward. The apple slipped from her grasp and tumbled off the passenger seat onto the floor. She gripped the steering wheel, heart pounding. The seat belt tightened across her chest as she fought to pull the truck out of a skid. The snowy highway was too dangerous a place for reckless games. The driver's actions were nothing short of suicidal on this winding stretch of road in a snowstorm. What the hell was he doing? Was he asleep at the wheel? She glanced in the mirror, but the truck's cab was too high to see the driver.

She'd get his license plate number and report him. The resort was another ten minutes away—the first opportunity to pull off the road. She pulled the seat belt off her chest and exhaled. The snowplow backed off slightly, giving her a view of the cab. This time she could make out the driver, but only barely. A slight man, or teen maybe? A baseball cap covered his eyes.

The gap closed. The snowplow rear-ended the truck bumper again, harder this time.

Her truck fishtailed. She headed across the opposing lane. Instinct kicked in and she hit the brakes. She knew it was a mistake even before her foot fully pressed the pedal.

CHAPTER 47

THE SNOWPLOW SIDESWIPED THE TRUCK box, sending it skidding sideways across the highway. Kat gripped the steering wheel as Jace's truck tipped and careened onto two wheels. It teetered momentarily before smashing back down onto all fours. Kat's neck whipped back from the force. Again her foot searched for the brake pedal. But it was futile.

The truck skidded into a 180, pulling Kat into its vortex as shades of white spun by the windshield. She lurched forward, hitting her forehead on the rearview mirror. A split-second later, the seat belt tightened and pulled her back into her seat.

The plow backed up and accelerated again. It slammed against the truck, shattering the windshield. Kat bounced back and forth before lurching to a stop, tilted down on the driver's side. Kat peered through the side window. She was perched precariously against the guardrail. One more hit and she'd be over the edge in a 300-foot freefall to the bottom of the canyon.

She braced herself for another hit as her stomach churned. Nothing.

Kat loosened the seat belt and listened. She slid over to the passenger side. The truck creaked and the apple rolled to the far corner of the floor.

Silence.

The truck had stalled from the impact.

She searched for the snowplow through the cracked windshield.

She saw nothing.

Nothing at all. Just white snow, falling.

Muffled silence.

She turned around in her seat and searched for the plow out the rear window.

Gone.

Nothing but her, the truck, and a bent guardrail holding her back from a plunge off the rocky cliff.

She inched her body back into a forward position slowly, feeling the truck settle against the guardrail metal.

Solid. Despite her earlier fears, the truck's four wheels still rested on the highway.

She felt relieved and scared at the same time. Had the plow driven off—or gone over the edge? She peered out the window again. The guardrail was still intact, at least on the section within her field of vision. She wasn't about to get out to inspect further. In case it shifted the balance of weight. In case that guy was still around.

She turned the ignition and restarted the truck. She slowly maneuvered the truck, inching backwards and forwards until she had disengaged from the guardrail. She steered the truck away from the edge and around so she now faced the right side of the road.

Kat drove a few miles up the road and pulled over onto a logging road, empty and unused in winter. Her hands still shook as she released the steering wheel. She took a deep breath and instinctively grabbed her cell phone and dialed.

Without thinking, she realized she had called Jace. She was about to disconnect when a woman answered.

"Yeah?"

Kat tried to place the background noise. Loud, like machinery operating. It could be anywhere—a manufacturing plant, a construction site. Where exactly she couldn't tell.

"Who is this?" But the woman disconnected as soon as Kat spoke. The voice sounded familiar, yet she wasn't sure why. It was hard to tell with all the noise. A busy place somewhere, like an airport or a shopping mall.

All her other calls to Jace had gone directly to his voicemail. Had she dialed wrong? Impossible, since his number was programmed into her phone. Who was using his phone and why? Was it someone involved in his disappearance, or just someone who had found his phone?

At any rate, she couldn't stay here in the middle of the road. She debated going back to town. She should report the snowplow driver to the RCMP. On the other hand, the police had done absolutely nothing about Jace, so it was another waste of time. It also delayed her search for him.

What if the snowplow waited on the road ahead, looking for more trouble? Unlikely, she thought. Anyone that impatient wouldn't stick around. He was probably inflicting his road rage on the next vehicle, if there was one.

In the end she decided to continue driving. The resort was only minutes away now, and once there she would be safe from the crazy driver. She'd report him to police tomorrow. After she searched the Pinnacle Trail and Kurt's cabin. By then she might have found Jace.

Kat pulled away from the shoulder slowly, looking for evidence of the plow. But the snow had already obliterated any tire tracks. Already the road ahead appeared as though it hadn't been plowed for several hours. But hadn't the driver had his plow down? She couldn't remember.

One thing was certain: she'd feel safer once she was off the road. Daylight was already ebbing, leaving her little time to reach the Summit trailhead for the hike to Kurt's cabin. At least in the wilderness you knew who your enemies were.

CHAPTER 48

KAT CAUGHT HER BREATH AS she trudged up the last few feet of the Summit Trail, snowshoes heavy on her feet. It was just a thirty-minute side trip from the main trail to the place where Svensson had plunged to his death, but her detour yielded nothing. No trace of the economist or his mysterious female companion. No sign left by the police, or search and rescue either.

Had Jace followed this same trail before her? There was no way to know for sure, not with the new snow. Other than some deer tracks crossing on either side of the trail, the mountain would keep its secrets.

She paused for a moment as she took in the breathtaking view of the inlet. Not a place that inspired suicide, if any place actually did. It was also remote—getting here took quite an effort for someone intent on giving up on life. She was weary after two hours of almost constant uphill. But it wasn't the physical exertion that tired her. It was the mental anguish, not knowing where to find Harry or Jace. She had always turned to Jace, but this time he wasn't here to help her.

After arriving at Hideaway Bay, she changed her mind and decided to report the snowplow before embarking on the trail. But the Hideaway Bay RCMP station had been locked up, a *Be Back Soon* note taped to the door.

What kind of police station locks its doors? The same kind that don't return phone calls about missing people, she thought. It made no sense. But then Hideaway Bay was a bit of a sleeper town. Other than the resort, not much happened there. She'd return tomorrow, but first she wanted to check the one place she might find Jace.

Kat still held a thin sliver of hope that Jace had gone to Kurt Ritter's cabin. Kurt and Jace had become close friends through search and rescue, even though they covered different territories. Assuming he escaped Nathan, Kurt's cabin was the only shelter within hiking distance.

Jace had been anxious to retrace Svensson's last steps. They had even argued about it, with Kat thinking it was a waste of time. Jace always kept his search and rescue gear in the car, so it was plausible that he had retrieved it from the resort parking lot. Maybe he was hiding out at the cabin? She felt a surge of hope.

Kurt headed the Sunshine Coast Search and Rescue team, and was likely on scene when Svensson's body was recovered. At the very least Jace would be itching to talk to him. The big German's cabin was a further forty-five minutes once she backtracked to the main trail, and Kat and Jace had overnighted there on backcountry hikes many times. She'd have to spend the night this time too, as the sun had dropped almost to the horizon. Even at the forty-ninth parallel, dusk came quickly at this time of year.

No cell phone reception meant whoever had answered Jace's phone earlier today wasn't here. It was also possible that Jace was here and had no way of contacting whoever she was. She felt a surge of hope as she bent down to refasten her snowshoes. She turned around and set off back down the hill.

The descent went much faster than the climb. Without exertion, her now-damp clothing chilled her. Her thoughts wandered to Jace. If he hadn't been so insistent on covering the World Institute, she would have wrapped up the Edgewater fraud case by now. She had all she needed with those documents in hand, but Jace had insisted on collaborating with Roger Landers. She never should have brought him, knowing that for him a story scoop overrode everything else. Especially after he was dumped by the *Sentinel*. But she had underestimated the World Institute, power, and what it did to people.

Finally the cabin came into view and it couldn't have been a more welcome sight. Kurt had built the log cabin himself from local timber. It was rustic but functional, comfortable and comforting. Kat wouldn't have traded it for a luxury suite. Exhaustion overtook her as she reached the front door. She couldn't take another step. She unfastened her snowshoes and felt under the clay flowerpot for the hidden key. Kat always chided Kurt for keeping a flowerpot at a cabin surrounded by alpine meadow. Both were now invisible under the heavy blanket of snow.

She opened the door and trudged inside. She was weary to the bone, though it was still only late afternoon.

The small cabin was furnished in a masculine, functional sort of way. The A-frame had stairs to a loft upstairs with two bedrooms. She had stayed in one of them with Jace last summer. She scanned the room, feeling the weight of all her troubles. Jace was gone, Harry unaccounted for, and Hillary was scheming up something that could only be trouble. She had never felt so alone.

Kat sighed and dropped her pack on the large pine table. She stooped to gather an armful of wood from the neatly stacked pile beside the wood stove. The stove was cold. No one had been here recently. She lit the stove and stoked the fire until it burned steadily. Then she headed outside to replenish the kindling before darkness fell. Cold air gusted in as she opened the door. The stove's heat hadn't permeated the cabin yet, but the building's log-and-chink construction still provided excellent insulation from the cold.

She circled the building, trudging through the snow, hoping against hope for any sign of Jace, Kurt, or any other visitors. No human or even animal tracks within sight. Even the woodpile stacked against the side of the cabin seemed undisturbed from when she and Jace visited in September.

Untouched.

A twig snapped. She jumped as she caught a flash of movement in her peripheral vision. It was just a rabbit racing for the cover of bush a few yards away. She stood still for a moment as she adjusted to the quiet. Snow slipped off the branches of the tall jack pines, landing with a soft plumpf. The trees surrounding the cabin usually gave it a cozy feel. But in today's late afternoon they seemed eerie, casting long shadows across the white landscape.

She loaded the wood onto her arms and trudged back to the front door, wincing as her arm hit the doorjamb. Her bicep still smarted from Victoria's needle jab. Enough fuel to last the night. She dumped the wood beside the stove. Tomorrow she would return on a different route, hoping for some sign of Jace. Maybe he was injured, unable to reach the cabin. A long shot, but she had nothing else to go on.

She kicked off her Sorel boots and laid her wet clothes out in front of the stove before collapsing into the oversized armchair facing the stove. She knew she should eat, but couldn't even muster enough energy to open her pack on the table a few feet away. Instead, she closed her eyes and felt the heat slowly warm her bones. Wilderness trekking always reminded her how truly immense the world was. Why was it controlled by so few?

CHAPTER 49

KAT JERKED AWAKE TO POUNDING on the cabin door downstairs. Someone rammed the heavy wood door, trying to force it open. She sprang out of bed only to hit her head on the low loft ceiling. She swore under her breath when she remembered where she was: Kurt's cabin in the second bedroom upstairs. Her heart thumped in her chest. Whoever was outside wanted in badly.

She inched her way towards the ladder leading downstairs and peered over the edge. Even in the dark, her bird's eye view from the loft gave an advantage over the intruder. The cabin door was already open a crack, the moonlight outlining the doorframe. She was trapped. No escape route.

The door gave way with a final crack. A man burst in, his dark form silhouetted in the doorway against the moonlit sky. Kat held her breath as he turned to shut the door.

Kurt had mentioned a cabin break-in once before. Transients sometimes looked for cabins to crash in. This guy might just grab food and leave. Unlikely in the middle of the night though, since it was too dark to travel and there were no other cabins nearby. He would stay until morning, which meant he would check out the whole cabin, including the loft. When he did, she'd better be ready. She felt around on the floor for a weapon but found nothing. She cursed her stupidity at leaving her pack with her pocketknife downstairs.

The stove. Even if it wasn't still burning, it would be warm to the touch, a sure sign the cabin was occupied. And her backpack sat in plain sight on the kitchen table. With the door shut it was dark again, but Kat could follow the intruder's shadow as he surveyed the cabin. He crossed the room and headed straight for the loft ladder. He stepped on the bottom rung and hesitated as he looked around.

Kat ran to the bedroom and grabbed a ski pole from a pair hanging on the wall. She tiptoed back to the ladder and stood at the side. She waited for the man's hands to reach the top rung. He would be stronger than her; the element of surprise was her only advantage. Her pulse quickened as she waited, knowing she'd only get one chance.

She stabbed at the intruder's knuckles, then dug the pole into his flesh and twisted. To her horror the hulk kept advancing, reaching the top with his free hand.

"Hey, what the—" He abruptly stopped.

"Back off!"

But the man had already wriggled his hand free. She stabbed at his other hand as he dropped down one ladder rung. She recognized him at the exact moment he saw her.

"You!" Landers stared up at her, eyes wide with shock. "How did you get here?" He paused and shook his right hand out.

"I should ask you the same thing." Kat jabbed his remaining hand with the pole. This time she kept it there, impaling the soft fleshy part with the tip of the pole. "Get out!"

"Kat, what the hell? You're hurting me. Get that thing off my hand."

"No way. Turn around and leave. Now."

"Calm down—I can explain everything."

She dug in harder. "Explain what? That you betrayed us? Get out."

"I can't go anywhere until you release my hand."

Kat lifted the ski pole and held it high as Roger Landers stepped back down the ladder. But he only dropped two rungs, just enough to be out of reach. "Keep moving."

"We need to talk first." He studied her.

"There's nothing to talk about." She pointed the ski pole at him, but kept it just out of his reach.

Landers didn't move. "You don't understand. Just come down here and we'll talk."

"Not a chance." He wasn't getting anything else from her.

"I know where Jace is. Just come down here, okay? I promise not to do anything."

Kat lowered the ski pole. Was it a trick to get her downstairs? But what if he could find Jace? Landers had been in the room with Jace at some point. Surely Nathan and Victoria were involved in Jace's disappearance. "Where?"

"Locked up. At the Hideaway Bay jail. He told me to come here if things went sideways. To hide from Nathan." ·

Had Jace been imprisoned at the precinct when she visited, mere feet away?

Landers couldn't know about Kurt's cabin unless Jace had told him. At least that part must be true. Kat lowered the ski pole and slowly descended the stairs, careful not to take her eyes off Landers. She followed him to the table and watched him sit down. She remained standing, wary.

"I'll give you five minutes to convince me. Then you're gone." She knew she wasn't a threat to Roger Landers without a weapon. The ski pole worked only while she was in the loft, where she had a height advantage. Still, she wasn't giving in.

Did Kurt keep a gun in the cabin? If so, she'd better find it before Landers did. Even if she didn't know how to use it.

"Why is Jace in jail?"

"Nathan had him hauled into Hideaway Bay for

questioning." Landers unzipped his jacket and placed it on the chair nearest the door, like he was planning to stay awhile.

"What for? Jace didn't do anything wrong." Nathan Barron might be powerful, but unless the Hideaway police were corrupt, they wouldn't arrest Jace without proof of a crime.

"Nathan wants him charged for theft. For stealing those documents out of his hotel room." Roger Landers sat down at the table, holding his hand. "I think you broke my hand. And it's bleeding."

Kat felt a momentary pang of guilt. Then she remembered Landers's inaction when Victoria injected her. He didn't stop Victoria, leaving Kat to be dumped unconscious at the train station. She didn't owe Roger Landers anything, especially not sympathy.

As a matter of fact, he owed her. She crossed her arms and ignored him.

"Didn't you hear me? I'm bleeding. Where's your first aid kit?"

Kat glared at Landers. "Why didn't they arrest you? You were in the room too." Was he working with them? Jace had disappeared and she got a needle poke. Only Landers had escaped unscathed. Too many parts of his story didn't make sense.

"Jace said he acted alone. I have no idea why they left me out of it, but we need to work together. Let's focus on getting Jace out of jail, and the real criminals behind bars."

"The real criminals?" He hadn't answered her question.

"Nathan and the World Institute, of course." He winced and wiggled his fingers. "The World Institute is committing the biggest crime of all."

"They haven't broken any laws," Kat said. Nathan, Victoria, and the World Institute might be unsavory, but the World Institute itself hadn't done anything illegal. Only Nathan had, with the Research Analytics fraud. Not to mention his assault on her and probably Jace. Maybe the World Institute was reprehensible, but discussing world domination wasn't a crime. She was sick of Landers and his conspiracy theories. It was his fault they were in this mess.

"They will. Or else they'll change the laws to suit their needs. Now they're putting their plan into action. The debt crisis was just the start, orchestrated by World Institute members. Their banks made big fees off risky loans, not caring if they failed or not. Enough bad loans and the government had no choice but to bail them out. Why? Because letting them fail has a cascading effect. The same people running government are or were running the banks. All those treasury secretaries and bank governors come from the banks. It's incestuous."

"You're implying the bank failures happened on purpose?" Kat walked over to the kitchen table and struck a match. She lit the kerosene lantern and sat at the opposite end of the table from Landers, wishing she'd never met him.

"Sure. A few profit, but the majority pay. Not only do bad loans enrich the bankers; they also further the goals of the World Institute. When governments bail out the banks, they raise taxes to remain solvent. When they can't raise taxes any higher, they simply print more money. At best, the currency devalues. At worst, it becomes worthless. No matter what they do, we taxpayers ultimately foot the bill. Eventually the currency fails, and the World Institute swoops in as savior."

"Why didn't you say all this to Nathan Barron when you had the chance?" Here she was, stuck in a cabin with no power and no cell coverage. Was it with a friend or an enemy? Roger Landers said the right things, but his actions spoke otherwise. "Why should I even listen to you? You didn't help me at the hotel."

"It's complicated." Landers leaned back in his chair, nursing his sore hand.

"How complicated can it be?" Exactly the sort of thing people said when there was a cover-up.

"If I say anything too soon, they'll suppress it. Once my new book is out, they won't be able to stop it. It will expose them, and they can be charged."

"Charged with what, exactly? This is just all about you—your book, your investigation. Getting famous, and getting credit." Everyone else was collateral damage. Like Jace.

"I don't know—the lawyers will figure that out."

"You've just told me they're ruining people's lives. Yet you're willing to let them continue so you can publish your second book?" Kat rose. She'd heard enough lies tonight.

"I'm not giving up years of research for nothing. The book is payback. If other people are harmed by it, there's not much I can do."

"Sure there is. If writing a story is the answer, why not do it right now and expose them? Sooner is better." Suddenly it occurred to her—that was exactly what Jace wanted to do. Jace was a threat to Landers. Publishing now meant Jace could get the scoop on Landers.

"A few more weeks or months won't make much difference. They aren't going to dismantle the currencies and governments overnight. Where's that first aid kit? I really should bandage my hand."

Kat shook her head. Suddenly she knew what was bothering her. If Jace really did tell Roger Landers to meet at the cabin, why didn't Landers know about the key under the flowerpot?

CHAPTER 50

KAT SENSED THE MORNING LIGHT before she even opened her eyes. She blinked as a soft, diffused glow filtered through the loft window's curtains. She shivered and pulled the comforter up around her shoulders. There was no heat upstairs, and the stove had burnt through the wood fuel sometime during the night. The firm mattress dug into her back. She winced and rolled over. Her breath vapored in the cold, damp loft as she inched towards the window. She wiped a small circle from the thin layer of ice that had formed on the inside of the window and peered outside. Exactly the same view as yesterday. Quiet, desolate, and deceptively serene. Too quiet for the drama playing out in her life.

She'd slept fitfully, worried about Jace. Was Landers really telling the truth about Jace's whereabouts, or was it just another lie? He had already deceived her about meeting Jace at the cabin. Was he lying about Jace at the Hideaway Bay RCMP station too? Just because the station had been closed when she checked didn't mean no one was locked up inside. She wanted to believe, but maybe that was naïve.

But what if Landers was telling the truth? Then she'd convince Jace to forget about the story, hand Zachary his report, and be done with it. Let Landers have the story. Nothing was worth this.

She shivered as she eased out of the covers. The sooner she got moving, the sooner she might see Jace. She stood and dressed quickly, pulling on her clothes from yesterday. She would have left last night if she could, but the winter weather and terrain made it impossible to hike in the dark.

Dishes clanked downstairs, reminding her she wasn't alone. A knot settled in her stomach at the thought of spending any more time with Roger Landers.

She peered over the loft edge and felt the heat rising from the wood stove. The smell of coffee and toast wafted towards her, reminding her of Uncle Harry. Was he with Hillary? The thought of Hillary making him breakfast, let alone staying with him for more than a few hours seemed extremely unlikely. She pushed the thought out of her mind and loaded her still-damp clothes into her pack.

Kat descended the ladder, carrying her pack.

Landers glanced up from the table and smiled. "Coffee?"

"Sure." Kat dropped her pack by the door. If she had to spend another few hours with him hiking out to Hideaway Bay, she'd at least be civil. And decide once and for all whether he was friend or foe.

Thirty minutes later, Kat waited outside the cabin. Landers hammered nails into the broken cabin door with an axe blade. Kurt wouldn't be happy about Landers's butchering of the hand-carved door, even if it was secured. She would get it repaired before Kurt returned from wherever he was, since it was unlikely Landers would contribute anything beyond the primitive job he was doing right now. He wasn't the kind of person to feel obligated or apologetic enough to fix it right. He'd be a good match for Hillary. They both had that sense of entitlement, never willing to lend a hand to anyone else. On second thought, maybe even he was too good for her.

"Just a minute—I forgot something." Kat trudged around the side of the cabin and scrounged inside her pockets for pencil and paper. She scribbled a note and wedged it into the woodpile, making sure it stuck out enough to be noticed without blowing away. No matter what happened, at least Jace or Kurt would know she had been here.

~~~

Ten minutes later they were on the trail. It was a crisp, clear day and the trail flattened out after the first hill out of the valley. Kat stepped in her snowshoe tracks from yesterday, undisturbed until now. Small animal tracks beside the trail traced tangents from one stand of firs to the next, undercover and out of sight of coyotes or cougars.

The return trek to Hideaway Bay was mostly downhill, easy except for a few technical descents. Landers had helped himself to Kurt's snowshoes, and Kat wondered how he'd managed the mostly uphill hike to Kurt's cabin in the first place without snowshoes or skis. She'd have to remember to bring Kurt's snowshoes when she returned to get the door repaired.

Landers was already short of breath. She'd ditch him in a minute, except he was her only remaining chance to find Jace. Only he knew the truth of what had happened that night with Nathan and Victoria. But he deftly avoided the subject every time she brought it up. He insisted he was equally a victim of Nathan and Victoria, though he was very short on details.

"Don't you care about democracy, Kat?" Landers stopped at a fork in the trail and turned to face Kat. Sweat beaded on his forehead, and he had already unzipped his jacket.

"Of course I care. But the World Institute isn't at the top of my list of worries right now." Like Landers actually bought into the whole democracy concept. He'd probably just use her opinions as fodder for his book. He'd been at her the whole trip, trying to gauge or sway her opinion about the World Institute. It didn't take a genius to see that his actions were designed to achieve what was best for Roger Landers, period.

"How can you say that? Give them free reign, and they control the world's currency. The Euro was only the start. They're working on a common Asian currency. After that it's North America. Governments won't be able to have much control."

"What's wrong with a common currency?" Kat poked at the snow with her ski pole. "There's less foreign exchange fluctuations, fewer currency conversion costs. It benefits the consumer."

"That sounds about right in theory. But it also means fewer people control the currency. Instead of dozens of countries and their central banks, thousands of traders and speculators, it's reduced to a few."

"And that's bad?"

"It is when it's the World Institute. It's the same men who control world trade, the global media, and—"

Kat interrupted. "I don't care. Why didn't you defend me against Nathan and Victoria? You're working with them, aren't you?"

"Absolutely not. I had to cooperate, or they'd make sure I never worked again. And they promised they wouldn't harm you."

Kat couldn't imagine either Nathan or Victoria uttering such a statement. Did Landers really expect her to believe that? She stabbed her pole into a snow bank. "What about Jace?"

"I already told you. The police took him away."

"Why Jace and not you?"

"It was all part of our plan. Once we knew we had been

discovered, Jace would take the fall, leaving me to expose the conspiracy."

Kat tried to recall the bed in the adjoining room. When Nathan had pushed her down onto the bed, it had been made and unwrinkled. Landers had to be lying. She wanted him to be lying. The alternative—Jace abandoning her for a story—was unthinkable. He would never do that. Not even for a blockbuster story. Would he?

"I don't believe you. Stop feeding me all this World Institute crap and tell me what really happened to Jace. You were in the room. How did Nathan know you were both there? What did you tell him?" Kat pulled her pole out of the hard-packed snow and turned to go.

Landers followed. "Nothing—I swear."

"I don't believe you." Landers, like most people, had a price. She just didn't know what it was yet. Why would Jace volunteer himself like that? Kat motioned him forward. If she had to hike with him, she'd make sure it wasn't easy. "Tell me what happened in that room."

"I never said a word. Nathan just barged in." Landers slowed and fiddled with his gloves, removing them. "It's warmer than I thought."

Kat stared at his bare hands but decided not to say anything. Frostbite might teach him a lesson.

"Nathan had a pass key. Two RCMP officers were with him."

"Police? Why?"

"I guess because of his room break-in. I don't know for sure—they wouldn't say."

Kat detected a catch in his voice. "Police don't show up at random. Someone called them." Why take Jace but leave Landers?

"Well, it wasn't me. I don't know how—but they knew Jace's name." Landers clenched and unclenched his hands, then put his gloves back on.

A lie, Kat thought. Jace hadn't been asked for identification. Other than the front desk staff and Angelika, the housekeeper, no one else at the hotel had even seen Jace. And besides Kat, only Roger Landers knew his real name. The resort only had the name of the audiovisual company. "Why didn't anything happen to you? You were in the room too."

"Jace told them I wasn't involved. That left one of us free to expose the conspiracy."

Or profit from it. Landers couldn't let Jace's story to break before he finished his book. Jace was his competition. How far would Roger Landers go to protect his story? Would he kill for it?

"We need to get moving again." She couldn't waste any more time and decided Landers didn't deserve a rest either.

Kat pointed to the right trail fork with her ski pole. "I don't believe you. Nathan wouldn't know where to find Jace in the first place. Or have any reason to go after him. Unless you told him." Only hotel staff knew which rooms were occupied, and they were prohibited from disclosing guest information.

Landers sighed and followed her. "You think I'm paranoid? You should hear yourself. Why would I be working with them? I'm on the same side as you."

Kat said nothing but picked up the pace. She could lose him if she wanted to. He was out of shape, and wouldn't last long picking up his feet in this heavy, untracked snow.

"Okay, fine. It was a ploy to lure Nathan. I pretended to co-operate in order to corner him. He promised me a story if I proved someone had infiltrated the World Institute and knew their agenda. Of course Jace was in on it too." Landers's breathing grew heavier as he struggled to keep up.

"Really?" Kat's instinct about Landers were right. He was obviously lying. How much had Jace shared with him?

"I've been following Nathan Barron for years. He's very egotistical. When I told him I was doing a story on the world's most powerful men, he agreed to be interviewed."

"What's Jace got to do with all this?"

Landers coughed. "In order to get something, I had to give something. I show how Jace infiltrated the conference, buy

Nathan's trust, and get him to talk about the World Institute. When Nathan admits it exists, it lends credence to our story."

"Jace agreed to this?" Kat fought the urge to impale him with her pole. It was hard to keep talking to him knowing he had betrayed Jace.

"Of course he did. And our plan worked. Nathan was so pissed off about Jace infiltrating the conference that he spilled a few secrets."

"Like what?" The trail took a sharp right into a clearing and the tiny hamlet of Hideaway Bay came into view below. It was less than a kilometer away, but with the numerous trail switchbacks, it would be another twenty minutes before they reached the sleepy town.

"Read the book. Until then, my lips are sealed."

CHAPTER 51

THEY REACHED THE RCMP STATION just after noon. Kat unfastened her snowshoes and stomped her feet, shaking caked snow off her boots and gaiters. She pulled on the door handle and to her relief, the door opened this time. She entered the deserted room with Roger Landers right behind her. A row of chairs on one wall faced an unmanned counter. A radio talk show played from a ghetto blaster that sat at the far end of the counter. Static.

"Hello?" No answer.

The radio commentator blathered something about the world economy.

Kat's ears perked up when she heard Svensson's name mentioned alongside the Nobel prize in economics. Due to Svensson's death, another economist had been awarded the prize. An economist who happened to support a common global currency.

She glanced at Landers who grimaced as he rubbed his hands. He didn't appear to be listening to the radio. Just as well, since she didn't want a reason to talk to him either.

Their argument had deteriorated to the point that they weren't speaking to each other. Kat didn't know what to believe, with Landers changing his story every five minutes. Was Jace's arrest yet another lie?

Landers let out a loud sigh as he plopped down on one of the vinyl chairs lined up against the wall. Kat watched him from the corner of her eye while she stood at the counter. She scanned the counter for a bell but found nothing. Except for the functioning lights and heat, the place seemed deserted. She hadn't expected a welcome party, but after a three-hour hike in the −20-degree cold, she didn't plan to patiently wait either.

A plain wooden door behind the counter led to what Kat assumed was the inner office and whatever else existed behind closed doors at police stations. Maybe a jail cell with Jace in it?

"Hello?" Kat shifted on her tired feet and leaned on the counter. Snow slid off the bottom of her snow pants and melted into puddles on the worn linoleum floor. She glanced back at Landers, who still rubbed his frozen fingers, his face contorted with pain. Condensation formed on the windows above him, the air humid from damp clothes and a heater in overdrive.

She was mad as hell. Mad at Landers for tricking her and then denying it. Mad at Nathan and Victoria. And she wanted to be mad at Jace for chasing the story. But she couldn't. She just wanted him back.

She turned back to the door. She was considering boosting herself over the counter just as the door opened. An overweight officer emerged.

"Can I help you?" His labored breathing was evident as he lowered himself into a worn vinyl chair. The bottom two buttons of his uniform strained against a pot belly bursting to escape.

"I'm here to see Jace Burton."

"Who'd you say?" His face flushed as he rubbed a hand

across his forehead. He wiped his hand on his shirt before reaching under the counter to pull out a worn manila folder. He opened it and flipped back a quarter-inch of pages before settling back in his chair.

"Jace Burton. He was arrested at the Tides Resort."

"Jason Burton?" He peered over his reading glasses. "No one here by that name. What makes you think he's here?"

Kat read the name on his uniform. *Officer Kravitz.*

The same officer from Roger Landers's TV interview.

"Jace Burton—you arrested him. A couple of nights ago. I'm told you're holding him here."

"News to me," Kravitz said. "If I arrested someone, I'd know it."

"Maybe another officer did."

Kravitz scoffed. "Not likely. No one here but me."

"Roger, tell them what you told me." Kat turned to face Landers, but the bank of vinyl chairs was empty. All that remained were Kurt's snowshoes in a puddle of smelted snow on the floor. "That guy that was just here—he said he was there when you arrested Jace."

"I don't see anyone."

"Officer? How could you miss him? He was just sitting over there. Seconds ago." Kat pointed to the bank of chairs.

"No one here but you 'n me. What did you say your name was?"

Officer Kravitz turned up the radio volume. The news had been replaced by a talk show host, droning on about consumer debt.

Kat moved closer to Officer Kravitz and raised her voice. "Katerina Carter. Officer Kravitz, Roger Landers was just here. He's a journalist with the..." Her voice trailed off when she realized the officer wasn't listening.

Kravitz dropped the file he had been carrying under his arm and placed it on the desk. He pulled out a notebook from his shirt pocket and flipped it open. He scribbled something in it, studiously avoiding Kat.

"Excuse me, Officer Kravitz."

"Carry on, I'm listening." He opened his file folder and licked his finger each time he turned a page.

"No, you're not. You're waiting for me to finish talking so I'll leave. Except I'm not going anywhere. Jace has to be here. I want proof he's not." The clock above Kravitz's head read twelve-forty-five. Twenty-five minutes till the ferry sailed.

"Are you the same Ms. Carter that reported another missing person a few days ago?" He looked up and raised his eyebrows. Then he flipped through the folder again. "Says here it was Roger Landers. Now you've lost him again and lost another guy?"

"I'm here about Jace. Is he here or not?"

Kravitz smiled. "The RCMP isn't in the habit of verifying who they have or don't have in custody."

Kat crossed her arms and smiled back, barely containing her anger. "Then I'll just wait here until you do." What did small town police do anyways? Crossword puzzles? What was Kravitz so anxious to get back to?

"Fine."

She headed over to the row of plastic chairs and dumped her stuff. She made as much noise as she could, hoping to annoy him.

It worked. Kravitz glared at her.

"You still here?" He turned down the radio.

"I told you, I'm not leaving without some answers."

He pursed his lips but didn't say anything.

Kat met his stare. "I know you've got Jace here. Roger Landers saw you arrest Jace. You brought him here. Where else could he be?"

His face reddened. "He's not here and never was."

"Prove it. This is the second time I've been here. I'm not leaving until I know for sure Jace isn't here."

The phone rang. Officer Kravitz answered on the first ring. He held his hand up as he lifted the receiver.

Kat strained to hear. Something about an accident and

highway closure.

"How soon can they get him out of there?" Long pause as Officer Kravitz listened to whoever was talking on the other end of the call. "When? Okay, I'll meet them here."

He listened.

"Got it. I'll do a press release at five. That should give you enough time."

What could possibly require a press release in this little dinky little town? Shoplifting at the general store? Stolen skis?

The press release had to be related to the World Institute. What were the odds of another newsworthy event in this place?

Officer Kravitz glared at her as he replaced the handset. "You still here?"

"I told you, I'm not leaving." All roads pointed back to this place.

On the other hand, she'd be better off at home. If there were an emergency involving Jace, someone would call home to tell her. Especially since she had left her cell phone behind at the resort.

"If I show you, will you stop? No one's in custody. Matter of fact, no one's even been in here for weeks." He motioned her towards the swinging gate adjacent to the counter. Somehow that phone call had changed things.

She stepped through the gate and followed Kravitz behind the counter. There was one large room on the other side, with another door to a lone holding cell. It was empty.

"Believe me now?" He stood by open door, arms crossed.

Kat stared at the empty cell, crushed. She had been so certain Jace was here that she hadn't considered any alternative. "When did you release him?"

Officer Kravitz threw up his hands. "Don't you listen? He's not here. Never was. I don't know anything about a—what did you say his name was?"

"Jace Burton. And I want to file a missing persons report."

"Fine. Then will you leave?"

Kat didn't answer as she followed him back to the

outer office.

Someone was lying, either Landers or the RCMP. She didn't know which, but there was one thing she was sure of. Roger Landers was somehow involved in Jace's disappearance. He simply he had too much skin in the game.

CHAPTER 52

KAT LEANED AGAINST HER FRONT door and pushed it closed. Outside the wind gusted and rattled the ancient single-paned windows. She kicked off her boots and dropped her gear in the hallway, exhausted. She'd barely made it onto the last Wednesday ferry, and her stomach still churned from the choppy crossing. The remaining sailings had been cancelled for the night, and she wondered what had become of Landers. She hadn't spotted him onboard.

She dropped her keys on the hall table and flipped the light switch on. She glanced beside the door, hoping to see Jace's shoes or some sign of his presence.

Nothing.

The hall chandelier illuminated the empty spot on the fire-damaged fir floor and erased any hope of finding him home. Her heart skipped a beat when she spotted Jace's sweatshirt hanging on the carved mahogany banister. Then she remembered. It was in exactly the same place when they'd left for Hideaway Bay. A stark reminder that nothing had changed.

The old house creaked as the wind blasted outside. She headed for the bedroom and grabbed the first warm clothes she could find. She glanced out the bedroom room window as she changed into fleece and slippers. Dusk had already descended, and the wind whipped leaves up into a cyclone funnel. She was glad to be inside, finally warm and dry.

Kat padded downstairs to the kitchen and realized she hadn't eaten since breakfast. She opened the fridge and peered inside, but the sight of food only made her nauseous. She closed the door without taking anything.

She headed back upstairs to the study and powered on the computer. Jace's disappearance was somehow connected to Roger Landers. She just needed to figure out exactly how.

One thing was certain. Landers wanted Jace out of the way because he was competition. But was there another reason? Maybe Roger Landers wasn't a story hunter at all. Maybe he was part of the story, or part of the cover-up.

Kat searched for everything she could find on Roger Landers. Other than his book from a few years ago, there wasn't much. If he really were writing an exposé, she would have expected at least a few more articles. But there were none.

She was so absorbed in her search that she hadn't noticed the house grow dark. She switched on the desk lamp, noticing it flicker as the wind howled outside. She wondered about Harry. Storms made him nervous, and he would be worried about his house. She dialed Harry's cell phone, but got no answer.

Hillary had surely tired of him by now, and would want to dump him off. Would she leave him alone somewhere? She called his house. Also no answer, and she didn't even have Hillary's cell phone number. She replaced the handset, torn between waiting for news about Jace or venturing back outside to Harry's house. Finally she decided to stay put. She might miss either of them if they came by the house while she was out.

The lights flickered again, the power interruption a few seconds longer this time.

Officer Kravitz had finally relented and filed a missing person report on Jace. Just a formality really, since he wasn't convinced Jace was actually missing. He probably wouldn't make any effort to search for Jace.

Was Kravitz, as Roger Landers claimed, even involved in Jace's arrest? Kat didn't know what to believe any more, or who to trust. She needed Jace's story to provide some evidence. That wouldn't happen unless she found Jace.

Kat worked on the Edgewater report for an hour, but couldn't concentrate. It was a downward spiral, she thought as she struggled to keep her eyes open. The computer's glare, her dry eyes, and sheer exhaustion were taking their toll. She was sick and tired of Hideaway Bay, the World Institute, and Edgewater Investments. She had her own problems to deal with.

All she wanted was Jace back home, Harry safe.

Of course that was stupid. The world, along with her need to earn a living, wouldn't stop just because she wanted them to. The sooner she finished Zachary's report, the sooner she could devote all her energies to finding Jace and Harry. She was so close—all she had to do was update the Edgewater report to include the weekend's findings and attach the World Institute agenda, proof of Nathan's involvement. That gave Zachary enough proof to prosecute Nathan for the fraud even if some of the key documents were gone. Ultimately it was his decision to report it immediately or hold off.

But something still gnawed at her.

Zachary. On the one hand, he called Nathan unethical, yet he did the same thing—capitalizing on others for his own personal gain. Like everyone else, he was out for his own piece of the pie. At any cost.

Her eyelids grew heavy and she fought to keep them open. She had to finish the report tonight if she wanted to deliver it to Zachary in the morning.

Wind blasted against the study windows and the lights flickered before going out completely. The desktop computer died too. Kat cursed under her breath when she realized she hadn't saved the latest version of her report. It would be at least morning before the power was restored. She might as well grab a few hours of sleep.

Kat felt her way along the hallway to her bedroom and collapsed on the bed without getting undressed. She drifted into a slumber, dreaming of Jace. This time she found him at Kurt's cabin, but each time she got closer, someone came between them.

CHAPTER 53

K AT JERKED AWAKE. SOMEONE POUNDED on the front
door downstairs. A car gunned its engine and
tires squealed into the distance. Then breaking
glass. Another firebomb? Or even worse, someone
trying to get inside?

She tripped over the steps to reach the front hallway. She
skidded on the hall rug at the same time the glass shattered.
Wind gusted through the front door's broken window panel.
She spotted the broken glass on the wood floor the same
instant something pierced her foot.

"Ouch!" Kat shifted her weight, but that only made the
glass dig in further. She lifted her foot and felt the bottom.
A shard of glass stuck out of the fleshy part of the ball.
She pulled it out. Something sticky oozed out and dripped
onto her other leg. Blood. She held her hand underneath to
prevent it from falling onto the hall area rug. "Ouch! What
the hell—?"

She grabbed the only thing close—Jace's sweatshirt—
to staunch the flow. As she wrapped it around her foot,

she spotted the cordless phone on the hall floor rug. The projectile that broke the glass. Relief washed over her—it wasn't a firebomb.

It was still dark outside, so she couldn't have slept for more than a few hours. Was the power was still out? Should she call the police? Her instincts kicked in before her common sense did. She turned the door handle and swung open the door, hoping to catch whoever did this before they got away.

She didn't have to look far. Uncle Harry stood in front of her, alone on the verandah in the middle of the winter storm. "Uncle Harry? What are you doing here?"

"That's some welcome, Kat. Geesh." He rubbed his hands together and shivered.

"Sorry, Uncle Harry. I—I'm just surprised to see you here. Where's Hillary?" The squealing tires must have been from Hillary's Porsche.

Kat rubbed the sleep from her eyes. What if she had missed the ferry and wasn't here to answer the door? Harry wouldn't have known what to do. He couldn't find his way home, and he would be stuck outside, all alone.

"I don't see Hillary here, do you?" Harry waved his hand. "Now, can I come in?"

"Of course." Kat ushered him inside. "I am really glad to see you—you just surprised me, that's all."

Harry's dementia had dramatically worsened in just a few days. Was it the stress of seeing Hillary again? The doctor had cautioned against significant changes. Hillary definitely counted as a significant change.

"Guess you didn't hear me knock. What were you doing?" Harry's teeth chattered as he stopped in the hall.

"Just working upstairs." Kat shut the door behind him. No point in telling Harry how late it was. "Did someone drive you here?"

Uncle Harry wore a light cotton windbreaker, cotton pants, and no gloves, attire suited more to late spring than to December in Vancouver. Despite the sub-zero temperature and freezing rain, his non-waterproof clothing was almost dry. Anything more than a dash from the curb would have soaked through.

"Nah. I just walked over. What are you and Jace doing for dinner? I thought we could go out." Harry stepped out of his shoes and hung his coat in the hall armoire.

Kat's shoulders slumped. She needed coffee to wake up. "Uh, that would be nice but—Jace isn't home right now. How 'bout I fix you something?" She studied her uncle. Harry's face was ashen. "Are you feeling okay? You don't look right."

"I'm fine. What happened to your foot?"

"It's nothing. Just stepped on that broken glass." She pointed at the mess that littered the middle of the entryway.

"That's no good. If you cleaned it up, you wouldn't have cut yourself."

"I know, Uncle Harry." Kat sighed as she followed behind him, carefully avoiding the glass. How could he not remember breaking the window less than five minutes ago?

"You sure Hillary didn't drive you here? You were with her, remember?" *Remember* slipped out before she could catch herself, but Harry seemed not to notice.

"Nope. Haven't seen her in ages." Harry wiped his brow. "Want to go out for a bite?"

"Uh, why don't I make you a sandwich instead? Come sit down while I get cleaned up." She guided him into the kitchen, ensuring he stepped around the broken glass.

"Okay." Harry shuffled over to the kitchen table and sat down.

Kat limped upstairs to the bathroom, trying to avoid dripping blood on the carpet. She held her foot across her knee as she rifled through the bathroom first-aid kit. The glass had worked its way in during her climb upstairs, despite her best efforts not to step on it. She studied the gash on the bottom of her foot. It was close to three inches long. She winced as she worked the tweezers to remove the shard.

It was hard to see with all the blood, but she finally

extracted an inch-long glass splinter.

Fifteen minutes later, after cleaning and bandaging her foot, she hobbled downstairs into the kitchen.

Harry stood. "You're limping—what happened?"

"It's nothing. Uncle Harry, why didn't you just knock?" Kat dragged her bandaged foot over to the fridge and pulled out cheese and a tomato.

"I did, but you didn't answer. Then I got worried something was wrong. Sorry about the window."

"It's okay." Alzheimer's in itself was puzzling. Sometimes Harry remembered nothing from a few minutes ago, yet with the same question a few minutes later he would recall everything. She sliced the cheese and tomato and layered it on two slices of whole wheat bread.

"You really walked here? All the way from your house?" Her foot was throbbing now, and she found it hard to concentrate on anything else. Crimson splotches of crimson seeped through the layers of white bandage.

"That's what I said, Kat. Did you forget already?" Harry stood and paced back and forth.

"Sorry. I'm tired and not thinking right. You really don't know where Hillary is?" Hillary must have brought him here since she couldn't return him to his house after emptying it out and putting it up for sale. Regardless of Harry's mental state, he would definitely notice all his stuff gone.

"Hillary? She's at work." Harry clutched the counter. "I need to sit down. The room is spinning and I feel sick."

Kat helped him back to the kitchen table. What she had taken for raindrops on Harry's forehead were actually beads of sweat. She felt his forehead. It was warm, despite his shivering. "You feel hot. Are you feeling okay?"

"I'm okay." Harry exhaled and collapsed into the chair.

"You sure?" She poured a glass of water and handed it to him, noticing his forehead had a bluish tinge to it. "You don't look very good. Maybe a sandwich will make you feel better."

"That would be nice—I'm starving. A cheese and

tomato sandwich?"

"I think I can do that. You just relax." She needed to find a caretaker pronto. She cut Harry's sandwich in half and brought it over to the table, setting it down in front of him. The thick bandage on her foot was now completely soaked through. She still felt glass embedded in her foot whenever she put weight on it.

Harry took a couple of bites of the sandwich, then put it down. He pushed the plate away. "I can't eat right now, Kat. Can't even look at it."

"But you said you were hungry."

"No, I didn't. How could I be hungry? I just ate dinner."

Kat sighed. That's how it was with dementia. One minute he was hungry, the next not. There was no point in reasoning with him. "Okay, let's go."

"Go where?"

"Just for a ride." The makeshift bandage wasn't enough to staunch the bleeding. She needed stitches. Not only that, but she'd have to drive herself to the hospital. At least it wasn't her driving foot.

As she grabbed Jace's truck keys off the hall table, her eyes locked on Harry's cordless phone. The projectile used to break the glass still sat in the middle of the entryway. How the phone escaped Hillary's housecleaning was a mystery, unless Harry had kept it in his pocket. At any rate, it was useless without its base station. Kat picked it up and deposited it on the hall table. She'd repair the window in the morning. She thought about securing it, but didn't have the energy to even search for duct tape. Not that it mattered. There was nothing in this house she couldn't afford to lose. Everything she treasured was gone—Jace, the old Harry before the dementia took hold, and most of all, any semblance of hope. She was simply too exhausted to fight anymore.

CHAPTER 54

KAT CRANED HER NECK TO watch the wall-mounted television in the Emergency waiting room. Like the stained fabric chairs, it was bolted down. Apparently without ergonomic considerations in mind, since it angled awkwardly, almost at ceiling height. How many emergency patients had carted off televisions or furniture to warrant such a decision?

Uncle Harry stared blankly off into space, oblivious to the background noise of screaming babies, late night drunks, and the general din of the overcrowded waiting room.

Kat strained her ears to hear the all-news channel above the noisy chatter. Type scrolled across the bottom of the television screen, and the updates sidebar flashed on the right. On what remained of the screen, a reporter stood in front of the Tides Resort at Hideaway Bay.

"Uncle Harry—we were just there!" Kat pointed as the camera panned out from the reporter, a petite blonde wearing a Gore-tex jacket with the television station logo. As the camera angle widened, a man came into view. It was

Roger Landers, wearing the same clothes as yesterday. It was still light out. It must have been filmed sometime after he disappeared from the police station.

"Huh?" Harry jerked his head.

"The TV. Look." Kat pointed to the monitor.

"Look at what?"

"Never mind." Kat rose and limped over to the television so she could hear better.

"I saw Svensson leave the resort unprepared—that's when I suspected the worst." Roger Landers gestured behind him with one hand and he held up a copy of his book with the other.

"What?" Kat blurted.

A couple of women seated opposite them gave Kat withering stares.

Liar. Roger Landers wasn't even at Hideaway Bay when Svensson disappeared. He couldn't have possibly seen Svensson leave on his fateful hike, since he had arrived on the same ferry as Kat. Svensson was already dead by then.

The reporter prompted him. "That's when you raised the alarm? That it wasn't a suicide."

"That's right. Lots of people wanted Fredrick Svensson dead. His views on currency reform were very controversial."

The camera zoomed in on the reporter facing the camera. "Fredrick Svensson was a Nobel nominee. His research on currency and monetary policy was revolutionary and the basis for the current discussions on currency reform. He had proposed one common global currency throughout his thirty-year career, then suddenly reversed his opinion. In a note written shortly before his death."

The screen switched to Svensson's speech in Stockholm. Again Kat saw the woman standing behind Svensson. This time she was absolutely sure. It was Angelika, the housekeeper at the Tides Resort.

Kat still puzzled over Angelika's housekeeper disguise. If they were lovers as Kat assumed, it explained Angelika's presence at Hideaway Bay. Was she involved in Svensson's murder? Could she be the woman who was seen with him the day he disappeared?

Did Angelika have some unfinished business at Hideaway Bay?

Kat realized something else. Why Landers had run from her on the ferry to Hideaway Bay. Being spotted on the ferry would discredit his chain of events. Landers couldn't claim to have seen Svensson if he wasn't there. According to the police, Landers was the only witness besides the unknown woman who could pinpoint the time of Svensson's disappearance. That left the timing of his disappearance suspect. What if he had actually disappeared much earlier?

Kat limped back to the chairs, suddenly aware of her throbbing foot again. She propped it up on the table in front of her, ignoring dirty looks from a middle-aged man across from her.

Landers was trying to set up a story. Was it sequenced to coincide nicely with what he postulated in his book? Or was it something more?

The reporter held her microphone in front of Roger Landers as the camera panned out.

"His abrupt change of opinion was a shock to everyone," Landers said. "After all, he was now dispelling his theory on currency reform. The basis for his Nobel nomination."

"Do the police have any new leads on Svensson's murder?"

It struck Kat as odd that these questions were directed at Landers and not the police. Surely the police of such a small detachment would want to appear on camera. Svensson's murder was the biggest thing to happen in Hideaway Bay for decades, maybe even ever. So where was Officer Kravitz?

"There is one lead in particular," Landers said. "Another man disappeared around the same time Svensson did."

Landers hadn't mentioned this in their hotel room.

Kat glanced over at Harry. He had dozed off, his head slumped into his chest.

"And who might that be?" The reporter appeared to be coaching Landers, as if she knew the answer.

"Jace Burton. He's a search and rescue volunteer familiar with the area. He recently lost his job and may have been distraught. He knows all the dangerous areas, including the cornice where Svensson fell. Or was pushed." The screen flashed a picture of Jace on the screen.

Kat's mouth dropped open. Landers was framing Jace? Landers knew Jace hadn't been on that trail. Would he go that far for a story? Was that what brought Landers to Kurt's cabin? To plant evidence?

If anything, Landers was the criminal, breaking into Kurt's cabin. Was he involved in Svensson's disappearance, or just covering up for someone else? Like Nathan Barron?

Jace was right.

Nothing mattered until it happened to you. Then it was always worth fighting for. Kat just hoped it wasn't too late.

CHAPTER 55

"K AT? THE NURSE IS CALLING you." Harry pointed at the heavyset nurse waiting in front of the double swinging doors. Her floral-print uniform accentuated rolls of fat straining to escape around her waist. She shifted her weight from one foot to the other, looking tired.

Kat couldn't believe she had dozed off in the waiting room. Sleep deprivation and the stress of running back and forth to Hideaway Bay were taking its toll. She rose and followed the nurse, motioning for Harry to follow.

He shuffled stiffly beside her. Even with her limp, she had to slow down for him.

The nurse arched her brows and regarded Harry.

"He's coming in with me," Kat said. She wasn't leaving him in any more waiting rooms.

The nurse met her eyes and nodded after a quick glance at Harry. She led them to a large ward with beds lined up against each wall. Curtains partitioned each bed but provided only an illusion of privacy. Voices rose and fell in tone and volume, and Kat's ears picked up several conversation threads as she hobbled by the adjoining beds.

The nurse stopped halfway down the ward and motioned for Kat to lie down. She propped up Kat's injured leg with pillows and unwrapped the bandages. Harry sat on the plastic chair beside the bed and stared off into space.

Minutes later the doctor appeared. He was thirty-something, thin, with pasty skin and a receding hairline. Kat recounted the accident as he unraveled her bandage and examined her foot.

The doctor held up a shard of glass in his tweezers. "Here's the problem. You still had a piece of glass in there. You'll need stitches and a Tetanus shot." He smiled and scribbled something on a notepad. "Wear shoes next time."

He whirled around on his stool and dropped his tweezers on a tray beside him. He turned back but stopped at Harry this time. "You're not looking so good. Are you feeling okay?"

Harry's face was flushed, and he was sweating despite the coolness in the big room.

"Yup." Harry wiped his brow. "My stomach's just a bit upset."

Dr. X grabbed a tongue depressor from his tray and rolled his stool over to Harry. "Open your mouth, please."

Harry complied.

"When was the last time you ate?"

"Uh, not for awhile. I haven't eaten all day."

Kat interrupted. "Actually, he ate about an hour and a half ago. A bite of a cheese and tomato sandwich." She pulled herself up in bed and smiled at the doctor. "He forgets sometimes."

Harry stared straight ahead, concentration evident as the doctor prodded with the tongue depressor.

The doctor turned to Kat. His face was a mask, the friendly banter gone. "I'd like to admit him, run some tests. It might be the flu, or something more serious. We'll need to keep him overnight."

Harry's ears perked up. "I'm not staying here overnight. I need to go home."

"You're not well, Mr. Denton. It's not advisable for you to go home."

"Well, in that case..." Harry's shoulders slumped. "I can't go home if it's not safe."

"We just need to rule out anything serious, Mr. Denton."

"Okay, doc." Harry shrugged and looked at Kat.

She nodded in agreement.

The doctor patted Harry on the shoulder and exited, avoiding Kat's gaze.

"Don't worry, Uncle Harry. I'll check your house, make sure everything's locked up. I'll be back in the morning to take you home." Harry did look ill. Even considering the dementia, he'd been acting strangely. It would be good for him to get checked out. It also solved another problem: she couldn't exactly take Harry to see his empty house. Maybe she could even track Hillary down and confront her about the house.

"You sure, Kat? You don't mind?"

"Of course I don't mind. And the hospital is the best place to be if you're not feeling well. They'll take good care of you."

The heavyset nurse reappeared and motioned to Harry. "Follow me, Mr. Denton."

Harry turned to Kat, uncertain. "Okay, Kat. I guess I'll stay."

"Okay, Uncle Harry. See you soon." Kat gave Harry a hug and the nurse led him away. But it wasn't okay. Harry was sick, all his possessions gone, and his finances had spiraled out of control. Jace was missing and a murder suspect— at least in Landers' eyes. What could she do? Their lives were shattering into pieces, so fast she couldn't pick them up anymore.

CHAPTER 56

KAT EXITED THE ELEVATOR ON the tenth floor Thursday morning, more relaxed despite only a few hours of uninterrupted sleep. Her foot felt much better, and she'd managed to board up the broken window. It had even stopped raining. She had come straight back to the hospital, having decided not to revisit Harry's house until she talked to Hillary.

She followed the signs to the Elder Care ward. She spotted Harry in a chair by the nurses' station, busily chatting with two nurses. She smiled as she headed towards them. Already Uncle Harry appeared much better, and his pallor had returned to normal.

"Uncle Harry? I'm back."

Harry turned and broke into a wide grin as he saw her. "What are you doing here, Kat?"

"I came to visit you. How are you feeling?"

"I'm fine." Harry lowered his voice. "Can't you see I'm working? I can't talk right now."

"You're in the hospital, Uncle Harry."

"The hospital? Don't be silly." Harry motioned to a row of chairs across the hall. "Just wait over there, and I'll talk to you on my coffee break."

The two nurses studied Kat, but their expressions remained unchanged. The older one said something to the second nurse, then rose and marched over to intercept Kat. "Dr. Konig would like to speak with you. Wait here, please."

"Okay." Kat walked towards Harry's chair just as a slim redhead sped around the corner, almost colliding with Kat and the nurse.

"Uh—Dr. Konig, this is Harry Denton's niece. She brought him in last night." The nurse returned to the nurses' station, leaving Kat face to face with the doctor.

The doctor nodded and studied Kat. She didn't say anything.

Kat held out her hand, but the doctor ignored it and crossed her arms instead.

"We have the preliminary test results back on your uncle." The doctor's eyes bored into hers, watching for a reaction.

"It's still the flu, isn't it?" Kat shifted her weight off her sore foot. "He was battling it a couple weeks back, although he seemed to be coming out of it."

"Not quite. He's been poisoned."

Kat almost fell backwards. "Poisoned? That's impossible. Are you sure?"

"Yes, I'm sure." The doctor nodded, her mouth set into a thin, hard line. "That's what the tests show. Harry said he lives alone—is that true?"

"He does—but I don't understand. I make all his meals. We usually have breakfast and lunch together. He comes to work with me every day and stays at our house for dinner. Usually, that is. I've been away for a few days."

"You haven't seen him for a few days? I thought you took care of him?" She snorted. "Just how often do you see him?"

Kat didn't like the tone in the doctor's voice. "Like I said— every day. But I was away for work the past few days. It couldn't be helped. But we eat the same food. Shouldn't I be sick too?"

The doctor scrutinized her. "In theory."

Kat felt uncomfortable with the way Dr. Konig was staring at her. "You can't possibly think that I—No!" Kat stepped back. "You think I poisoned him? That's crazy."

"It doesn't matter what I think, Ms. Carter. I've given my medical assessment to the health authorities. They'll determine the next course of action."

"What do you mean, the next course of action?"

Dr. Konig glared at Kat and handed her a business card. "Here's the number. A social worker will call you in the next few days. In the meantime, I hope you'll understand that we can't release your uncle to you. Furthermore, all your visits will be supervised."

Kat glanced at Harry. A security guard had materialized twenty or so feet away, near the entrance. His eyes met Kat's before he averted his gaze.

"Supervised?" Kat's voice cracked. "That doesn't make any sense. You don't think that I—I poisoned him?"

Dr. Konig pursed her lips but said nothing.

"I would never hurt my uncle. There must be a mistake."

"I've got to take precautions. Now if you'll please excuse me." Dr. Konig turned and strode away. Kat's eyes followed her as she retreated down the hall.

"You don't understand. I didn't do anything." Kat followed after Dr. Konig. She stopped when she noticed the security guard approach. She swallowed the lump in her throat. She felt like a criminal. She yelled after the doctor. "Can't you check the lab tests again? There must be a mix-up."

But the doctor kept walking. She disappeared around a corner at the end of the hall.

Kat shuddered. If Harry really was poisoned and she didn't do it...that left only one other person with twenty-four-hour access to Harry. Hillary. But even she wouldn't go that far. Would she?

"Kat?" Harry's voice increased in pitch, agitated. "Take me home."

The security guard stopped and studied his feet, again avoiding eye contact. He stood near the nurses' station, only a few feet from Harry. Probably waiting for her to leave.

"I can't, Uncle Harry." Kat's face flushed as she fought back tears. This was not how things were supposed to be. One by one, everyone she cared about was stolen away. She stared down at the card Dr. Konig had given her. The words blurred through her tears; some community health organization with a long name. Why would they believe her? She turned on her heels to leave, feeling ashamed, though she really didn't know why.

"What do you mean, you can't?" His face reddened. "Don't leave me here, Kat. You have to get me out of here."

"I'm sorry. I'll be back as soon as I can." Kat turned away, choked with emotion. Harry wouldn't understand.

She stopped in her tracks and blinked, sure she was seeing things. Except she wasn't.

Hillary strutted down the hall, bracelets jangling. She wore a long tailored black coat and designer boots with four-inch heels. No doubt bought on Harry's credit. Hillary waved in the direction of the nurses' station, then flashed her veneers at Kat. Kat ignored her.

Hillary rushed up to Dr. Konig. She smirked at Kat before disappearing with Dr. Konig into a small office. She shut the door behind her.

It was then Kat remembered the bitter-tasting orange juice in Harry's fridge. She had tasted it the same day she had felt ill. She had just assumed it had spoiled.

Harry drank a couple of glasses of the juice daily; much more than Kat's small sip. How long had it been spiked? She had to get her hands on that orange juice and get it tested. She just hoped she wasn't too late.

CHAPTER 57

KAT SAT ACROSS FROM ZACHARY Barron, preoccupied with Harry's prognosis and Dr. Konig's accusations. And, most of all, the orange juice at Harry's house.

Zachary leaned back in his leather armchair, hands clasped behind his head. "Find the proof yet?"

"Yes and no." Kat related the events in the hotel room with Nathan and Victoria, leaving nothing out. "I don't have the World Institute papers anymore, but it's all documented in my report." She'd quickly restored the lost version after leaving Harry at the hospital. She'd be dammed if she would let Zachary delay reporting Nathan's Ponzi any longer.

"When you get those World Institute documents of Nathan's back, we'll discuss the next steps." Zachary stood to dismiss her.

Kat wasn't leaving. He couldn't use the documents as an excuse to delay the inevitable.

"Zachary, you can't keep pushing this out into the future. You've got enough proof without the World Institute documents—they only add another layer. We both know Edgewater's a Ponzi scheme. You owe it to your investors to report it now."

"I'm not sure *owe* is the right word, Kat. Look at this." Zachary flipped his computer monitor around so Kat could see. "I'm up ten percent since yesterday. Ten percent. I'm trading for my own account, and I'll use all my profits to replenish the fund's losses. Give me another week and the investors will have every penny back, and more. I'll make them whole—like none of this ever happened."

"Something like this can't go unreported." How Zachary could possibly make back billions in less than a week? Even if it was possible, why hadn't he already done that with the fund previously? None of his previous trades even came close to that kind of return. Or, they wouldn't have had if they'd been actually executed. "It's not a game, Zachary."

"Of course it's a game. The whole monetary system is a game. Every country's currency gets manipulated. Surely you're not that naïve? I'll report Nathan's fraud, but only once I've made all the investor money back."

"Zachary, these are real people. With real losses. They deserve to know immediately. Now—not in two weeks."

"You think I don't know that? My investment in the fund is bigger than anyone's."

So that was the reason. Now Zachary's about-face made sense. It was all about self-interest.

Zachary walked around the side of his desk. "Look at it this way. As soon as we expose Nathan, they'll shut down the fund, freeze Edgewater's assets, and the losses will be permanent. Edgewater declares bankruptcy, and the whole mess turns into years of lawsuits and court battles."

Kat shook her head. "You can't be serious."

"Of course I'm serious. I'll get the money back first. Nathan's not going anywhere. He'll still be charged, but at least the investors won't be ruined financially."

"How can you possibly make that much money back in

two weeks?"

"It won't be easy, but it can be done. The whole global financial system is all artificial. My trading. The valuation of each and every country's currency. Even the World Institute's global currency, whatever they decide to peg it at. It's completely removed from the actual value of things, and has been for decades. Look at this." Zachary pulled his wallet from his back pocket and extracted a dollar bill. He dropped it on the desk. "What do you see?"

Kat played along. "A dollar."

"That's what it says on the face of it. But what is a dollar? It's just a promise to pay. A fancy IOU from the government. It's essentially worthless."

"An odd thing for someone like you to say. You trade currency for a living."

"No, what's odd is that we exchange our paper money for items of value in the first place. One upon a time that paper was backed by gold. Not anymore. Before gold, we bartered for things. Maybe gold for food. Something of value was given in exchange for something else. It's different now. This promise isn't worth the paper it's printed on. The paper money printed today exceeds the value of the assets that back it, by a thousand-fold, or more."

"What does this have to do with Edgewater and Nathan's fraud?"

"It's got everything to do with it. Reporting Nathan's fraud means unwinding it. We're talking about a huge sum of money, Kat. So much that it has repercussions far beyond Edgewater and the fund. Money's been leveraged to the point that no one even knows what's behind it—what's going on any more. Any sudden shocks and the whole financial system collapses."

"You're exaggerating. Edgewater's fund is just a fraction of the money in circulation. You can't seriously think it would destabilize the global financial system. That's not going to happen."

"I'm not talking about Edgewater itself, Kat. Look where the stolen money went. To a secretive organization that wants to replace the world's currency. If people get wind of this, they'll lose faith in all their governments, all their monetary systems. They'll cash in all their investments. A run on the banks. There's not enough money in the world to stop it."

"You can't be serious. And don't use this as an excuse to delay the inevitable."

"I'm not. I'm just saying—everything's connected."

"You're telling me the global monetary system is just created out of thin air?"

"Basically. It's a very big poker game. Everyone thinks theirs is a winning hand. As long as that's the case, they hold, and everything's good. The minute they fold we're in trouble. We can't have everyone cashing in their chips at once."

"But Nathan robbed Edgewater. You yourself said you wanted to ruin him."

He said nothing.

At that moment, Kat saw that Zachary wanted exactly the same thing Nathan did—absolute power. He just had a different means of getting it. Nathan wanted to control the monetary system itself. In contrast, Zachary used trading as a means to exploit it. Both had the same end result. Values manipulated for their own personal gain.

"I am going to bring him down. But not at the expense of the markets and my livelihood. I'm getting the money back first. Then I'll report it. Don't shaft Edgewater's investors, Kat. You'll be ruining it for yourself too. For everyone."

"Who's ruining it? Sooner or later they'll have to pay. Waiting just makes the inevitable more painful."

"Nothing's inevitable." Zachary turned the monitor back. "How many Ponzi schemes do you think are going on in the world right now?"

Zachary didn't wait for her answer. "Hundreds? No—thousands. All over the world, big and small. Most will never be uncovered unless and until there's a cash shortage. As long as returns, money supply, and investors keep growing, no one ever knows."

"It's the same with the global monetary system. The assets backing it are a fraction of the paper money circulating. It relies on everyone not cashing in their chips at once. As long as no one panics, enough stays invested and everything works. Money stays in the banks, and investors keep their money in our funds. If that's not a game, I don't know what is. It's dangerous to call a bluff when things aren't in your favor."

"I don't get it, Zachary. What happened to exposing Nathan?"

"He'll get what he deserves. After I recover the losses."

Kat jumped as her cell phone rang. She checked the call display. It was the hospital. She'd deal with Zachary later. "I have to take this."

The woman on the phone sounded in a hurry. "I've got a patient here—demanding to see you. How soon can you get here?"

Uncle Harry must be feeling better. This nurse sounded decidedly more polite than the two from last night. She probably didn't realize Kat had been the one that brought Harry to the hospital. "How is he doing?"

"Not bad. A little incoherent, though. Muttering something about globalization and money."

Odd. Harry usually tuned out her finance discussions. At any rate, she was sure he wouldn't remember them.

"I was planning to visit in a couple of hours," she said. This nurse's demeanor was quite a departure from the supervised visits and suspicious glares. What had changed their minds?

"I'm hoping you can get here sooner, maybe calm him down. He's threatening to leave, and I can't stop him. He really needs medical care."

"It's the dementia," Kat said. "He's easily agitated in unfamiliar places." Kat was surprised that Harry even remembered the World Institute and Nathan Barron, let alone talked about them.

"Dementia? I don't think so. He appears normal to me."

"He seems okay at first, but within a few minutes he'll repeat himself." How could a medical professional miss the signs? Harry would appear confused within minutes of striking up a conversation.

"He hasn't so far. I guarantee you this guy does not have dementia. At any rate, he's far too young."

"Too young?" Uncle Harry could pass for years younger than he was, but he was still a senior. "He's eighty."

The nurse laughed. "Eighty? I don't think so. Are we talking about the same guy? " She didn't wait for Kat to answer. "He doesn't have any identification. Just a cell phone. That's how I got your number. It's programmed into his phone as an emergency contact."

Kat's heart skipped a beat. "Brown hair, blue eyes? Six-three or so?"

"Sounds about right."

He's alive. "His name's Jace. Jace Burton."

CHAPTER 58

KAT RACED TO THE HOSPITAL in record time, despite snarled traffic, a four-car accident, and impossible parking. She parked in a tow-away zone, though she doubted the truck would be there when she returned. Who cared? It was worth it just to be here.

Jace stared up at her from the hospital bed. The right side of his face was covered in bruises, and his eye was swollen shut. "Take me home."

"Who did this to you?" Kat perched on the side of Jace's hospital bed and stroked his forehead. "Nathan Barron?"

Jace winced. "What's Nathan Barron got to do with anything?"

"Hideaway Bay? The hotel room? Don't you remember? You went next door with Roger Landers."

He scratched his head. "All I is remember being in the room with you and Roger Landers. You were mad because he ate everything in our mini-bar. I didn't see Nathan Barron. At least I don't think I did." Jace's brows creased. "How did I get here?"

"I don't know." Kat swallowed the lump in her throat.. "But you've been missing for days. I thought I'd never see you again."

"Days?" He reached for her hand and squeezed it.

"You don't remember going next door?"

"No." Jace shook his head. "It's all a big blank."

Kat filled him in on her altercation with Nathan and Victoria. "The same thing probably happened to you. Do you remember seeing him? Or Victoria Barron?"

"I—I don't know. Something else did happen—I just can't quite pull it from my memory." Jace frowned. "Somebody knocked at the door I think..."

"Try to remember, Jace. You went next door with Roger, taking the World Institute documents and my laptop with you. The laptop was still there when I was there. Do you know what happened to the documents? Did Roger take them? or Nathan Barron?"

Jace scanned the room. "I'm trying—but it just won't come back to me. Where are my clothes?"

Kat stood, feeling a surge of hope. Could the documents be right here in the room? They were the key to linking Nathan Barron to both Research Analytics and the World Institute. The agenda and meeting minutes were particularly incriminating, and a critical piece for Zachary's investigation.

She glanced around but saw none of Jace's personal belongings in the tiny hospital room.

"You were writing a story about the World Institute. You and Landers discussed the global monetary system and the World Institute's plan for a single global currency. You had my laptop and the papers."

And we argued. She hoped Jace didn't remember that part.

"The agenda? You didn't want Landers to have it." Jace tried to lift himself up to a sitting position. He swore and dropped his head back down on the pillow.

Kat held her hand up to stop him. She pressed the button on the side of the bed until the bed slowly elevated Jace to a half-sitting position.

"You do remember! What happened to it?" Kat surveyed the room and noticed several drawers built into the far wall. She moved around the bed and opened them one by one.

"I don't know." Jace yawned and stretched his arms. "I remember the room a little bit, but everything's a blur."

Jace hadn't mentioned his half-written story either. Did he forget that, too? "I've figured out why the *Sentinel* pulled your mortgage fraud story. See this?" Kat showed him the story. "Look at the address—422 Cedar Street."

Jace gave her a blank stare.

"Global Financial's address is 422 Cedar Street."

"I'm not following." Jace grabbed a plastic cup from his bedside tray and sipped through the straw.

"Global Financial, the company you exposed in your mortgage fraud story, has the same address as Beecham, Edgewater's fictitious auditors." Although Jace had researched Beecham, only Kat had actually visited 422 Cedar Street.

"They're connected?" Jace bolted up in bed, spilling water all over his hospital gown. "That's an awful lot of activity for a vacant lot."

"You were right about Pinslett, Jace. I'm still working out the details, but it appears that Global Financial's mortgage fraud was Pinslett's contribution to the World Institute. Just as Nathan Barron diverted money from Edgewater, so did Pinslett. Only Pinslett's funding comes through Global Financial."

"You followed the money and it led you to the crime." Jace brushed the water off with his palm.

Kat nodded. Finding the same address had been a lucky break. Then again, forensic accounting often involved creating your own luck. Searching for patterns in the data often provided clues, in this case a shared address. It was the catalyst that broke the case wide open. "It proves that whoever is behind that mortgage fraud is also connected to the World Institute. Who has the ability and desire to pull a story from the *Sentinel*—and is also connected to the World Institute?"

"Gordon Pinslett." Jace pulled the covers off and swung his legs over the bed. "My story. I've got to get out of here."

"You're not going anywhere, my dear."

Kat stopped her drawer search and turned to the doorway.

A plump nurse bustled in. Her rubber soles squeaked on the linoleum floor as she strode towards the bed. "Now lie back down. The more you relax, the sooner you'll be out of here."

The nurse held up Jace's arm. The same forearm blistered from the fire now sported a six-inch purple bruise on the inside of his elbow crease. Exactly the same location as the one on her arm. A small scab also decorated the top of his forearm. Either sloppy needle work or patient resistance. Probably a bit of both.

"I see you've got yourself a visitor." The nurse nodded at Kat as she walked around the bed and lifted Jace's uninjured arm. She wrapped a blood pressure cuff around it and pumped it up.

"He was incoherent when we picked him up. Didn't even know his own name." The nurse glanced at the monitor and undid the Velcro cuff. "Everything's good, except he's still not a hundred percent with the concussion. His memory will probably come back over the next few days. Hard to know for sure."

Jace protested. "My memory is back. I'm fine now."

The nurse ignored him.

So did Kat. "How did Jace get here? In the hospital, I mean."

"Same way they all come in, honey. By ambulance."

"Do you actually know that? I mean, is it in his chart, or did you see him come in?"

"I wasn't here, but I heard all about it. Didn't you?" The nurse seemed annoyed at Kat's question. "It's been all over the news."

The nurse noticed Kat's pause and gave her a disapproving look.

Kat shook her head. She had been busy getting dumped herself, except that she was lucky enough to wake up on a bench in the Waterfront train station. But explaining that to the nurse would just make her sound like a nutcase.

The nurse's timeline also conflicted with Landers' version of events. The whole jail story was obviously false, and she felt stupid for believing any of Landers's lies. The guy was a pathological liar. She resumed her drawer check.

"I don't even know what happened," Jace said. "I can't remember a thing before waking up here."

The nurse replaced his chart and turned. "You were lying on the side of the highway, unconscious. Police said someone dumped you there. You're lucky you didn't freeze to death. Or get run over." She turned to Kat. "He only woke up an hour ago."

"I sure don't feel very lucky." Jace grimaced and shifted on the bed.

Kat smiled as she opened the bottom drawer. It held Jace's clothing. Kat pulled out a jacket and patted the pockets. Nothing. She refolded them and dropped them on the floor.

"Believe me, you are lucky," the nurse said. "Mild hypothermia, frostbite on three fingers, and a concussion. It could have been a lot worse. You were almost run over."

The nurse turned and left the room, footsteps squeaking across the linoleum floor.

Kat extracted Jace's shirt and searched the pockets. Also nothing. Only his jeans remained. She lifted them out of the drawer and stuck her hand in a back pocket. Tucked into the pocket and folded in four was a copy of the World Institute minutes. The other documents were missing. Landers or Nathan Barron probably had them. Which of the two didn't matter, since they were probably co-conspirators.

"I had a run-in with Nathan and Victoria too." Kat recounted the events. "Landers just stood there and did nothing."

"Your client's ex-wife?"

Kat nodded and realized Jace had never actually seen Victoria. She explained Victoria and Nathan's relationship.

"Now I remember," he said. "She was with Nathan. I didn't know she was Russian."

"Russian?"

"Yeah. Isn't Angelika's accent Russian?"

"Angelika? You mean the housekeeper at the Tides Resort?"

"She's the one who injected me." He rubbed his arm. "She was in the room with Nathan. And Roger." Jace's eyes narrowed. "That traitor."

"Angelika?" Was that why the housekeeper had entered their room so early in the morning? She had been searching for something, or someone.

Jace nodded. "That's what I said."

Svensson and Angelika. Angelika and Nathan. Was Nathan somehow involved in Svensson's murder?

The nurse returned with a paper cup and some pills.

Jace smiled as he swallowed the pills. Whatever the pills contained made him oblivious to the World Institute, the *Sentinel*, and his story.

Kat's pulse quickened. The prepaid credit cards. Nathan had a bunch of them, and one of the same type was in the housekeeper's uniform. A uniform approximately Angelika's size. Was it a form of payment? If so, were there other services rendered?

The nurse interrupted her thoughts. "He's not going anywhere for awhile."

It was the best news Kat had heard in a very long time.

CHAPTER 59

KAT REACHED HARRY'S HOUSE JUST after noon. The front sidewalk remained un-shoveled, in stark contrast to the neatly cleared sidewalks on the rest of the block. She climbed the front stairs and knocked. If there was any chance Hillary hadn't emptied out the fridge, she needed to get ahold of that orange juice—it had to be the source of the poison. But there had to be another explanation. Food poisoning, maybe? She wanted the juice tested and to see if it tied in with Dr. Konig's theory. If the juice was tainted, it meant that she had been poisoned too.

No answer. Kat breathed a sigh of relief. Hopefully Hillary hadn't sold the house to the couple, or to anyone else just yet. It was highly unlikely that the sale would close so quickly, but anything was possible with Hillary. Especially if she was hard-pressed for cash.

Cutting off Hillary's cash supply had been nothing short of disastrous. It brought Hillary back to town, ruined Harry financially, and almost cost him his life. If Kat hadn't cut off Hillary's access to Harry's bank account and credit cards, none of this would have happened. It was all her fault. But choice did she have?

She was anxious to get inside. Instead she knocked again, and forced herself to wait another minute. Still no answer. She leaned against the door and listened for any sign of activity.

Harry's diagnosis of acute poisoning still seemed unreal. Since she and Jace had been together at Hideaway Bay during the time frame of the poisoning, that left Hillary. Why, then, wasn't she a potential suspect? How could she visit Harry unsupervised? Unless she had concocted a story to implicate Kat.

Kat shuddered. Harry was in imminent danger since Hillary still had unrestricted access to him in the hospital. There was simply no other explanation than Hillary for the poison in his system.

Kat peered through the side window as she waited on Harry's front porch. Still no answer, and no sign of activity through the sheer curtains. That was good.

Kat descended the stairs and followed the sidewalk around to the back of the house. The snow was untracked. No one had come or gone since last night.

She peered in the kitchen window. Deserted. Still devoid of furniture as it had been on her last visit. Even the dishes stacked beside the sink were untouched. She turned the key in the lock and went inside.

She headed straight for the refrigerator and grimaced when she remembered the orange juice's acrid aftertaste. It hadn't occurred to her that the juice was anything other than spoiled until the doctor's diagnosis. Both she and Harry became sick shortly after breakfast with orange juice. She had just a sip, which could explain her lesser symptoms. But the nausea after that sip had been unmistakable. Along with the bitter taste. Kat realized that she hadn't mixed Harry's orange juice for several weeks. It had been already prepared, a full jug inside the refrigerator. This despite the fact that Harry hadn't been eating, washing dishes, or even putting away food.

And during that time, Harry had complained of stomach aches, but his doctor had ignored it, focusing on his Alzheimer's diagnosis. Poisoning explained a lot—his pallor, sweating, and general malaise. His symptoms fluctuated, inconsistent with flu symptoms. But would Hillary go so far as to poison Harry? What other explanation was there?

Kat opened the refrigerator. The shelves were empty. Where else could she look?

Kat swore under her breath.

No doubt Hillary had destroyed any evidence after Harry's diagnosis. But the results had only come this morning. The absence of snow tracks meant the bottle must have been disposed of before last night's snowfall.

Kat pulled out her cell phone and called Connor Whitehall. More than anything, she just needed someone to talk to. Someone that would understand. She reached Connor's voicemail instead. She didn't leave a message. Instead, she slumped down the kitchen wall to the floor, and buried her head in her hands.

She was out of ideas, but had to do something. Poisoning seemed far-fetched, yet according to the hospital, it was true. She felt like she was part of a weird reality TV show she never asked to be on.

She could ask another doctor to examine Harry. But even she believed the hospital doctor's diagnosis. Poison made sense. Trouble was, suspecting her meant they weren't looking at anyone else.

Maybe the juice carafe was in the garbage? Kat stood so rapidly that she was dizzy.

After steadying herself, she checked the kitchen garbage. Empty.

She opened the kitchen door and ran down the back stairs. Once in the lane, she pulled off the garbage can lid. Even in the cold, the pungent odor of garbage wafted up and assaulted her. She opened the garage door and grabbed

Harry's gardening gloves from the workbench.

Returning to the garbage can, she began the unpleasant task of sifting through the full can of garbage. She stuck her hand down through the layers, through both saturated paper bags and soiled plastic ones. It wasn't long before a shard of glass dug into her canvas glove.

She lifted the top most layers off the heap and tossed them onto the garbage can lid on the ground. One quarter of the way down was a bunch of broken glass. It was the orange juice carafe, broken.

Now what? Even if she had the container tested, what did it mean? While it could corroborate the doctor's suspicions, it certainly didn't prove her innocence. Worse, it likely incriminated her more, since the hospital had already concluded she was the culprit. At any rate, she figured it was better to preserve it than lose it to the landfill. She retrieved the pieces and dropped them into a container.

She could ask Connor Whitehall what to do next.

Kat felt eyes on her and glanced across the lane to see Mrs. Brantford. Harry's neighbor stood by her open gate, eyeing Kat with a mix of suspicion and curiosity.

Kat waved.

Mrs. Brantford brought her arm up slowly, looking uncertain. She waved slowly, then turned away, closing her gate behind her.

Odd. Mrs. Brantford usually cornered her, eager to talk. But she had no time to spare anyways. She returned to the garage and searched for a container to put the broken glass into. She spied a small cardboard box and reached to pull it down when she saw three Garden Heaven shopping bags on top of the workbench. She was certain they hadn't been there the other day.

She peered inside one of the bags. Two-pound bags of No-Gro pesticide. She pulled out one of the packages and stopped when she saw the skull-and-crossbones poison symbol. Did Harry even use chemicals in his garden? She couldn't remember. In any event, six packages was enough to kill everything on a small farm, let alone a garden on a city lot.

She studied the receipt. The pesticides had been purchased two weeks ago, shortly before closing time. Where was Harry at that time? Did he buy the pesticides? She doubted it. Garden Heaven was a half-hour drive away, and his garage door had already been disabled as of the receipt date. That meant he wouldn't have been able to get the Lincoln out of the garage. The purchase was also made around dinner time, so he would have been with her and Jace at the time it was bought.

She skimmed the label. Just below the poison symbol was the ingredients list, all unfamiliar and unpronounceable chemical names. She hadn't heard of any of them.

She slipped the Garden Heaven receipt into her pocket. Who the hell bought pesticides in December?

CHAPTER 60

Kat FINALLY ARRIVED AT CONNOR Whitehall's office just before five. She brushed past the receptionist and blew straight into Connor's office.

"You have to help me. I'm positive Hillary's trying to poison Harry." She plopped down in the chair opposite his desk and just as quickly stood again.

Connor faced his computer screen. He swiveled around and eyed her. "Well, hello to you too. That's a pretty strong accusation. Are you sure?"

Kat recounted her suspicions about the orange juice and Hillary. "The only problem is—it's gone. The only evidence I've got are these shards of glass." She didn't mention the pesticide because she wanted to be sure before laying an accusation. She'd check out Garden Heaven first. Maybe she could find out who bought it.

She handed him the cardboard box with the broken orange juice carafe. It contained several inch-sized pieces of the glass along with part of the plastic handle. "I think she's trying to kill him."

"You need more proof than this."

"The proof is in the motive, Connor. She's desperate for money and tired of Harry. She wants him out of the way. So she can get whatever's left of his estate."

Connor shook his head. "Not enough. If these pieces of glass were analyzed for fingerprints, what would they show? Probably yours, Harry's, and Hillary's. Exactly who you might expect to be pouring a glass of juice. You need something more substantial to prove Hillary had a hand in this."

"But how? I'm at my wit's end."

"I don't know exactly. But I'm confident you'll find a way. You'll have to. The hospital will likely recommend the police file charges against you."

"Suspicions aren't facts. There's nothing that points to me either."

Connor waved her away. "Harry's around you all the time. You prepare his meals, and by your own accounts, Hillary is never around. Proximity is enough to make you a suspect. Which leads me to the next issue. I'm not a criminal lawyer. Should they go ahead, you'll need a good one to represent you."

"I can't believe this. I'm the only one taking care of Harry—watching out for him. And because of that, I'm accused of poisoning him!" Kat jumped from her chair. "It's not fair!"

Connor motioned her to the chair. "Calm down. You haven't been charged yet. Yes, the medical staff is pursuing that, but it takes more than just their suspicion to actually lay a charge. I'm just preparing you for what might come next."

Kat sat down. "But they're completely overlooking Hillary. Why aren't her visits supervised? Shouldn't they supervise all visits as a precaution?"

"Probably, but no one has given them a reason to do so. And somehow the doctor already suspects you. Did you poison him?" He peered over his glasses at her.

"Of course not!" Kat jumped up, knocking over a glass of water on the edge of the desk. "How could you even say such a thing?"

"I apologize, but I have to ask." Connor stood and grabbed a golf shirt off his coat rack. He sopped up the water with the shirt and dropped it on the floor. "You really need to calm down, Kat. This doesn't help matters."

"Sorry." Connor was right. "And sorry about the water."

He waved her off. "I brought one of the doctors to see Harry today. He certainly seems to be getting better in the hospital."

"That's because Hillary can't poison him while he's there." Kat leaned forward and rested her elbows on the desk. "I know how crazy it sounds. Even I can't believe Harry's been poisoned. But I didn't do it, and whoever did needs to be stopped. Why does the doctor assume it's me?"

"You're the obvious suspect. You brought him to the hospital. You said yourself you're taking care of him. Harry's with you at the office all day and after hours, too. Almost all the time."

"It has to be that way. Harry can't be left alone, Connor. You've seen his condition."

"I know. But you can understand the doctor's suspicions. She has to err on the side of safety where her patient's concerned. Anyways—I did have a chance to talk to Harry about his mental capacity. He insists he's perfectly fine."

"Of course he's going to say that. He can't see what's wrong." Kat felt a lump in her throat. It was all a vicious circle.

"He did agree to a medical assessment, though. To 'prove those doctors wrong,' as he put it. I'll try to have it done before the end of the week."

"He can't wait that long. He's now destitute, Connor. Pretty serious consequences for a family squabble. No one takes financial abuse seriously. Why?" Hillary might not have held up Harry at gunpoint, but she robbed him just the same.

"It's not that they don't, Kat. It's just that the onus of proof is on the victim."

"A victim who can no longer take care of himself? That's so unfair." Kat felt helpless. She couldn't do anything about the house, since Harry hadn't been proven incompetent at the time of the title transfer. The forged signature was a possibility, but charges and a court date were in the distant future. By then Hillary would be long gone.

"Surely the police can do something about this."

"Kat, you said yourself, there's no concrete proof."

Kat threw her arms up in the air. "He lost his house, Connor. His bank account has been emptied and he's got loans he'll never be able to pay. Hillary's now on his house title. She's driving a Porsche and wearing the jewelry he paid for. Look at who's benefitting. How obvious does the motive have to be?"

"I know. But the courts are black and white. You already know this. You need to build a case, with proof that she took the money without his knowledge or consent. Or prove he was unable to give his consent because of his mental incompetence. Don't let emotions cloud your judgment."

"But he doesn't have the capacity to understand what she's doing. She's ruined him."

"That may be. But we can only move forward—after he's been assessed as mentally incompetent."

"So everything to date is lost? His money, his house, everything? I can't believe this. How can the law be so unfair?"

"It might seem unfair. But we can't go back and question his mental incompetence at some point in the past. There was no objective assessment of his condition at that time. No matter how you recall his state of mind. Without a qualified medical doctor's opinion, it's just a matter of opinion." He patted her hand. "I'm sorry. I really am."

Harry's money was gone, and now his health was in jeopardy. What did it take to stop Hillary? If no one was going to help her, she'd do it the hard way. The only way to prove her innocence was to prove Hillary's guilt.

CHAPTER 61

EN MINUTES LATER KAT PULLED into Garden Heaven's gravel parking lot. There were only two other cars in the lot. Who bought plants and gardening supplies in the dead of winter?

The gravel crunched under her feet as she headed for the front door. A wind whipped up and snapped at a torn banner across the front of the store. She unzipped her jacket and went inside.

"Can I help you?"

Business must be slow. The fifty-something woman practically accosted her before she was even inside. She wore a Garden Heaven green golf shirt with the name tag *Rosemary*. She wiped her hands on the thighs of loose-fitting jeans as she smiled at Kat.

Kat smiled back and pulled the sales receipt from her pocket. "Actually, yes. I'm looking for some information."

Rosemary frowned. "I'm afraid this is nonreturnable. It's past our fourteen-day return policy." Her eyes darted to Kat, waiting for a reaction.

"I don't want to return it—I'm just wondering if you're the one who sold it." Kat held out the receipt.

"What difference does that make?" Nevertheless, Rosemary took the receipt. She pulled down the glasses perched on her head and studied it. "Yep, I rang this sale up. I remember that day."

Kat's hopes soared. "You remember the person who bought this?"

"Normally, I don't. But this one I do—it was my anniversary that day. I had closed a bit early. A woman rushed in here—I hadn't locked up yet. I told her we were closed, but she ignored me. She wouldn't leave, so finally I gave up asking her. She was out in five minutes and I hadn't closed my cash yet. So I just rang it up. It was the easiest way to get rid of her."

Kat pulled out a photograph of Hillary. "Is this the woman you saw?"

"Um...could be. Then again, maybe not. I'm not good with faces. Can't say for sure."

"Okay." Kat's shoulders slumped as her hopes faded. She thanked Rosemary and headed for the door. That's when she saw it.

Garden Heaven had a surveillance camera, right above the door. She turned around and pointed to the camera. "Rosemary, is that camera on all the time?"

"Should be. Why?"

"I'm investigating a fraud. Please save the footage—don't erase anything. It might be important for the case."

Rosemary's eyes widened. "What kind of case? A criminal one?"

"Yes." It wasn't exactly a lie. As far as Kat was concerned, Hillary was a criminal. And Rosemary hadn't specifically asked if she was from the police. She wasn't about to elaborate, either. "Someone could be in danger. I don't suppose—no."

"Suppose what?" Rosemary's eyes lit up.

Exactly the spark of interest Kat had hoped for.

Kat tapped her watch. "Well, I'm racing against time and

I've got several leads. If I could just have a quick peek at your video, I can rule this one in or out. But never mind, I don't want to get you in trouble or anything."

Kat let out a heavy sigh, hoping to elicit Rosemary's sympathy. It worked.

"It's no trouble. I'm the owner, so I can do what I want. It's dead slow today. We can access the footage on my computer." She motioned Kat to follow her over to a desk by the florist department.

Less than a minute later they sat in front of Rosemary's computer. Rosemary started a program and within a few mouse clicks they were viewing the film from that day. Another slow day from what Kat could see. Rosemary played it in fast-forward mode. The door opened and closed, and people came and went in rapid motion. Less than a dozen customers so far. Exactly what you'd expect in December.

"Wait. Go back a minute." The latest woman was blurry, but there was something familiar about her. Kat's pulse quickened.

Rosemary slowed the footage to play mode.

The sound on the tape was garbled, but the picture was clear. A woman in black entered the store and strode towards the rear. Rosemary followed her, motioning towards the door and saying something Kat couldn't make out. Probably protesting that the store was closed, no doubt. The woman's back was to the camera, and she wore a long coat. Hillary always wore black.

No one entered or left the store for the next few minutes. Rosemary fast-forwarded the tape until the figure stepped up to the cashier. She pushed a shopping cart filled with bags about the same size and color as the pesticide bags in Harry's garage.

"Now I remember her," Rosemary said. "She was dressed different, you know? Most gardeners don't wear high heels. The occasional one maybe, dropping by on their lunch break or on their way home after work. But this was right before closing. Another thing—absolutely no one buys pesticides in December."

"What's the pesticide used for?"

"It's broad spectrum, meaning it kills anything. But you'd need a serious infestation to use something this strong. It kills absolutely everything it comes in contact with."

Kat shuddered. "Even people?"

Rosemary's mouth dropped open. "Well, it is poison. Did someone die?"

"Almost. Any chance I can have a copy of that tape?"

After an eternity fighting her way back home during rush-hour traffic, Kat sat in her upstairs study, wondering how to link the pesticide to Harry's toxicology report. A report she didn't actually have. A CD copy of Garden Heaven's footage lay on the side of her desk.

Finding Hillary on tape making the purchase had been a huge step forward. It wasn't yet enough to charge Hillary, but it was enough to make her run. Kat wanted to ensure she faced justice for her actions.

She'd visit Connor Whitehall's office in the morning with the footage and to get his advice on the next steps. Was the receipt enough evidence? No way was she going to simply hand it over to the police. After all that had happened in Hideaway Bay, she couldn't blindly trust them without a back-up plan.

Now she turned her attention back to the pesticide itself. One by one, she typed each ingredient listed on the label into the computer. She wanted to rush to the hospital—and the police—with her suspicions, but knew she had to build a case first. Otherwise they'd never believe her.

Even though she had expected it, the words still astonished her:

Contact your poison control center and seek immediate

medical attention if product is ingested, inhaled or contacts skin, eyes, or mucous membranes. May cause blindness.

Ingestion may cause gastrointestinal distress including stomach cramps, nausea, vomiting and stomach cramps, pallor, dizziness, fainting, seizures, mental confusion, delirium or death.

Kat focused on the last word. She was running out of time. So was Harry.

CHAPTER 62

KAT RAN THE TWO BLOCKS to Harry's house in the rain. After the snowplow incident, she'd avoided driving Jace's truck as much as possible. It gave her the creeps after such a targeted attack. She sprinted around the corner, relieved to see that Hillary's black Porsche wasn't parked out front. Neither was Harry's Lincoln, or any other cars for that matter.

She hoped she wasn't too late. She cursed herself for leaving the pesticide at Harry's place. A major misstep, since it was additional potential proof of what had poisoned Harry. What if it was gone? The receipt alone wasn't enough evidence that someone was trying to harm him. Leaving the pesticide at Harry's also meant ample supply for future poison doses. What had she been thinking?

Hillary would be long gone by now, having already harvested Harry's money, credit line, and everything else. Including his house, his last thing of value. And soon, possibly his life.

Kat puzzled over why Hillary would take such an extreme step. She already had all his money and his house. What else was there?

A split second later she realized there was something else. Harry had a life insurance policy. She tore down the driveway towards the garage. Hillary wasn't going to get away with this. Not if she could help it.

The freezing rain pelted down loud and hard, splattering mud up onto her running shoes. Kat shivered, wishing she'd worn something waterproof.

She landed in a puddle and winced as cold water seeped into her shoes. They squished as she jogged the last few steps down the driveway to the padlocked garage door. She shoved her frozen fingers into her pocket and fished out the key. She fumbled with numb fingers, trying to work the rusty lock. Finally the sticky tumbler turned.

She opened the garage and placed the padlock on the door latch. She sighed in relief when she spotted the pesticide bags still above the workbench, untouched. She hesitated, uncertain. Was this a crime scene? If so, was removing the bag tampering with the evidence? But she couldn't leave it to be used again.

The thundering rain increased in volume as she entered the garage, as if on cue. It drowned out her thoughts like a conductor's crescendo. Kat glanced at the open door. It was black outside except for the cold sodium light of a streetlamp across the street. It glistened off the spikes of rain as they charged to the ground. She'd better hurry before she froze to death.

Should she take the pesticides, or leave the bag here?

In the end she decided to take it. Of course Hillary could simply buy another bag, but at least this way she had removed the poison source, and preserved the evidence. She pulled the bags down one by one and deposited them on the workbench.

Evidence. She stared at her hands. She had touched the bag too.

But the most important thing was to remove the poison. Maybe she could tie these particular bags to the Garden

Heaven video footage. Lot numbers could be tied to dates, and so on. Of course, it all rested on her hunch about this pesticide. Nothing was proven yet.

She regretted not driving over in the truck. The thought of lugging ten pounds of pesticides for two blocks wasn't exactly appealing. She searched through Harry's garage, looking in drawers and boxes for a plastic bag to protect the bag from the rain. The plastic would also preserve the fingerprints on the bag. Of course, that included her own.

She bent down and searched through a pail of plastic bags.

A shadow blocked the outside light and Kat turned towards the door.

"What are you doing in here?" Hillary's voice was unmistakable.

Kat rose to her feet to face Hillary. She kicked herself for not realizing sooner that Hillary would be back for the poison. And to cover her tracks.

"Answer me. Why are you here, Kat? This isn't your house." Hillary stood in the doorway, arms crossed. She wore jeans, boots, and a black pullover. "You don't belong here."

"I—I'm just checking on something for Harry." Kat shivered.

Hillary scoffed as she entered the garage. "Checking on what? Harry doesn't need anything. Certainly not from you."

Kat glanced at the workbench, glad she hadn't already picked up the bag. At least Hillary wouldn't know she was after the pesticide. "Why are you here, Hillary? It's not your house either."

Hillary smirked but said nothing. Instead, she shook her plastic water bottle and stepped towards the workbench.

"I don't have time for your ridiculous accusations, Kat. I've got enough problems of my own without you harping at me." Hillary glanced at her watch.

"I'll bet you do. Late for something? Or maybe things aren't wrapping up as quickly as you hoped they would?"

Hillary dropped her water bottle on the workbench, right beside the pesticide bag.

Hillary wore gardening gloves. Had Hillary been wearing them when she administered the poison?

Kat flashed back to the Garden Heaven video. Hillary had gloves then too. Were Kat's fingerprints the only ones on the pesticide bag?

She shuddered. Maybe she was just being paranoid. The garden center visit was the one anomaly that couldn't be explained away. Hillary had never been a gardener. She certainly didn't nurture and grow things. She killed them.

"I think you should leave now," Hillary said.

"I'm not going anywhere." Kat stood her ground.

Hillary pointed a trigger finger at Kat and laughed. "I'll give you thirty seconds to disappear. Or else." She marched towards Kat, blocking the light from the open door.

Kat felt all semblance of self-control vanish. Enough was enough. "How could you do this, Hillary?"

"Do what?" Hillary flashed her whitened veneers. But her smile was cold.

"You think I don't know what you're up to?" Kat didn't mention the poison. "The credit cards, the bills? Your name on Harry's house title? A new low, even for you. Are you so desperate that you have to steal an old man's last hope for a comfortable life?"

"How dare *you* accuse me of stealing! You should know. You stole my life." Hillary backed against the workbench, in front of the pesticide bags.

"What are you talking about?" Kat moved closer. "You're responsible for your own life. Nothing I do changes that."

"He's my father, Kat, not yours. I'm sick of you muscling in, getting half of everything. You have no right to anything."

"Half of what?"

Hillary didn't answer. She grabbed a screwdriver off Harry's workbench and stabbed the pesticide bag. She ripped it open and lifted it above her head, releasing a dusting of powder. Then she charged Kat.

Clouds of powder burst from the bag, enveloping Kat's

head and face. Kat gasped as it covered her face, neck and shoulders, invaded her nostrils and lungs. She dropped her head, and shielded her eyes with her arms. But it was too late. The powder was everywhere. It stuck to her wet clothes, covered her shoes and coated the garage floor. She gagged, inhaling the pesticide into her lungs. She flailed her arms and thrashed, momentarily blinded as the powder stung her eyes.

Kat's eyes burned as she slowly opened one. She rubbed her eyes and staggered forward. She had to flush the poison from her eyes, but the nearest sink was inside the house.

"Everything here is mine. Is that clear?" Hillary turned and walked away, the half-empty bag in one hand.

Then the door slammed and the padlock clicked.

"Oh, and cuz—I'll be sure and tell Dad you said goodbye."

CHAPTER 63

KAT STUMBLED BLINDLY TOWARDS THE workbench and ran her hand across the surface. She let out a sigh when she touched Hillary's water bottle. She squirted a drop onto her finger and tasted it to be sure. Plain water.

Why had she given Hillary the benefit of the doubt? She should know by now that Hillary's actions were meant to benefit one person only. Even if that meant betraying Kat, Harry, or anyone else.

She held up the bottle and squirted the contents into one eye, then the other, flushing them until the burning stopped. She used the remaining water to rinse off her face as best she could. Her eyes still teared, but at least she could open them to see.

All the Garden Heaven bags were gone.

Kat pushed on the door, knowing it was futile. She had heard Hillary relock the padlock. How could Hillary just leave her here? Kat scanned the garage. She considered breaking the window when she realized there was another way out.

The garage door opener.

She pressed it. A minute later she stood outside in the lane, gulping the fresh air and letting the rain wash the poison from her skin and clothes.

She no longer had the pesticide bags she had come to collect as evidence. Hillary had taken care of that. Regardless, she should gather some powder to get tested. She headed back inside and grabbed an empty yogurt container from the stack Harry kept under the workbench. She scooped up as much as she could from the garage floor.

She called Connor Whitehall but got no answer. She left a message with instructions on retrieving the sample and video from her house, along the location of her spare key. She had no time to wait for him. She had to get to the hospital before Hillary did.

An hour later, Kat rushed down the hospital corridor, only to discover Hillary already there. She sat in a chair outside Harry's room, wailing.

Despite her wet clothes, Kat broke into a sweat. Had Hillary done it? Had she killed him? She froze outside Harry's room. What could she do?

At that instant Hillary looked up. If she was shocked at seeing Kat, she didn't show it. "You don't belong here." She shooed Kat away with a manicured hand.

Kat ignored her and ran into Harry's room. A half-dozen nurses and doctors huddled around Harry's bed with carts of equipment and instruments. A nurse glanced up at her as she entered. It was the same nurse who had been rude to her earlier. She held up her palm, motioning for Kat to stop.

Kat's heart stopped. Was she too late? She retreated outside to where Hillary sat, stone-faced.

Hillary's audience was gone, as were her tears. Her cheeks were dry and her makeup appeared no worse for wear. She knew better than to talk to Hillary, but she couldn't help herself. "What did you do to him?"

Hillary smiled. "What makes you think I did anything?"

"I don't think—I know, Hillary."

The nurse emerged from Harry's room. She ignored Hillary's sniffles and stared directly at Kat. "He's worse."

"Huh?" Kat was shocked that the nurse was even speaking to her. Not only that, but her eyes belied concern. Why wasn't she telling this to Hillary? "Worse how?"

"He's in shock. All his symptoms have returned, worse than ever. He's ingested poison again."

Without me being here. Suddenly Kat realized why the nurse was sympathetic. She now knew Kat hadn't done it. But did she realize that Hillary had?

The nurse shifted her gaze to Hillary, whose sniffles had morphed into a wail.

Hillary's bawling sounded convincing, but her eyes gave her away. They darted between the nurse and Kat, hoping for a reaction.

Hillary must have given Harry one final dose. One bigger than the rest. While the medical staff tried to save a life, Hillary was intent on taking one. And she had almost succeeded.

Kat punched in Connor Whitehall's number. By now she hoped he would have the Garden Heaven video footage, as well as the pesticide sample. If all went according to plan, Connor Whitehall was handing it over to the police at this very moment. The sample would match the toxins found in Harry's blood test, and the authorities would be forced to take action.

Hillary stood outside the room. She wailed, louder and louder, like a sole survivor of a disaster. Every few seconds she glanced around to check on her audience.

Within a minute, the hallway was completely empty as all available medical staff had rushed into Harry's room. Only Hillary and Kat remained outside, forbidden to go inside.

Hillary's crocodile tears disgusted Kat. Did she really

think she could fool everyone?

"Why'd you do it, Hillary?"

"Do what?" A sly smile played on Hillary's lips. "I have no idea what you're talking about. Even if I did, you'll never know. No one will."

"I do know. I've got proof."

Hillary raised her brows. "Really? What exactly?"

"They know it's you, Hillary. They know about the money and the poison."

"Who's *they*?"

"The doctors, the police. Blood tests have confirmed the poison, and the police have proof. It's all on video. You at Garden Heaven, you poisoning the orange juice. You can't get away with this." Kat added the orange juice just to gauge Hillary's reaction.

"You're bluffing."

"The police are on their way over right now." Even if Connor had provided the footage to the police, she doubted they'd be this quick. But Hillary wouldn't know that.

"Say anything and I'll make you sorry you ever lived," Hillary whispered as she peered around the corner into Harry's room.

But no one heard her except Kat. The medical staff were intent on their work.

Hillary pulled a compact from her purse and flipped it open. She dabbed at her mascara with a tissue and glared at Kat. Gone were Hillary's hysterics, switched off like they always did when her audience vanished.

"Don't leave town, Hillary. You've got some explaining to do."

Hillary stared back at her, dead calm. "Just try and stop me."

"I already have."

Hillary glared at Kat, hatred burning in her eyes. "I'll get you for this."

"Too late for that." Kat met Hillary's stare, wondering why

she had ever been afraid of her in the first place. She had also been blind to the fact that Hillary was incapable of caring for anyone but herself. With that realization, Hillary no longer held any power over her.

Kat did belong, and she had a right to be here. No matter what Hillary said or thought.

"Accuse me of anything, and I'll make you sorry you did." Hillary scowled at Kat.

"The truth will come out, Hillary. It already has."

Hillary glanced towards Harry's doorway and rolled her eyes. She paused momentarily, then turned on her heels and marched down the hall and through hospital ward's double doors. Her heels echoed off the walls, followed by the ding of the elevator.

If Kat ever saw her again, it would be too soon.

CHAPTER 64

KAT SAT IN ZACHARY'S OFFICE a few hours later, stunned by what Zachary had just told her.

"You bet it all?" Kat's mouth dropped open, astounded that Zachary would bet everything on one trade. "Why, Zachary?"

Zachary stood in front of his computer terminal, his shirtsleeves rolled up. Coffee stained the front of his wrinkled shirt, and he looked like he hadn't slept in days. For the first time, Kat felt better dressed than him.

"I can get it all back, Kat." He smiled. "My model works. I just need to prove that—"

"Zachary, it's too late. It doesn't matter anymore whether your model works or not. Edgewater investors and the authorities need to know about Nathan's Ponzi scheme. Now."

Zachary pointed at his trading screen. "They will, after I get the money back. Watch the screen. The Euro's up, and I've already made back some of the losses. Almost a billion so far." He pulled a handkerchief from his pocket and wiped his forehead. "A billion, Kat. I've got to ride this thing while it lasts."

The television droned on behind Zachary. The dollar was collapsing against the Euro. Dozens of harried-looking traders sat glued to their computer screens, the polar opposite of the scene playing out in front of her with Zachary.

"It's the investor's money, Zachary. Cut your losses and get out while you can."

"That's crazy. I make a hundred million for every ten basis points the Euro appreciates against the dollar. Why stop now?"

A hundred basis points equaled one percent in trading terms. A billion dollars equaled half of Edgewater's losses from Nathan's fraud. "It can easily go the other way, Zachary. Let it go."

Gone was the naked panic etched on Zachary's face when she told him about Nathan's Ponzi. His expression had changed from vulnerable to smug.

Kat stared at the graph on screen. The Euro's trend line was green, already up one percent against the greenback today.

"Sell it, Zachary. Get out while you're ahead and report the fraud. The investors will understand that it was all Nathan and not you."

"Not yet."

"What if you lose what little is left? It's a gamble you're sure to lose."

"Don't jinx me. It's not a gamble at all. My bet is big enough to move the market by itself. Once it gains momentum, I'll be back in the black within days, if not hours."

"You can't be serious. After complaining about Nathan ruining Edgewater, you're about to do the same."

Zachary snorted. "Rich people won't understand a loss this big, Kat. They'll be out for blood once they hear what Nathan did. They'll assume he's taking the fall for me too. Or that I'm a complete idiot, too stupid to notice a massive fraud right under my eyes. I'm either incompetent or a thief. Either way, I lose."

"With enough proof they'll believe you." Kat pointed to the screen. "Those profits aren't locked in. They can easily swing the other way. Instead of a two billion loss, you could lose much more. Unload your position, Zachary, and face the music. You haven't done anything wrong—yet."

"And I'm not going to. This is perfectly legal. There's nothing in the fund prospectus that says I can't."

Technically it was legal, but was it right? "But surely your investors don't want you to bet everything on one trade. What would they do if they knew?"

Zachary didn't respond, so Kat answered her own question. "They'd pull their money out." The Euro's graph line plunged again, reversing all of the gains from a few minutes ago.

Zachary was just as morally bankrupt as his father—the only difference was that he didn't cross legal lines.

"They don't have to know," Zachary said.

"This isn't a Las Vegas crap shoot." Kat stared at the screen. The graph line had turned red. Now it showed a one percent loss. Almost all the gains of yesterday were gone too. "Just like I said—you're losing."

"Will you shut up?" Zachary waved his arms in the air. "It's not a hunch—it's my model and it's working. At least it was until you interfered."

He waved her over to a chair opposite him. "You're distracting me. Either take a seat or leave. If you want to watch history take its course, you'll see what I mean."

Kat sighed and sat down. The last thing she wanted to see was Zachary making history. Disaster loomed as the Euro dropped another hundred points. Now the loss was two billion.

They stared at the trading screen in silence.

Then, just as all seemed lost, the Euro stopped dropping. Slowly it rebounded, a few basis points, then a dozen, then thirty. Now the loss was only 1.7 billion. Only.

"See that, Kat?" Zachary's panicked expression from a few minutes ago had changed to a smug one. "That's me. My bet's working now."

"How can you be so sure?" To Kat, the graph line angled like the steepest climb on a never-ending roller coaster. In a few seconds it would plunge off the precipice, repeating the wild ride of the last twenty minutes.

"Momentum, Kat. It's turning around." Zachary pointed to a sharp trough on the graph line. "Everything works if the bet's big enough."

In less than ten minutes it was up again. Now Zachary needed a billion.

"How can it be that simple?"

"It's a zero sum game. Whatever I win, someone else loses. If I bet enough, I can move the market in any direction I want. When it moves, others follow."

The graph line continued its ascent. Now it turned green as Zachary's fortunes continued to rise.

"But the economists are predicting—"

"Who cares what the economists think? Traders make the markets. Anyone who thinks otherwise is a fool."

"What about Svensson and the other economists? If their work is meaningless, why don't they give Nobel prizes to the traders?"

"You think markets are based on science?" Zachary laughed. "It's more like poker. You can bluff your way to a fortune."

Zachary leaned back in his chair. He clasped his hands behind his head and smiled.

According to the green line, Zachary was up two percent. He had made back all of Edgewater's losses. Kat wouldn't have believed it could happen so quickly. But it did.

"But your model—you said it was based on quantum game theory. That it was infallible."

Zachary laughed. "Just marketing hype. I tell people that to impress them, and it works like a charm. After all, what I'm really betting on is greed. No one wants to miss out on a sure thing."

"But it's not a sure thing at all."

"*Au contraire.* Who do you think creates the currency fluctuations in the first place? If they're big enough, I can lock them in. I sell once all the little people follow."

"Just like the World Institute would? At the expense of the Edgewater investors?"

"Sophisticated investors who know what their risks are. And if they're not sophisticated, they shouldn't be in the game. It's that simple. Everyone's out for self-interest. It's just a matter of whose interest has the most clout."

"Everything's manipulated? The end result a foregone conclusion?"

"Of course. Everything's decided, Kat. Just like Las Vegas. Only I'm the house."

Kat remained silent, transfixed by the screen. The Euro continued its climb, seemingly unstoppable. Zachary hadn't just recouped all of Nathan's losses; he had also made an extra billion.

"I'm back." Zachary clapped his hands together and let out a whistle. "Not only is the fund whole, but I've made a profit. And a nice little fee for Edgewater. How do you like those odds?"

Las Vegas odds. In favor of the house, naturally.

Kat stared at the screen. "Time to lock in your profits?"

"In a few minutes." Zachary turned to Kat. "Now—about my divorce settlement. We'll need to rework the numbers, go back to court. Victoria's not getting a red cent." Zachary was more concerned about the dollars than Victoria and Nathan's affair.

Since the divorce settlement had been based on falsified numbers, Victoria was entitled to even less than she had been awarded. But could the case be re-opened?

"I can have something for you tomorrow." Kat rose and turned to leave.

But Zachary wasn't listening. He hunched over his computer terminal, biting his lip until it bled. "What the hell—?"

Kat stopped and leaned over to view the screen. Though it wasn't her money, she still felt physically sick. The graph line had changed from green to red. Once again it plunged in the wrong direction.

This time, Zachary wasn't the house. Edgewater's reversal of fortune was just as sudden as the gains. Someone else had bet even bigger.

And won.

CHAPTER 65

KAT STOOD IN THE FOYER of the land title office late Friday afternoon and checked her watch. Hillary should have arrived thirty minutes ago. Would she actually show before the office closed for the weekend? Of course she would. Kat's plan gave her no other choice if she wanted to avoid criminal prosecution.

Not that Kat wanted things to go that route. A case like this would take years to wind through the courts. Maybe even more years than Harry had left. Kat didn't like to resort to blackmail, but it was the only way to ensure swift justice for Harry.

Five minutes later, Hillary stomped up the front steps and pulled open the door.

Kat's stomach knotted like it always did when facing off against her cousin. Would Hillary actually do what she had asked of her? Hillary's promises were empty ones, so Kat had taken steps to ensure her cooperation.

"Did you like the video?" Kat had emailed Hillary a copy of the Garden Heaven video with instructions to meet her here.

The pesticide receipt and empty containers were further evidence to support Hillary's intent to poison Harry.

"Don't you threaten me." Hillary scowled. "I'm here. Isn't that enough?"

"It's not a threat," Kat said. "It's a promise. If you ever do anything like this again, I will expose you. My copy goes to the police."

Before the cops arrested Hillary, there was something she needed to do. The wheels of justice turned too slowly to fix some injustices she intended to put right.

Kat had insisted on meeting Hillary here to be absolutely sure that Hillary did remove her name from Harry's house deed. That meant nothing short of official confirmation that his property had reverted back to his sole ownership. She wasn't about to take Hillary's word for it.

"Let's go inside." Kat held the door for Hillary.

Ten minutes later, all the paperwork had been completed. Hillary had removed herself from Harry's house deed, and Harry's ownership was restored.

The police would deal with the funds Hillary had stolen from Harry. Not that Harry would ever see it again. The money had already been spent, and trying to recover it from Hillary was futile. But at least his house was his again.

Hillary stood by the door, fumbling in her purse. She looked a mess. Her black hair was teased out and tangled, and her mascara-smudged eyes kept flitting to her watch.

"Late for something?" Kat asked.

Hillary's eyes narrowed. "You should be grateful I signed it. I didn't have to."

Yes, she had. "Don't expect a thank you."

"You're going to regret this, Kat."

Kat doubted it. Hillary's threats had scared her once, but now they rang hollow. Hillary was not only full of empty promises, but empty threats as well. Like Nathan Barron and Gordon Pinslett, Hillary Denton was out for herself. They circled like sharks for the kill, consuming their prey and gaining every advantage they could. Only their tanks got smaller and smaller, until they were the only survivors. Sharks couldn't survive alone for long.

CHAPTER 66

TWENTY MINUTES LATER KAT ARRIVED home, exhausted but happy. Harry was expected to make a full recovery and would be discharged soon. You couldn't put a dollar figure on that.

While she did get his house back, there was no escaping the fact that he was now saddled with debt. It was tragic, really. The fact that Hillary would face fraud charges was little consolation.

Kat kicked off her shoes at the front door, dropped her coat on the stairway banister, and headed upstairs. She was still astounded that Zachary's trading fiasco earlier today had ruined what little was left of Edgewater Investments. Why he had gambled away whatever he had left was a mystery. He had barely avoided personal bankruptcy himself. Maybe he just wasn't used to losing. Too bad it was the investors' money he was playing with.

Kat reached the top of the stairs and froze in her tracks.

Someone was in the study. The chair creaked, the way it did when someone sat in it and swiveled. Whoever it was also tapped on the keyboard.

Kat spied a broom in the open hall closet and grabbed it. She brandished it above her head as she peered inside.

The intruder sat at the desk with his back to Kat.

She was about to turn and run when the chair suddenly spun around.

"You're here!" Jace grinned and jumped out of the chair. He stopped and held up his arms in surrender. "Don't hit me."

Kat dropped the broom and rushed over to embrace him. "You're out of the hospital? I thought you had to stay a few more days. Why didn't you call me?"

Jace pulled back to study Kat. "I figured I'd surprise you."

"They discharged you already? But I thought—"

"I've got to get my story out, Kat. Before someone else does." He kissed her.

"You checked yourself out? With a concussion?" Kat pulled back and touched his forehead. Jace's bruises were turning purple and he looked like a crash victim.

Jace didn't answer.

"Jace, you should have stayed in the hospital." She pulled on his good arm. "I'm taking you back. Just tell me what you need done and I'll do it."

Jace shook his head. "I feel fine, and besides—I need to—and want to—do this myself. I want to see Pinslett and the rest of these guys nailed."

"You're not usually one to hold a grudge."

"I'm not letting them get away with this, Kat. They can't keep taking whatever they want without impunity. Laws are meant to be followed by everybody—including the rich. Even Hillary."

Kat couldn't argue with that. "I know, but you should at least rest. We can pick up on your story once you're recovered."

"Too late." Jace smiled at her. "Pinslett can't hide the truth. He might own a lot of radio, television, and newspapers. But he can't control social media. Look."

He pointed to the computer monitor. "My story's gone

viral—it's everywhere. Pinslett can't deny his involvement in the mortgage fraud. I've got the proof."

Kat studied the screen. It was true. Pinslett had hastily organized a press conference. For once the media tycoon was on the defensive.

"And my story's finally out there." Jace smiled. "I've got something to say, and Pinslett can't stop me. Now that it's in the public eye, the authorities are forced to investigate it. Unless they want a public outcry."

Kat studied the video clip, a repeat from a news conference earlier today. Gordon Pinslett sat at a table with several his media henchmen at a long table. *The Sentinel* logo was prominently displayed prominently on the wall behind them.

A defiant Gordon Pinslett denied any involvement in the fraud, insisting he had no part in the mortgage fraud and real estate flipping.

But even without the proof, Kat could spot a liar. He was stammered as he struggled to find the right words to get the reporters off his back.

"I don't see what's changed. He's still denying—"

"Wait for it, Kat."

The story moved to a second clip, just minutes ago. Kat listed to the reporter voice-over as Pinslett was led, handcuffed, out of the main doors of his media conglomerate. Half a dozen reporters stood at the entrance, peppering him with questions. The disgraced media tycoon ignored them. He dropped his head as he was ushered into the waiting police car.

"My story came out during his news conference. Once it was public, it couldn't be ignored. Even the traditional media had to report on it. No one's above the law. Not only that, but Roger Landers has the goods on him too. Apparently Pinslett asked Landers to *stop the story.*"

"Landers fire-bombed our house? I'll kill him."

"Relax, Kat. Pinslett asked him to, but Landers didn't do it. He did, however, record the conversation, and dozens of others he's had with the guy. All very incriminating. Landers might be self-serving, but at least he's transparent about it. He only wanted the story—an exposé on the World Institute, just like I did."

"What about all that stuff about Svensson's murder?"

"Fishing for a story, I guess, or trying to throw us off the scent. At any rate, it's something the police will sort out."

Kat kind of doubted that. Just as she figured, Landers was still trying to steal Jace's story. But Jace was right. Landers really was harmless compared to Gordon Pinslett, Nathan Barron, and the rest of the World Institute. And with Jace's story now public, there was little Landers could do to steal his thunder.

"You did the right thing, Jace. Even if it did cost you your job." She hugged him. "Do you really have no hard feelings towards Landers? He gave us up."

"Maybe, but I kind of feel sorry for him. He's so desperate for glory that he's willing to fabricate a story out of thin air. He's ruined as a journalist. Who will take him seriously now?"

CHAPTER 67

Angelika reclined in first class and smiled at the man beside her. He beamed, blushing at the attention. Fiftyish, confident, and assured. Would his impression change if he knew her secrets?

In a few short hours she would be back in London, away from Hideaway Bay, the World Institute, and Nathan Barron. Away from the man who had stolen her trust and betrayed her.

She wiped her hands with the moist cloth as the flight attendant removed their trays. She never doubted Nathan would cop a plea deal to save his own skin. He would have given her up in a minute if it gave him an advantage. He left her no choice but to kill him. She hated messy endings.

By now housekeeping would have discovered Nathan hanging in the closet, his belt a makeshift noose. Another broken, ruined man. Another tragic suicide. There had been a rash of them at Hideaway Bay lately.

Was it the gloomy weather? Nathan Barron's financial ruin? Guilt over betraying his son? The Ponzi scheme had surprised her, but it fit her plan perfectly. Whatever the cause, Nathan's suicide would fuel speculation for months. Then he would be forgotten.

She had done Nathan a favor. Instead of facing criminal charges and hordes of irate investors, he was in his final resting place. She had put him out of his misery.

Murder was such a harsh word. Mercy killing was more like it.

Nathan. How could she have been so wrong about him?

Angelika had met him on the African plains. Selous, Tanzania, on a hunting trip. In that remote and wild place, he had serenaded her. She had fallen hard for him, drunk from his attentions, enveloped in his circle of power. She would do anything, even kill for him.

And she had.

Nathan understood the dance between hunter and hunted. Each was necessary to sustain life, to live it. Like the special relationship she had with her victims. Svensson had trusted her completely, even at the moment of death.

After flip-flopping over the cause of Svensson's death, the coroner had ultimately ruled it a suicide. Angelika liked those best.

No loose ends.

Angelika glanced over at her seatmate. He faced the window, his back to her. Outside the indigo sky flew by, stuck somewhere between night and morning as they travelled east.

People never appreciated everyday life, or considered when or how it might end. Hunting taught her that.

But Nathan had fooled her. She thought their partnership was special; he as one of the most powerful men on the planet, and she, the professional assassin no one ever expected. She didn't fit the stereotype, but that was part of her success. No one ever expected a female assassin, much less a young and beautiful one.

Until he stood her up in London. She had delayed Svensson's hit as punishment. She hoped for a panicked call from Nathan, but none came. So she travelled with Svensson to Canada, to Nathan's conference, hoping to up the ante before she killed Svensson at Hideaway Bay. There was something intimate about spending the last few hours of a man's life with him. Especially when he had no idea that those last few hours had come to pass.

Besides ignoring her, Nathan also stiffed her on the final Svensson payment by not topping up her prepaid credit cards. The cards were convenient and untraceable, useful for carrying large amounts of cash across borders. Non-payment was bad enough, but Victoria was the final straw. Did Nathan really expect her to do all his dirty work while he played around with that Botox bitch? Angelika hadn't counted on another woman.

Men didn't leave Angelika. If they tried, they left the world on her terms, not their own.

Angelika glanced out the cabin window. She sipped her coffee as the plane chased the sunrise.

All in all, a perfect day. And another one on the horizon.

CHAPTER 68

KAT SAT AT **HARRY'S KITCHEN** table, amazed at the difference in her uncle. Gone were the blank stares, the shuffling gait and the forgetfulness. It was a miracle.

There was an explanation, though she still had a hard time believing it. The poison's effects had mimicked the symptoms of dementia, resulting in Harry's Alzheimer's misdiagnosis. Harry never had dementia after all.

Sure, he was forgetful sometimes, but no more than any eighty-year-old.

Now, after a week in the hospital, the poison had been purged from his system. Harry had bounced back quickly, though he didn't remember much of the last few weeks and months. His recovery was nothing short of amazing.

Kat glanced at the stack of seed catalogues that sat on the table. Harry was planning next year's garden and even getting back in touch with his lawn-bowling buddies.

"Hillary's got a new job, Kat. Out of town."

"Good for her," Kat said, wondering how much of this

story Harry actually believed. Or wanted to believe, because the alternative was unthinkable.

Of course Kat had bought into plenty of Hillary's lies herself over the years, wanting to give Hillary the benefit of the doubt. But now she saw her for what she really was. A parasite.

Amazing, Kat thought. Harry's financial nightmares began around the time his dementia symptoms started. Kat had naturally assumed his delusions and forgetfulness were from the dementia, as had Harry's family doctor.

In retrospect, Harry's health had spiraled downward quite suddenly. When Kat cancelled his credit cards and confronted the bank, she exacerbated the situation. It cut off Hillary's source of money. His health decline hadn't caused his financial mess; it had been the other way around. In her efforts to protect Harry, Kat had conjured Hillary up out of the woodwork.

Harry was idealistic, refusing to believe that his own daughter was taking advantage of him financially again. He kept believing her excuses and gave her money; each time sure she would extricate herself out of her current mess.

"One egg or two?" Harry retrieved the egg carton from the fridge and slammed the door.

"Two." When the money stopped, Hillary returned, this time with a more desperate attempt to liquidate Harry and his assets.

"Orange juice?" Harry held up the carafe.

While Harry didn't remember a lot from his months of hell, Kat was certain Dr. Konig had mentioned the doctored orange juice. But she couldn't blame him for refusing to believe his daughter had tried to poison him. That was a truth too painful for anyone.

"I think I'll pass."

Harry turned to Kat. "She's just a bit reckless, Kat. She'll learn."

Even now he was making excuses for Hillary's behavior.

But what else could he do? To think it was premeditated was too much to consider.

Kat said nothing. She was distracted by noise coming from the front of the house.

"Be right back." She rose from her chair and padded into the living room. As she got closer to the window, she saw a figure bent down in front of the Porsche.

Her heart stopped as the hood of Hillary's Porsche jerked forward. Hillary had returned for her car, despite the restraining order prohibiting any contact with Harry.

Kat braced herself. Why was Hillary violating the terms of her restraining order after only one day? She was already in enough trouble—charged with attempted murder and fraud. The police had charged her, despite Harry's protestations. Now it was up to the courts to decide her fate.

Kat flung the door open, anxious to intercept her before Harry did.

Only it wasn't Hillary.

The tow truck lifted the front end of the Porsche.

Kat ran outside. "You can't tow that car—it's parked legally, and there's no ticket."

"Sure I can. The bank's repossessed it. Overdue payments."

"Oh." Kat backed away as he hoisted the car. One way or another, the fraud would be unwound and sorted out. At least if the finance company towed it, it would be locked up securely and safe from Hillary. And the payment notices would stop. "Have a good day."

The tow truck driver smiled back at her. "Now that's something I don't hear too often." He gave her a thumbs up and hopped into the truck cab.

The tow truck pulled away from the curb, pulling the Porsche behind it.

Kat watched the truck ascend the hill. Finally it reached the top, to where the hill touched the sky, where the world tipped away.

The morning sun glinted off the Porsche's bumper

momentarily as it crested the peak. Then it slowly dipped below the horizon and disappeared.

This time, she wasn't the one running away.

AUTHOR'S NOTE

I HOPE YOU ENJOYED READING *GAME Theory,* book two in the Kat Carter Fraud Thriller Series.

While most of the settings in *Game Theory* are real, Hideaway Bay is not. It is a composite of several small communities that dot the Sunshine Coast, part of Canada's southwestern coast. The World Institute is also fictitious, but certainly not outside the realm of possibility.

No-Gro pesticide is also from my imagination. When the

stakes are high, people will go to extraordinary lengths to gain both money and power.

Fraud also fascinates me, and I'm always amazed by what motivates people to enrich themselves at the expense of others. Despite what these criminals think, it's only a matter of time until they are caught. Sooner or later they slip up or become complacent. Forensic accountants like Kat have a number of methods to track down and expose fraudsters, but they all focus on one thing. Following the money eventually leads to the perpetrator.

You might also enjoy *Exit Strategy,* book one in the Kat Carter Fraud Thriller Series. Find out more at http://www.colleencross.com/.

Thank you for choosing to spend some of your valuable time with my books and me. I hope I've succeeded in temporarily transporting you to another world, away from your cares and worries. Above all, I hope I've entertained you.

If you enjoyed the book, won't you please tell a friend and consider leaving a review?

You can find my books and leave reviews at your favorite retailers and reading sites.

ABOUT THE AUTHOR

COLLEEN CROSS IS THE AUTHOR of the Katerina Carter Fraud Thriller Series. She is also an accountant. She lives near Vancouver, Canada.

To keep up to date with Colleen's latest books and events, please visit her website and blog at http://www.colleencross.com.

You can also become a fan on Goodreads, Facebook, or follow her on Twitter: @colleenxcross

15428586R00200

Made in the USA
Charleston, SC
02 November 2012